W9-DBI-005

The Lively A R T

The Lively
ART

A TREASURY OF CRITICISM,
COMMENTARY, OBSERVATION,
AND INSIGHT FROM
TWENTY YEARS OF THE
AMERICAN REPERTORY THEATRE

Edited by Arthur Holmberg

*With an Introduction by Robert Brustein
and Reflections by Robert J. Orchard*

Jan Geidt and Lynn Kasper
ASSOCIATE EDITORS

IVAN R. DEE
Chicago 1999

THE LIVELY A R T. Copyright ©1999 by the American Repertory Theatre. All rights reserved, including the right to reproduce this book or portions thereof in any form. For information, address: Ivan R. Dee, Publisher, 1332 North Halsted Street, Chicago 60622. Manufactured in the United States of America and printed on acid-free paper.

Library of Congress Cataloging-in-Publication Data:
The lively A R T: a treasury of criticism, commentary, observation, and insight
   from twenty years of the American Repertory Theatre / edited by Arthur
   Holmberg ; Jan Geidt and Lynn Kasper, associate editors ; with an
   introduction by Robert Brustein and Reflections by Robert J. Orchard.
      p.   cm.
   Includes index.
   ISBN 1-56663-244-7 (alk. paper)
    1. American Repertory Theatre—History.   2. Theater—Massachusetts—
   Cambridge—History—20th century.   I. Holmberg, Arthur.   II. Geidt, Jan.
   III. Kasper, Lynn.
  PN2297.A53L58   1999
   792'.09744'409045—dc21   99-19564

Preface
by Arthur Holmberg

Robert Brustein is not only a theatre practitioner but also a formidable critical mind and master teacher. He has built into the life of his theatre various conduits to offer A.R.T. audiences a vast array of materials to deepen both the pleasure and the profit they receive from our productions. In our newsletters and programs we publish literary articles by eminent critics and interviews with directors and playwrights. For each production we organize a symposium. Here again both scholars and artists participate. Scholars lend their erudition and critical insights to our productions. Reflecting on an artistic experience is an important and necessary enrichment of that experience. Artists describe their creative processes, enabling audiences to understand the meticulous craft and the visionary gleam that join forces to produce great theatre.

All these activities attest to Mr. Brustein's conviction that theatre should not only enchant or provoke, it must also educate in the broadest sense of that word. It ought to lead out from the self, broaden perspectives, and enlarge our sympathetic understanding of ourselves and our world. The articles gathered together in this anthology are testaments to that belief.

In putting this collection together, I and my associate editors, Jan Geidt and Lynn Kasper, had to choose from articles of a consistently high quality of writing. In addition to a chronicle of our endeavors over the past twenty years, we have tried to put together a selection that represents a broad cross section of different methodologies by literary scholars. We have also included interviews with artists and pieces written by them that help explain both the inspiration and the hard work that go into writing or directing a play. Many different voices and many different viewpoints are here assembled, for theatre implies dialogue, and dialogue implies a lively exchange of ideas. From this exchange, from these different and opposing viewpoints, the experience and meaning of a play and its ability to reverberate increase exponentially. This book, then, is the intellectual, artistic, and spiritual memoir of our collective effort to create theatre.

Acknowledgments

The American Repertory Theatre wishes to express its gratitude to the National Endowment for the Humanities, which for many seasons supported our symposia and enabled us to commission articles for our newsletter from distinguished scholars and humanists. We also thank the Playwrights' Platform of Boston and the Dramatists Guild of New York (the professional association of playwrights, composers, and lyricists) for excerpts from their seminar hosting Marsha Norman and Robert Brustein.

All photos are by Richard Feldman, company photographer, excepting those for *Henry V* (page 261) and *The America Play* (jacket and page 269) by T. Charles Erikson.

The editors also are grateful to the members of the A.R.T. staff, notably Christopher Dearborn, Henry Lussier, and Gideon Lester, as well as Lisa Cohen, Dyana Kimball, Richard Parr, Emily Tarvin, and Blythe Yee.

Contents

The Lively A R T

Introduction
by Robert Brustein

If every play has a plot, every production has a story and every theatre has a history. The production history of the American Repertory Theatre begins in the summer of 1979.

A sizable number of us—actors, directors, designers, administrators, technicians—had just decamped from New Haven, having completed thirteen seasons at the Yale Repertory Theatre. Now we were in a new town, associated with a new university, trying to develop an audience for theatrical work that was, to put it mildly, not exactly mainstream. To our astonishment, we attracted thirteen thousand subscribers with our very first season (having never played to more than six thousand at Yale). Single-ticket sales, the hardest to promote, were also selling like hotcakes. Theatre-parched Boston was prepared to soak up our plays like a thirsty ground soaks up rain.

Beginning with the hugely popular A *Midsummer Night's Dream* in Alvin Epstein's shimmering interpretation (complete with Henry Purcell's music from *The Faerie Queene* and featuring such founding company members as John Bottoms, Carmen de Lavallade, Jeremy Geidt, Karen MacDonald, Steve Rowe, Ken Ryan, and Max Wright, as well as a large portion of Yale's 1979 acting class, including Mark Linn-Baker, Eric Elice, and Marianne Owen), three of the four offerings of our first season were revivals of successful productions in New Haven. For the fourth we took a chance on a young Harvard senior named Peter Sellars, who had impressed us with his puppet version of Wagner's *Ring* cycle, compressed into a single hour and crammed into a very small space. Not yet twenty-one, Sellars was offered the opportunity to stage a full-length version of Gogol's *The In-*

spector General. It became our fourth and most controversial production. (His 1981 production of Handel's *Orlando*, set in Cape Canaveral, on the other hand, was among our most popular successes, as well as being the longest run of this opera in history.)

From the beginning, the American Repertory Theatre featured a literary and scholarly component, in the guise of symposia, preshow talks, newsletters, and copious program material. No doubt this reflected the fact that our theatre employed a full-time dramaturg/literary director (sometimes two) and was being led by a director who doubled as a dramaturg and trebled as a professor of dramatic literature and part-time theatre critic. This humanistic side of our work—*The Lively A R T* constitutes a fair sampling of a great deal of this material—was also a consequence of our association with a formidable scholarly institution, many of whose faculty had strong opinions about the theatre, pro and con. We were eager to find a productive way to vent these feelings lest they explode in our face. The various forms of intellectual outreach we employed were, therefore, partly educational devices, designed to explain our methods to a not always appreciative public, and partly an opportunity for our audience to speak out about theatrical issues, particularly whether a company should try to reinvent the classics (our view) or perform them in a traditional manner (the view of most of our critics).

Despite these steam valves, and the addition of such new company members as Cherry Jones, Tommy Derrah, Tony Shalhoub, and Harry Murphy, serious doubts were beginning to emerge at the end of our second season in Cambridge about whether we would have a third. The thirteen thousand subscribers the A.R.T. had managed to attract to a mini-season in the spring of 1980 had swelled to fourteen thousand for the second season in the fall of 1980. By the beginning of the third season, half of these had vanished, along with the goodwill of much of the press.

What had happened? Well, for one thing, our second season was perceived as a kind of avant-garde typhoon threatening to engulf the entire Boston area. Audiences had grown suspicious after Sellars's *The Inspector General*, which featured, among other anachronistic jokes, portraits of Stalin being carried along the back wall of the stage. By the next year the public was growing openly hostile. We began the season with a production of *As You Like It*, in which Hymen, the goddess of marriage, wore a headdress consisting of penises and breasts. We followed this with the Brecht-Weill ballet/

Robert Brustein
(left) with Robert
Orchard.

oratorio *The Seven Deadly Sins*, a hit in New Haven but like most of
our German plays, poison in Boston; then, performing in repertory, a
British play called *Has Washington Legs?* involving strong language
guaranteed to bring a blush to the cheek of the young person; and,
most scandalous of all, Lee Breuer's version of another German classic, Wedekind's *Lulu*. The latter was not only sexually but artistically
provocative. It was cutting-edge theatre, all right, to the point of ending with the character of Jack the Ripper cutting the heroine's throat
(then washing his bloody hands in a toilet bowl and exiting through
the audience, murmuring "I'm so lucky"). Local critics were surprisingly positive about this *Lulu*, and it was invited to tour major festivals in Europe, Israel, and the former Yugoslavia. But it hit
Cambridge like a slap in the face. We were lucky to keep half the audience by the end of each show.

Many of our subscribers didn't even bother to attend our last two
productions—a fairly straightforward *Marriage of Figaro* and Jules
Feiffer's *Grownups* (which went on to enjoy a brief Broadway run).
They had angrily canceled their subscriptions. And it didn't help
when, in trying to account for the exodus, I opened my big mouth on
radio to speculate that perhaps we had overestimated the extent of
Boston's theatrical sophistication.

I had been looking gloomily at the seven thousand who left us. I
should have been celebrating the seven thousand who remained, be-

cause they became the nucleus of a loyal following. It took a few more years to build our subscription base up to ten thousand. But we never again attained the dizzying heights of that second year. A new theatre called the Huntington, associated with Boston University, was now attracting mainstream audiences with the kind of fare we were unlikely to provide. The establishment of two resident theatres in an area that previously could boast none was a blessing in many ways. Importantly for us, it relieved the A.R.T. of the obligation to be all things to all spectators.

In our third season we established the New Stages series, devoted to the presentation of new plays, often in a smaller space, usually the historic Hasty Pudding Theatre. In succeeding seasons we had the privilege of producing new plays by, among others, Sam Shepard, Marsha Norman, Robert Auletta, David Mamet, Christopher Durang, Don DeLillo, William Hauptman, Dario Fo, Arthur Kopit, Ronald Ribman, Alan Havis, Heiner Müller, Keith Reddin, Larry Gelbart, Howard Korder, David Lodge, Derek Walcott, David Gordon, Han Ong, David Rabe, Peter Feibleman, Steve Martin, Paul Rudnick, Suzan-Lori Parks, and Susan Sontag, as well as two of my own. These were often met by surprising audience indifference. It is a curious fact that unlike New York and Chicago, cities that invariably prefer new plays to the classics, Boston may embrace the most recherché Greek tragedies and seldom-produced Shakespeare but shows very little interest in new work. There is one clear exception to this rule—David Mamet, who has developed a strong following in the Boston area. A resident of Newton, he has also become our resident playwright in recent years, having given us premieres of *Oleanna*, *The Cryptogram*, *The Old Neighborhood*, and *The Boston Marriage*, along with a powerful adaptation of *Uncle Vanya*, directed by David Wheeler, that featured Christopher Walken, Dan Von Bargen, Lindsay Crouse, Alvin Epstein, Pamela Gien, Priscilla Smith, and Bronia Wheeler in the cast. But many of the other works we've proudly presented in the New Stages series have rarely filled more than a third of the house.

Robert Wilson, on the other hand, is an example of an experimental artist who gradually developed a large following in the area among single-ticket buyers, though we invariably dropped a fair number of subscribers every year we included a Wilson production. Bob's first work with the company was the hypnotic Cologne section of *the CIVIL warS* in 1984, with music by Philip Glass. (Glass also gave the

A.R.T. premieres of three of his mesmerizing operas—*The Juniper Tree*, *The Fall of the House of Usher*, and *Orphée*—as well as providing us with incidental music for quite a few of our plays.) We watched the audience hemorrhage out of previews of *the CIVIL warS* in helpless dismay until Bob conceived the idea of taking an intermission after the first scene. This didn't stanch the bleeding altogether, but it did manage to persuade some people they were not being insulted, that this unique *auteur* was eager to communicate his vision to the public.

Wilson always avoided doing published plays because he hated what he called the "ping-pong" of dialogue. I pride myself on having persuaded him, essentially a visual genius, to undertake his first classical text. It was Euripides' *Alcestis*, performed against the background of a massive mountain with rocks slowly tumbling down the face and a dark river over which floated the body of the heroine in a plexiglass coffin, trailed by the figure of death. *Alcestis* was invited to the Festival d'Automne in Paris, where in 1986 it won a prize for Best Foreign Production. At the A.R.T., Wilson also directed *Quartet*, a play by the German writer he claimed to have inspired his most brilliant images, namely Heiner Müller. For his third text he staged my adaptation of Ibsen's *When We Dead Awaken*, set against the gloomy fjords and mountains of Norway, and later performed at the Bienale in Saõ Paulo, Brazil, in the fall of 1991.

By that time we were touring regularly through Europe, Asia, and the United States. The most popular of our earlier touring vehicles was Andrei Serban's production of Molière's *Sganarelle*, a romp performed so many times, in so many different venues, and in such an arduous fashion that the muscle-weary actors rebelled and refused to play it anymore. Equally popular touring shows were the Serban/Julie Taymor version of Carlo Gozzi's *The King Stag*, featuring some of the most beautiful puppets and masks ever devised in this country before *The Lion King*, and, in repertory with it, my own production of Pirandello's *Six Characters in Search of an Author*.

With these two shows in repertory, we were positioned to demonstrate the immense advantages of a permanent company doing plays in rotation. *Six Characters* began with the company actors rehearsing parts in *The King Stag* (under their own names) in preparation for a tour before being interrupted by the appearance of the ominous, ethereal, otherworldly six, swaying gently under an eerie light. Moving in and out of their own personas, our company was able to contribute ideas, dialogue, and business to the production and then, a night or so later, transform themselves into the *commedia dell'arte* figures of another Italian play, Carlo Gozzi's *King Stag*.

From the beginning, Andrei Serban was a key director with our company, mixing his Romanian spirituality with an American sense of mischief, both seasoned by his fiery and tempestuous nature. He did seven brilliant productions at the A.R.T., many of them featuring our leading lady, Cherry Jones—most notably a luminous *Three Sisters* and an enchanting *Twelfth Night* (with Diane Lane, who first acted under Serban in *Fragments of a Trilogy* at the age of seven). After a few years away, Serban returned to the company in 1998 with a hilarious and curiously spiritual *The Taming of the Shrew* and a bold rendering of *The Merchant of Venice;* he is again one of our most valued and most inspired collaborators.

Serban was not the only Romanian to direct with our company. His mentor Liviu Ciulei staged a production of Chekhov's first play, *Platonov,* for the A.R.T. after relinquishing the reins of The Guthrie Theater, and Andrei Belgrader directed seven productions for us, most of them farces, including *Rameau's Nephew* with Jeremy Geidt and returning company member Tony Shalhoub, and Belgrader's absolutely loopy, scandalously funny version (with co-adaptor Shelley Berc) of Jarry's *Ubu Roi.* Featured among many other outrages in this production was a patter song performed by Tommy Derrah playing a half-crippled, half-blind general. The song went on for so long that the audience began throwing programs, eggs, water, and shoes at the stage—like a replay of the heady days of Dada.

Among our American directors, Adrian Hall—former artistic director of Trinity Rep—staged for us Ronald Ribman's *Journey of the Fifth Horse,* Ibsen's *Hedda Gabler* with Candy Buckley and Stephen Skybell (a production that stimulated an interesting debate among feminists), and a controversial *King Lear* featuring F. Murray Abraham playing Shakespeare's dispossessed king as if he were a homeless derelict. A.R.T.'s congenial resident director David Wheeler was responsible for most of our Shaw productions (including *Misalliance, Major Barbara, Heartbreak House,* and *Man and Superman*) and two of our Pinters (*The Homecoming* and *The Caretaker*), almost all of them popular hits in a community that adores British plays. Anne Bogart did productions of Calderón's *Life Is a Dream* and Paula Vogel's *Hot 'n' Throbbing* (a play about a female pornographer that also stirred up a feminist hornet's nest). Richard Foreman abandoned his own plays for a moment to stage for us a Glass opera (*The Fall of the House of Usher*) and Arthur Kopit's *End of the World* (*With Symposium to Follow*). And I did most of the Ibsen, Strindberg, and Pirandello productions, staging my own adaptations of *Ghosts*, *The Father*, and (in addition to *Six Characters*) *Tonight We Improvise* and *Right You Are* (*If You Think You Are*). In our twentieth year, I have teamed with a recent graduate of the A.R.T. Institute for Advanced Theatre at Harvard, the visionary Kate Whoriskey, to direct my adaptation of *The Master Builder*—a play about a young woman, representing the coming generation, knocking at the door of an aging architect.

Our penchant for hiring daring, adventurous directors who liked to turn the classics upside down often got us into trouble—never more so than in the notorious tempest over the 1984 production of *Endgame*. We had been doing Beckett for years without much controversy—indeed, our very first production at Yale was an *Endgame*, set in a wire cage with a soundtrack featuring the voices of old comics. Andrei Belgrader had staged a *Waiting for Godot* in the 1981–1982 season that was hardly reverential, with no complaint from Beckett. But when JoAnne Akalaitis set *Endgame* in an abandoned subway station, cast two black actors as Hamm and Nagg, and commissioned an overture from her former husband, Philip Glass, all hell broke loose.

What had happened? Well, for one thing, a vacuum had developed after the death of Alan Schneider over who was going to be Beckett's most faithful American disciple, and people were working overtime to demonstrate their loyalty. At all events, Beckett's publisher, Barney Rossett, sent a representative to Cambridge to watch and report on a preview performance. That this man happened to be the director of another *Endgame* currently playing in New York may have been entirely coincidental. But his report so incensed the playwright that Beckett demanded we cancel the production.

He had been informed (apparently on the basis of Philip Glass's three-minute overture) that the A.R.T. production had "musicalized" his play. He objected to our racially mixed cast (odd, since Beckett had not protested an all-black *Godot* performed in New York). But the thing that maddened the playwright most was the fact that our production had ignored his stage directions. The action was set not in a room with a window, as specified in the text, but in an abandoned New York subway station, apparently after a nuclear war. Beckett's lawyers attempted to get an injunction blocking the production from going forward; failing that, Beckett asked that his name be removed from all programs and posters.

We were unwilling to obey that demand because what the audience was seeing, after all, was Beckett's play, regardless of the setting, every word in place. We produced our witnesses; Beckett and his agents produced theirs. It was a cliff-hanger right up to opening night as to whether the curtain would be allowed to open on the play. At the last minute Beckett agreed to withdraw his demand for cancellation provided he be permitted to air his dissent in a program note ("The American Repertory Theatre production which dismisses my directions is a complete parody of the play as conceived by me. Anybody who cares for the work couldn't fail to be disgusted by this"). Since freedom of expression seemed to us the very basis of the conflict, we were happy to agree. But I insisted on responding on behalf of the theatre. Both statements are included in this book.

Following this controversy, Beckett's contractual control over all future productions of his plays became very strict indeed, to the point where he and (after he died) his estate could sue any theatre making changes in the text or the stage directions. This seemed to us an excessively restrictive way for a playwright to relate to his collaborators, especially after his plays had been performed often enough to benefit from fresh interpretation. Pirandello, a considerably more flexible playwright, recognized that drama could not survive without continual renewal and reimagining—he was willing to risk a complete misinterpretation of his text (a text that, after all, continued to exist regardless of production) rather than watch it freeze into an artifact.

There was no resolving this debate, and there were good arguments to be made on both sides. But it was regrettable that an artist we revered as much as Beckett should have developed such a strong aversion to our theatre. A few years later, when Robert Scanlan, later president of the Beckett Society, became our dramaturg, he received permission to stage a couple of Beckett productions in the New Stages series with the blessings of the estate. And the A.R.T. was even allowed to remount *Waiting for Godot* in a new version directed by David Wheeler, with veteran actors Jeremy Geidt and Alvin Epstein playing Didi and Gogo, and younger company members Remo Airaldi and Ben Evett playing Pozzo and Lucky.

Our problems with Beckett—and occasionally with our audiences and critics—arose out of our incorrigible tendency to deconstruct theatrical texts. This was always less of an issue with dead authors—Aeschylus, Shakespeare, Middleton, Ibsen, Chekhov, Pirandello—than with living ones. But even with the dead we would often run into trouble with the living. (François Rochaix's unorthodox productions of Aeschylus's *Oresteia*, which first brought Randy Danson to the company; Euripides' *Bacchae*; and Molière's *Tartuffe* seemed to please classics departments, though they upset some of the critics—but then his *Wild Duck*, with Will LeBow, Steve Rowe, Jeremy Geidt, Karen MacDonald, and young Institute actor Emma Roberts, pleased everybody.)

With the coming of Ron Daniels to the A.R.T. as associate artistic director for a five-year period, complaints over reinterpretation seemed to abate. It was not that Daniels's productions were conservative. Far from it. He did a *Hamlet* featuring Mark Rylance in pajamas, and presented Bill Camp as Hal, and Jeremy Geidt as Falstaff drinking beer, eating pizza, and watching television in *Henry IV*. But these interpretations were radical in a manner more pleasing to audiences familiar with British theatre—sometimes historically anachronistic but clear, concise, beautifully designed, and elegantly staged, most notably in Daniels's two Chekhov productions (*The Seagull* and *The Cherry Orchard*) and in his penetrating staging of *A Long Day's Journey into Night*, which featured Claire Bloom, Jerry Kilty, Bill Camp, and Michael Stuhlbarg.

After Daniels left the A.R.T. to pursue an independent career, we managed to discover a few new wild men, as well as to bring back a number of our theatrical terrorists from the past—Serban with his controversial Shakespeares, Belgrader directing an outrageous "commedia dell'farte" version of *The Imaginary Invalid*, Bob McGrath devising a postmodern Charlie Chaplin evening (with Tommy Derrah playing The Tramp) based on a Robert Coover story, Marcus Stern transforming Büchner's *Woyzeck* into a concentration camp study; Robert Woodruff staging a harrowing version of *In the Jungle of Cities* (and winning Best Production of the Year from the local critics, though audiences still wouldn't sit still for German plays).

I don't mean to suggest that all twenty years at the A.R.T. have been experimental. We've had our share of popular successes, among them the musicals *Big River* and *Shlemiel the First*, both of which originated at the A.R.T.; Marsha Norman's *'Night Mother*, which went on to Broadway with both members of the original cast (Kathy

Bates and Anne Pitoniak); David Leveaux's version of *A Moon for the Misbegotten* with Kate Nelligan, Ian Bannen, and Jerry Kilty, which also had a nice run on Broadway; Larry Gelbart's *Mastergate*; all of David Mamet's plays; and Susan Sontag's production of Milan Kundera's *Jacques and His Master*, an adaptation of a Diderot story, which, oddly enough, did the best business in our history (I told you Cambridge was a strange place). It's been a generally exhilarating, if occasionally bumpy ride—an extended holiday in which the pleasure we've been able to give to the public has been more than equaled by the pleasure we have taken in each other's company. Here's to the next twenty years!

A MIDSUMMER NIGHT'S DREAM

Erotic Dreams
by Arthur Holmberg

Is sex an anti-social instinct? *A Midsummer Night's Dream* forces the question upon us. Like all good dreams, this play sticks its nose into the dark corners of the libido. What it finds there has varied wildly in different eras, different societies.

Even for a play by Shakespeare, *Midsummer* has had an unusually checkered production history. Originally performed, in all probability, at a noble wedding, by the end of the seventeenth century the text had become a pretext for baroque stage machinery: amidst dragons and Chinese gardens, some incidental lines from Shakespeare. In the nineteenth century, Felix Mendelssohn's music took over, and the balletic tradition of romantic sylphs flitting about a wedding-cake stage persisted obstinately until just the other day.

Harley Granville-Barker dragged the play kicking and screaming into the twentieth century with his ormolu fairies, and Peter Brook's acrobatic circus production of 1970 delivered the *coup de grâce* to the tradition of moonlit arbors and grottoes. Now Alvin Epstein has left his mark on the play, changing the way the text looks, sounds, and feels. Epstein's production jolts us into new perceptions of *Midsummer's* complexity and beauty.

His production fuses, miraculously, the bright, shimmering surface of the play with its dark undertones, pushing textual ambiguities about the tortured nature of love to the point of undecidability. Can the sex and aggression the sweet young lovers stumble over in the woods be channeled into the holy sacrament of matrimony? Yes, maybe, this production says; but then again, maybe not. It is through

Carmen de Lavallade (Titania) and Kenneth Ryan (Oberon) in
A *Midsummer Night's Dream*.

his scenic daring that Epstein signals his agreement with Marjorie Garber, who argues in her critical study *Dream in Shakespeare* that the play finally gives primacy to "imagination over reason."

The fairies hold the keys to the kingdom of dreams, and Epstein has found an inspired way to actualize Titania and Oberon and their spritely retinues. What does a fairy look like? No one has ever photographed one, and Tinkerbell has joined the romantic sylphs in the trashcan of theatre history. Epstein eroticizes these airy nothings, giving them beautiful bodies of flesh and blood. This uninhibited celebration of the play's sensuality—and an attendant willingness to plumb its shadowy, menacing depths—carries us beyond Brook to a distinctively American vision of Shakespeare's fantasy.

Epstein's *Midsummer*, first mounted during Robert Brustein's tenure at the Yale Repertory Theatre in 1975, was restaged at the American Repertory Theatre in 1980 as its first production in its new home in Cambridge. Rather than basking in the glow of a beneficent moon, Epstein's production inhabited the dark side of that satellite. Designer Tony Straiges's eerie, lunar landscape was dominated by a giant sculptural scoop, and subhuman fairies slithered to and fro across it like misbegotten reptiles, slimy, scaly, evil. In contrast to these lizards of night, creeping through the sewers of sex, Oberon and Titania were tall, chiseled creatures in fleshtone tights, glorifications of the body in motion. Sliding down the scoop, playing sexual tag, or blessing the mortal nuptials, they charged the stage with erotic energy. The beauty of their sexual love, expressed through movement, finally triumphed over the anger, jealousy, and aggression that had separated them.

"I wanted to create the impression of nudity," Epstein says of his visual concept, "because Oberon and Titania are forces of nature, and forces of nature don't wear clothes. I studied with Martha Graham, and for me the body in motion is one of the most powerful ways humans communicate. *Dream* is a physical play about physical realities. Any director who tackles it must find a way to physicalize the complicated poetry and emotions."

In his efforts to do that, Epstein turned to Henry Purcell's 1692 score for *The Faerie Queene*, interrupting Shakespeare's play with musical interludes. This postmodern layering was his way of questioning the play's meaning; harmony answered discord.

"You can't reduce this play to any one meaning," the director elaborates. "Love in the play unleashes destructive forces. On the other hand, the lovers yearn for harmony and order. Purcell's music counterpointed the cruelty of my production. The music is elegant, formal, controlled, while everything in the woods spins out of control. The music reminded the audience of the desire to regain harmony."

In this American *Dream*, the body in motion becomes a primary means of theatrical expression. Music and dance weave through the dramatic structure (in contrast to eighteenth- and nineteenth-century productions, in which music dominated the play). Epstein eroticizes the body and pushes his sexual explorations to the point of menace. He seizes upon the possibilities of the nocturnal world of spirits to explore Freudian depths and Jungian reflections, and he plays a dark reading of the play off against a bright one.

"There will always remain two interpretations of *A Midsummer Night's Dream*: the light and the somber," writes Shakespeare critic Jan Kott in *The Bottom Translation*. "And even as we choose the light one, let us not forget the dark one."

Epstein's production refuses to choose between the two. It dramatizes both possibilities, sounding ominous notes of carnality and mortality beneath the beauty and laughter. And, opening up the ambiguities of Shakespeare's text to the point of undecidability, it suggests that ambivalence might be the best response to love.

The above piece was excerpted from a longer article Mr. Holmberg wrote for American Theatre *(April 1989) in which he analyzed other major productions of the play: Mark Lamos's at the Hartford Stage (1988), A. J. Antoon's at the Public (1988), and Liviu Ciulei's at the Guthrie (1985). The A.R.T. production and Mr. Holmberg's notes on it and responses to it occurred several years before he had any professional connection to the theatre.*

THE INSPECTOR GENERAL

A Note on the Translation of The Inspector General
by Sam Guckenheimer and Peter Sellars

Gogol provides a special problem for the translator, as his characters frequently speak ungrammatically, mispronounce words, choose the wrong words, or invent new ones, stumbling over themselves in desperate attempts to communicate. In this language, sound becomes highly important—the speeches are peppered with snores, buzzes, coughs, and sneezes, which merge into a more phonetic than denotative pattern.

Gogol's intention is facilitated by the qualities of his native tongue. Russian, at the time of his writing, was less than a hundred years old as a standardized literary language, with six cases, no articles, a flexible yet innately convoluted word order, continuous juxtaposition of consonants, and unlearnable stress. The author's use of linguistic peculiarity we have tried to render in the closest possible English equivalent, without conversion of Gogol's rough idiom into a glib adaptation. Russian expressions have been imported wholesale, such as "both have fallen finger-first in heaven" (translated elsewhere with "you're both talking through your hat," and "you're way off, both of you") or "it turns on its moustache" (previously rendered as "they are noting it"). Our approach has been a stubborn literalism with a dash of imagination.

Jeremy Geidt (Osip) and Mark Linn-Baker (Khlestakov) in *The Inspector General*.

Certain connections defeated us, when English couldn't approach the density of Russian. For example, Khlestakov calls Osip a "crude animal." In doing so, he uses a word whose first two syllables mean stomach, and thereby he unwittingly reminds himself in mid-insult of his gnawing hunger. Hunger as Khlestakov's dominant urge recurs in his ecstatic cry "Labardan!" To him, this fish embodies ecstasy, hardly conveyed by the English, "Salt cod!"

The Russian director Meyerhold compared Gogol's language with that of Mayakovsky: "Certain passages produce a remarkable impression when you read them—it isn't prose, it isn't verse, but some new linguistic formulations This new linguistic formulation is what we have tried to capture. Gogol knows our problem:

With a profound knowledge of the heart and a wise grasp of life will the word of the Briton echo, like an airy dandy will the impermanent word of the Frenchman flash and then burst into smithereens; finickily, intricately will the German contrive his intellectually gaunt word, which is not within the easy reach of everybody. But there is never a word which can be so sweeping, so boisterous, which would burst out so, from out the very heart, which would seethe so and quiver and flutter so much like a living thing, as an aptly uttered Russian word! [*Dead Souls*, Chapter 5]

THE INSPECTOR GENERAL

A Note on Names in Revizor
by Donald Fanger

Gogol's genius in naming characters is on a par with that of Dickens. Like his English contemporary, he exploited the radical associations of his language with perfect tact and lively suggestiveness; in *Revizor* (*The Inspector General*) he gives us the Russian counterparts, linguistically speaking, of Twist, Gamp, Chuzzlewit, Dedlock, Veneering, Cratchit, Micawber. The names of Gogol's personages, in other words, establish a certain comic level of response (as does the mechanical doubling we find in the hyphenations of Skvoznik-Dmukhanovsky and Lyapkin-Tyapkin, the generational repetitions in Anton Antonovich and Luka Lukich, the near identity of the two Peter Ivanoviches or Dobchinsky and Bobchinsky). They do not characterize, hence they do not invite simple translation. A Russian, recognizing in Zemlyanika the ordinary word for wild strawberries may well try to repress the recognition; certainly he will seek plain meaning in it at his own peril. With this much by way of warning, some of the etymological presences latent in Gogol's cast of characters may be indicated.

Skvoznik suggests an inveterate rogue—also, incongruously, a draft; Dmukhanovsky, a vaguer matter, may suggest self-importance and is indisputably, demeaningly comic when pronounced. Khlopov comes from the onomatopoetic word for bang, slap, clap, or clatter. Lyapkin-Tyapkin inverts tyap-lyap (slipshod or slapdash), with further overtones of spanking and stupid speech before the hyphen and taking or stealing after it. Whipping and swilling lurk in Khlestakov—a name that, Nabokov assures us, "conveys to the Russian reader an effect of lightness and rashness, a prattling tongue, the swish of a slim walking cane, the slapping sound of playing cards, the braggadocio of a nincompoop and the dashing ways of a lady-killer (minus the capacity for completing this or any other action)." When the German doctor's surname, Huebner, emerges in Russian transliteration as Gibner, it does so bearing suggestions of death and destruction. There is lullaby in Lyulyukov; Rastakovsky is Mr. Such; Korobkin takes his name from korobka (box) and is not far from korobit (to jar or grate on); there is a twisted ear in Ukhovertov, a whistler in Svistunov, a button in Pugovitsyn (alongside a shadow of intimidation), and Poshlyopkina might be Englished as Spancks. As for Derzhimorda the policeman, his name is an ominous injunction involving the way your mug or kisser should be held.

These are (to cite Nabokov again) "nightmare names," nicknames in fact "which we surprise in the very act of turning into family names." Such metamorphoses are part of the central action in Gogol's writing. His hero is language.

GROWNUPS

Feiffer on <u>Grownups</u>
by David Edelstein

Jules Feiffer sees his impulse to write plays as an extension of the one that made him a cartoonist—to create scenes. One of his scripts, *Hold Me!*, contains actual translations of cartoons to the stage, and two of his plays—*God Bless* and *White House Murder Case*—are, according to Feiffer, enlarged political cartoons. *Grownups* is a departure—a painful, though still comic, treatment of domesticity, a disturbing look at three generations of a family whose members pull each other apart.

"In *Grownups* I have tried to write about the minutiae of life," he says, "the day-to-day pettiness that drives people up the wall—the material that is almost never treated except in situation comedies. We are trained by sit-coms to laugh at stuff that in fact drives us crazy; we're educated by television and before that by radio to swallow the things that are really serious in life, that really frustrate us, that really drive us wild, the situations to which we overrespond because the incidents are rarely as strong as the emotions they pull out of us. These emotions are so strong that we don't know how to deal with them, so we mock them in our entertainment."

In *Grownups*, a decision to allow a little girl to stay up and watch *Charlie's Angels* becomes a political struggle between father and mother; a visit from meddling parents, a painful test of endurance; and a character's inability to finish an anecdote without being interrupted, the sad reflection of a life without recognition. "It's not a play about good guys and bad guys," Feiffer stresses. "The characters are creatures of frustration. They are holding onto their lives and by saving themselves, destroying all those around them."

Feiffer wrote the first draft of *Grownups* in 1973 but was not willing to have it produced then. "Robert Brustein disagreed from the beginning and wanted to do it back then—he was very enthusiastic. But I just put it away and forgot about it. When I looked at it again, I decided he was right."

Although *Grownups* is personal, Feiffer stresses that all his plays are. He cites as an example *Knock Knock*, which opened on Broadway in 1976. "It was generally reviewed as a far-out farce and escapist entertainment, but I consider it a serious play and very personal. . . . I don't write autobiography, though," he says. "I've never known how to do that, because whenever I start to write anything that really happened to me, I lose control of it. I have to invent situations and then characters to go forth and enact an emotional truth."

Feiffer will stay with the company in Cambridge for the duration of the rehearsal period. He believes it is his responsibility to assist the cast and director. "When things are going well you feel kind of dopey being around . . . but there is always a crisis." Feiffer has found himself becoming less and less possessive of his plays the longer he works in the theatre. He is able to put more trust in the instincts of the director and cast than he did with his first play, *Little Murders*. In his notes to the published version of that play, Feiffer writes, "the author, while always correct in his intentions, is sometimes mistaken about the means to fulfill them."

Next he plans to write a political play. "I feel it's time, " he says, "but I still don't know what it will be about. I've always been interested in this fragmented land of ours. I wrote about that in *Little*

Murders, but it's become even more splintered since then, and I'd like to be more specific about it."

SGANARELLE

Seeking the Source of Farce
by Andrei Serban

Like the colleagues of my generation, I looked at Artaud as a prophet. He inspired in me the magic of a theatre that goes beyond the rational and the psychological. Later, assisting Peter Brook, I witnessed in practice that the essence of theatre is not in narrative nor in literal language.

My own experience in Greek tragedy convinced me that the theatre event should not illustrate the text but that performance must be a creative art in itself, as Grotowoski suggested. It should be true for farce as well as tragedy, since they are closely connected. For instance, in my production *Fragments of a Trilogy*, I used the incantation of Greek and Latin sounds to stimulate the imagination of the actor to transmit to the audience a primitive human reaction. The same reaction was sought in the Molière farces. It is known that in the *commedia dell'arte* the performers did not rely on words. A group of actors with a scenario prepared by themselves, freely improvising lines, movement, and sound in shifting tempos, were reaching at the root of our art. In the same way, we found in Molière's early farces the best material for our purpose. If Greek tragedy used the archaic elements of sacred origin, in comedy we illuminate the opposite: the parody of the sacred in the cosmic force of farce.

"The Flying Doctor," "Sganarelle," "The Forced Marriage"—one-act sketches of a young Molière, who like the young Mozart was creating from instinct canvases of pure transcendence—became in our hands a collage for the actors to improvise upon and to reinvent the *commedia* but with respect for tradition. This was physical theatre, wild and explosive, a challenge to taboos, a violation of the accepted stereotypes of the classical style. For example, in "The Doctor in Spite of Himself," we used an invented language (replacing the translation of the text in good Artaudian fashion), but this chaotic

Cherry Jones, Tony Shalhoub, Karen MacDonald, and John Bottom in *Sganarelle***.**

pattern of sounds did not correspond precisely to the detailed situations in the play. Rather, it brought to light the subconscious energy hidden in the comedy. The attempt was to search for a made-up, ersatz theatrical language that asked: What is human, immediately recognizable? In farce, ever since Roman comedy, there has been a recognition of our ancestral foolery, perpetuated through to our days.

We were experimenting with a new vocabulary, imagining a situation similar to the young Molière, learning the discipline of the old craft while inventing spontaneously this new theatre.

SGANARELLE

Bravos for A.R.T. in Europe
by Jeremy Geidt

Sganarelle *is one of the most traveled productions in A.R.T. history. Following its premiere at Yale, it played at Harvard's Loeb Drama Center, the Public Theater in New York, the Goodman Theatre in Chicago, and the International Fortnight of Theatre in Quebec. In the summer of 1982,* Sganarelle, *with three other productions, embarked on an eleven-week European tour. One of the engagements was at the Avignon Festival in France. The following is an excerpt from a three-part report published by the* Boston Globe.

Inhabited for over two thousand years, Avignon became a place of great importance with the arrival of the Papal Court from Rome, and in 1309 the building of the magnificent Palais des Papes began. In 1947 the Avignon Festival began—the most prestigious theatre event in Europe. We were understandably scared at the thought of playing Molière, France's great playwright, to French audiences in American English. We said as much at a press conference, then left, swallowing our stage fright of acting their national monument and plunged into festival life.

While we battled the ubiquitous festival mimes, our crew fought the elements. The Mistral was blowing, that majestic wind that rushes down the Rhône Valley, drying the air and sending glasses crashing off café tables. We were playing outdoors in the beautiful courtyard of the Faculté des Science, and our production manager, Kris Kinet, was skeptical at rigging the *Sganarelle* set, virtually a series of large canvas sails, in such winds. Her French counterpart said go ahead. Up went the set, along came a gust of Mistral, and down crashed the set, bringing with it a chunk of nineteenth-century architecture. The set was abandoned, except for "The Flying Doctor" house, and we played on a bare white stage surrounded by stunning oleander bushes.

Curtain time was 10 p.m., and under a full moon, the actors' voices overcoming the roar of the Mistral, Tommy Derrah assumed his roles of twin Sganarelles in "The Flying Doctor." Two hours later we were being called back from our dressing rooms, costumes half

Christine Estabrook (Arkadina), Jeremy Geidt (Sorin), and Stephanie Roth (Nina) in *The Seagull*.

off, to take yet another curtain call, the sound of clapping and stamping in unison, music to our ears.

It's one thing to please the public and another the French critics. We were delighted with our reviews but were told by the French we should be ecstatic, these being the toughest critics in France. "A miracle has come from the U.S.," said *Le Matin*. "You must run there with blankets, but you must run. . . . Molière of the Melting Pot . . . no longer belongs to us and so much the better," the critic added. *La Marseilles* said, "The actors who come from the austere city of Boston are comics of rare quality. Absolutely astonishing. Those damned Americans, it would have to be them who make us discover the comic force of these four plays." *Le Monde*: "More Molière than Molière. A devilish display, totally American. This show is astonishing, Molière spat out whole, not travestied a single second. Merci to the actors of the A.R.T. of Boston, to Robert Brustein, its artistic director, and Andrei Serban, their guest director, for the joyous, American Molière-ish evening."

At that we took ourselves off to Ousteau de Baumaniere, awarded five spoons and forks and three rosettes by Michelin, perhaps the best restaurant in France. I mean you've got to do something, haven't you? Or else we might start believing those wonderful French.

ORLANDO

Handel's <u>Orlando</u>: Scenes, Machines, Songs, and Dances
by Peter Sellars

Ariosto's epic poem *Orlando Furioso*, first published in 1516, was in some respects the science fiction of its time: a fabulous serial of heroic adventures set at the geographical and psychological frontiers of the then-known world, with a full panoply of alien armies and fantasy monsters, mingled with realistic detail, close observation of human beings in day-to-day life or *in extremis*, and the occasional moral truth. Ariosto was able to weave chatty asides; blood-spattered tragedy; delicate, luminous love poetry; maddening psychological torment; and pure adventure into a single, sustained form. *Orlando Furioso* was one of the most widely read books in Europe for several centuries, with spin-offs beginning almost immediately: hundreds of operas were derived from it (Handel composed three), and the central romance of Angelica and Medoro (the subject of Handel's *Orlando*) was the standard choice for love-in-the-woods scenes in the visual arts right up through Tiepolo's magnificent suite of drawings.

Opera, in the words of Dryden, is the consummate union of "scenes, machines, songs and dances." Operas were advertised with "Particularly, the Fountain Scene," or "Mlle. Crail will do her Spanish dance," whereas the name of the composer was often left off the bill. Handel's *Rinaldo* in 1711 featured "two huge Dragons," a "Black cloud descending, all filled with dreadful Monsters spitting Fire and Smoke on every Side," plus mermaids, waterfalls, and "thunder, lightning, and amazing noises." *The Spectator* dryly noted after this performance that the dragons were not very impressive and there was "a very short allowance of Thunder and Lightning," though the spitting of fire and smoke was exceedingly generous. It also mentioned that "the sparrows and chaf-finches fly as yet very irregularly over the stage." This latter effect was in fact something of a disaster: a large flock of live pigeons was released on stage, whereupon they immediately flew out over the audience and spent the rest of the evening covering George I and his royal party with rather unceremonious droppings. Extreme divergences of tone were reconcilable in music, literature, cuisine, and theatrical entertainment. In a London theatre of the eighteenth century, the performance of the most solemn tragedy would be attended with a ludicrous farce as an afterpiece and songs and dances as interludes, along with trained dog acts, acrobatics, or even equestrian ballets. It was by no means unheard of for a leading actress to follow a particularly rousing speech with a bow and then a rendering of some of her favorite airs.

"Theatrical, or Opera Dancing" fell into the categories "serious, grotesque, and scenical." Possibilities ranged from the "Tub Dance" to the "Union of Two Nations." "Droll attitudes, leaping, and contortions of the body" alienated with the "natural, fit and proper." The grotesque and melancholic were thought especially suitable to opera.

There are many accounts of card games, gossip mongering, snoozes, and sexual adventures in the private boxes. Aaron Hill in his broadside *The Prompter* found the music itself not "beautiful" so much as "titillating" and the very presence of castrati a corrupting influence upon the morals, having "the eyes, ears, and thoughts of our ladies conversant with figures they cannot well see, hear, nor think of without a blush." A large number of gentlemen of quality wrote passionate letters to Mlle. Celestina, who created the male role of Medoro in *Orlando* "in travesty." They repeatedly confessed that the sight of her sweating in a helmet was very arousing indeed. But for all this, there are also accounts of audience members fainting at dramatic high points in performances. Reactions were strong, and stage action could provoke "a civil broil among the subscribers."

Baroque opera was a question of the manipulation of clichés, in the most positive sense of the word. In terms of the performer, the parts were written to order—exactly the way one had Cary Grant or John Wayne roles in Hollywood, where the persona of the star was inseparable from the character. For example, in *Orlando* Handel wrote the role of Dorinda (a personage who does not figure in Ariosto) as a showcase for Signora Bertolli, a woman who was possibly the first Italian *commedia* actress to arrive in England. Zoroastro (again not in Ariosto) was invented as her seriocomic foil for Signor Montagnana, "whose formidable pipe may excite terror in the most intrepid," in the words of a contemporary fan. A great deal of audience excitement was derived, as in a Broadway musical or cabaret act, from the star performer stepping to the front of the stage to present a specialty number, frequently a song in ABA form in which we wait for the singer to improvise on the reprise of the main section, adding his own personal stamp to the music. The ornaments on these *da capo* arias in baroque opera are in many ways the equivalent of scat singing.

The other aspect of cliché dominating eighteenth-century opera concerns characters, plot, and setting. Handel's audience didn't need to be told who Orlando was, as audiences today do not need to be told about Captain Kirk or Mr. Spock. As soon as the characters appeared, the audience had a set of collective expectations and was ready for action. Thus I think the logical choice is to update these clichés in modern performance.

These clichés were for Handel (as for Ariosto or any great artist) not end points but starting points, and in every case he went beyond them to tackle major musical, emotional, social, and moral issues.

The beauty in the music is hard-won, through desperation and persistence. Handel is daring. He freely mixes tragedy and comedy in a way that leaves us breathless, bewildered, and grateful. He condenses a half-hour of action into fifty seconds and spins a moment out across a whole act.

ORCHIDS IN THE MOONLIGHT

Carlos Fuentes Turns to Theatre
Interview by Arthur Holmberg

"When I was a young man," Carlos Fuentes confesses, "I wrote to live. Now, at fifty-four, I write not to die. Like Scheherazade in the *Arabian Nights*, I'll live as long as I have another story to tell." *The Death of Artemio Cruz* and *Terra Nostra* established Mr. Fuentes's reputation as one of the world's leading novelists. Now *Orchids in the Moonlight*, his first play to be produced in America, will have its world premiere at the American Repertory Theatre.

The title comes from a Vincent Youmans tango danced by Dolores del Río and Fred Astaire in the 1933 movie musical *Flying Down to Rio*. The play is a dialogue between Dolores del Río and

María Félix, two Mexican screen goddesses. A third character, an American movie buff, precipitates the play's tragedy. All the costumes are visual references to films made by both actresses and evoke the glamour of a bygone era.

In one of the play's emotional climaxes, the two aging film beauties watch clips from their old movies. Their faces and bodies were once symbols of erotic fantasy onto which millions of mute spectators projected hidden desires. Past their prime, they no longer have any tangible relationship to those far-off images, and one cannot be sure if those shadows flickering across the wall promote self-definition or self-deception.

"Movies," Mr. Fuentes notes, "are bearers of the collective unconscious, the warehouse of modern myths. It would be difficult to overestimate the impact of movies. Hollywood manufactures the archetypes we need to understand our collective life. Marilyn Monroe is one of the great totems of the tribe. She arose from the same realm of the imagination as Venus. She fulfills the same need. American pop archetypes have permeated the world from the mountains of Tibet to the jungles of Brazil.

"My play is about the myth of culture and the culture of myths. But even more it is a play about memory. About the movies I saw years ago in Mexico. The interesting thing about modern archetypes is that they are embedded in fashion, they go in and out of style. Our icons are ephemeral, our gods disposable. We throw them away. Our civilization is based on amnesia. So writing this play was a journey into the past and an evocation of two beautiful Mexican women who were important to me in my youth. Growing up, I used to say that I descended from Montezuma, Hernando Cortés, María Félix, and Dolores del Río. They were my ancestors.

"I loved those two actresses because they were strong and independent. They shattered all the macho myths. They were not what Latin women were supposed to be. They were not little dolls men could cuddle. María Félix was a Pancho Villa in skirts."

Mr. Fuentes flashes a matinee-idol smile. He has dark good looks and the easy grace of one descended from a solid line of bankers, merchants, and landed gentry. The son of a diplomat, he grew up in Washington and served as Mexico's ambassador to France. He is an aristocrat in style, a revolutionary in thought.

Why did Mr. Fuentes, one of the acknowledged wizards of the novel, turn to the theatre?

"I write for the stage from a deep urge," he said. "I don't believe in pure genres. Genres are not vital unless they are contaminated, cross-fertilized. My two literary models, the two authors I live with, Cervantes and Shakespeare, created works where the various genres speak to each other, engage in a dialogue. Every genre has a voice in *Don Quixote. Hamlet* is a play within a play within a novel. Hamlet's desperate attempt to recall the past is an act of the narrative imagination. The past is a memory that must be dreamed again.

"Also, writing and reading a novel is a private experience. The theatre is a public art. I wanted to communicate with others beyond the printed word. I had something to say which could be said only if my words were given faces and voices. I wanted to give my language a body. The stage is a vacuum which I want to fill up physically with my language.

"The theatre is a unique experience. Language comes alive on the stage as nowhere else. You have a living, human voice interacting with other voices. No experience can replace this verbal presence. The word incarnate cannot be filmed or taped or canned.

"I love movies as well, but the theatre is the real thing, a living, breathing organism made up of author, actors, audience. The audience actually finishes writing the play for me. They recreate it in their own mind. My play opens up windows for them into their memory and imagination."

Joann Green, who is directing the premiere at Harvard, sees the play as an exploration of the possibility of friendship between women. "The vital fantasy of *Orchids in the Moonlight* exists because of the strength and beauty of a bond between women," she said. "It is rare to have two such vibrant female presences stage center. These women reflect for each other the power of fame and glamour and the wisdom of revolution and nostalgia. They hold each other tighter as time slips away."

Why did Mr. Fuentes choose America for the play's premiere?

"American actors," he replied, "are the best in the world. I just saw Mickey Rooney in *Sugar Babies*, and I realized that he would be perfect in Molière. He was born to play *The Bourgeois Gentleman* or *The Imaginary Invalid*. His comic fire matches Molière's.

"English actors can be splendid, too. They know how to pronounce well, but they are obviously an artistic fabrication. Brought to its highest pitch with a Gielgud or an Olivier, this type of acting achieves a polished beauty I respect and enjoy, but there's an intimacy in American acting I find more exciting. American actors are not afraid to show their vulnerability, and this vulnerability creates a tension that for me is the essence of drama. It's precisely this kind of acting that I needed and wanted for my play, and I'm most pleased at what the American Repertory Theatre is doing with it."

Orchids in the Moonlight represents a significant departure from Mr. Fuentes's earlier work. It depends much less on the surface reality of Mexico for its local color and themes; its preoccupations are more personal and less political; and its style is more playful and self-consciously theatrical. It is also the first important work that Mr. Fuentes, who is perfectly bilingual, has written in English.

"My work is probably becoming less and less 'Mexican,'" agreed Mr. Fuentes, who spends most of his time in the United States. "I've been living outside my country for a long time. Maybe I've paid my nationalistic dues by now. Nonetheless, even in *Orchids* there is an element of identification with Mexico. But it never entered my head that I should write a Mexican play. I was writing a play about two women who need each other desperately. It's a play about loneliness, and loneliness is universal. Anyone who has been in love will understand my play.

"I wrote the play in English and Spanish at the same time. It's very curious. I had the two Mexican actresses in mind, so I started in Spanish. But the third character, the fan, was American, and this character ran away from me. He started doing a series of puns on the words "Citizen Kane" that simply wouldn't work in Spanish. They had to be in English. There were some jokes I could not say in Spanish. I had to fall back on English, which has this tremendous, protean capacity for word play that we don't have in Spanish. The demands and opportunities of Spanish are very great and very exciting, but they are other. The particular kind of humor I wanted I could get only in English.

"English has such comic life in it. Whenever it threatens to wane, along comes another Irishman to give it a good kick, and here we go again. English will always live as long as there is an Ireland."

Serban's Three Sisters: While the Light Lasts
by Arthur Holmberg

When the lights go up on Andrei Serban's new production of *Three Sisters*, they reveal a stage full of darkness. As one's eyes readjust to the dimness, three monolithic silhouettes take shape and, ghostlike, float across the stage bearing flowers for the dead. An eerie, disembodied voice-over fills the theatre with bits and pieces of memory, skimming the surface of consciousness. Then the three sisters begin to talk, slightly out of sync with their own recorded voices. This indelible stage picture sets the mood for Serban's ruthless probing of the play's central tensions between past and present, hope and despair, life and death. Throughout the production, darkness threatens to close in.

But while the light lasts, it is pure glow, brilliant and warm. Serban has stripped away the usual bourgeois interior. Only the beautifully crafted costumes and a few crucial stage props—a samovar here, a gramophone there—anchor us to a specific time and place. By paring down, the director uncovers the archetypal encoded in the realistic. Instead of a claustrophobic drawing room, Beni Montresor has designed a playing space delineated by two massive red velvet curtains in the back and banks of footlights on either side of a mirrored floor. And beyond the lights, infinite, palpable black. The Prozorov house becomes a small *theatrum mundi* onto which the familiar poor players strut and fret their hour.

But what exuberant fretting! Using the fluid rhythms of silent films, Serban has so accelerated the movement that without betraying the play's elegiac sadness, he gives the audience a dense impression of life—even in its petty, stupid details—lived to the hilt. The director doesn't miss a moment for energizing the stage picture. Anfisa (Anne Pitoniak) doesn't walk in the birthday cake, she scuds across the boards. Lost in silent dreams, Masha (Cheryl Giannini) twirls herself to a Chopin mazurka. Vershinin (Alvin Epstein) leaps atop a chair to philosophize, wigwagging his handkerchief like an SOS. Irina (Cherry Jones) spins in circles, hoping to fly away like the birds overhead. Olga (Marianne Owen) rakes in leaves with a furious haste in order to avoid Vershinin. Solyony (Tony Shalhoub) falls into a wild Cossack dance to gloss over his social insecurity. Natasha (Karen MacDonald) scatters Vershinin's flowers underfoot while making plans to chop down the Prozorovs' fir trees. But Serban does not employ this manic agitation and strangely dislocated stage business merely to create striking visual images. His characters use gestures the way they use language—as a narcotic.

The search for oblivion is summed up by Chebutykin, the army doctor richly portrayed by Jeremy Geidt as a pixilated, addlepated nihilist. As the three sisters struggle to hold on to their memories, Chebutykin—with the help of a seemingly endless supply of vodka—seeks to forget. Combing his beard and burbling about smallpox in China, he shows how easy it is to withdraw from reality into current events, from truth into facts. He protects himself from the world by rattling a newspaper, and Geidt turns this desperate buffoon, who long ago discovered that he and all other members of his species were *de trop* in the universe, into a prophet of the absurd. Before Beckett, Chekhov had discovered that farce and tragedy inhabit the same human kingdom.

And Serban, aided immeasurably by the brilliant ensemble playing of the A.R.T. actors, has unearthed other similarities between Chekhov, the master of realism, and Beckett, the clown of existentialism. By emphasizing the random, episodic flow of events, this production explodes the mirage of a well-made play. The characters spend their lives talking and waiting and waiting and talking, and, in the meantime, time passes, bringing not fulfillment but despair. Serban accentuates this despair by letting the various characters drift off into private, solipsistic reveries. Dialogue becomes monologue. No one listens to anyone else. When Andrei (Thomas Derrah) tries to confess to his sisters in Act III and seek their forgiveness, Masha runs off to meet her lover, and Olga and Irina doze off. When Masha tries to explain her secret happiness, Olga shuts up her ears. Irina pours out her soul to Chebutykin, who ducks into a newspaper. Not merely the best modernist Chekhov I have seen but, simply, the best Chekhov.

Against this bleak, existential nightmare of physical and metaphysical dispossession, what enables the three sisters to carry on? The title of the play gives the answer, and Serban etches in the life-sustaining bond between these three women with delicate force. We wait, expectantly, exaltantly, for those few precious moments when

Members of the company in *Three Sisters* (Thomas Derrah, Cherry Jones, foreground).

the three sisters make contact with each other. In the final act, Serban has strewn the ground with red and yellow leaves. Autumn has come, the soldiers have left, and the three sisters are alone on the stage, exactly where they began. As they disappear again into the dark, they hold each other tightly in a community of love.

Arthur Holmberg wrote this piece for the Performing Arts Journal *in 1982, five years before he had any professional association with the A.R.T. The article was later anthologized in* Theatre: A Way of Seeing *(1986) by Milly S. Barranger.*

Marsha Norman on Playwriting
Interview by Robert Brustein

Q: Is there anything in your past that accounts for your development as a theatre artist?

MARSHA NORMAN: There were things, yes, that seemed to be curses at the time, that turned out to be blessings. Things I would need as a writer. I was very isolated. Not lonely but definitely cut off from other children. Mother was afraid other children would tell me things she didn't want me to know. So I read and read. Also, it was a cheerful household. I was not allowed to frown. Consequently I spent a lot of time imagining what I would say if I had somebody to say it to and if I didn't have to smile all the time. I lived on imaginary conversation. I still do. My plays are always conversations I would like to hear, conversations people have—or would like to have but don't, for fear of what would happen if they did.

'Night, Mother is just such a conversation. What on earth would you say if I came over to your house one night and said, "I'm going to kill myself, Bob"? What is there that is enough to say? Can we really understand the people we live with? I don't know. I wrote the play to find out.

So many of the things that we need to say to each other are unsayable. The only place we can hear them, in fact, is in the theatre. In a sense, it's my responsibility in writing to say the unsaid, to show you how these unthinkable things go, when they happen. Because they do happen.

Someone once told me the characters in my plays were all the people Mother wouldn't let me play with. Maybe that's true. I did live in a very secret world. But then, I still do.

Q: What is there, Marsha, about this highly public and exposed art called theatre that attracts you?

MN: Well, it's real simple. I'm a listener. I'm a great eavesdropper. You can go to lunch with me, and I can tell you what's happening at tables all around the restaurant, and you'll still think I'm listening to you. Listening is the only thing I do all the time. Sometimes I talk, sometimes I don't. Sometimes I make jokes and entertain; sometimes I seem to disappear. But I'm always listening. I don't notice things that, say, a painter would notice, but I do notice how people say things. And what people say is never as interesting as how they say it. There are at least fifteen ways to say, "Pass the salt." How you say it is what you mean.

Q: That explains why you like quiet food like ice cream, rather than noisy food like celery: so you can overhear the people at the next table.

MN: I do love ice cream.

Q: But you love your isolation more.

MN: I am happiest when I am absolutely alone, yes, when it is completely quiet, and nobody knows where I am. But the significant isolation is more than a simple solitude. It is the ability to keep from thinking about the critics or the audience, to keep the doubts away until the play is written.

Writing a play is like designing an automobile. You can't just know what one looks like. You have to know how the thing is put together and how it moves down the road. You have to know the mechanics: how it works. Plays are vehicles of transportation. In order to be successful, they have to take you someplace. How pleasant the ride is, how nice the seat covers are, how good the view is, what kind of talk there is along the way—those are all important but not nearly as important as moving down the road. It's not very entertaining to sit and talk in a car that won't go anywhere.

It is so easy to lose your way as a writer. You can write too fast, you can talk too much, you can begin to think you're special. You can break the rules. I know these are mistakes because I've made them all. But this business about the rules is the most interesting. There *are* rules for plays, and they cannot be broken. Rules like "You must have an active, central character," and "Something has to change by the end." I no longer see rules as restrictions. Now I want to know why they have worked for so long and what it is, exactly, that makes them work. I feel like I'm fighting a battle that is so old—one that's been going on for thousands and thousands of years in the theatre, this struggle with the form. But it's exciting to be providing new evidence for the sturdiness of the ancient structures. Those old Aristotelian unities are still the standard as far as I'm concerned. I like to write in real time. *'Night, Mother* plays in exactly the amount of time it takes on stage. I'm a purist about theatrical time.

Q: You have had five plays produced now. Which of these plays is your favorite, and why?

MN: I don't fall in love with my plays. I've only seen *'Night,*

Kathy Bates (Jessie) and Anne Pitoniak (Thelma) in *'Night, Mother.*

Mother five times in the nine months it's been running on Broadway. The last time I saw it, I knew I could do better now. But that's not to say it's easy to separate from them in the beginning. That moment, when you understand that this fragile thing is actually going out into the world, is terrifying. If you are fortunate, there are good people at dinner with you that night. But if the play doesn't leave your control, it will never have a life. The moment of separation is terribly important, and I think I do it pretty well. You have to. You have to say,

"Well, all right, there it goes. God bless it, and I hope I can get out of the way if it falls."

It's sad when writers follow their work around, I think. If you design a skyscraper, you must not spend all your time riding the elevators after it is built. For one thing, you won't design any more buildings if you do, and worse than that, you will never see what it looks like from the outside.

I ask for help as soon as I have a first draft. I will ask three or four people to read it and tell me what they think. Then I generally ask actor friends to come read the play for me. Wonderful actors are so helpful. Simply by reading the play, they can tell you when it isn't clear, when you've made it up, and when you've got it right. It's not their conversation that tells you that, it's how they read the play, how they respond to it as they are reading. Good actors can't help but show you what you have in a play. It's their gift.

There is a danger, though, in listening to any comments about your work. You must never listen for the solutions; you must listen for the problems and then go back to your study and find the solutions.

Q: One final question. Why did you decide to do *'Night, Mother* in a resident theatre outside of New York?

MN: The reasons are so clear, Bob. At the A.R.T., you feel supported and secure, encouraged and challenged. It's a great job when someone says, "You may have this theatre for six weeks." Working here is not just a way to avoid the pressure of New York. It's a way to enjoy the process. In New York, people disappear after rehearsal and you never get to know your cast, much less the staff of the theatre. But there's a better reason. Last year I would occasionally listen to the performance in the green room instead of watching it from the theatre. Then, after the show I would come out into the house, and there would be these small groups of people, still in their seats talking to each other. That's what the play had done—taken people who had been facing the front all night and turned them to face one another. We can't do that in New York. We can't let the audience talk to each other after the play. We have to send them out into the streets. Resident theatres like the A.R.T. are places where people can stay and talk. And I don't know why else I do this other than to get people to stay and talk; so naturally, this is where I want to do it.

This article was supplemented with additional remarks published in an interview by Stephanie Carroll in the 1982 A.R.T. News.

Jonathan Miller Rehearses
by Arthur Holmberg

Dr. Miller's speech falls naturally into the graceful cadences of Augustan prose. Meanwhile, his hands, which seem to number not two but twenty, carry on a Socratic dialogue of their own. His tongue is nimble, but his limbs are nimbler, now tugging his hair, now rubbing his chin, now palming his knee. Arguably the finest conversationalist in the English-speaking world, his sign language does not so much emphasize his main point as render visible his process of thinking.

"I wanted to do *The School for Scandal* because it dramatizes the importance of gossip," he says. "Talk is a pleasurable act. It is also a creative act, and talking about other people constitutes an enormous part of what we call social life. Gossip is a form of laser holography. When millions of beams of talk coincide around a person, a three-dimensional image begins to hover in the otherwise thin air, an image more vital than any elaborated by a single eye or ear. We are, to a large degree, a composite of the talk different people have about us— of their views and opinions of our personality.

"Of course gossip can turn sour. Talking exorbitantly about people behind their backs can denature relationships, and the constant repetition of bad judgments and seductively persuasive condemnations can be unfair and encourage an appraisal in the worst possible light. Gossip is dangerous in direct proportion to the gullibility of the audience. Sheridan's play shows both sides of the coin. He establishes an antiphony of cynicism and sentimentality. Few people today can gossip with the energy, intelligence, or malice of Sheridan's characters. Gossip is a highly advanced and highly elaborate form of discourse. Most great literature, in fact, is simply elegant, printed gossip. *Remembrance of Things Past* is gossip of the highest order."

Watching Mr. Miller in rehearsal is to see a master strategist and shrewd diplomat at work. He wheedles, coaxes, and cajoles his actors into giving the performance he wants. First a compliment, then a gentle suggestion. If the interpretation really misses the mark, Mr. Miller engages the actor in a lively discussion that might begin, "Have you ever noticed in a moment of awkward silence the kinds of faces people make?" And, step by step, he then nudges the actor along. He's a good director because he's a good audience. He doesn't

Alvin Epstein (Sir Peter Teazle), Tony Shalhoub (Joseph Surface), and Cherry Jones (Lady Teazle) in *The School for Scandal*.

miss a detail. "The sound of that laughter isn't quite right," he observes at one point. "Why don't you try less of a giggle and more of a cackle?"

During a five-minute break, he launches into a theory of social justice, bringing to bear on the discussion Plato, David Hume, Adam Smith, Immanuel Kant, and John Rawls, the Harvard philosopher. Between breaths he sucks on a seemingly endless supply of sugar cubes. His mind is a warehouse of Western civilization, but he intimidates no one. The warmth he feels for his colleagues, generous and genuine, creates an atmosphere of trust.

"Working with the A.R.T. has been a very special experience for me because of the company spirit," he says. "What makes the theatre special is not making 'art' but making friends with the people who make the art. There's a special and irreplaceable bond that grows between directors, designers, technicians, and actors. There is no substitute for this fellow-feeling. We players know that the theatre—like life itself—is a doomed enterprise. Putting on a show is like being on a mad, shipwrecked vessel with the engine gone. You keep it all afloat for a while and then it disappears into the night. This knowledge makes actors very companionable."

Later, Mr. Miller begins drilling the actors on their exits and entrances. He makes the company repeat one entrance fifteen times before he's satisfied. "Don't waltz in," he advises. "It's more like a gavotte!" He encourages the right movement by tripping through the door himself on tiptoe. "Exits and entrances," he observes, "are often the most crucial moments of social intercourse. They are moments of highly concentrated psychological incident. It's not just a question of getting someone on or off the stage. The first five seconds are vital. The moment we enter a room, we encounter gazes, questions, criticisms, welcomes, or hostility—a whole network of highly charged verbal and nonverbal signs that establishes a magnetic field. Therefore, on entering, we must make some kind of statement to the assembled company, summing up our attitude to the group. We enter apologizing, smiling, blustering."

After all the actors have exited from the day's strenuous rehearsal, Mr. Miller falls atop a table and rolls himself up into a hedgehog ball. After a few moments he stretches his enormous frame up to its full height, groaning. He rubs his eyes and blinks back at the world.

"People don't believe what hard work the theatre is," he says. "It's like pushing a heavy rock up the side of a steep mountain, and once you get there it stays for only a few moments. Surgery, by comparison, is easy. All you have to do is cut the body open and sew it up." An angelic smile sweeps across his face as he strolls over to the sugar bowl. He turns it upside down and shakes it violently. It's empty. "Oh dear, oh dear, oh dear," he says. "We're out of sugar. Whatever shall we do?"

David Leveaux on A Moon for the Misbegotten
Interview by Laura Rice

Q: What do you find challenging about O'Neill's writing that drew you to it?

DAVID LEVEAUX: I wanted to work with actors who could encompass both a vocal and emotional range that most twentieth-century dramas do not require. I was seeking work that demanded an operatic aspiration and commitment. This is not so obvious with O'Neill, who is often regarded as one of the great naturalist dramatists. From my reading, I guessed he was not a naturalist first and foremost. He was writing on the cusp of the classical age meeting the modern naturalistic age and inventing a language for the stage that bore no resemblance to colloquial parlance and that required a technical facility in the actor similar to that required by Shakespeare.

Q: What place does *Moon* hold in the course of O'Neill's work, and what attracted you to it rather than another of O'Neill's plays?

DL: Reading the play is like reading again the oldest dream one has ever had. It is a baby compared to the other great plays in terms of its running time. It is marvelously economic in its writing and language.

Finally, it is a very simple tale, and that deeply attracted me. I was also intrigued by the fact that the play takes place outside and is not domestic.

Long Day's Journey into Night and *The Iceman Cometh* are more familiar and more often done. For many people, they tend to be the beginning and the end of Eugene O'Neill, but that is inappropriate. *Moon* is the most Irish of O'Neill's plays, and O'Neill's Irishness was a vital strength for him.

Q: Some critics and biographers view *Moon* as a sequel to *Long Day's Journey*. Do you agree with this notion?

DL: There is an autobiographical vein in both plays. James Tyrone of *Moon* and Jamie of *Long Day's Journey* are drawn from O'Neill's brother, Jamie, who died of alcoholism in 1923. *A Moon for the Misbegotten* is, in some sense, a continuation of the family fortunes but with a focus on Jamie. Undeniably there is an autobiographical link but not necessarily an artistic one. *Moon* is more unashamedly classical and more tightly achieved than *Long Day's Journey*.

Q: *A Moon for the Misbegotten* was O'Neill's last play. Do you think he realized that when he undertook its writing?

DL: He knew he was very ill and that his nervous disorder was making it physically harder for him to write. He wrote in longhand; he did not type or dictate. For him writing was a physical activity, the act itself intimately connected to the process of imaginative creation.

He finished the play in 1943 and by June of that year was incapable of further writing. He devoted the next ten years to getting his plays produced.

It is always tempting to say, as with Shakespeare, "*The Tempest* was his last play because Prospero buries his book." I think O'Neill was too obsessed with the theatre to stop writing for an abstract reason, but *Moon* is, in some ways, the most mellow of his plays.

Q: Do you sense some special reason for his writing the play?

DL: I think it was mainly written as a way of getting out of his system something about Jamie, who had died twenty years earlier, but of course O'Neill was a dramatist and continued to write for grander reasons still.

Q: You've said that the character of James Tyrone was probably drawn from Jamie O'Neill. Where do you think the character of Josie originated?

DL: A combination of sources. I like to imagine O'Neill was familiar with a number of very old Irish folktales in which a figure of a woman occurs who has very definite qualities of pride, great strength, and a sort of divinity.

Some women have mentioned that Josie has suffered abuse and then is called on to understand and forgive a man who, after all, wrecked himself. It's not that simple. Josie, too, longs for and receives something from Tyrone that she did not have before.

Q: But not what she expected?

DL: No, not at all. The fascinating thing about the play is that it is not at all what anyone expects. The early part of the narrative ends up going out the window.

Q: Could you suggest a motive for such a dramatic plot shift?

DL: It's a careful and deliberate technique that casts upon the audience a sense of deception that is analogous to the way the characters deceive themselves and each other. The plot is one of the most extraordinary red herrings in the world of drama. In fact, the whole play is full of blarney. Some of it is obvious from the beginning; some is not. It is an extraordinary, extended joke with wonderfully comic, Irish moments.

Q: From what you have said, I gather you devote a great deal of attention to the structure of the play's language. When you begin a production, how do you approach the text?

DL: First I read the play very fast all the way through. When I do that the shape and form of the play yields to me something that I don't get when reading in great detail. This immediate impression is vital. I keep it as a touchstone throughout the production and often ask actors to do things that are rooted in the play's form rather than in character.

After a quick reading, I work through the text in more detail. This is especially important with O'Neill, whose lines are composed of phrases with phrases. I mark the periods and gear changes in the play where one thing ends and another begins. O'Neill has a few pauses because his is a very vigorous, fluid language, but there are clear breaks in the dialogue, which give it dimension. At first I am more interested with the form of the lines than the psychology of the character.

Q: Do you do much research beyond these readings of the play?

DL: I immerse myself in the landscape of the writer to understand the play better, but I also want to come to the play without any sophisticated notions. I read other plays by the writer and, in O'Neill's case, I read a lot about him because I was fascinated with the strong autobiographical content of his work.

Q: What follows all the reading and study?

DL: Rehearsal. The minute I hear a play, I get something that I never get from the page, especially if it's a good play by a dramatic poet like O'Neill.

Huckleberry Finn and the Stage: Will the Twain Ever Meet?
by Glenda Hobbs

Throughout his lifetime Mark Twain was obsessed with the stage. Although his only successful stage play was *The American Claimant*—a collaboration with William Dean Howells, based on a character from Twain's novel *The Gilded Age*—Twain wrote stage adaptations of *Tom Sawyer*, *Roughing It*, and *The Prince and the Pauper*. He also collaborated with Bret Harte on *Ah, Sin!*, a comedy set in the Mother Lode country, and planned many others, including an abolitionist melodrama and an historical drama set in Oliver Cromwell's time. Twain worked zealously on a burlesque of *Hamlet*, which he discussed with Edwin Booth, but he abandoned it when he couldn't think of a satisfactory way to do it without corrupting Shakespeare's poetry.

Years later he would overcome his hesitancy to tamper with the Bard's words in a hilarious parody of "Hamlet's Immortal Soliloquy" in *The Adventures of Huckleberry Finn*, performed by the bogus Duke of Bridgewater in his theatrical fiasco, "The Royal Nonesuch." Misremembering some of Hamlet's lines to read, "To be or not to be; that is the bare bodkin," the Duke humorously illustrates Twain's precept that "the difference between the right word and the nearly right word is the difference between lightning and a lightning bug."

In the A.R.T.'s *Big River*, "The Royal Nonesuch" becomes a play within a play. Adapting such a beloved and influential American novel (Hemingway said, "All modern American literature comes from one book by Mark Twain called *Huckleberry Finn*") was a considerable challenge for William Hauptman. As a dramatist, he says he was attracted by Huck's character, who is "almost always, (except when Jim is there with him) the only sane person in an insane world. Huck is fleeing from many things, but he's also fleeing toward growing up." Hauptman was also intrigued by the way the story moved in two directions at once: "A flight down a great river through the heart of a troubled country, and at the same time a journey back into Twain's own boyhood past."

Director Des McAnuff sees the form of *Big River* as more akin to Thornton Wilder's *Our Town* and Tennessee Williams's *The Glass*

Menagerie than to classics of the musical stage: "The novel *Huckleberry Finn* is written in retrospective; it's past tense. And like *The Glass Menagerie* or *Our Town* it has a single narrative voice. We're maintaining Huck's strong voice in *Big River*, so in terms of point of view, *Big River* is a memory play."

McAnuff wants the stage enactment to be in some way equivalent to reading the book. To accomplish this goal, he'll go back and forth between "presentational" and "representational" scenes while keeping Huck's own perspective central. The director wants the audience to believe that all the events in some sense really happen; he doesn't want "Wonder Bread theater." In early rehearsals, McAnuff demonstrated his commitment to historical accuracy by engaging the actors in round-table discussions and readings from actual slave narratives, accounts of temperance revivals, and even a profile of the real Duke of Bridgewater.

William Hauptman chose the title *Big River* because he believes that the metaphor contains all the themes in the novel: Huck and Jim use the raft as an escape from the cruelty they encounter onshore. Much of director McAnuff's confidence and enthusiasm comes from his faith in Hauptman: "Bill is a Southerner, from Texas, and he sees the novel from both instinct and logic. . . . He's found a way to lay it out dramatically and leave out what's not relevant onstage."

Hauptman describes his method of adaptation as "taking a tangled piece of wire and yanking it, straightening it out." His aim was "to uncover, by selection, the essential *Huckleberry Finn*," which meant at times simplifying some of the more labyrinthine, or what he calls "devious," plot contrivances, and "condensing, purifying." Hauptman says he lifted out the subtext and clarified the throughline to make a cleaner, more dramatic story for the stage. "I took what I thought were the best parts from different sections of the book and ran them all the way through in an attempt to try to see what was the best book—the best *Huck Finn*."

This dramatization, coming one hundred years after the novel was published, poses challenges Twain never faced when he adapted his own novels for his own time. Hauptman felt he should "bring it into our century" by smoothing out some of the dialect and deleting some racist remarks. "I felt that a living, breathing, twentieth-century actor would feel uncomfortable with these comments, so I thought it was appropriate not to use them." McAnuff feels that "the idea of satirizing slavery is quite a dangerous thing to do," and he doesn't think

Twain always succeeded with the satire in the novel: "It's not always clear in the book; occasionally sections are ambiguous, and I think Bill's dealt with it very sensitively."

Hauptman's other writing suggests his affinity with *Huckleberry Finn*. His tough, comic plays question American cultural myths. Many characters in Hauptman's plays, such as his Obie Award–winning *Domino Courts* (1976) and *Heat* (1974), are like Huck: they encounter violence, struggle to find ways to escape loneliness, and love the journey for its own sake. Hauptman's elegiac short story "The Desert," about his boyhood trip to the Arizona desert, recalls Twain's ambivalent lament for his boyhood in *Huckleberry Finn*.

Both Hauptman and McAnuff credit Rocco Landesman with the inspiration for *Big River*. Landesman's first notion was to lure country singer/songwriter Roger Miller into the theatre. McAnuff explains: "Rocco is a great fan of country music and a lover of Roger Miller's lyrics. He saw a certain parallel between Twain and Miller: a sense of irony, a way of finding the unobvious, wit and irony, and a wonderful way with language. Song is one way to evoke the atmosphere of the period." Hauptman was thrilled to work with Roger Miller; he too perceived a connection between Miller and Twain: "Roger's music is verbally brilliant, like Twain's prose, and is simple, like a folk song. The novel just naturally lends itself to music, and country and western is the natural choice."

Musical director Michael S. Roth is arranging the music to make it sound as authentic as Miller's lyrics and Twain's prose. "It's refreshing that Miller isn't a musical theatre person," Roth said. "He doesn't deal with theatre songs conventionally—that is, that the action has to reach an emotional climax, the strings come in, and the character sings. We'll establish a mood, for example, when Huck and Jim are on the raft, and they'll simply sing a folk song—straight from the heart."

Roth is a contemporary composer whose work is predominantly chamber music, although he once played guitar in a jug band. "My instincts are classical. My writing is spare, and my orchestrations tend not to be thickly textured. Listeners usually hear everything the individual instruments are up to when I orchestrate, which is akin to the simple clarity of what Roger does with his guitar. Rather than try to make this music theatrical, I'm hoping to use a little distance to achieve a straight-ahead classical sound. If this is heard as fresh nowadays it's only because most contemporary theatrical orchestrations are so bombastic."

Hauptman's untangled wire, Miller's honest lyricism, and Roth's uncluttered arrangements all support McAnuff's vision of a poignant American memory play.

Of his own attempt to adapt *Tom Sawyer* for the stage, Twain wrote that however hard he tried, it just "did not arrive." Twain's A.R.T. collaborators are hoping that *Huckleberry Finn* will arrive fresh from the big river and rarin' to go.

Big River *went on to win seven Tony Awards in 1985, including Best Musical.*

SIX CHARACTERS IN SEARCH OF AN AUTHOR

Brustein's Hall of Mirrors
Interview by Arthur Holmberg

Q: Why Pirandello? Why *Six Characters in Search of an Author?*

ROBERT BRUSTEIN: It's a seminal play. It raises issues that are central to the twentieth century: What constitutes reality? What constitutes character? Are we nothing but fragmented, incoherent creatures in a constant state of change? Or do we have a fixed reality? The play deals with the major metaphysical, psychological, and aesthetic concerns of the modern consciousness. It bears on our notions of time, truth, and selfhood. It also bears on our notion of art and the theatre.

"Art is a lie," Picasso observed, "that leads to the truth," and Pirandello explores the way art lies and the way it leads to the truth. He juxtaposes the fixed form of art with the flux of life, and this confrontation creates the major conflict of the play. Pirandello was one of the first to question whether realism was a viable form on the stage anymore.

Q: But the play turns on good old-fashioned melodrama. How would you characterize Pirandello's attitude toward the conventions he inherited from the nineteenth century?

RB: Maybe that's the reason Pirandello originally abandoned the characters, because the piece he was writing ended melodramatically.

The Family: Lise Hilboldt, Seth Goldstein, Linda Lavin, Nicole Shalhoub, and Robert Stattel in *Six Characters in Search of an Author*.

He grew dissatisfied with existing formulas. Then he hit upon the genial idea of putting these conventional scenes into a frame that would question them and at the same time give them a new lease on life.

Q: Twentieth-century theatre frequently turns to itself for subject matter and metaphor, not just the major playwrights like Pirandello, Beckett, or Genet but also the run-of-the-mill Broadway extravaganza. *The Real Thing*, *42nd Street*, *Noises Off*, *A Chorus Line*, *Dreamgirls*, *La Cage aux folles*, *On Your Toes*—all these plays are about putting on a show. Why does our theatre keep looking at itself in a mirror?

RB: Well, they tell us we live in an age of narcissism. But then there's nothing new about theatre reflecting on itself. *Hamlet* and Calderón's *Life Is a Dream* are plays that also talk about life as a form of playacting. But today the theatre is thinking about itself because it's in a crisis. With the coming of movies and television, the theatre can no longer take itself for granted. It has to define what it is and how it differs from other performing arts, in the same way that painting in the nineteenth century had to redefine itself in relation to photography. Once playwrights began asking themselves these fundamental questions, a new form of theatre emerged. It turned its back on realism to explore the nature of theatricality. Human consciousness is self-reflective, and it is precisely this kind of issue that intrigued Pirandello. He no longer saw the theatre as a fourth wall that lets us eavesdrop on middle-class domestic squabbles but as a self-reflecting hall of mirrors.

Q: This play is one of the acknowledged literary masterpieces of the twentieth century. Isn't it rather risky of you to adapt it?

RB: The text of a play, no matter how great, doesn't live in a library. It lives on stage, and on stage it is merely one element, though the most important, in the theatrical occasion. The other elements—the actors, the design, the lights, the director, the audience—also contribute to the occasion. A piece of stage business invented to convey an actor's conception of a character is in itself an adjustment of the text. Every performance is a kind of adaptation, because every text conforms to some extent to its actors and audience. A text undergoes many changes throughout history: time deconstructs it. When we think of a text as sacred, we're really talking about an idea we have from our reading or even the last good performance we saw. But that is to freeze something living. It is the obligation and the responsibility of the theatre, without vulgarizing a written work, to make it as fresh, as original, as direct in its relation to the audience as on the day it was first produced. And that means cutting past contrivance, past convention, past all our inherited ideas, cutting past criticism and analysis to the immediate and living event that can move people to a fresh, immediate response.

One of the main difficulties with this play is that when the audience enters the theatre, they are expected to believe that they have stumbled into a rehearsal. Pirandello wrote *Six Characters* about an Italian company rehearsing one of his other plays, *The Rules of the Game*—a wonderful bit of self-mockery. But if a modern American audience comes into the theatre and sees a group of foreign-looking actors rehearsing a Pirandello play, they're not going to believe that it's a rehearsal, and the very spirit of the play is already invalidated. So we had to find an equivalent to help the audience believe they were actually walking into a real rehearsal, and to keep that disbelief suspended during the period they remain in the theatre. Therefore we decided to rehearse our regular company—actors our audience is familiar with—in *Sganarelle*, a play we will actually be rehearsing at that time for our tour.

Six Characters is a great play because of its ideas and its highly theatrical situation, not because of its language or even its action. It's not like Chekhov where every nuance, every subtlety, every detail of character and action is crucial. You cannot cut Chekhov without doing serious violence to the play. The same is true of Ibsen. These two playwrights create intricate, interdependent mosiacs, and every bit and piece of that mosaic is essential to the total dramatic design. Pirandello is a different kind of artist. He doesn't create mosaics. His genius lies in the power of ideas and theatrical situations.

Q: When I talked to Susan Sontag about her brilliant production of *As You Desire Me* in Rome, she mentioned that the major hurdle in producing Pirandello was that his characters tend to ride off on long-winded tirades and that during these interminable speeches it's difficult to energize the stage, difficult to find meaningful stage action for the other characters.

RB: She's right. That is a problem. The exposition in this play is hard to make theatrical. The six characters have had only two scenes written for them by their author before he abandoned them. Before they can do those two scenes, they have to provide the background leading up to and connecting the two scenes. It's important to make clear what that background is because it's a convoluted, confusing, and protracted story. Pirandello does tend to go on a bit, long past the moment when the audience has grasped his meaning. So it's a service to the author to trim and barber those speeches—not to change the sense but to compress the sense when it's being repeated. The philosophical issues Pirandello brings up are very much worth hearing, but they are most powerfully invoked in the dramatic action itself. Pirandello spoke of himself as the first playwright who turned intellect into passion. He wasn't the first, but he is certainly the first to turn what one might call the abstract intellect into passion. What we mustn't lose, in listening to the intellect, is the way its passion expresses itself through a profound and moving theatricality.

Q: One of the questions Pirandello raises in this play is whether art is an exercise in futility. What answer does the play propound?

RB: Resoundingly, gloriously, triumphantly NO!

Taking the Imaginary Seriously
by Andrei Serban

The unknown cannot be captured by logic. But in the theatre of the magician Carlo Gozzi, the experience of the unknown becomes available to us. Much of twentieth-century art luxuriates in despair. It gives the impression of a room that is locked up and sealed off from anything that can receive life. Look back to Dostoevsky. He wasn't a stranger to the misery of light. His novels take us underground, in the sewers of existence, into the prisons of the self. But in Dostoevsky there is always in that dark prison a little window above, and through that window one can catch a glimpse of a tiny streak of light. You know there is something to hope for, to strive for—the possibility of escape. I believe that art is a tool to help us clarify something about our existence, not just to embrace the confusion. That's not enough. We must acknowledge the prison wall but also the window above. Gozzi lets us see the window above.

With *The King Stag* I am continuing my "year of Gozzi"—begun with Puccini's *Turandot*, which was presented at the Olympic Arts Festival in Los Angeles and Covent Garden, and followed by Prokofiev's opera based on *The Love of Three Oranges* in Geneva. For me the theatre of Gozzi remains an important point of reference and the source to which I had to return to unravel the threads of theatricality that the opera composers set in motion with their music. Here an opposition comes into play, embodied at one time in the quarrels of Gozzi and Goldoni and renewed at the turn of the century in the quarrels of Meyerhold and Stanislavsky. Meyerhold took Gozzi as his master and entitled the publication in which he set forth his theatrical theory *The Love of Three Oranges*. It is well known how fundamental this quarrel has been ever since for the choices that have been made in the contemporary theatre. What Gozzi wanted to affirm is that *the theatre's truth exists only within the theatre, that the theatre's function is not to copy or mimic any sort of reality, and that naturalism is a perversion of art*. This is obviously equally true of opera, which in its essence is an art of convention and imagination by the simple fact that in opera one expresses oneself in song.

Very important to the creation of *The King Stag* is my collaboration with Julie Taymor. Her inspired use of masks and puppets has

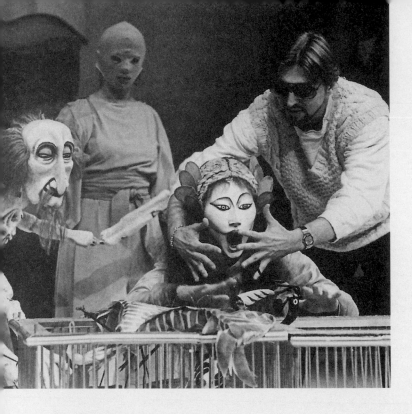

Andrei Serban directing *The King Stag*.

not only enriched the visual beauty of the production but exercised the muscles of our imagination.

Gozzi's scenarios represent first and foremost an homage to the theatre, to art—and the power of art to create laughter, healthy, athletic laughter that can heal—an homage to this intentional game that engages the imagination, the emotions, the intellect, the longing. For this reason we must play it truthfully, which means that we must not at any price undercut the joyous craziness of the work with a true-to-life lie that would be contrary to its nature. We must take the imaginary seriously in its extreme creative liberty, which leads to a very naive style of playing, like that of children's theatre. It is also a matter of going back to the primary function, that of the medieval mysteries, with their power, solemnity, and sacredness. Opposite of Goldoni, Gozzi turns *commedia dell'arte*, into an irrational windmill spinning about, mixing the comic, the absurd, the grating, and the irritating in an invented reality, joyous and sparkling. Here the theatre is king, joy bursts forth, gestures crackle, agitated by a kind of organic pulsation that must be made to surge from the story—perhaps finding, along the way, the path to the biomechanics that Meyerhold talks about: an energy, a pattern of rhythms, a system of gestures. If the mill of images and sounds works right, the audience will feel pulled into this great wheel of made-up reality—and reach out to the cosmic laughter.

ENDGAME

Statements of Samuel Beckett, Barney Rosset of Grove Press, and Robert Brustein of the American Repertory Theatre

For background of these documents, see Robert Brustein's Introduction, pages 9–10.

Bare interior.
      Grey light.
      Left and right back, high up, two small windows, curtains drawn.
      Front right, a door. Hanging near door, its face to wall, a picture.
      Front left, touching each other, covered with an old sheet, two ashbins.
      Center, in an armchair on casters, covered with an old sheet, Hamm.
      Motionless by the door, his eyes fixed on Hamm. Clov. Very red face.
      Brief tableau.

Clov goes and stands under window left. Stiff, staggering walk. He looks up at window left. He turns and looks at window right. He goes and stands under window right. He looks up at window right. He turns and looks at window left. He goes out, comes back immediately with a small step-ladder, carries it over and sets it down under window left, gets up on it, draws back curtain. He gets down, takes six steps (for example) towards window right, goes back for ladder, carries it over and sets it down under window right, gets up on it, draws back curtain. He gets down, takes three steps towards window left, goes back for ladder, carries it over and sets it down under window left, gets up on it, looks out of window. Brief laugh. He gets down, takes one step towards win-

dow right, goes back for ladder, carries it over and sets it down under window right, gets up on it, looks out of window. Brief laugh. He gets down, goes with ladder towards ashbins, halts, turns, carries back ladder and sets it down under window right, goes to ashbins, removes sheet covering them, folds it over his arm. He raises one lid, stoops and looks into bin. Brief laugh. He closes lid. Same with other bin. He goes to Hamm, removes sheet covering him, folds it over his arm. In a dressing-gown, a stiff toque on his head, a large blood-stained handkerchief over his face, a whistle hanging from his neck, a rug over his knees, thick socks on his feet, Hamm seems to be asleep. Clov looks him over. Brief laugh. He goes to door, halts, turns towards auditorium (Endgame [New York: Grove Press, 1958], 1).

Statement of Samuel Beckett About This A.R.T. Production

Any production of *Endgame* which ignores my stage directions is completely unacceptable to me. My play requires an empty room and two small windows. The American Repertory Theatre Production which dismisses my directions is a complete parody of the play as conceived by me. Anybody who cares for the work couldn't fail to be disgusted by this.

—Samuel Beckett

Statement of Barney Rosset, Publisher of the Play

As personal friend and publisher of Samuel Beckett, Grove Press is charged with the obligation of protecting the integrity of Samuel Beckett's work in the United States. The audience of the American Repertory Theatre production can judge for itself how the stage before you differs from Beckett's directions as they are reproduced here from the printed text. In Beckett's plays the set, the movements of the actors, the silences specified in the text, the lighting and the costumes are as important as the words spoken by the actors. In the author's judgment—and ours—this production makes a travesty of his conception. A living author of Beckett's stature should have the right to protect himself from what he perceives to be a gross distortion of his work. We deplore the refusal of the American Repertory Theatre to accede to Beckett's wishes to remove his name from this production, indicate in some way that this staging is merely an adaptation, or stop it entirely.

—Barney Rosset, President, Grove Press, Inc.

Ben Halley, Jr. (Hamm) and John Bottoms (Clov) in *Endgame*.

Statement of the American Repertory Theatre

Samuel Beckett's plays are among the most powerful documents of the modern age—but except in published form they are not etched in stone. Like all works of theatre, productions of *Endgame* depend upon the collective contributions of directors, actors, and designers to realize them effectively, and normal rights of interpretation are essential in order to free the full energy and meaning of the play. Each age, furthermore, brings fresh eyes to the works of the past—it was Beckett's *Endgame*, ironically, that inspired Peter Brook's radical new reading of Shakespeare's *King Lear*. We believe that this production, despite hearsay representations to the contrary, observes the spirit and the text of Mr. Beckett's great play—far more so, in fact, than a number of past productions, which to our knowledge evoked no public protests from Mr. Beckett's agents. One of these, recently performed in Belgium in 1983, was set in a warehouse flooded with eight thousand square feet of water; another, produced in New York in 1972, substituted American colloquialisms for Beckett's language.

Indeed, when directing his work, Mr. Beckett makes significant revisions in his own text and stage directions, suggesting that even he recognizes the need for changes with the passage of time. But even were our own production far more revisionist or radical, it is the public that must be the final arbiter of its value. This is not the first appearance of *Endgame*, nor is it likely to be the last. Like all great works of theatrical art, the play is open to many approaches, and each new production uncorks new meanings. To threaten any deviations from a purist rendering of this or any other play—to insist on strict adherence to each parenthesis of the published text—not only robs collaborating artists of their interpretive freedom but threatens to turn the theatre into a waxworks. Mr. Beckett's agents do no service either to theatrical art or to the great artist they represent by pursuing such rigorous controls.

—Robert Brustein, Artistic Director

JACQUES AND HIS MASTER

On Jacques and His Master
by Susan Sontag

The Master and Jacques are in the great tradition of the odd couple that begins with Don Quixote and Sancho Panza and includes Beckett's Vladimir and Estragon, Hamm and Clov. Kundera's play seems at moments Beckett-like—and, in its self-reflexiveness about theatre and theatricality, Pirandelloesque as well. But many of the most modern features of Kundera's dramaturgy come from the astonishingly "modern" Diderot novel on which it is based.

Jacques the Fatalist and His Master was written in the early 1770s and remained unpublished in Diderot's lifetime. (Diderot died in 1784.) Milan Kundera wrote his play *Jacques and His Master* almost exactly two centuries later, in 1971, when he was still living in Prague but no longer allowed to publish. (He left Czechoslovakia in 1975 and has been living in Paris ever since.) The eighteenth century of Diderot's novel is a late eighteenth century, shortly before the French Revolution. Kundera's play was written very much "after the revolution" and is suffused with *that* pathos, one unknown to Diderot's sensibility.

No one before Kundera had ever tried to make a play from Diderot's novel, which though written mostly in dialogue, is not play-like at all. It is one of those open-ended structures in which it is possible to do almost anything: to tell stories, to muse, to insert bits of so-called reality. This is one of the leading models for the novel—for, among contemporary novelists, Kundera himself. But it does not seem so appropriate to the stage, where unities rather than digressiveness have flourished.

(The one dramatic adaptation made from Diderot's novel, *Les Dames du Bois de Boulogne*, Robert Bresson's second film, with dialogue by Jean Cocteau, relates not the process of storytelling—Diderot's subject—but a story; it is the single most famous episode in the novel, the story of the revenge that the Marquise de la Pommeraye wreaks upon her faithless lover. Kundera proposes a cubist form of dramatic narrative in which it is possible to relate the story of the Marquise's revenge *as told by* the Innkeeper. Which is as Diderot invented it.)

The play exists in two historical periods—as the action in the play exists simultaneously in the present and in various times in the past.

Kundera calls his play "an homage to Diderot." There are, of course, many forms of homage. Kundera's play is both ingeniously faithful and unfaithful to the novel—which is as it should be, I think. And the playwright has made the fact that he has intervened in Diderot's world, appropriated it as well as paid homage to it, part of the work itself. Kundera has Jacques and the Master be ruefully aware that they are characters who have been not only "written" (by Diderot) but "rewritten" (by himself). Actually, Diderot was also doing a fair amount of rewriting, inspired by Laurence Sterne's *Tristram Shandy*, and his novel could be called "an homage to Sterne."

My staging provides a further reworking, both of the Diderot original and of Kundera's selection and transformation. Instead of the bare stage imagined by Kundera, I have set the action in a vast, empty, but theatrical space—a Roman ruin as reinvented by the dark brain of Piranesi (who was Diderot's contemporary) and presided over by a bust of Diderot, "the master of us both," as Jacques and the Master call him. This is ghostly space—the stage is both a stage and a theatre of ghosts. The personages in Kundera's ghost-play about the *ancien régime* are phantoms, survivors. Both presences and absences. In a word, actors.

Milan Kundera: The Paradox of Play
Interview by Arthur Holmberg

Q: Primarily you are a novelist. Why did you turn to theatre?

MILAN KUNDERA: *Jacques and His Master* is a *pièce de circonstance*. In 1971, after the fall of Dubček, the new regime looked on me with wary eyes. My books were banned, and I was stripped of all legal means of earning a living. A friend who directed a theatre suggested I write a play for his troupe using a pseudonym. So *Jacques* saw the light of day due to dire economic straits. But in addition to external circumstances, I was tempted by the call of adventure. I had never written a play before, so I wanted to try my hand creating a work that would take me, its author, by surprise.

Q: Does the drama as a genre offer you strategies of expression not found in fiction?

MK: The playfulness inherent in theatrical expression appealed to me. The theatre is a game, and playing games is an important source of pleasure. Real life is linked to a series of deceptions. It disappoints us with its futility. But when we consciously play games, as on stage, we already know that the game isn't serious. Thus the tragic futility of life becomes the joyous futility of play. In totalitarian regimes one quickly learns the importance of humor. You learn to trust or mistrust people because of the way they laugh. The modern world frightens me because it's rapidly losing the sense of the playfulness of play.

Q: Why Diderot? Why dramatize *Jacques le fataliste*?

MK: The friend who commissioned the play wanted a dramatization of a novel. In fact, he tried to shove Dostoevsky's *The Idiot* down my throat, but Dostoevsky nauseated me, not only because Russian tanks had occupied my country but also because of his streak of sentimental melodrama. I wanted to get as far away as possible from the bombastic Russian soul; I longed to take refuge in the smile of reason of French classicism.

Jacques le fataliste is one of my favorite novels—it's one of the few important novels constructed on the principle of play as play. It achieves greatness by refusing to be serious. The novel dramatizes the terminal paradoxes that ushered out the Enlightenment. Diderot was one of the first to explore the tragi-comic split between human intentions and human acts. The results of what we do get out of hand, and the rippling out effects of seemingly insignificant gestures often form a noose around our necks. After Diderot, novelists could no longer look on action and plot in quite the same way. Diderot knew that paradox is the basic law of human life.

But my play is not so much an adaptation of Diderot's novel as a dialogue across two centuries with its author—a confrontation between the eighteenth and twentieth centuries. Diderot looked on the future as infinite space to be filled with unlimited progress. We look to the future with fear and distrust. If Diderot can see my play from the other side of the tomb, he may not agree with me, but if he takes into account everything our century has seen, I don't think my play would anger him. He would understand why we've lost faith in man.

Q: What do you like best about your play?

MK: The monologue about bad poets and bad poetry. Diderot gave me the beginning of this speech, but I elaborated on it, and the end is pure Kundera. Nobody reads novels anymore, but everybody—at least in France—is writing one.

Q: Will you write any more plays?

MK: No. Never. *Jacques* is my first and last. I find that as I grow older I want to concentrate more and more intensely on my specialty—the novel. I want to learn as much as I can about its possibilities. I want to explore its secrets. When I was a young man, my attention was more dispersed. The cinema, the theatre attracted me much more than today. Now I'm quite content to sit in an easy chair and read a novel.

I think I've also lost interest in the theatre because of the productions I see around me in Paris. They're loud and tawdry and worthless. You'll see what I mean when you go to Strehler's *L'Illusion*. Listening to actors scream bores me. So I virtually stopped caring about theatre after I moved to France. It always left me so disheartened. The theatre I liked took place in those small pocket theatres of Prague in a black room where two or three actors would create magic with almost no props or scenery. Out of a void they would bring forth life. But that Prague no longer exists, and here in Paris there's no point in going to the theatre.

Susan Sontag: The Odd Couple in Extremis
Interview by Arthur Holmberg

Q: What are the main differences between Kundera's play and Diderot's novel?

SUSAN SONTAG: The emotional balance is different. Kundera's play is sadder—the ebullience of Diderot filtered through a central European melancholy. Kundera turns a rambunctious, picaresque novel into a ghost sonata about the *ancien régime*. Kundera is more skeptical about human relations and the possibility of pleasure. The range of human options has shrunk. A sense of *lacrimae rerum* pervades his play. Diderot lived before the revolution. Kundera lives after the revolution has failed. So you have a clash between pre-revolutionary hopes and post-revolutionary sorrow. The end of the play can be read as a political reference. The stage directions of Kundera force the issue. Forward, without enthusiasm, into a glorious future we now know isn't going to be glorious at all. Kundera imposes this pathos on Diderot's full-blooded material.

The play is a portrait *in extremis* of the odd couple that ranges in literature from Don Quixote and Sancho Panza to Hamm and Clov— the eccentric, helpless master and the indulgent, clever servant. But the servant has no desire to leave. Kundera, in fact, reinforces the social implications of the mutual dependence of the master/slave bond.

What I find difficult in staging the play are the roles Kundera writes for women. With the exception of the innkeeper/Marquise, the other female parts are little more than caricatures, and the actresses and I have to work hard to try to give them some presence.

Q: *Jacques* is the second play you've directed. The first—Pirandello's *As You Desire Me*—was presented in Italy. What are the main differences between working with American and European actors?

SS: Whereas European actors tend to be more cultivated than Americans—they have a large frame of reference from literature and art to draw on—Americans tend to be more intellectual. Therefore the process of working is quite different. It's more democratic here. American actors love to do improvisations. This rehearsal process makes Europeans uneasy. Europeans, by and large, view the theatre as a director's medium and do what they're told without quibble or comment. Americans, on the other hand, are always formulating questions based on detailed and precise critical readings of the text. They're obsessed with the whys and wherefores. I keep saying, "Let's go back to the blocking," and they want to talk about the theory of the play. That's unlikely in Europe. Italian actors are very different from American actors. They use everything differently. The body language varies greatly between the two cultures. And working with *Jacques*, a modernist, self-reflecting drama, I realized again what a central presence Pirandello is in the theatre. He is the single most influential playwright of the twentieth century. He was the last of the great playwrights of bourgeois intellection. He raised the private agonies of the drawing room to a metaphysical pitch.

Q: I find the way you choreograph the actors' movements through space extremely potent. It's been five years since I saw your Pirandello, but I can still see in my mind's eye the fluid patterns you created on stage. How did this *plaisir du plastique* enter your work?

SS: My hero is George Balanchine. I attend ballet regularly, and by watching his work I learned a great deal about what real stagecraft is. Acting is physical work. A good part of the director's task is to teach actors how the foot and mouth connect—how the mouth can say these particular words while the feet move in that particular direction without tripping over furniture. And once foot and mouth get connected, it's hard to disconnect them. I found this out with the Pirandello. Right before opening I decided to change some blocking. Suddenly foot and mouth no longer connected, and the actors were either bumbling over the lines or stumbling over their feet.

Q: You've directed four movies as well. What are the main differences you've found between your role as a director of film and of theatre?

SS: Film really is a director's medium. The final product is constructed in an editing room and can look very different from what the actors did on the set. The theatre belongs to actors. After a play opens, the director disappears, but the actors go on living with the play night after night. Changes creep in. I remember how different *As You Desire Me* looked at the end of its run. A play is never the same on any two nights. Once you finish a film, it stays finished. And one constructs stage pictures completely differently from movie sets, which one sees in bits and pieces.

Q: What appeals to you most about theatre as a genre?

SS: What I cherish in the theatre are those dazzling visual images the stage can generate that rattle inside your head forever. And the human contact in the theatre is intense. Underneath all the banter of this play, I hope it communicates Kundera's anguish and sorrow. I want it to tug at the heart. I'm happiest in the theatre when I cry. The theatre liberates. It frees our deepest feelings.

THE CIVIL warS

A Conversation with Robert Wilson and Heiner Müller
by Arthur Holmberg

Robert Wilson and Heiner Müller collaborated for the first time in 1983 on the Cologne section of the CIVIL warS: *a tree is best measured when it is down*. Much of the material for Müller's text came from the earlier play *Gundling's Life Frederick of Prussia Lessing's Sleep Dream Scream*. Wilson conceived of the CIVIL warS as a twelve-hour multilingual epic, exploring the theme of civil war from many different cultural perspectives. Wilson worked on the CIVIL warS for more than six years on three continents. Sections premiered in Japan, Minneapolis, Rotterdam, Rome, Marseilles, and Cologne. Wilson intended to present the entire work at the Olympic Arts Festival in Los Angeles in 1984, but the project was canceled for lack of funds.

In February 1985, Wilson and Müller came to Cambridge, Massachusetts, to restage the Cologne section. The Cambridge production, a multimedia phantasmagoria, explored the problem of civil strife by juxtaposing images from the life of Frederick the Great of Prussia with scenes from the American Civil War. Müller's kaleidoscopic text embedded fragments from such diverse writers as Racine, Shakespeare, Goethe, Kafka, Hölderlin, Empedocles, the Brothers Grimm, the Bible, Hopi Indian chants, and Frederick the Great. David Byrne, Philip Glass, Frederick the Great, and Franz Schubert contributed to the sound track.

On February 28, 1985, Wilson and Müller discussed the A.R.T.

production of *the CIVIL warS* with members of the audience, who had just seen the piece and who were invited to direct questions at either Mr. Wilson or Mr. Müller. The artists were seated on two futuristic chairs Wilson had designed for the production. The conversation that follows is drawn from that discussion.

Q: What is your view of the social role of your work? Do you intend your theatre to preach or to change the world?

ROBERT WILSON: No, I'm not trying to preach. I'm not trying to change the world with my theatre. Maybe it's different with Heiner.

HEINER MÜLLER: I think we both want to change the theatre. Maybe that's possible. What do you think, Bob?

RW: Yes . . . maybe that's possible.

Q: Do you think the world can be changed and that theatre can help it change?

HM: It's changing anyway, with or without the theatre. But I think this is too general a question for the beginning of our conversation.

Q: What is the role of the audience in your theatre?

RW: The audience has the same role as the author, the director, or the actor. All of us are engaged in the process of asking, "What is it?" We don't try to say what it is or what it means. So we're all the same from that point of view. Our theatre is an open-ended form, and the audience has the responsibility to bring an open mind.

Q: You have stated that all an actor has to do is be able to count, that actors shouldn't interpret. You choreograph your movements meticulously. So it seems to me that you are in control.

RW: It's only when we are completely mechanical that we have the chance of beating a machine. So it goes beyond being in control. It's being automatic. At that point freedom begins.

Q: I didn't understand that. [audience roars with laughter]

HM: Maybe I could try to say more and also go back to the previous question about if we think we can change the world. There is a problem between man and machine. Changing the world depends on this relationship. Once I tried to find a formula for the theatre of Bob regarding this problem. I think Bob's theatre is one step toward a marriage between man and machine. The unification is very important for the future of mankind. . . . But I see you still don't understand.

Q: But if the actor's movements are precisely choreographed, I'm not sure what the actor is then.

Priscilla Smith (Snow Owl), Jeremy Geidt (King Lear), Frances Schrand (Earth Mother), and Diane D'Aquila (Abraham Lincoln) in *the CIVIL warS*.

HM: Look at this chair I'm sitting in. It was designed by Bob, made by Bob. I'm sitting in one of Bob's chairs for the first time, and this chair demands a special attitude. It is a frame, and this frame is a precondition. Bob's theatre is also a frame, and within this frame the actor is free. On stage you need a frame.

Q: Does what you say work with the words as well? What is your attitude toward the text?

HM: What is your attitude toward the text?

Q: It seems to be an attempt to create meaning from a series of non sequiturs. After a while you stop asking questions like "Why is Frederick the Great in a Model T Ford?" and just sort of roll along with it. Your text seems to work against constructing a meaning. On the other hand, there's a lot of citation in the work, self-citation too. You're frequently self-referential. Sometimes I can relate what Wilson has created on stage to the words you wrote, sometimes not.

HM: This play is a montage of quotations—a collage of texts. This structure takes its time to get a meaning. Two days from now you will have another attitude. Two weeks from now, another. And my attitude is changing each time I see the show and hear the text.

Q: Has your idea of the fragment-as-text been worked into the structure of Wilson's piece?

HM: That's a very dangerous question, and fragment is a very dangerous word. Once in an interview I told somebody that I like to do fragments. Now, in all reviews, especially in Germany, whatever I write is called a fragment.

I think the most fragmentary thing is a perfect square because you have to exclude so much to make it perfect, to make it not be fragmentary. You have to exclude curves and circles. So I think your question is just an exercise in scholasticism.

Q: I was very moved by the performance, but I also felt that the technical means of the theatre were shaping the performance. Sometimes I thought effects were used simply because the technology was there.

HM: Everything that takes place during the process of writing for the stage belongs to the text.

Q: How does this production differ from the Cologne production?

RW: It differs because the house is different, the actors are different, the technicians are different and the audience is different. Whenever you restage a work, you have to adapt it to where you are and who's there. The timing and structure remain, but how they're filled out will always be different.

I do have to admit that I prefer the original German text to the English translation. The text doesn't really work for me in English because the edges become rounded. In his writing, Heiner puts things on edge. I don't speak German, so I'm talking about a quality of sound. Heiner's language is like a stone, and my stage pictures have strength because his word blocks are placed in a certain arrangement so that what you see does not necessarily illustrate what you hear. With Heiner's language I felt I could sometimes do something against my beautiful pictures. But in English the text becomes too soft.

What's the point of painting a white horse white? I don't want the visual simply to illustrate the verbal. In Cologne I had directed scenes with no text—not knowing what the text would be. After Heiner arrived with a text, some of the scenes worked with the text, some of the scenes worked against the text.

Q: You said earlier that you don't speak German. At the same time you say you prefer the production in German. Does that mean you concentrate on the visual images and on the audio sound?

RW: I think normally you could say yes. What interests me about Heiner's writing—and I'm sure this frustrates him—is how it sounds. Listen to the beautiful text he wrote for the White Scribe in German [Müller reads the German text]. Now listen to it in English [Shirley Wilbur, an A.R.T. actress, says it in English]. You hear how awful it is! It's terrible. In English the language has no edges. It's not a problem of the quality of translators but of translation. In German literature, everything that is a good text is an act of violence against the language. And this is possible because of German grammar and German syntax. It's not so easy in English. It's impossible in French.

Translating a great work of literature from one language to another always presents problems. Heiner says that Samuel Beckett's plays don't work in German.

HM: Beckett's humor gets lost in German. On the German stage, he's a very serious author, very metaphysical, and the clown is cut. That's one loss.

Q: I found a lot of humor in this production. Do you think people take your work too seriously? Sure there were some dark moments in this work, but I often felt like laughing.

HM: Nothing is really serious without humor. And I like the attitude of the American audience. If they can't stand it, they walk out. That's okay! [big laugh from the audience] No, I really like that. Because in Germany the audience will sit and sit and sit, even if they hate the play, growing more and more angry. Walking out is a better way to deal with that.

Q: The play reminded me of the Western collective unconscious. I felt I was watching a dream.

HM: I think that's great, but I would like to say one thing more, maybe. For me, in a certain way, you see in the fourth act, or I can see it now, the meeting or collision or conflict between a German subconscious and an American one. And this is very moving for me. Because they don't quite come to the same level. And it's floating and sometimes you get the feeling they will find the same level, and then it's again different and colliding. This is one of the movements throughout the show.

Q: What is the difference between the American and German subconscious?

HM: Who would like to answer this question? [audience laughs] America is the most subjective, the most innocent nation in the

Western world. Now, even more than the first time I visited America, I feel the danger of being too innocent. There isn't a nation in Europe that didn't experience the Holocaust. This makes a difference in the subconscious. And it makes a difference in this production.

Q: What is it you like about Robert Wilson's theatrical formalism?

HM: Bob's works demonstrate that the basic thing in theatre is silence. Theatre can work without words, but it cannot work without silence.

THE CHANGELING

Robert Brustein Discusses The Changeling
Interview by Jonathan Marks

Q: Why did you want to direct *The Changeling*?

ROBERT BRUSTEIN: For a number of reasons. First, *The Changeling* has always been one of my favorite Jacobean plays. It is peculiarly modern, perhaps the most modern of all Jacobean plays, because of its cloudy ethical construct. Also it leads to so much later Western drama. I see real connections between *The Changeling* and *Miss Julie*, for example; the relationship between Jean and Julie is similar to that between De Flores and Beatrice-Joanna.

Q: In other words, Middleton caught on to an unchanging psychological truth?

RB: Yes. He had a peculiar affinity for women's psychology, which he also explored in *Women Beware Women*. The emphasis on psychology, especially aberrant psychology, was so unusual at the time that one wonders where he got it, what he was reading, what he was thinking to have come up with these advanced perceptions. This kind of investigation of a woman with an ethical blind spot falling in love with the thing she most abhors is quite a remarkable idea, and it has roots not only in psychology but also in fairy tale, for example, "Beauty and the Beast."

Q: So Middleton made a real leap in portraying women?

RB: I think Middleton was born out of his time and seems to be writing like Racine, rather than like any of his contemporaries. Indeed, in the cutting we've done of the play, it comes out like a French neoclassical tragedy, like *Phèdre*. So he is not of his time, and he is not even of his country. Also, he is writing in an essentially naturalistic vein that we seldom see in Jacobean or Elizabethan drama, which is more often heightened.

Q: "Naturalistic" is a surprising word for a play over three hundred years old. How will you convey this naturalism?

RB: Through the acting. We're trying to get as contemporary an approach to the play as the actors can handle while maintaining the verse. An actor's normal inclination is to approach this sort of thing classically, but the play is not classical in any conventional sense. If we could find a really contemporary approach to the language, I think it would work. Brecht called this "making the familiar strange."

Q: You don't think that betrays the language?

RB: No. If you look carefully at the verse, even though it is stressed, it's got rhythm, it's got imagery. It's the language of everyday life, the language of declarative speech. "I loved this woman in spite of her heart."

Q: You seem to have a great affinity for the Jacobean period. Would you have liked to live then?

RB: [laughs] Heavens, no. Even though we live with the shadow of extinction over our heads, I can't think of a better or more exciting time to live. I would hate to think of life without my compact disc, word processor, or VCR [laughs]—I get real pleasure out of technology, and despite its destructive side I share with a lot of people the enjoyment of its constructive, creative side.

Q: Why your attraction to the dramatic literature of the Jacobean period? Is it nostalgia for sex and violence?

RB: We have plenty of that now! No, I think the more we know about other times, the more our own is enhanced. I was a history major in college, as well as doing my doctoral dissertation on Jacobean drama, and I've never lost my appetite for it. I also love the color of Jacobean drama, the primal emotions that it shamelessly evokes, and I love the great mythical actions that these playwrights were able to create.

Diane D'Aquila (Beatrice-Joanna) and John Bottoms (De Flores) in
The Changeling.

Robert Brustein: Why Do Theatre?

Q: Most artistic directors come from the ranks of stage directors. Few come from the ranks of critics. Your background is unique. How does the fact that you come to the theatre from a different angle change the face of this theatre?

ROBERT BRUSTEIN: That's for other people to say. [laughs]

I'm lucky in having wide-ranging experiences. I began as a theatre practitioner before I became a critic and gave up the practice. I was an actor and director associated with two early postwar theatres: a modern experimental theatre called Studio Seven, which performed at the Provincetown Playhouse in New York, and one of the earliest resident classical theatres (though it just functioned in the summers), called Group 20, also known as Theatre on the Green in Wellesley. I worked with one or the other of these companies from 1949 to 1957. It was only in 1957 that I began writing regularly, first for *Harpers* and then as a play reviewer for the *New Republic*.

I stopped reviewing for thirteen years when I was dean of the Yale School of Drama, but now I have the best of all possible worlds (for myself, though I'm not sure others might say the same)—I can now write criticism and work in the theatre at the same time.

Q: We've had five-and-a-half seasons in Cambridge, and we're entering our twentieth year as a producing organism. Since we're looking back, how has the A.R.T. changed in its six years here, and how does it differ from the company that existed in New Haven?

RB: I don't think we've changed in any essential way over the twenty years we have existed. We still do the three varieties of work we've always done: new plays (preferably American); classical plays in a fresh way; and little-known classics of the past, usually with music. That's been our program since 1966, and it's still true.

Perhaps there has been more of a tendency in the last two or three years to mate avant-garde directors with classical plays. It's something we did in 1966, when Andre Gregory came to Yale with an experimental version of *Endgame*, and when Clifford Williams did a Fellini-esque version of *Volpone* in 1967. We also did an updated version of *Prometheus Bound*, in an adaptation by Robert Lowell, directed by Jonathan Miller and set in the Spanish Inquisition.

This is the way we started, but then something happened to the avant-garde as America got further embroiled in Vietnam. The avant-garde got anarchic, it turned against culture, it turned against history, it turned against text. The Living Theatre was the primary example. Having gone into exile in Europe, Judith Malina announced that she didn't want to play Hedda Gabler anymore, she wanted to play Judith Malina. The group wouldn't do texts that were not totally transformed by their own immediate political or artistic needs. And that counterculture became the enemy of culture for a while, and if you remember there were people at a Living Theatre symposium shouting expletives at Chekhov and Ibsen. Those expletives summed up the attitudes of the avant-garde toward the past.

It's only in the last ten years or so that there has been a reconsolidation of experimental theatre and the avant-garde with classical text and tradition. I've always believed that combination to be potentially one of the most exciting developments in the theatre. We have gone further in that direction over the last few years as more and more of the really stunning experimental directors have opted to work with texts. And so we now have the delightful prospect of a Robert Wilson willing to do *Alcestis* and *King Lear*, JoAnne Akalaitis working on *The Balcony* and *Endgame*, and Andrei Serban doing Molière and Gozzi—all of these gifted directors working with classical theatre.

Q: You don't think we're shouting expletives at Beckett and Euripides?

RB: Not at all. The link is there, the text is there, the text is not being obliterated. Admittedly, abuses can result from this collaboration, and I dislike the abuses as much as anyone.

Q: Do you think there are such abuses in our theatre?

RB: None that I would admit to. [laughs] Classical drama can become a springboard for your own careerism, your own opportunism, your own signature. But I think as long as you feel the director is trying to enhance the text and taking liberties with the letter of the text in order to enhance its spirit, the liberties are justified.

Q: How has the acting company changed? Is the American Repertory Theatre acting company the same organism as was the Yale Repertory Theatre acting company?

RB: No, it's different because the constituents are different. As the actors change, the company changes—the same veins, different blood corpuscles. But there is one actor who has been with the company for twenty years, and that is Jeremy Geidt. It is also a fact that we have fewer and fewer Yale-trained actors in the company than we used to. We now have five or six in all, and we're drawing from other areas; we're drawing locally from Boston, from New York, from avant-garde theatre groups; we're drawing from wherever we can get an appropriate actor, because we don't have an institute or conservatory at the moment [the Institute for Advanced Theatre Training at Harvard was established in 1986], many of our Yale-trained actors are so successfully ensconced in films or commercial theatre that they can't come back for a whole season. So really it is quite different.

Q: There's been an even more fundamental change. In the early years, and even at the end of our residency at Yale, the permanent acting company existed more in theory than in reality. Now it really exists.

RB: You're right. We used to have a nucleus company. We always had five or six actors, and then we had a lot of students who were with the company over a period of one to three years. We also had people jobbed in for specific roles who'd acted with us in the past but were not permanent members of the company insofar as they were with it all year. We never had a solid and sizable company such as we have here, with people who are willing to stay on from year to year, and that makes a real difference.

Q: Do you think it's not just the nucleus but the entire constellation that has become fairly fixed?

RB: Yes that's true—actors, staff technicians, designers—and that has changed my way of operating. The company is now more of an organic whole, and that has made me change in the sense that I choose plays now for the company instead of choosing the play and finding the company to fit it.

Q: You also used to pull the plays off the shelf, texts you wanted to see done—and then you'd go looking for a director and a company. Now the mating of text, director, and cast takes place at the same time. Now projects are often suggested by a director you're interested in.

RB: That's right. Now I will ask a director what play he wants to direct with our company, and that is not a question I would have asked fifteen or twenty years ago. I would have asked, "Would you direct this particular play?" and let the other elements fall into place. But now we ask, "What play would you like to direct *with our company, with our actors?*" All three things are considered.

Q: We're getting a lot of new funding. How does that help us, and what are the difficulties?

RB: Well, the funds, as you'll notice, are virtually all matching funds. The only incremental grant among those monies is for our permanent ensemble; what that helps us do is bring more people into our resident company, to develop from what is now only twelve or fourteen actors to a company comprising twenty, including not just actors but voice consultants, movement people, resident designers, and directors. So I don't see that as a *pitfall*; I see that as a necessity, because we are doing five to eight plays a year with a small acting company, and that is just backbreaking for all of them. Nobody has a play off.

Robert Brustein (left) with Andrei Belgrader.

One worry is that the public will perceive that we have a lot of money and won't contribute. We don't have a lot of money. We have the beginning of what we hope will be an endowment that has to be matched, and when that endowment is achieved within the next four or five years, assuming that it will be achieved, then we will have guaranteed ourselves against future deficits.

Q: For years I got the feeling we were on the brink of the void, that our existence was not assured. Is that still true?

RB: It's less true now, but the existence of no theatre is ever assured. An endowment is better insurance against the precipice, better insurance against extinction, than anything else, and that's why it's so important for us to raise this endowment.

It goes back to funding. Theatre is a bottomless well that always needs priming. The money you get each year is spent, and each year you need more money. Just because you get the money doesn't mean you are saved forever from extinction—you have to keep improving your financial situation.

Our budget is not enormous, but we have a small theatre of only 556 seats, so we can take in only a certain amount of money at the box office. We have to supplement that continually with contributions. Once we get the endowment, the ability to make up the deficits will be guaranteed. That is as close as we will get to being insured against extinction.

Q: So the brink is still there, we're just a little farther away from it.

RB: The brink is there, as the brink is there with all human endeavors. Remember Captain Shotover in Shaw's *Heartbreak House*? He lived with five hundred pounds of TNT under his house to remind himself that he could be blown to smithereens at any given moment.

Q: What about the university connection? We've always had it. Is it important?

RB: It's very important. It has saved us from a fate that has afflicted so many resident theatres in this country, popularly referred to as the "artistic deficit." We have never felt pressure from the university administration to do popular plays or to make more money at the box office. Universities, being nonprofit institutions themselves that support experiment in science and sociology and literature, are more willing and able to recognize the need for that in the arts, and we do have access to a highly intelligent and literate public. Also, it is a great value to have students in the area because it is good to work with them on stage, and I think they make wonderful audiences and keep the atmosphere lively and youthful.

Q: Is there a disadvantage to the university connection?

RB: There is the disadvantage of a certain suspiciousness on the part of the academic community toward any practical arts. There always has been. We have been lucky that it hasn't been expressed toward us too vocally in the last few years, and we feel a lot of moral support coming to us from the university administration. I can't think of too many disadvantages to this kind of situation.

Q: Why do you do theatre?

RB: It's the most exciting thing I can conceive of doing. Sometimes it's irritating, sometimes terrifying, sometimes disappointing, but the privilege of expressing oneself and helping others express themselves creatively is invaluable.

Theatre is a microcosm of society. It captures contemporary life better than any other art form. Working together with a collective of people you respect and love is a rare luxury, and of course the response that we've been getting is enormously satisfying. In olden times, one of the justifications for the opposition to the institution of theatre was that it wasn't a real way of working, it was a way of playing. It's interesting that a drama is the only thing that is called both a work and a play; it has elements of both work and play in it. My work is playful and my play is work. It's considered frivolous because it's play. Well yes, but playfulness is important, both for the city and for the academic community. It's important also to recognize that these texts we do—texts that are being studied not too far from here in Harvard Yard—are living organisms. They are not simply historical artifacts but have something to do with our lives. Our lives today as well as the times in which they were written.

Q: Now imagine you're on the Vineyard, a long time from now, in your retirement. You hear someone say, "This is what the American Repertory Theatre did for American theatre." What would you enjoy hearing next?

RB: "The American Repertory Theatre, along with other theatres of its kind, demonstrated that theatre exists not just for entertainment but for revelation, enlightenment, and the nourishment of the soul. It helped to show that theatre includes entertainment but has a purpose that doesn't fade when the curtain goes down, and that it is as important an art form as literature or painting or serious music or dance. The American Repertory Theatre helped to restore respect for the art of theatre."

Robert Brustein Defines Theatre: " . . . works that assume the power of dreams . . ."

I am often asked (and sometimes told) what the identity of the American Repertory Theatre is. How would I characterize its purpose, ambitions, and future direction? One approaches the task of self-definition with hesitation, if not reluctance. Defining a theatre, like defining a human being, is perhaps a way of limiting possibilities, of putting boundaries around an entity that would like to consider itself indefinable, unclassifiable, unpredictable. Still, the request is not unreasonable. Our patrons and supporters have a right to know what to expect, even if my seemingly evasive answer is: Expect the unexpected.

Some people have concluded that our theatre is avant-garde, regarding our work as a kind of kaleidoscope of special effects, extravagant visual displays, directorial gimmickry. Although I can understand the reasoning behind this conclusion, I do not believe it is accurate. First of all, the term *avant-garde* has all but lost its meaning in the present climate, where innovative artists, who in previous ages used to languish in obscurity until after their death, are often quickly absorbed by the culture, lionized by the media, and then cast off before they have reached their full maturity.

Secondly, when our theatre—satisfying the requirements of certain contemporary theatre artists—has employed a variety of visual and conceptual images, this has not been for the sake of dazzling audiences with external displays; rather, it is to find fresh pathways into the heart of the text. Sometimes we fail—but not, I believe, for lack of intention. For those drawn to new theatrical experiences—and our audiences are unique in their appetite for innovative forms and images—Robert Wilson's Delphic mountain in *Alcestis*, Andrei Serban's animated projections in *The Juniper Tree*, and JoAnne Akalaitis's abandoned subway tunnel in *Endgame* (to take just three examples) represent revelations about these works that assume the power of dreams.

It is true that these are not literary approaches, but as the visionary Russian director Meyerhold said half a century ago, "Words in the theatre are only a design on the canvas of motion." The stage is not a study or a closet—it is a focus of the collective art of the playwright, actor, director, composer, and designer, perhaps the only form where so many elements share so much importance. It is also true that we generally eschew works primarily realistic and domestic in nature (though even there we may surprise you, and ourselves, with a play such as Marsha Norman's *'Night, Mother*). But I believe movies and television have long since preempted these styles from the stage, permitting the theatre to return to its traditional role, which is to be theatrical, nay more than theatrical—metaphysical, philosophical, vatic, prophetic.

The contemporary stage is blessed in the kind and quality of

Kristin Flanders (Ann Whitefield/Doña Ana), Jeremy Geidt (Mendoza/Devil), Alvin Epstein (Roebuck/Statue), and Don Reilly (Jack Tanner/Don Juan) in *Man and Superman*.

artists who are working in it; some see the present time as representing the third great age of Western theatre. The American Repertory Theatre provides a forum for the finest contemporary theatre artists, letting them use our stage as a crucible for their imagination. These artists may be playwrights or directors or actors or designers or composers. They may work best on a stage with striking visual images—or on a stage without scenery. *Six Characters in Search of an Author* and *Waiting for Godot* took place, respectively, in an empty theatre and on a bare platform. *the CIVIL warS* and *The King Stag*, on the other hand, stretched our versatile facility to its limit. In each case, theatre artists were trying to find the most appropriate means by which to serve the production and the text. Our role, indeed our obligation, is to identify and invite to the A.R.T. those people we believe most likely to excite you and advance the theatre.

Duets, Trios, Quartets, and Quintets: World Premiere of The Juniper Tree
by Donna DiNovelli

No fairy tale is the work of an individual. Not even Jacob and Wilhelm Grimm, those indefatigable German collaborators, could claim to be the sole authors of the story they called "The Juniper Tree." Their life's work was to enlist the help of spinning wives and spindle-bearers, nurses and fishermen, who told them the stories they had heard by the fireside, stories that had been passed down for generations.

Now, in the bicentenary year of the brothers' birth (Jacob in 1885, Wilhelm in 1886), another collaboration brings their story of a murdered child and his revenge and regeneration to the A.R.T. stage—this time in the form of an opera with music by two avant-garde composers at the forefront of their art (Philip Glass and Robert Moran) and a libretto by an award-winning writer of children's books, Arthur Yorinks. The stage director of this world premiere will be Andrei Serban, who last season in *The King Stag* revealed a sense of childlike wonderment and a particular sensitivity to the fantastical world of fairy tales.

Glass and Moran had wanted to collaborate on a musical piece for some time, and Maurice Sendak, one of the most successful writers of children's books, suggested that the two composers take a look at "The Juniper Tree," the title piece in a collection of Grimms' fairy tales that he had illustrated. Moran had always been attracted to the Grimm stories "because they are so bloody and unbelievably great for opera." The two composers then approached Arthur Yorinks, author of several children's books, to fashion the libretto.

Although writing is usually a solitary adventure, Yorinks thought of himself as collaborating with the Brothers Grimm. "I didn't want to change the story dramatically but to flesh out what drama was already in the story." He found the essence of the story in "how families relate to each other," noting the ambivalence and struggle involved. As he continued writing, the work became more complex technically and gradually evolved into its final form as a chamber opera for eighteen voices.

During the development process, the three collaborators decided to meet at Glass's retreat in Nova Scotia, where they secluded themselves in individual cabins in the woods (no phones) to finish the opera. The Nova Scotia days gave the artists both the solitude to work alone and the ability to run to the cabin next door to check on one another's progress. The libretto was complete, but Yorinks added "a trio here, a duet there to accommodate the music."

The composers worked in different ways. At one point Glass wrote a theme and Moran composed variations on that theme. "We didn't try to sound the same," said Glass. "We used our differences in style to extend the range of the piece." They also divided up various sections of the opera between them, paying particular attention to the transitions from one scene to another. Much of the running between cabins was to ensure that "the ending of one segment glued onto the beginning of the other."

Glass has had ample experience wedding his music to a text. "I'm more of a theatre composer than anything else," said Glass, composer of *Satyagraha*, *The Photographer*, *Einstein on the Beach*, *Akhnaten*, and *the CIVIL warS* (the Rome section), most of which have been called operas. During the course of his career, he has also composed music for numerous Mabou Mines theatre productions, including *Dead End Kids* and *Cascando*, both directed by JoAnne Akalaitis.

Because of his work as a composer for the theatre, *The Juniper Tree* will be presented by the A.R.T. Last fall the company produced *Endgame*, also directed by Ms. Akalaitis, which included a prelude and incidental score by Glass, and in the spring another of his compositions was heard at the Loeb—music for the "Smilers" section of Robert Wilson's *the CIVIL warS*.

Richard Pittman, founder and conductor of Boston Musica Viva, was engaged as conductor for the opera. Pittman thinks audiences will have no trouble appreciating the Glass/Moran score. He noted the growing popularity of Glass's music among audiences not normally drawn to opera and believes that American audiences have responded well to the cyclical style of repetition and variation common to both composers.

Yorinks is mindful of these qualities of the music and observes similarities to the essence of the Grimm tale; the repeating cycles of nature are important to the story. He highlighted this particularly in his prologue, which emphasizes the interrelationships among animals, birds, humans, seasons, birth, death, and rebirth—all around and beneath a tree that stays green forever.

But this continuum of cycles and collaborations that began at a hearth in nineteenth-century Germany will not be complete until, as Pittman says, the opera goes before its final collaborators, the audience. "Music does not exist until it is listened to. It's a living organism. You don't know how any piece works until you've done it in front of an audience."

THE BALCONY

JoAnne Akalaitis Discusses Genet and The Balcony
Interview by Erin Mee

Q: Do you have a philosophy of directing?

JOANNE AKALAITIS: Not really, no. It depends on the project. I don't feel that a director is an aesthetic general. I'm opposed to the God idea of directing. I don't want to say the director is the team captain, or the leader, or the mother, or facilitator, or observer—the director is all of those things and not one of them. But for me the process of being a director is stimulating because I get to bounce ideas off a lot of people, like the designers, the lighting people, the actors. The director has a dream one night, and she wants a lot of other people to share that dream, or nightmare as the case may be. One of the primary things is to try to get all of us to dream the same dream.

Q: As I understand it, you are setting the play in Central America but not in a specific country.

JA: Yes. To set it in a specific country would take Genet's play and make it a polemic for Central American activism, and I think that would be a misuse of the play. To set the play in El Salvador specifically would be limiting, because it would undermine Genet's imagination. Genet is too complicated to assign a specific political agenda to him. *The Balcony* is a great work of art, a work of poetry, and one of the most exciting things about it is that it is not separate from the world. It is in the world, and the world is political.

Q: Much of the criticism of Genet centers on the idea that he takes our established ideas and turns them upside down.

JA: People will think that in their deepest unconscious, but they won't know that they are thinking it. It takes a tremendous kind of courage to confront that in yourself.

One of the powerful aspects of theatre is that it should leave people gasping and sobbing and crying, in a metaphorical way, and nothing but theatre can do that. We are not allowed to be passive in theatre. In film we are, because we're sitting in the dark, and the image is so big that it dominates; we look at it, and we can get sucked into it. But in theatre we are always reminded that there are people involved, and if you sit close enough to the stage you can see how imperfect they are, and that they are as perfect as any of us. We all want to have that nakedness and vulnerability in our lives, but actors are brave enough to make a career of constantly baring and exposing the self. Film is put together in such a way that the actor winds up looking the way the director and editor and actor have decided he should look. That is wonderful too, it's another kind of art, but what has always drawn me to theatre, the strength of theatre, is the humanity of it.

Q: What draws you to Genet?

JA: Genet is in the grand tradition of classical theatre from the Greeks on. He exposes social and personal dilemmas in grand and powerful images that seem formal but are *so* extreme that people have no place to turn but to themselves. There is a wonderful quote from Genet: ". . . let evil explode on the stage, show us naked, and if it can, leave us haggard and without recourse except in ourselves." There is no way to say that you *enjoy* a play like this, even though it is terribly entertaining and beautifully written and funny and sad.

Genet is someone who has been completely rejected by society, and his plays target society in high poetry that uses the "toilet" of experience. He is one of the few writers who is able to glorify the obscene and use it as a metaphor, which is what is so brilliant about his writing. No one else thought of this. Genet uses what sex does to us—which is that it excites us—and he uses the voyeuristic and curious tendencies that live in all of us, and turns that against us.

Q: Many people think that Genet is saying that revolution is doomed to failure. By setting the play in Central America, are you saying that the revolutions in Nicaragua and El Salvador are doomed to failure?

JA: I don't think that Genet is saying that revolution is doomed to failure at all, because at the end of the play, when things are winding down, we hear the crackle of machine-gun fire, and Madam Irma says: "Whose is it? Ours, or theirs? Is it guerrillas, or . . ." ; and The Envoy replies: "Someone dreaming, Madam." I think that line must be taken in two ways: that a particular revolution can be stopped but that the dream of revolution can never be stopped. In one corner of the world or another, someone is always dreaming of revolution. And what is revolution but an idea about making life better?

ALCESTIS

Robert Wilson: The Stage as Mask
Interview by Nina Mankin

Q: What attracts you to Greek theatre after doing so many of your own works?

ROBERT WILSON: I am attracted to the mask. With the Greek mask, we have an image and we have a sound. And it is the same in Japanese classical drama, say, with the Noh play; all the actors are masked. Here the actors won't physically wear masks, but in some sense I think of the stage picture as being the mask. It is a bit like a voice-over.

Q: I don't understand.

RW: Well, for instance, if you take a silent movie, you can only see the text, but you can still think about the way it sounds. There is so much space for the listener because we can hear the sound of the text in our imagination. If we take a radio play, the boundaries of the images are limitless because we can imagine whatever we want. There's a voice in both and there's an image in both; one is external and one is internal.

In a talking film or a naturalistic play, the image and the text are put together in such a way that it is more difficult to have that kind of space. So in a sense what I am trying to do is like trying to take a radio drama and a silent film, and place the radio's voice over the visual image. And it's like the Greek theatre in that when the actor was on stage he wore a mask, which presented an image that was different from what he was saying. It's in this way that what I'm trying to do is similar to Greek theatre—the entire stage is a mask. That's one reason I use microphones—to create a distance between the sound and the image.

Q: Is this why you use electronic voices in the play?

RW: An actor from last fall's workshop, Tim McDonough, told me recently of a scholarly theory he had read which said that as late as the period of the *Iliad*, internal verbalization was just developing in human consciousness. Prior to this time, words were spoken only out loud; in the absence of speaking there was silence. At a certain point in the development of human consciousness, words began to be internalized, but the experience of this was at first mysterious, as if voices were being heard—the gods whispering to characters, either in confirmation of or in contradiction to their impulses. So the Greeks were accounting for the emergence of inner dialogue by way of their mythology. They experienced hearing voices and could not account for this.

Q: How does the work of the Japanese choreographer Suzushi Hanayagi relate to Greek theatre?

RW: It is appropriate to have a Japanese choreographer whose training is in the traditional theatre working on a Greek text, because there is something so similar in the formality of presenting ideas instead of expressing them.

Q: Is there a distinction between what is dance and what is theatre in your work?

RW: I don't think about it. I don't see the separation between dance and theatre. It is what it is. I think about the line of an arm, or a neck, or a shoulder, or the space between fingers in all my work; so in a sense it is dance. But whether we call it "theatre" or "dance theatre" is unimportant. The Noh theatre is a dance theatre; when you see a Noh actor you ask, are they singing? Acting? Dancing? It's all one thing.

Q: What is the theme of *Alcestis*?

RW: Among other things, death, because the word "death" repeats all the time. And after a while it comes to mean something else.

Q: What does it become?

Rodney Scott Hudson (Death) and Paul Rudd (Admetus) in *Alcestis*.

RW: Through repetition it comes to mean something different, something mysterious. Something you cannot say because it will be different for each person. There was a man who did an experiment in Chicago in the sixties where he took the word "cogitate" and he made a tape loop: "cogitate . . . cogitate . . . cogitate . . . cogitate. . . ." He just repeated the word for half an hour. And he asked everyone what they heard—people on the street, scholars, all kinds of people—"What do you hear?" They began to hear all sorts of things—"meditate," "tragedy." So the image of a word becomes internalized differently by different people.

Q: What is the relation between *Alcestis*, the Heiner Müller prologue, and the Kyogen epilogue?

RW: [pause] Birds. I hear birds all through the Heiner Müller text, and through *Alcestis* too. Then of course, there is the epilogue: *The Birdcatcher in Hell*.

Q: Say more.

RW: I can't, that's all I can say.

Q: Did you approach Heiner Müller about this project?

RW: Yes. I asked him to write a prologue for *Alcestis*.

Q: What did you talk about?

RW: I talked about the blink of an eye, about the deaf hearing and seeing—a little bit about these things—and he incorporated them. Heiner's text is very compressed; it's all one sentence and thirteen pages long; all the ideas are compressed in this space. It's like a rock, but by compressing the space he has perhaps created more space.

This rock of a text can be fragmented like molecules breaking apart, but even in the end it can't be destroyed. We start out with a man on tape sounding like a Shakespearean actor and then add another voice—Chris Moore sounding very neutral, androgynous—a simple way of speaking; then Chris Knowles, who erases some of the words, putting holes in the text; then we have Harry Murphy sounding like a newscaster; and finally the ghostlike voice of Death. So the prologue sets up these different ways of speaking, of thinking about language, of presenting ideas through words that anticipate the situation that is to follow.

Q: Do you mean the use of different acting styles?

RW: Yes, because sometimes the actor should sound formal, sometimes very naturalistic. There are many different levels to this text. Sometimes the text has been taped and altered electronically.

Q: So the prologue sets up the style of acting for the *Alcestis* story. How?

RW: Well, there are jumps in the story: from the very domestic scenes, like the deathbed scene, to very ritualistic, surreal scenes, like the Crocodile King sitting at the banquet table.

Q: Your work is often referred to as "epic" because of its sheer dimensions.

RW: There is something extraordinary in the theatre that people don't experience every day. You go to the theatre to have another kind of experience; I think this is one of the attractions of seeing a play of epic proportions. So, yes, it serves a unique function in society because of that.

Q: What are some of the images that stand out for you in *Alcestis*?

RW: The river is important; it stands for so many things. Death—Charon—is seen on the river in the beginning, so it is a river of death. Then we see the women cleansing themselves, washing their hair, washing their clothes in the river. So it is also an image of purification.

Q: Was that one of the first images you had when you read *Alcestis*?

RW: The river, yes, I came up with that, and the rocks, mountain, buildings, the stone wall, the fact that the rocks are falling and collecting—in the beginning a rock has been chiseled from a mountain range similar to the one in Delphi where the Temple of Apollo is—and in the end it's replaced by a future city. There is a sinking down, yet a building up.

Q: You create a relationship between the audience and what's on stage that is very different from what people usually experience in the theatre.

RW: Normally what happens in theatre today, Western theatre, is that the edges of the frame become so clearly defined that, to me, they limit the space. If we can break away and destroy that frame so that there's more space—then we have a different kind of experience.

The stage is like a battery: you set up all these activities that are generating totally different states of mind—vibrations, so that one can be totally awake, one can be in a semisleep state; so that it is not just "look at this, this is happening," forcing the audience to participate, to pay attention; one can daydream, come back in, then phase out. I want people to have time to think about what's on stage. I don't want to impose so much that they don't have time to reflect, to dream.

Q: You're also directing another *Alcestis*—the opera by Gluck in Stuttgart.

RW: Yes. The Gluck opera is baroque, and it is much more formal. I think about it in a formal way: as lines being drawn in space, asymmetrical lines echoed by the way the body is placed and moves, which also draws a line in space that we look at. That's baroque gesture, and that started ballet as we know it today. It's completely formal, and the same with the Noh play. This *Alcestis* is more naturalistic—the trees look like trees, the mountain looks like a mountain, the river is water, the rocks are rocks. And the crocodile looks like a crocodile. Are people going to laugh when they see the crocodile walk on stage?

Q: They are.

RW: I hope so!

Q: Is there anything you want to communicate to the people reading this interview? Should they come to the theatre with any expectations?

RW: No, no expectations. We want them to come and to look and to listen—that's basically it. To be able to hear and see. It's not that difficult; you're just looking at these pictures and hearing this text. Then you go home, think about it or not think about it. But it doesn't come to a big conclusion. I think the piece should be left open for people to wonder about, particularly at the end, when Alcestis comes back. It can be done very "Hollywood," and everyone is happy, and the king and queen walk away into the sunset. But not here. I'm not convinced we know who she is at the end. We have to wait three days.

Q: In a way, the fact that we don't know makes it more mythical.

RW: Sure. And that's why we're still involved with the myth. Because it remains mysterious. We really don't know what has happened. That's why it can exist all these years. We can still think about it, we can interpret it in a multitude of different ways.

THE DAY ROOM

The Door Inside The Day Room (Notes Toward a Definitive Meditation)
by Don DeLillo

It was late March or early April, with a gusty rain sweeping across Harvard Square. I decided to slip into the theatre even though there was no rehearsal scheduled. I wanted to sit in the dark and think about my play. I opened the outer door, walked through the lobby, opened the inner door, and entered. [Enter.] The stage was occupied by strangers, by people and equipment. Eleven men and women, young, urban-rustic, with gum boots, sleeveless Gore-Tex jackets. They wore electrician's belts with claw hammers dangling. A couple of stepladders, a man with blueprints, a woman cranking up a bed. I didn't know who they were; they didn't know who I was, if they saw me at all.

It was the set, of course. They were putting up the set for Act I. I hadn't realized this was scheduled to happen today. Who did they work for, exactly? Where had they come from? As the author of a

Carmen de Lavallade, Gayle Keller, Charles Weinstein, Jeremy Geidt, and Thomas Derrah in *The Day Room.*

mystery play, a play about master strategies of performance and deception, I couldn't help wondering who was running the show.

The stage was dimly lit. The workers spoke a private jargon. [Dialogue.] For me, it was a curiously deep-reaching moment. To see an idea I'd had in a room in New York, eighteen months earlier, drift and thicken into three dimensions a couple of hundred miles to the north, nailed and boxed together by a group of strangers.

I think what intrigued me most was the sense that I'd become an audience for my own work, subject to the same mystery and surprise I was trying to summon up for others.

I had the distinct feeling I shouldn't stay too long.

Half a block away I ducked into a sprawling café. A service person approached and asked in which part of the room I wished to sit.

"Smoking or non-smoking? Croissant or non-croissant? Sandinista or anti-Sandinista?"

Back in the world, I thought. The world of categories, choices, and regrets.

Robert Brustein on Auteurs, Authors, and Actors
Interview by Jonathan Marks

Q: In the upcoming season, I see a continuation of what we've been doing in the last few years, and also some divergences from what we've been doing. For example, we'll be doing several new American plays. Does this mean that the word is again being brought forward?

ROBERT BRUSTEIN: Actually, that is not a departure, because our first priority in this theatre has always been to seek out the best new American plays, and by great good luck we came across three brilliant new American plays this year. If we had four, we would have done four. However, there is one interesting departure this season. The *auteur* director has often been charged with being indifferent to the word, which is the playwright's contribution, because he or she is more interested in his own effects. Now, to my knowledge for the first time, the *auteur* director is forming a union here with the American playwright: Andrei Serban directing a new play by Ronald Ribman, and Richard Foreman directing a newly rewritten play by Arthur Kopit. I've always believed one of our purposes at the American Repertory Theatre was to unite the various, sometimes warring factions in the American theatre and bring them into harmony. I've always hoped for that, and it will be interesting to see if it can happen without bloodshed.

Q: What exactly is an *auteur* director, and why do you call Serban and Foreman *auteurs*?

RB: For one reason, directors like Foreman rarely do material other than their own. He did a *Threepenny Opera* for Joe Papp at Lincoln Center and a *Don Juan* for Liviu Ciulei at The Guthrie Theater. But aside from those, I believe he has pretty much kept to creations written, devised, directed, and even designed by himself. Serban is a different case. He works almost exclusively with classical plays, from the Greeks to Chekhov. With the exception of a play called *Zastrozzi* he directed at the New York Public Theater, he has never done a new play. This will be a wonderful opportunity for him and for us because he is doing a play of genuine significance— Ronald Ribman's *Sweet Table at the Richelieu*. He's terribly excited

Robert Brustein (center) and Frederick Wiseman (right) with members of
the company in *Tonight We Improvise*.

about this play, which, I think, will benefit enormously from his
poetic imagination.

Q: Doesn't the *auteur* director usurp the function of the playwright? Won't they be in conflict? Aren't these directors inflating
themselves to a position that should be held by the playwright?

RB: Your question uses loaded phrases like "inflated" and "raising
themselves to positions," but my guarded answer is that the *auteur*
director, when working with traditional texts or his own scenarios, is
in effect a creator and a playwright himself. This was the argument of
Meyerhold, one of the earliest of the *auteur* directors, and it has also
been argued in some recent books on the subject. One—*Great Directors at Work* by David Jones—called the twentieth century the century of the director, recognizing that in theatre as in the movies, the
director is frequently the animating force.

There are at least two different kinds of directors. One sees it as
his or her function to serve the playwright exclusively and to realize
the literary intentions of the text. He or she functions as a kind of
playwright's adjutant, subordinate to the playwright's vision. Another
kind of director believes, particularly in relation to classical plays,
that certain works have been seen so many times that it is necessary

to bring a fresh, rejuvenating imagination to them in order to see them anew, through contemporary metaphors.

I don't mean just a contemporary setting—that's not very imaginative—but rather to find the pulse at the heart of the play that has not yet been discovered. It's the difference between simile and metaphor. Some directors approach plays as similes; they see analogies with something in the modern world and therefore transfer the play to a contemporary setting. "The Vienna of *Measure for Measure* reminds me of Freud's Vienna; therefore, I'll set it in nineteenth-century Austria." Now I believe this kind of updating is the activity of an essentially prosaic mind, simile being essentially a prose device, whereas the metaphorical director functions more like a poet. What he seeks is something at the heart of the play that cannot be specified precisely as being *like* something else but is rather a congeries of images that reverberates as a poem reverberates and communicates through a variety of meanings.

Q: So there is more to theatre than divining what the playwright has in mind and reproducing it literally on stage?

RB: There is certainly more to the classical theatre, because at this point nobody is in a position to divine what the playwright originally had in mind; and quite often even if the playwright is alive, one can't divine what he had in his mind when he wrote the play. You know Robert Browning's celebrated remark when he was asked the meanings of one of his poems? He said, "When I wrote that poem only God and Robert Browning knew what it meant, and now, ten years later, only God knows." Once the playwright or the poet releases a work, it becomes part of the atmosphere, open to interpretation by everybody, including the poet—and who *knows* which interpretation is correct?

I don't mean to take an entirely relativistic view of the question, but I do want to emphasize that there is no definitive production of any play. Culture, particularly theatrical culture, is a dialogue, and one production really should stimulate another production in response. Peter Brook's circuslike *A Midsummer Night's Dream* was provoked by all those airy-fairy *Midsummer Night's Dream*s that preceded it; and then Alvin Epstein's and Liviu Ciulei's *Midsummer Night's Dream*s were stimulated in response to Peter Brook's.

So a great play is always there to be confronted, to be reinterpreted, to be refreshed through the vision of a great director.

Q: There are some elements to this season that are definitely new: the expanded company and the new A.R.T. Institute for Advanced Theatre Training at Harvard. How will they affect the company internally, and how will the audience notice a difference?

RB: Both of these new instrumentalities represent expansion. We are expanding the number of actors in our company with the generous aid of a National Endowment for the Arts grant, and our Institute will also expand the company insofar as we're bringing young people into training who will work both in Institute projects and in A.R.T. productions.

The expansion of the company will relieve the incredible pressure that has been on seven or eight actors to perform an enormous variety of roles in all eight plays of the season. It spreads the roles more evenly, and it allows people a little more rest than they've had in the past. We've a number of wonderful new faces in the company, which I think will flesh it out and give it more variety.

The Institute clearly is an organic part of the company in that it is training young people for our theatre and for theatres like it. One of our problems—our major internal problem since we came to Cambridge—is that our younger actors have grown older, and we've had difficulty finding young people to take their place. Our Romeos have turned into older Montagues, and our Juliets into older Capulets, but now as before in New Haven, we are in a position to train new Romeos and Juliets and bring them into the company with the same vocabulary, the same aesthetic, the same experience that our older company actors enjoy.

Four of the seven Institute actors are appearing in *Tonight We Improvise*, one of the Institute directors is my assistant, and one Institute dramaturg is working on the production; those actors who are not performing are understudying featured parts, which they may get a chance to play at a matinee. I can safely say that all of these Institute actors will be performing in two, three, or more productions during the course of this year.

Q: One part of our operation the Cambridge audience never sees but only hears about in the *A.R.T. News* and other press organs is our tours. What is the importance of the A.R.T.'s tours?

RB: They have many important functions. First and foremost, of course, we see it as one of our obligations as a theatre to cross-pollinate, to bring our productions to areas that may not have seen that kind of work before. We hope it can stimulate activity from theatres in those areas of a similar ambition. Second, it appeals to our actors to travel. Loyal as they are to one city, they generally do want to see other places, and touring gives them a chance to visit Paris and Venice and Los Angeles and La Jolla and the various other cities that invite us. Third, we tour by necessity, because for six weeks in the fall we don't have a theatre; we're homeless, so we have to find other theatres—in the Midwest, in the far West, in New England—where we address ourselves to new audiences and get refreshing new responses.

Q: *Tonight We Improvise* is the second Pirandello play you have directed at the A.R.T. What about Pirandello attracts you?

RB: We are celebrating the fiftieth anniversary of his death this year, so it's appropriate to have a Pirandello play on our stage. But he's also attractive because he addresses himself to the question you asked earlier. What is the relationship between the play and the director and the actors? It's a question that haunted him, and, as an essentially modest writer, he recognized that his work was only one element in the theatrical equation. Yet as an artist with his own needs for self-expression, he recognized that any playwright who submits his work to actors and directors is going to be disturbed by the way that work is changed; the very fact that an actor speaks your words changes the nature of how they are perceived. The theatre imposes its own obligations, its own imperatives on a playwright's product, and this obsessed Pirandello all his life. It fascinated him as a philosophical animal. He wrote three plays on this subject.

The other thing that fascinated him was the continuing dialogue between what happens on stage and what is happening in the audience. Pirandello did not believe that the stage event was self-enclosed, something the audience peeked at from a safe distance. He thought that the stage was coextensive with the audience—could not be separated from the audience—and he never pretended that what you saw in the theatre was real, except on the occasions when he created the appearance of reality in order to undermine it. He was the first modern to play with this notion, to break down that illusionistic "fourth wall"—even more than in the Elizabethan theatre or the Greek theatre, where there was direct address to the audience. In Pirandello the actor went right through the wall and sat in the audience's lap.

Q: How do you like the change of pace when you lay aside your artistic director's hat for a few hours and go into rehearsal wearing your stage director's hat?

RB: Well, it certainly changes your focus. Instead of being scattered among a large number of projects—production projects, fundraising projects, actors' problems, or the troubles of the office—you have to concentrate intensively on one thing alone and try to blinker yourself off from other distractions. That takes a lot of persistence and a lot of energy.

It's a process that is a compound of joy and frustration. Just as the playwright is frustrated at not seeing his vision precisely on the stage at the first rehearsal, so the director experiences frustration at not seeing his ideas realized at the first rehearsal. If he has any sense, he steps back, recognizes that his idea is much less important ultimately than what emerges from the collaborative and collective effort of the entire company—and that includes not just the actors but the designers and technicians and dramaturgs—and the spirit of the playwright as well, which hovers over us always both as rebuke and encouragement.

END OF THE WORLD (WITH SYMPOSIUM TO FOLLOW)

Richard Foreman: Directing with His Head and His Feet
by Donna DiNovelli

Traditionally a play begins to become living theatre around a table. It is there that actors gather for the first time; rehearsal scripts are distributed, and the play is read from cover to cover, each player taking a part. It is a sedentary beginning, and one that does not sit well with the peripatetic director Richard Foreman.

Foreman, the avant-garde director of more than forty productions, directs on his feet, moving himself and his actors around the space that will envelop the dramatic material. Yet for the first rehearsal of Arthur Kopit's *End of the World (With Symposium to Follow)*, Foreman sat at the head of the table for this traditional read-through of the script. He said it was only the third time he had begun a rehearsal period this way in a career that spans two decades. However, he considered this reading important, not for himself but for the man sitting next to him, Arthur Kopit, who was completing a thorough rewrite of the text.

Immediately following the read-through, Foreman moved into action, tackling the real job of turning the playwright's words into a theatrical production. The first thing he did was put the play on its feet by beginning to block the action. The chairs and table were removed, and the actors began walking around a mazelike construction of wooden rails that Foreman had devised with the designer Michael H. Yeargan.

As they walked through the makeshift set and read their lines, music from several of Foreman's tapes filled the rehearsal hall. The tapes, which were labeled with such names as "Oscillate," "Bongo Rat-a-Tat-Tat," "Fire Music," and "Piano Trip," created an eerie, menacing world. Foreman owns a library of between seven hundred and eight hundred tapes, many of which he made in France from pirate radio stations "that play great American music you don't hear in this country." An A.R.T. Institute actress commented that Foreman is so effective in creating a mood that when she enters rehearsal "it's like entering another planet."

With the rehearsal in movement, Foreman would add his own rapid directions: "keep moving all the time . . . you're on a merry-go-round . . . a big, cosmic swirl of life." Yet within this constant motion he often took time to talk head-to-head with actors who had questions about their characters. At such times Foreman became a different director; the movement stopped and the world of the mind came into the play.

When asked if he would emphasize the psychological, Foreman says, "I never think in those terms. When you get a play on its feet, what surfaces surfaces. I don't plan which aspect is going to surface. I certainly want a lot of psychological tension between the characters, but the poetry of a piece is always overdetermined. I want to have all the possible interpretations playing with each other at the same time, otherwise it will become a one-dimensional illusion."

Foreman often speaks of a character's subconsious, but he does not impose a Freudian interpretation on the characters' relationships. Instead he approaches the characters as Jungian archetypes. "A lot of people see my work only as choreography and think I don't care about characters. It's true I don't think of character in a normal sense, but I do spend most of my time thinking about which archetype the character is manifesting each moment and what side of his unconscious personality is coming to the fore."

As the rehearsal progressed, Foreman would bounce back between these two worlds: the mind of the actor and the movement on stage. He warned the actors, "I can only think by doing things." Later he explained that even though he is considered an intellectual, "when I'm creating, when I'm working, I do not operate out of that kind of analytical basis. I operate intuitively. To make art is to try to find responses and feelings that you're not aware of in yourself or in the material. Art comes intuitively, in trying different things vis-à-vis the material until something clicks. Most of the time your first ideas don't work. The problem is you always have to get the play staged before you can see all the things you're doing that are wrong."

A playwright himself, when Foreman decides to direct something by another playwright, it is because the text contains "a web of associations" similar to the web he spins in his own writing. But Foreman makes a large distinction between directing his own works and the work of others. "I believe that in my own plays I am speaking more directly to the energies that run the universe; those same energies are the *subtext* of plays that seem to have more normal subject matters. What's important to me, always, are the unconscious and cosmic and archetypal forces that are driving everything, be they decisions made at General Motors or decisions made at the Vatican or in monasteries in Tibet.

"The necessity of the universe is at work sometimes through institutions and forms like the U.S. government or the Pentagon (which might be represented in this play). At other times, it's at work through an individual's psychic struggle, as in my plays."

At the core of *End of the World (With Symposium to Follow)* Foreman sees an "archetypal central myth," a myth that is also embodied in the Edgar Allen Poe piece "The Imp of the Perverse." As Poe states it, "We stand upon the brink of a precipice. We peer into the abyss— we grow sick and dizzy. Our first impulse is to shrink from the danger. Unaccountably we remain . . . upon the precipice's edge. There grows into palpability a shape, far more terrible than any genius, or any demon of a tale and yet it is but a thought . . . of what would be our sensations during the sweeping precipitancy of a fall from such a height. And this fall—this rushing annihilation—for the very reason that it involves that one most ghastly and loathsome of all the most ghastly and loathsome images of death and suffering which have ever presented themselves to our imagination—for this very cause do we know we most vividly desire it." This myth, Foreman told the actors, is "what we're working for."

"The world is full of contradictions," he says. "There's always a war going on." The tape "Oscillate" begins to play. Pages of a script flutter and fall to the floor. The actors are in motion. Richard Foreman is at work.

This article was supplemented by additional material from an interview conducted by Mary Coleman in 1987 during Mr. Foreman's rehearsals of The Fall of the House of Usher *at the A.R.T.*

THE GOOD WOMAN OF SETZUAN

Brecht Is No Longer Dangerous
by Andrei Serban

Brecht wanted to achieve two things: transform the theatre and transform the world.

He did not quite succeed in either. He used to be called a dangerous man, but he is no longer dangerous. As the century ends, the old anarchist becomes a classic. Brecht's message that art should resist and fight and that theatre has a social and political function is today a subject for late-night dinner discussions among Wall Street corporates after watching *Chicago* or *Cabaret* on Broadway.

Once, it was difficult to separate Brecht from his political ideologies and see him as a theatre craftsman. But with the disintegration of communism, one notices that Brecht's strength lies in his innovative technique: the composition of elaborate, precise structures that provoke the audience into reevaluating the ways in which they observe. The stops and starts of Brecht's episodic style force audiences to break their habits of observation and encourage them to see and hear freshly. Brecht the author is also a director who needed to work closely with actors. In this way he bridged the two strains of twentieth-century theatre. One, the "natural," connects the experiments of Stanislavsky to the journeys of Grotowski. The other, the "unnatural," found its roots in the Asian theatre that was explored by Meyerhold and Vakhtangov. Meyerhold, the maker of spectacles and the auteur of the performance, worked differently from Stanislavsky, who attempted to reach what he thought the playwright intended by a coauthorship with the actors. Between them was Vakhtangov, who was Stanislavsky's pupil but was fascinated by Meyerhold's work and invented fantastic realism. Brecht intelligently stole from them all, understanding that tradition means investigation and interrogation, the only way that theatre can advance.

Chekhov disliked what the "playwright-friendly" Stanislavsky did with his plays as director. But the auteur Meyerhold was roundly applauded for his faithfulness to the spirit of Gogol when he directed his highly experimental *The Inspector General*. The paradox is that sometimes one can be faithful only by appearing unfaithful. Brecht provides the perfect example of this in his methods as a director because of his disrespect toward his own writing in rehearsals. He often asked actors to improvise and did not hesitate to make major changes in the text from these experiments. Brecht recognized that practical work is more trustworthy than words or theories.

While writing *The Good Woman of Setzuan*, what fascinated Brecht from the Asian theatre was the element of contradiction: going in one direction briefly, then turning in another. From this friction vitality flows. Brecht also shows this contradiction in his acting method. While often misinterpreted as artificial because of the lack of inner process, the chilly execution, and the nonidentification with one's role, Brecht's "unnatural" style tries to make the actor both "doer" and "observer." Grotowski once said that Brecht's use of montage structure—no continuity but bits and pieces of images—is done at such speed that, although interrupted by stops, it gives the impression of continuity. The controversial *Verfremdungseffekt* (the so-called alienation effect or, more accurately, the defamiliarization effect) that Brecht desires is not a tool for distancing the audience but rather one that illuminates ideas.

Brecht's message today seems as dogmatic as an old Hollywood movie: "This is the victim, this is the villain, things are bad, therefore it's somebody's fault." Compared with Shakespeare, the message lacks complexity. But in working on his plays today, it is important to recognize Brecht the craftsman on the stage: the explosive situations, the sharpness of character, the chameleon-like transformations, the rich material for actors. Even though Brecht lived through one of the grimmest periods of history, he explored its horror with joyful imagination, creating extravagant grotesques. The challenge for us is to take his stories and structures and use them as inquiries in terms of energy, rhythm, and color. We need not fall into the trap of pretending that political theatre can change anything. Recent history unmasks Brecht's dogma. But by avoiding the pedestrian realism that Brecht abhorred, we can find in his theatre an opportunity to bring fresh clarity to our lives.

He takes theatre away from the sacred and transforms it into a sporting event.

See photo on page 153.

ARCHANGELS DON'T PLAY PINBALL

Dario Fo: Andiamo a Ridere
Interview by Arthur Holmberg

Q: Recently we've seen two plays by Pirandello at the A.R.T. His works also deal with illusion and reality. Did he influence you?

DARIO FO: The emotional climates of our plays are different. Pirandello is a pessimist. His plays wound. They pile catastrophe on catastrophe. You leave the theatre distressed. Pirandello and I deal with the same themes, but I'm an optimist. Even when I face tragedy in my plays, I face it with a positive mental outlook. It's a question of personality, not philosophy. One finds a philosophy that suits one's personality, not vice versa.

Q: Underneath the jokes, *Archangels* is an enchanting romance. Why did you embed a tender love story in a farce?

DF: In my North Italian dialect, the idiom we use for making love is *andiamo a ridere*—let's go have a laugh. Moping about and sighing is not my idea of love. Love isn't tragic. It's joyous. Shakespeare always framed his love stories with farce and ribaldry. How better to dramatize love than by putting it in the realm of the comic?

Q: You've said that satire and tragedy are related. How?

DF: Satire is born of tragedy. Take *Archangels*. It begins as tragedy with a dude who survives by turning himself into a buffoon and a girl who survives by selling her body. They've both lost their battles with life and have to invent reasons to go on living. Both live in spiritual misery, in a society that tells Sunny he's not a man but a hunting dog. But from Sunny and Angela's grotesque encounter, hope is born. The play ends in elation. Satire, like tragedy, ends in catharsis. The difference is how each genre achieves catharsis, that moment of liberation and release. Catharsis is the end-all and be-all of theatre. It exorcises anguish and gives you the courage to face life. You cannot have a catharsis at home watching television or reading a novel. Catharsis can be achieved only in a community as a result of a social ritual. It transcends the individual; it enlarges the individual. It makes him feel passions with an intensity he could never feel alone. It is the confrontation of a society with its gods and its devils.

Q: You've chosen an intriguing title for your play. Why did you use pinball as a symbol?

DF: I wrote *Archangels* thirty years ago. At that time, pinball had just come to Europe from America, and we were all wild about it. It was like Aladdin's lamp—a physical object that puts you in touch with the marvelous. Franca and I became fanatics. We bought one for our house to practice day and night. At that time, pinball machines were rare, and you couldn't count on finding one in every bar, and there were always endless lines of people waiting to play. Franca and I became the champions of the town.

Q: But in the play you use pinball as a symbol for the randomness of fate.

DF: Sunny, my hero, accuses the archangels of banging him around like a ball in a pinball machine. In Italy we tell children that archangels invent dreams, but Sunny feels that life has mocked his dreams. At the end, he says "Archangels don't play pinball." He means we must learn to take our dreams seriously. Archangels don't lie. Dreams are a paradox; they're both true and not true, so we must fight to make the impossible possible.

Q: You use many techniques from classical comedy—quid pro quo, mistaken identities, disguises. Why?

DF: Why not? If it worked for Shakespeare and Machiavelli, Molière and Goldoni, it will work for me. And the *commedia dell'arte* is an indispensable primer for studying what's effective on stage: how to create comic confusion to introduce a large number of characters, how to spin off an imbroglio, how to plot a double-cross. Gags are the life force of comedy.

Dario Fo and Franca Rame during rehearsals of *Archangels Don't Play Pinball.*

Q: So you learned how to write comedy by reading the masters.

DF: Reading? No. One learns next to nothing about the theatre by reading plays. I learned by seeing them performed.

Q: During rehearsals you work extensively on gestures, facial expressions, and body movement.

DF: What I call the false Stanislavsky—a misinterpretation of what the Russian director really taught—has exerted a pernicious influence on theatre by encouraging an overreliance on words. I always say you must not act words, you must act a situation. A situation is not just words.

How can I convey to the audience the despair of a man on the verge of suicide? With words? Should I say "Life has done me in. I prefer death"? How flat. Now watch me. Through my face and body I can make an audience experience my pain. [Here Mr. Fo launched into an improvised sketch of a suicide. He slumped over in the chair, moaned, and whorled his face into the living image of Edvard Munch's *The Scream*.]

My work with grammelot proves the point. [Grammelot is a stage language made up of sounds, rhythms, and inflections but no words.] I can communicate with an audience for an entire evening without using a single word because I'm acting situations. Great mimes use no words but say everything.

I'm not against words. They're important. But they mustn't dominate. Theatre is a dialectic between words and stage images, between sounds and silence. That's why rhythm is the basis of theatre—verbal and visual rhythm. You don't create theatre with words. You create theatre with rhythm, and you create rhythm through contrast—black against white, high against low, square against circle, soft against loud, stasis against movement, tragedy against comedy. Rhythm gives everything else value and significance. Rhythm establishes the proper relationship among the various elements, and there is no art which uses so many different elements as theatre—language, music, scenography, movement. All the arts converge in theatre. That's why theatre is an art of equilibrium, and equilibrium is difficult to teach actors. The easiest thing to do is fall back on words. But theatre is the art of synthesis. And economy. Second-rate actors and directors always do too much. They're too busy. Braque once said, "Too many colors equal no color." The great actors are masters of understatement and restraint. Whenever you hear an actor shouting, you know you're in the presence of an amateur.

Q: You are one of the great clowns of the twentieth century. Why does everyone—young and old, sophisticated and naive—love clowns?

DF: Clowns are the most ancient figures in world theatre. They antedate the theatre. Long before tragedy, there was the chorus of satyrs. Clowns represent the oldest living theatrical tradition. We have records of clowns from the Renaissance, the Middle Ages, Rome, and Greece, and they all used the same gags. Clowns concretize our obsessions, our fears, our desires. They act out our repressions and transgress our taboos. They laugh, they cry, they fall down, they jump up. They play out for us the absurdities of our life. They're also violent and cruel. It's the cruelty of clowns that appeals most to children. Clowns are grotesque blasphemers against all our pieties. That's why we need them. They're our alter egos.

RIGHT YOU ARE (IF YOU THINK YOU ARE)

Reflections on Reflections
by Arthur Holmberg

"On or about December 1910," Virginia Woolf noted, "human character changed." Human character may or may not have changed in that precise month, but the way artists began to portray character was undergoing a major shift. The self, no longer seen as a sharply defined entity, was now felt as a tumble of multiple selves—slippery, uncertain, mysterious. Proust's *intermittences du coeur*, Picasso's Cubist portraits, Kafka's *Metamorphosis*—these landmarks of modern art point to the centrality of this new sense of a broken self.

The turning point in the novel came with Dostoevsky. Before him, the great European Realists, from Stendhal to Tolstoy, created memorable characters by a logical analysis of an individual's inner world set within a specific environment. Enter Dostoevsky, who, according to Woolf, understood that human consciousness is a "shower of innumerable atoms." Logical explanations fail; the human soul is a "seething whirlpool."

The turning point in drama came with Pirandello. When his six characters, uninvited and unannounced, elbowed their way onto the stage, they brought with them the relativity of Einstein and the uncertainty of Heisenberg. Pirandello gave these twentieth-century dogmas a local habitation and a name. Beautiful poetry, Mallarmé observed, is not made with beautiful ideas. Pirandello's genius lay in his ability to give dramatic flesh and bone to this new sense of a fugitive self.

Right You Are demonstrates how Pirandello pumped theatrical blood into abstract ideas. His story line is easy to follow. A new family arrives in a small Italian village and soon sets idle tongues buzzing with their unusual living arrangements. Apparently the son-in-law refuses to let his mother-in-law visit her daughter. Called on the carpet by the city councillor, mother and son give opposing explanations. The old woman—Signora Frola—claims that Signora Ponza is her daughter; Signor Ponza claims that the old woman's daughter, his first wife, has died and that he has remarried. Who is right? Who is Signora Ponza? The town gossips, presented by Pirandello as a chorus of buffoons, decide that only Signora Ponza can solve the riddle. The tensions build rapidly to her appearance and the play's unexpected denouement.

Pirandello coopts a popular genre—the mystery story—and uses it to demonstrate the relativity of truth. Who is the woman who passes for Signora Ponza? What dark secrets do her husband and Signora Frola wish to bury? As in all good mystery stories, a series of clues—including official documents—are dug up as the buffoons blithely set about their task to lay bare the naked truth. Their method? To gather as many verifiable facts as possible, sift through them, and, with the aid of reason and logic, arrive at a solution—the same method all great detectives from Sherlock Holmes to Miss Marple have employed. But Pirandello turns reason on its head and overthrows the tradition of the detective story. The very structure of the play is ironic. It twists the well-made thriller into a philosophical parable. The play ends as it begins—with an unsolved mystery.

The master of the revels is Laudisi, a stand-in for Pirandello who nudges the chorus of buffoons into a discovery, not of the truth they wanted but of the elusive nature of all truth. In Act I he dramatizes the relativity of truth by having different characters look at him from different angles—everyone sees him, but they all see different parts of him.

> You see me, don't you? Now you touch me. Okay, you've seen and touched me—and so you are absolutely certain of my existence. But don't tell each other—your husband here, my sister and my niece— don't tell any of them what you've concluded, because they'll all say you're totally wrong. On the other hand, you might be right because I really am what you think I am. But that doesn't mean that my sister, my niece and your husband aren't right, too, even though their opinions may all be completely different from yours.

With this little piece of metatheater, Laudisi proves that every production is a perpetual hypothesis. Pirandello does not deny that something exists exterior to and independently of our minds. What

Pirandello dramatizes is the process through which each human consciousness must first perceive and interpret the sense impressions that bombard it from outside. The very act of seeing—and *to see* is one of the key words of Pirandello's text—is an act of cognition, a subjective process by which an individual constructs a subjective and partial view of reality. We can never see the thing in itself. We can never embrace the reality of another person. Our field of vision is limited. Our consciousness, as Husserl noted, is locked into a narrow horizon. Laudisi introduces his play-within-the-play by indicating that we can never know for certain anything or anyone. All we can do is represent a fact or a person to ourselves and each other.

The crisis of representation—the keystone of Western art—has moved to the forefront of postmodern criticism. Art, Pirandello wrote, "is not a question of imitating or reproducing life; for the very simple reason that there is no life which constitutes a reality in itself to be reproduced. Life, infinitely varied and constantly changing, is a continual and indistinct flowing and has no other form outside of that which we give it from time to time."

Pirandello came up with brilliant visual images to dramatize this problem. The metaphor he uses in *Right You Are* is a mirror. Left alone for a moment in Act II, Laudisi stops before a mirror and engages his own reflection in conversation:

My God, it's you. Now tell me, are you the crazy one or me? I say it's you and you say it's me. One of us has to be right, no? Okay, have it your own way. I don't want to argue with my alter ego. We get along fine, the two of us, don't we? But the trouble is, others don't think of you the way I do, and if that's the case, Professor, you're in a helluva fix. I think I know who you are. But what are you for other people? Just a reflection, Professor, an image in a mirror. Everyone of them is carrying around just such a phantom inside themselves, and yet they all want to meddle with the phantoms in other people. Peeking in private keyholes. What can you do but laugh.

In this scene from *Right You Are*, the mirror exists as a concrete dramatic metaphor for a wide range of Pirandello's concerns. First, the mirror image dramatizes how we must objectify the self in order to think about the self. But each of these self-reflecting images—necessary to define the self—becomes a trap. Consciousness is constant flux. A reflection defines self but also limits. It hardens into a false image that captures only one aspect of self at one moment in time. It cannot catch the essence of self—spontaneous, free-flowing, ever-changing consciousness. In "The Mirror Stage," one of Lacan's most influential essays, the French psychoanalyst explores the neurotic consequences that follow when a subject identifies with his mirror-image. This mirror-image—Lacan calls it a mirage—"fixes . . . in contrast with the turbulent movements that the subject feels are animating him." This "fixing," according to Lacan, leads to self-alienation.

Pirandello always sets up a tension between the necessity of these self-defining images and their absurdity. We need to define the self to avoid sinking into chaos and schizophrenia. But our consciousness always moves away from each self-definition, refusing to be pinned down by any one formulation. Each image of the self immobilizes the self; consciousness is movement and anarchy. Pirandello's plays dramatize this endless struggle. In *Right You Are* this dichotomy is portrayed as the dynamic interplay between self and others' reflections of self. In other works the conflict emerges as a dialectic between life and art. In *Enrico IV* and *As You Desire Me*, self becomes defined and ossified by a portrait. In *Six Characters in Search of an Author* the characters fight the actors, who want to shape the characters' lives into meaningful form through theatre. Once written down and interpreted by others, the characters no longer recognize themselves—only grotesque reflections of themselves.

But *Right You Are* dramatizes that self has an objective existence beyond self. Signora Ponza exists not only in and for herself. She also exists in the consciousness of her husband, in the consciousness of Signora Frola, and in the consciousness of each of the buffoons. All these contradictory images of the self crash and collide, yet each has its own validity. "For myself, I am nobody," Signora Ponza explains. "I am whom you believe me to be." Self can never see self, all we have are twisted reflections.

"When a man lives," Pirandello wrote, "he lives and does not see himself in the act of living." Passing before a mirror "he is astonished at his appearance, or else he turns his eyes to avoid seeing himself. Then again, he may spit at his image in disgust, or clenching his fist, break the mirror, but always there is a crisis, and that crisis is my theatre."

A theatre of crisis for an age of crisis. As our century slouches toward its end, Pirandello's importance for the theatre looms larger and larger. No other modern dramatist is so closely attuned to the post-modern sensibility with its emphasis on self-reflection, the dissemination of meanings and local rather than grand narratives. Postmodern theatre forces the spectator to see events through several contradictory lenses at once, baffling the most dogged effort to construct a unified viewpoint. On the postmortem stage, reality is not represented. Representations are deconstructed. We can find no better guide than Pirandello through this unraveling of consciousness.

QUARTET

Machiavellis of the Bedroom—
An Erotic Endgame
by Arthur Holmberg

The eighteenth century was a century of doubt. The smile of reason mocked all social and political institutions, ushering in the Age of Revolution. By the end of the century, philosophers of enlightenment had become firebrands of revolt. The culmination of this most reasonable of centuries was Thomas Jefferson and the Marquis de Sade.

Whereas American philosophers turned their attention to the *res publica*, the French divided their energy between politics and sex. Love, after all, had become as encrusted with silly ideas as government, and if men and women wanted to free themselves from the tyranny of superstition, what better place to begin than love? The eighteenth century was an age of great political thinkers—Montesquieu, Edmund Burke, Benjamin Franklin. It was also the age of Don Giovanni and Casanova.

What was left of love after reason had desiccated it? Not much. "The pleasure is momentary, the position ridiculous, the expense damnable," Lord Chesterfield warned his son, and the French naturalist, the Count Buffon, asserted that "Nothing is good in love but the physical part. Animals do not make the same mistake as men. Animals do not look for pleasure where pleasure is not to be had. Men, on the other hand, want to invent pleasures and thus spoil the pleasures that nature offers. By trying to conform to romantic sentiments, men abuse their true nature and hollow out in their hearts a vacuum nothing can fill." In his maxims, Chamfort sums up the thinking man's attitude acerbically: "Love as it exists in society is nothing but the exchange of two fantasies and the contact of two epidemises."

Americans find it hard to believe that, once upon a time in a faraway kingdom called Versailles, aristocrats idled away their lives and fortunes pursuing pleasure, not happiness. No one who did not live before the French Revolution, sighed Talleyrand, can know how sweet life can be. What made life sweet? Hunting, gaming, and love. But hedonism is hard work, and love, the greatest of pastimes, obeyed a strict set of rules that turned a simple pleasure into an elaborate ritual called seduction. The purpose of seduction was to glorify the reputation of the seducer. An affair that did not create a scandal was no affair at all, and if a seducer wanted to be admired—and what seducer doesn't?—he had to observe piously the four stages of seduction: the choice of quarry worth chasing (ugly or promiscuous women do not add luster to a seducer's reputation); courtship (Don Juan assumes the role of romantic lover); the fall (self-explanatory); and rupture—also called *la mise à mort*.

Libertinage, as the French aristocrats defined it (and they invented the word), was the opposite of passion. It was an intellectual exercise of the will, a social pantomime played to the gallery. One becomes a seducer to be applauded. The performativity of seduction and sex as self-conscious role-playing: the seducer as comedian. Diderot's "The Paradox of Acting" (1773) might serve as a manual for any would-be Don Juan: "The actor must have in himself an unmoved and disinterested onlooker. He must also have intellectual penetration and no sensibility. If an actor were full of feeling, how could he play the same part twice running with the same spirit and success? At the very moment when the actor touches your heart, he is listening to his own voice; his talent depends, not as you think, on feeling, but on rendering the outward signs of feeling so that you fall into the trap. The player's tears come from his brain, not his heart."

Novelists rush in where angels fear to tread. A series of worldly-wise writers from Crébillon fils (*The Sofa*, 1745) to Restif de la Bretonne (*The Perverted Peasant*, 1776) and de Sade (*Juliette or the Rewards of Vice*, 1797) painted this new philosophy of the boudoir. The summa of worldliness and the greatest novel of seduction, *Les Liaisons dangereuses*, by Choderlos de Laclos, created a scandal when it appeared in 1782 because the author had failed to glamorize seduction. His first readers, expecting an erotic uplift, accused the author of blaspheming sex. He was too parsimonious with details about the moment of pleasure. The nineteenth century, on the other hand, feared that Laclos had made sex too tantalizing. The novel was condemned by the French courts for obscenity and was not reprinted until 1894. Laclos gained his rightful place in the pantheon of great writers slowly. Baudelaire said the novel "burns like ice." Twentieth-century critics have come to admire Laclos's psychological insights into the antagonisms of sexuality and the delicate minuet he dances between cynicism and morality. No one doubts his stylistic virtuosity. The novel, in epistolary form, articulates a different voice for each of its thirteen letter writers, from the biting intellect of the Marquise de Merteuil to the sentimental gush of Cécile de Volanges. These different voices—and the attitudes toward love they espouse—set up a counterpoint that makes it difficult to draw any easy lessons.

The novel charts the strange complicity between two aristocratic libertines—the Vicomte de Valmont and the Marquise de Merteuil—as they plot the seduction of an innocent girl, Cécile de Volanges, the Marquise's niece, and Mme. de Tourvel, a virtuous wife (also called la Présidente after her husband's title). Although both the Marquise and the Vicomte find time for desultory sex along the way, they concentrate their satanic energy on debauching the virgin and ruining the wife. Why? Valmont claims it's to enhance his reputation as an irresistible Don Juan. Merteuil claims it's for revenge. The Count Gercourt, who has just been engaged to Cécile, had once rejected Merteuil's advances, and she wants to see his bride deflowered before the wedding night. But these conscious aims touch only the surface of their motivation, and Laclos suggests deeper, darker motivations that reach a bedrock of hostility underlying all sexual arousal and an invincible will to power that dominates all sexual relations. Images drawn from warfare color the letters both seducers write.

In contrast to these two Machiavellis of the bedroom, the pious Mme. de Tourvel suffers a moral crisis. Married as a girl to an older man chosen by her family, she awakens to physical desire only after meeting Valmont. This sexual attraction to a man other than her husband precipitates an interior dilemma that forces her to question what she owes society, what she owes her family, and what she owes herself. Her decision to sacrifice all for love heralds the romantic revolution. After seducing her, Valmont himself is seduced into the dangerous world of affections. "The intoxication was complete and mutual," he writes. "For the first time the emotion outlasted the pleasure." The sentimental education of Don Juan. This Napoleon of the boudoir is embarrassed to learn that feelings, not sensations, define love. Merteuil, however, cannot forgive Valmont for preferring another to herself, and her jealousy sets in motion the machinery that will destroy all three.

The Marquise de Merteuil dominates the novel. She can take her rightful place alongside Clytemnestra, Medea, and Lady Macbeth as one of the most awesome women ever imagined by male paranoia. It is difficult to understand what Laclos intended with this hellhound of fury unless one knows his "Essay on the Education of Women," in which he asserts that woman in society is a slave of man and powerless before a social and legal system that institutionalizes her slavery. Woman, he argues, is the equal of man in a state of nature. Why has she become his slave in society? He ends by noting that no slave ever won freedom without a revolution.

To prepare for this revolution, Laclos insists that women must gain access to knowledge, which men have withheld to keep women dependent. The first step to freedom is education. In Letter 81 the Marquise explains how she educated herself. Like other women of her class, she was raised to be an idiot. But after her husband had the good grace to die and leave her a rich widow, she entered the forbidden territory—the library—and spent her days soaking up the wisdom of the ages. There are two classes of women, she explains to Valmont: "The more numerous one, which comprises those women who have had nothing but youth and beauty to recommend them, falls into a feebleminded apathy, from which it never emerges except to play cards or practice a few devotions. These women are always boring, often querulous, and sometimes a little meddlesome. . . . They have neither thought nor being, and merely repeat indifferently and uncomprehendingly everything they hear, retaining within themselves an absolute void. The other, much rarer class, and the really valuable one, contains those women who, having been possessed of a character and having taken care to cultivate their minds, are able to create an identity for themselves when the one provided by nature has failed them."

Merteuil has created an identity for herself. Unfortunately, although her program of education follows closely Laclos's recommendations, she has perverted the goals. Laclos saw education as a means to free the self, not to control others. Merteuil, however, identifies with the aggressor and rather than fighting the patriarchy wants to beat it at its own game. "I was born to revenge my sex," she warns Valmont, "and master yours." She does, but in the process destroys Valmont and herself.

Les Liaisons dangereuses announces and explains the French Revolution: *après moi le déluge*. Laclos died a general in the Army of the Revolution, and most French critics interpret his novel as a bitter indictment of an aristocracy that had lost its historical role but still retained political power. At heart, both Valmont and Merteuil wage war against a sense of their own futility. By exposing sex as the deadliest weapon, Laclos laid bare the social tensions that would rip through France seven years after he wrote his novel.

Quartet, Heiner Müller's play, is a contemporary reverie on Laclos's novel. Writing exactly two hundred years later, Müller peppers French cynicism with German nihilism. Although the psychopathology of erotic obsession and the eternally returning battle of the sexes remain an important part of Müller's text—the images of death at the end relate to the suicide of Müller's first wife—most German critics interpret Müller's play as a political allegory.

Müller is a revolutionary. Although committed to socialist experiments, his play *Hamletmachine* explores why all political ideologies based on Western philosophy—communism as well as capitalism—have failed to achieve social justice. Western liberals who wish to criticize their governments are products of Western civilization. Consequently their criticisms are trapped in the vocabulary and assumptions of the system they wish to attack. Müller implies that correcting a system with tools provided by that system corrects symptoms, not causes. The only escape would be to invent a new political agenda outside the pale of Western categories of thought. Since no Westerner can escape the categories of his own mind, Western history stumbles into the same nightmares over and over. Thus Müller refutes Marx's belief in historical progress.

Because Müller believes that Western thought and Western history are self-perpetuating systems, he often situates his plays in two superimposed time frames—a historical past and a political present—to dramatize the endless repetitions of the same tragic patterns. *Quartet* takes place simultaneously in a French salon shortly before the Revolution and in an air raid shelter shortly after World War III. For Müller, the bourgeoisie has outlived its historical usefulness as the French aristocracy had outlived theirs. But the atom bomb has replaced the guillotine as the instrument of retribution; the play abounds in apocalyptic images. A sense of urgency runs through Müller's works, but he is not a pessimist. He believes that we are products of a historical moment but that we can and must change that moment.

In Müller's play, Valmont and Merteuil are reunited after many years of separation. Both have aged and both have withdrawn from an active sex life. To idle away the few seconds before extinction, they reenact the two greatest moments of their sexual glory: the annihilation of the virgin (Cécile) and the wife (la Tourvel).

Some German critics interpret Valmont and Merteuil as symbolizing the two superpowers—Russia and the United States, who nonchalantly amuse themselves by seducing and destroying third-world countries as they edge the world closer and closer to nuclear doom. Müller frequently uses sex to mirror politics: the will to power drives eroticism. The way people relate to each other sexually exposes the deepest values of their society. "Our destiny is to conquer!" exalts Laclos's Valmont—a line echoed ironically at the end of *Quartet*.

Müller is no less a revolutionary in theatre than in politics. European critics point to him as the prime example of postmodern drama. Traditional drama depends on characters, dialogue, and plot. In *Theory of the Modern Drama*, Peter Szondi discusses why contemporary European thought rejects the assumptions behind these triple pillars of Western drama. Müller's texts negate the notion of a stable, unified self; the ability of language to bridge the alienation of individuals; and the possibility of forging the chaos of experience into a coherent story. Müller's theatre represents another important aspect of postmodernism: intertextuality, or two texts talking to each other (*Les Liaisons dangereuses* and *Quartet*). Many of Müller's works are intertexts—ironic assemblages of bits and pieces of the European canon of great literature. Müller does this to question the privileged voice of authority we confer on masterpieces.

Instead of traditional, realistic drama, Müller offers metaphoric visions. His mind works through analogy and image. His style is dense, elliptic, poetic. His dramatic texts are really dramatic poems, and many German critics consider him their greatest stylist writing today. The beauty of his language sets up a tension with the brutality of his subject matter. As in Laclos, elegance and animality walk hand in glove.

Artaud, Genet, and Beckett showed Müller the way to his own version of the theatre of cruelty—an erotic endgame. Self-conscious role-playing is the central metaphor in both *The Balcony* and *Quartet*. Müller believes that the only way an oppressor can experience the humiliation of his victim is by becoming a victim himself. Hence Valmont must assume the part of the women he has destroyed. And, like Beckett in *Waiting for Godot*, *Quartet* fuses comedy and tragedy. Müller often complains that German productions miss his playfulness, and it is the humor of his text that Robert Wilson has understood and dramatized to counterpoint the anger.

But one does not have to agree with Müller's politics or his existential philosophy to enjoy his plays. "An ideological approach to theatre is inadequate and unartistic," Müller contends. In *Against Interpretation*, Susan Sontag argues that theatre is first and foremost a sensuous experience. Müller is a brilliant magician of the stage who never fails to catch an audience off guard and jolt them into a new perception.

Müller is subversive. He tosses his plays at audiences like Molotov cocktails. "The only thing a work of art can do is awaken the yearning for another condition of the world. This yearning is revolutionary."

THE FALL OF THE HOUSE OF USHER

Philip Glass: Emotion in Pure Form
Interview by Arthur Holmberg

Q: *Einstein on the Beach*, which you wrote with Robert Wilson, forced theatre critics to invent a new vocabulary to describe a new experience. How did this work influence your evolution as an artist?

PHILIP GLASS: My personal involvement with music theatre began with *Einstein* in 1976, a turning point for me and for American music theatre. It was the first avant-garde piece that got out of the lofts and galleries of downtown New York to reach a wider audience. Artists today see their work as firmly rooted in the culture of our time. This

Francine Torres (Ma Ubu) and Charles Levin (Pa Ubu, standing right) with courtiers (Will LeBow and Thomas Derrah, on left) in *Ubu Rock*.

started with Andy Warhol. Artists wanted to be significant players in the events of their own day. Pop artists broke out of that small downtown community into the larger cultural scene.

Q: Besides proving that the avant-garde could be anchored in the mass culture of its own time, was pop art important in any other way?

PG: Pop art taught us to take a very American vocabulary and turn it into an idiom of the fine arts. The first exhibition of Warhol's "Brillo Boxes" was revolutionary. In the early sixties, the idea that the vernacular of popular culture could become the language of high art was unimaginable. The aesthetics of pop art affected people like Sam Shepard, Bob Wilson, and . . . myself. We were all beneficiaries of that.

Q: In addition to pop art, did the experimental performance groups of the sixties—the Living Theatre, the Open Theatre, Mabou Mines, and the Wooster Group—influence your approach to music theatre?

PG: They changed our attitudes toward theatre and the process of creating theatre. The ideal of collective creation and theatre as intense collaboration is a legacy of these groups. We're in a period of collaborative work. Artists want to work together today. All my pieces are collaborations. In *Usher* I'm collaborating with Arthur Yorinks on the libretto, and with Richard Foreman, who is designing and directing.

Q: Many gifted composers can't write for the theatre—Schubert tried and failed. What makes music dramatic?

PG: When I take on a dramatic work, I spend time with the subject matter. It can be a book, a play, a person, or an image. In the case of *Usher*, I began with the story. Arthur Yorinks and I studied the tale together and reached an interpretation. Then Arthur did a fifteen-page libretto. Before I began the music, I spent a great deal of time on the libretto, looking for the dramatic structure that I could articulate musically. In my view, what makes dramatic music dramatic is the point of departure. In this case, the libretto. It can also be a series of images, which is how I work with Bob Wilson.

Q: When you were working on *Einstein on the Beach*, the music, the words, and visual images were juxtaposed in startling and unexpected ways. Is the relationship between words and music different in *Usher*?

PG: Yes. *Einstein* was a collage; words, music, and movement were layered on each other like images superimposed on transparent paper. *Usher* began as an interpretation of Poe's story.

Q: What attracted you to this text by Poe?

PG: I read Poe as a boy growing up in Baltimore, one of the cities Poe lived in. He's a local literary hero. When I went back to his work in 1984, to compose a dance–theatre piece based on his short story *A Descent into the Maelstrom*, I began to see him as the precursor of Kafka and Beckett. The French Symbolists admired him because Poe focuses on intense images dreamt by the mind. He's interested in psychological responses to the outside world—very much the way modernist writers are—and the macabre aspect of Poe appealed to me.

Q: So you wanted to explore the dark side of the human psyche?

PG: Yes. And Poe leads you there. For him, fear and terror become so persuasive and emphatic they break free from their object and become abstract states of mind. Poe presents emotion in a pure form.

Q: What do you mean by pure?

PG: By dislocating fear from a rational source, Poe transmutes it into existential angst. It becomes metaphysical. Poe was interested in transcendent experiences. But he transcends through descent, not ascent. Transcendence down through the dark side.

Q: Once you said you grew up in a musical tradition that was not literary, that it would never occur to you to take a play or literary text and set it to music.

PG: That was true until 1985.

Q: What changed?

PG: I'd done enough of the other. I'd written four operas, a trilogy, and sections of *the CIVIL warS* with Bob Wilson. So I decided to work with writers. At that point I began to collaborate with Doris Lessing, Arthur Yorinks, and David Henry Hwang.

Q: It seems as if you have now become more interested in character.

PG: That's right. I think it's a measure of how my interests continue to change as I explore various aspects of theatre. My career is an ongoing process of discovery. At various points in my life as an artist, I'm interested in certain aspects of theatre because that's what I'm concentrating on. Later, other aspects interest me.

Q: Your attitude toward the structure of an artistic work has also changed. Once you said you admired Beckett's plays because the emotional climax came at a different point each time you saw the play. But a work like *The Juniper Tree* is structured to reach a definite climax.

PG: With *Juniper Tree* I composed a musical epiphany within a clearly marked dramatic structure. But in regard to the participation of the audience in the interpretation of the piece, it remains fundamental to the way I work. I still depend on the audience to complete the meaning.

Q: You used two interesting terms to talk about these epiphanies. One was contemplation, the other, catharsis. Could you define the difference?

PG: I have to use musical examples. With *Descent into the Maelstrom* there is a moment of quiet in the storm. The moon comes out, the storm abates, and the character looks around and begins to understand the meaning of death. The music invites us to contemplate. It's a moment of detachment. In catharsis, say with the spaceship in *Einstein*, the audience is swept along with the music. It's a moment of involvement, not detachment. It's very different. Both catharsis and contemplation occur in almost all my works. This is how a work achieves texture and balance.

Q: Your earlier compositions privileged rhythm, but melody seems to have reasserted its appeal to you.

PG: Melody has always been there. It's a question of whether you hear it in the foreground or background. My collaborators influenced the way I write. I've been working with singers trained in opera. Singers have to have something to sing. Once you understand how the human voice works, how it stays fresh over a four-hour performance, you compose with that in mind. Singers have changed the melodic nature of my work.

Q: What aspects of Poe's story did you try to capture in your opera?

PG: The first act is about the relationship of Madeline and Roderick, the second act about their relationship to the house itself. The opera explores the relationship of the children to the tradition of the Ushers that finally overwhelms them. In this piece, Poe presents us with a series of forbidden activities—the relationship of the brother and sister, the relationship of the house to the children, the relationship of the visitor to Roderick. Poe focuses on bonds that break taboos. We come to empathize with people caught up in forbidden sexual encounters, sacrifice, death, and suicide—all the good things that make a horror story. We're fascinated because everything about *Usher* is forbidden. Everything.

Q: Even the music?

PG: I've tried to carry out Poe's ideas in musical language. So the music, too, enters forbidden territory. It violates taboos. There are some musical surprises at the end of the piece that will shed new light on the old tale.

Tragedy Could Go No Further: Reflections on Ford's 'Tis Pity She's a Whore
by Harry Levin

The sensational title of this drama can be intriguing or off-putting, depending on one's point of view. It is spoken by the Cardinal, a moralist whose morality does not carry much conviction. " 'Tis pity"— it's just too bad—is the least we could say, confronted with so fearful a denouement. And the monosyllable that characterizes the heroine is, of course, a calculated shock. Annabella is far from being a blithe professional. She earns her epithet when, on her wedding night, her husband discovers that she is already pregnant and proceeds to denounce her as a "whore of whores." That is not the only point in the play when a double standard prevails, since the sexual background of Soranzo himself—like nearly everything else about him—is shady.

Annabella's whoredom may have been prefigured in the name of her "tut'ress," Putana, who prates on and on like Juliet's nurse. At the lover's side, Giovanni has his own confidant in Friar Bonaventura, whose admonitions are even sterner than those of Friar Lawrence to Romeo. If the play begins amid such plaintive reverberations from *Romeo and Juliet*, it moves toward a climax that resonates with *Othello*: Giovanni's fatal resolve, attended by the Iago-like perfidies of the cynical Vasques. "O Iago, the pity of it . . . !" Coming a generation after Shakespeare, reaching his dramatic prime in the decade before the Puritans closed the London theatres (1642), John Ford took a belated, retrospective, and self-conscious stance. Robert Burton's recently published *Anatomy of Melancholy* was for him what Freudian psychoanalysis would be for many a modern writer. His critics do not hesitate to speak of decadence—an outlook that can foster artistic sophistication as well as the pursuit of extremes.

Pressing beyond his predecessors for an unexploited subject, Ford was bold enough to challenge a fundamental taboo. Incest, as T. S. Eliot has described it in this connection, seems to be "a perversion of nature which, unlike some other aberrations, is defended by no one." Yet it finds an apology here in the irresponsible tutelage of Putana. "Your brother's a man, I hope, and I say still, if a young wench feels the fit upon her, let her take anybody, father or brother, all is one." The mutual attraction of brother and sister is presented sympathetically, though sooner rather than later—within nine ominous months—they must face the direst retribution. Other dramatists had touched upon the forbidden deviance; Shakespeare had treated it most expressly through a pageantlike episode in *Pericles*. Beaumont and Fletcher had dallied with it: over *A King and No King* it hangs like a melodramatic cloud, only to be blown away by a timely breeze of mistaken identity.

But it remained to Ford to embrace the theme fully and forthrightly. When it is enunciated by his hero, in confession at the arresting start, he is solemnly warned by the Friar: "O Giovanni, hast thou left the schools of Knowledge to converse with lust and death?" Having now dropped out of the University of Bologna, this brilliant student applies his dialectical and rhetorical talents to rationalizing his forbidden passion, motivated—he convinces himself—more by fate than by lust. "Love reigns only in death" is a last refrain in the best of Ford's other tragedies, *The Broken Heart*, and Eros is coupled with Thanatos throughout *'Tis Pity She's a Whore*. "Must I now live, or die?" is Giovanni's proposition to Annabella, and on those terms their lives are overwhelmingly shortened. On their knees they both exchange the same vow: "Love me, or kill me, brother (sister)." Both alternatives will soon be realized. The continual outer movement that strives to part them is contrasted strikingly with the two intensive and intimate scenes where the lovers are alone together: when they plight their unsanctioned troth in Act I and when their amorous consummation turns into a murderous deathbed in Act V.

Ford's diction, energetic and direct, is relatively simple for a Caroline poet; quite frequently the blank-verse rhythm is weighted with a line consisting of ten monosyllables. As the dialogue plunges into a collision course between its individualistic spokesmen, two key words figure with increasing emphasis: "blood" and "heart," each reechoing more than thirty times. Visually and violently these two related symbols are brought together in a startling gesture of the grimmest actuality. Soranzo's birthday marks a fitting occasion for the grand finale. Annabella underscores the tragic irony when she perceives the invitation as "an harbinger of death." The manner of her immediate demise was foreshadowed when Giovanni—in their earlier scene—had offered her a dagger, telling her to rip up his bosom and read the message on his heart. Now he enters the banquet hall alone to enact his object lesson before the assembled dignitaries, with his sister's bloody heart impaled on his dagger.

"Tragedy could go no further," in the view of Taine, the French historian of English literature. In the view of some, it might indeed have gone too far, by transposing moral and psychological disaster into sheer physical carnage and then gloating over it. Recoiling spectators have sometimes reacted to Giovanni's macabre demonstration with uneasy laughs. The tradition in which Ford still worked to some extent, reducing the vagaries of human nature to allegorical dumb-shows or to the personified emblems of the morality play, would have posed no special problem here.

Action had been previously formalized in Act IV with another banquet, preceding the birthday party and celebrating the marriage. A masque, with appropriate music and dancing, serves a purpose sometimes performed by a play-within-the-play: it is utilized as an instrument for vengeance. Soranzo's cast-off mistress, the ghostly Hippolita, emerges from it conspiring to poison him and ends by quaffing her own lethal toast.

All of those machinations and tergiversations take place "in another country," in the Italian city-state of Parma, not a ducal court but among a mercantile elite. English playwrights of the Renaissance tended to keep evil at a picturesque distance by setting some of their darkest scenes in the homeland of Machiavelli, in an atmosphere of popery, poison, and plot. Leading through conspiracy into complexity, Ford's central plot around the star-crossed siblings is intricately ramified into subplots, as each of Annabella's three suitors pursues his own designs. The hypocrite who gains her hand, Soranzo, is saved from one revenge to be cut off by another. The victim of that first attempt is the rejected lout, Bergetto, who has subsequently become engaged to the niece of Hippolita's vengeful husband, Doctor Richardetto. The third suitor, Grimaldi, is the bungling hatchet-man who assassinated one rival while aiming at the other and who is allowed—under anti-papal protest—to take sanctuary in Rome.

Out of the fifteen articulate characters, there are seven deaths at the final count. The only person to survive untainted by the contagions of intrigue is the Friar, and he too must play a somewhat ambiguous role when he abets and conducts the wedding; ultimately he gives up his lost "pair of souls" and returns to academic Bologna. His lecture on the horrors of hell may have reached Annabella's conscience, but Giovanni's "conscience is seared" against compunctious second thoughts. To the end an arrant hedonist, he dismisses any apprehension of hell or of heaven: "My world, and all of happiness, is here." The outer world, as Ford depicted it, looks so malign and repellent that we can well understand—if not altogether condone—their desire to take occluded refuge in the inner world of one another. When this resort is closed, the self-destruction becomes an act of dual sacrifice, a hecatomb among the ruins to reprehend the survivors.

'Tis Pity She's a Whore, not surprisingly, made its debut in a private playhouse, the Phoenix. Briefly revived on the Restoration stage, it was viewed by Samuel Pepys as "a simple play"—perhaps because he chanced to be sitting next to "a most pretty and ingenious lady, which pleased me much." Through the eighteenth and nineteenth centuries it seems to have gone unperformed. But the twentieth century has seen numerous revivals, both amateur and professional, notably including the Donald Wolfit company (1940), Bernard Miles's at the Mermaid Theatre and Luchino Visconti's at the Théâtre de Paris (1961), Kenneth Haig's at the Yale Repertory Theatre (1967), Ron Daniels's at the Royal Shakespeare Company (1979), Michael Kahn's at the McCarter (1974), one at the Ashland, Oregon, Festival (1981), and a television broadcast from the B.B.C. When in the 1930s Antonin Artaud was projecting his subversive ideas for a "Theatre of Cruelty," the best poetic example he could point out was Maurice Maeterlinck's French adaptation, *Annabella*. He threw light upon the play's contemporary significance when he spoke of choosing "themes and subjects which respond to the agitation and the disquietude characteristic of our epoch."

THE SERPENT WOMAN

Gozzi's Theatre: Clowns as Challengers
by Andrei Serban

The comic characters challenge the serious themes of the main plot. The clowns provoke, question, tear apart; they make the worst out of what is tragic for some and comic for others.

The masters have ideals. The masters try to reach the clouds, but the servants bear the weight of existence. The brain has to go through the stomach, and what the stomach needs at each moment decides the future. Through comedy every ideal is deflated, every holy action demystified, challenged to the maximum. The laughter of the clowns is at times cruel, at times compassionate. They question the hero's search for the ideal, for love, for perfection. The clowns remind us that while we strive for heaven, we live on shaky earth.

The clowns comment on the main action. Through the *lazzi*—the free improvisations between the lines—they catch us off guard. They set in motion a paradox. The weapon of the *commedia* clown is to create surprise, to illuminate the text in indirect ways, from unexpected angles. The audience must never be lulled into a comfortable position, must never be allowed to believe easily, but be provoked by a conflict of opinions, an action that awakens the spirit of contradiction. Like the clowns, the audience doesn't naively believe in miraculous things; they have to be convinced. That's why they buy a ticket. They come to the theatre wishing to acknowledge the incredible but demanding proof.

The *commedia* masks represent essential types of humanity. The mask is almost a sculpture that captures (if the attitude is right) an expression of ourselves frozen in motion, universal states recognized in us, the everlasting human comedy from Aristophanes to Chaplin. The actor looks at the mask, studies its expression. Somehow there is some rapport, and the mask becomes a mirror. A sensitive relationship between the mask and the actor must exist before putting it on. And by putting it on, something happens, a meeting between what is caught in the mask from time immemorial and something immediate the actor feels at this very moment.

The mask is connected to the mystery of the cat. The cat is metaphorically a twin of the actor, so for an actor to observe the movements of a cat is as important as learning his lines. If one studies the cat, one notices the impulse comes from the center. The legs are grounded but ready to open and move in any direction. One should be able to listen with feet, arms, back—the whole self. High intensity in a frozen position. Now the actor/cat Truffaldino attacks with lightning speed, now he's relaxed and feeling good, now lazily lying in the sun and playing with a fly. The fly annoys him, and he decides to eat it. The actor's attention in the body should equal the intelligence of the cat.

Cherry Jones (Cherestani) and Derek Smith (Farruscad) in *The Serpent Woman*.

In the *commedia dell'arte*, there are three main types of characters (masks):

I Vecchi—or the Old Men, come down from Roman comedy in a line of direct descent that includes Pantalone and Tartaglia. The physical movements of these characters are rooted in the earth, close to the practical side of life.

Gli Amorosi—or the Lovers, developed later into what we know today as ballet dancers or the first lovers in opera. Their movement is connected to the air. They are always trying to reach upward toward the heights, to search out the ideal (ethereal).

And in the middle are the Servants:

I Zanni—or the Clowns, trying to catch everything from earth and air, from above and below. They control their movements from an impulse in the middle of the body. The upper part—the face and eyes—are alert and fast, but the legs are well grounded.

Clowns grounded in the earth, lovers seeking the skies. *Commedia dell'arte* should be dream material for actors and directors. It ranges from something close to life, familiar and recognizable, to the most paradoxical connections with other worlds.

THE SERPENT WOMAN

Elliot Goldenthal: Big Music for Big Mythic Themes
Interview by Christopher Baker

Q: What was your approach to composing music for this production?

ELLIOT GOLDENTHAL: *The Serpent Woman* has four layers of reality: the fairies, who call for a very fantastical and mysterious atmosphere; the clowns, who need naive and tactile music; the lovers, who elicit passionate and sensual themes. And the last layer is a tongue-in-cheek smile in the spirit of Gozzi and Serban. One of the reasons so many opera composers like Prokofiev or Puccini have been turned on by Gozzi is the breadth of emotion. One needs big music to match the big, mythic themes. Gozzi requires active and dramatic music to complement the shifting moods and textures. I've composed a lot for puppets, and I'm attracted to them for the same reason I'm attracted to Gozzi: it allows for a bigger emotional gesture. We have an interesting psychological reaction to puppets. In *The King Stag*, the Bunraku puppet of an old man was charming and effective. But when the character Angela caressed it, the interaction between this fantastical, animated creature and a real human being elevated the emotional impact of the scene.

Q: You spoke of different levels in the music. Do you also use individual character motifs?

EG: Yes. There will be leitmotifs. Not as strict as in Wagner or Prokofiev but certainly ones the audience can hang their hats on.

Q: Talk a little more about the specific process you are using in rehearsal.

EG: The last time I worked on Gozzi, I was in rehearsal every day, playing piano and percussion. Now, away from rehearsal, I use a little four-track portable tape recorder to write music that is more layered and closer to what it will finally sound like. The technology helps a great deal in the translation from mind to music to rehearsal. For example, I might come up with five approaches to one particular theatrical problem, which might be how to describe Truffaldino talking to Brighella about a mysterious event. The music might have a buffo quality about it, so the audience is hearing the story from the point of view of Truffaldino. You could also, for the same scene, have music that is evocative and mysterious, and then it is like what Brighella might be imagining. Each one is valid, but the rhythm and pacing of the production will determine which one will ultimately be used.

Q: How much do you influence the actors in rehearsal, and how much do they influence you?

EG: I remember a scene in *The King Stag* in which the actress playing Clarice runs in to tell her father that she loves Leandro and doesn't want to marry the King. She was very quick and animated. I asked Andrei Serban to let me do something else; let me write something that is bittersweet and Pierrot-like, the way Leandro is, as if she were thinking of him and their dilemma. The actress, who was wonderful, was completely thrown off by the slow tempo in rehearsal. Andrei was convinced by my logic, though, and it worked because it was interesting counterpoint. She ran in very fast, and her costume was a beautiful, shimmering garment so you got the quickness; what you heard was that other layer, what she is thinking of and what's motivating her. Maybe the other would have worked just as well, but I think this made it richer.

Q: When one thinks about this production, or *King Stag*, one thinks about eclecticism. What sources do you draw on?

EG: Let me preface my remarks by talking about the term *eclecticism* when it comes to my collaboration with Andrei. Yes, we draw on various world influences, but we hope the personality is clear enough to express one artistic sensibility. I usually work with instruments from all over the world. A typical percussion section might have temple blocks from Korea and instruments from Indonesia or Central America. In an orchestral piece memorializing the Brooklyn Dodgers, I had hubcaps from a '57 Chevrolet because it was the last time the Dodgers were in Brooklyn, and I wanted an authentic sound. It's important to find acoustic instruments that have singularity and personality to play against and work in harmony with the synthesized sounds.

PLATONOV

Liviu Ciulei: Sculpting Shapes for the Stage
Interview by Arthur Holmberg

Like the sequence of Shakespeare's sonnets or Georg Büchner's *Woyzeck*, Chekhov's *Platonov* is a riddle without answer. Surviving in only a rough first draft, the play requires directors to fidget with the text to work on stage. The unwieldy, overcharged play needs to be cut, sewn, mended. Working from a new translation from the Russian by Vlada Chernomordik, the playwright Mark Leib worked on the text to make it flow smoothly. Then Liviu Ciulei performed the operation of chipping away at the overly long play, a process the director refers to as "cutting into the flesh." Some scenes have been transposed, and the sequence of some lines switched, but the new adaptation remains close to the original. "The best adaptation I know," says Mr. Ciulei, "is the film script by Nikita Mikhalkov called *An Unfinished Piece for Player Piano*. It takes only half the play, but still we have the sensation of the whole. He eliminated the melodramatic and let the tragi-comic rise to the surface. A director has no choice but to go with his own intuition, knowing the whole time that the best adaptor would be Chekhov himself."

Internationally known, Mr. Ciulei was for many years head of the Bulandra Theatre in his native Romania. Mr. Ciulei likes to shake up classic texts by infusing them with a contemporary sensibility. His productions of *The Tempest, Twelfth Night*, and *A Midsummer Night's Dream* revolutionized the world of those plays. Prospero's island in *The Tempest* emerged from a moat of blood on which the *Mona Lisa* and other relics of civilization (books, scientific instruments, and a flute) floated by. *Twelfth Night* took place in a circus world, and the characters in *A Midsummer Night's Dream* were projected on a shiny red floor and wall to emphasize the sensuality of the play and bring to the surface the deepest dimensions of the fairy world.

"There is no such thing as an authentic Elizabethan production," Mr. Ciulei asserts. "We don't know enough to be able to reproduce with archaeological precision a play as it looked or sounded in Shakespeare's day. We know, more or less, what the living room in *'Night, Mother* is like, but what does Illyria look like? For every production of Shakespeare we must reinvent anew his universe, limited only by our understanding and our contemporary aesthetics.

"The reason I liked Peter Brook's production of *A Midsummer Night's Dream* so much was that it showed our society at the crossroads between a humanistic and a technological society—both elements were in his set. A production should not only capture the aesthetic of the play but also tell us something about where we are today." Mr. Ciulei, who studied architecture as well as theatre, often designs his own productions, as he did with *Platonov*.

Q: You studied architecture and theatre at the same time. What led you to combine these two disciplines?

LIVIU CIULEI: What is the subject of architecture?

Q: To create meaning in space.

LC: Theatre does the same thing, always on a human scale. Architecture and theatre have the same unit of measurement, the human being, and the same subject: man as individual and as social being.

Q: At the first reading, you said the set must look tired and worn out. Why?

LC: It must suggest an estate in Russia at the moment when the aristocracy has lost its energy and economic power. No money has been reinvested to maintain the buildings. Paint peels, walls crack. This atmosphere creates a note of elegiac sadness.

Q: You said that in your youth you built realistic sets but now you like to put sets in quotation marks so that they refer to their own theatricality. Why?

LC: I learned that the artist can't compete with nature. It is much stronger than the world of art, so why try? I like to create an alternative reality that does not represent nature so much as refer to it semiotically. I prefer Turner to Constable. I like a set to let you be aware that it's a theatrical reality—objects that can be invested with reality only in the space of a stage.

Q: Many of the scenic elements move fluidly across the stage during the play, creating a kind of mechanical ballet.

LC: This is a kinetic technique, influenced by film. Like a camera that zooms in and out on an object, making it larger or smaller, that was what I had in mind when the set slides. Maybe this movement also catches the frailty, the ephemeral nature of this world on the verge of collapse.

Q: After seeing and admiring several of your Shakespeare productions, I was surprised by this Chekhov set, because your Shakespeare sets are more abstract and symbolic.

LC: The historical context of this play is important in a way that it isn't in Shakespeare, so I think there must be some visual references to that historical reality.

Q: Is your approach to directing Chekhov different from your approach to Shakespeare?

LC: You always try to follow the arc of the play. But Shakespeare's characters are monuments called Macbeth, Lear, Hamlet. If you were a sculptor, you would place a colossal statue in the center of the city square. If a sculptor made a statue of Chekhov's characters, they would be those little domestic tombstones you see in nineteenth-century cemeteries, where an angel reaches down to embrace a pot-bellied bourgeois in frock coat and vest. These statues are ridiculous, yes, but also touching. In directing Chekhov, even more difficult than to recreate the characters is to give shape on stage to the air, the unseen nets, between them. Chekhov should be like silk kept for a long time in a drawer. You take it out and it dissolves into the air.

MASTERGATE

Larry Gelbart: Covert Comedy / Scandalous Satire
Interview by Arthur Holmberg

Q: What was the genesis of *Mastergate*?

LARRY GELBART: I first thought of it as a film that would depict a series of scandalous events that might be the result of a shotgun, or rather a missile marriage between Washington and Hollywood. But from experience, I know how long, how too long it takes to get a movie made and that a faster and perhaps better way to tell the story would be by turning the focus onto the investigation of the events without dramatizing the events themselves. Also, I am more interested in the people we see on both sides of the witness table than I am in their actions. Beneath their poker faces, I wanted to explore their passions and motives; I wanted to see what makes them tick.

Q: Why did this subject appeal to you?

LG: I had to vent feelings that have been accumulating in me for eight years

Q: What feelings?

LG: Anger. Outrage. Frustration. Amazement at the ability of certain people—not just those in office during the last eight years but going back to Watergate—to behave in such a fashion and get away with it for so long. Read this morning's headlines. There is no end in sight for this behavior, which is so contrary to what we expect of people in high office.

Q: You said the original idea that prompted you to write this play was the diabolical marriage between Hollywood and Washington.

LG: I was watching TV news last night. They were describing the downing of two Libyan jets. In lieu of actual footage the network broadcast clips from *Top Gun* with Tom Cruise. This is right out of *Mastergate*. *Mastergate* talks about substituting movie footage for newsreels to give the illusion of war reportage.

Q: Daniel Boorstin, who coined the phrase "pseudo-event," says that media images are taking the place of reality.

LG: Exactly. We think something is beautiful in life only if it's as good as something we've seen on television.

Q: What concerns me about this substitution of image is that nothing is validated unless it becomes a TV image. Therefore most people's lives, feelings, and experiences are never validated.

LG: It is terrifying and it is here.

Q: What part does television play in American politics?

LG: Originally the role of TV was to show events as they happened. Now political events are staged for TV. Television has changed the character and quality of many institutions—religion, education, sports, entertainment itself. We know that the Reagan administration's first meeting of the day was what the six o'clock news should be. Television is no longer a bystander. It is the master puppeteer.

Q: Another theme in *Mastergate* is the role of corruption in crystallizing political thought. How does the American public react to scandals unearthed in Washington?

LG: Political corruption no longer alarms us. We have been

steeped in it for so long we don't even blink when we hear about it. We have been so inundated by muck, it has reduced us to impotence. We no longer react. The play also deals with the corruption of language in Washington.

Q: What is the major degradation of language in politics today?

LG: Bloated words. Politicians always find an extra syllable or two. It comes from the need to obfuscate what is being said. Language becomes camouflage. Politicians talk to hide their thoughts.

Q: Could you give me some examples of how Washington has degraded language?

LG: I refer you to any presidential press conference in the last few years. They are marvels of jerry-built sentences that can only be connected if three dots are in there. Men in high places are not just leaders but teachers. Today young people learn that it is all right to speak so badly on important subjects. Official Washingtonese is a language of obfuscation, approximation, and evasion.

Q: So this political language of evasion is calculated to pretend to have a message but say nothing.

LG: However like *The Manchurian Candidate* it may sound, I think our top leaders have been chosen by powerful interests for their ability to sound and look earnest. But they never really address any given problem or question.

Q: So politicians accede to supreme power only because they are good messenger boys.

LG: There has never been a more skilled messenger than Ronald Reagan. Born a sports announcer, he then had all those years of being spokesman for General Electric. He can say anything in the most affable way without knowing what he is saying. Bush is not an actor. I can't tar him with the same brush. Reagan, it seems to me, feels very little and says it all beautifully. Bush demonstrates feelings but expresses them miserably. Having grown up when I thought Franklin Roosevelt would be president for my whole life and hearing him and Adlai Stevenson and John F. Kennedy speak, it is difficult for me to settle for the impoverished language and ideas in Washington today.

Q: So this perversion of language is a barometer of political perversion.

LG: It is part of it. Orwell warned us of doublespeak. Washington has invented halfspeak.

Q: Literary critics say every satirist hides in his heart a disillusioned idealist.

LG: Most Americans are idealists. We all want to believe the best. It's hard to go on doing that when our front pages seem like satire.

Q: One area where Americans have lost their idealism is politics. Most Americans used to believe in Washington.

LG: The politician as joke has always existed. Graft, pomposity, and stupidity are part of every country's political culture, but we never thought of all politicians as that. We knew as a class they contained scoundrels, but now it seems—especially through the last administration—that the quotient was especially high. The day Kennedy was shot, idealism began to disappear from our national soul. Then Robert Kennedy and Martin Luther King fell. When people of that quality and daring could be removed so easily and randomly from our lives, the descent into darkness began. Faith in our leadership died in Vietnam. During Watergate we got a president appointed, not elected, by one who was about to be impeached. It has been an insane slide into the abyss. God must love America to let us get away with it . . . if we have gotten away with it. At least we haven't been blasted off the embarrassed face of the earth yet.

Q: In talking about satire, Northrop Frye says it is a militant genre that assumes moral standards against which the grotesque and absurd are measured. What moral standards does your play assume?

LG: The backdrop for the play is an enlarged photo of the famous painting of the signing of the Constitution—a graphic way to show what our standards are and how these ideals contrast with the action on stage, a total debasement of those ideals.

Q: What is the most valuable characteristic for a satirist to have?

LG: A satirist can never stop being offended. My responses to all you've asked me are good examples of self-importance run wild. Next question, please?

Andrei Serban Introduces The Miser

The Miser is a comedy, but the laughter takes on tragic undertones. Molière wrote it four years before he died, and life had darkened his vision. Because of *Tartuffe*, he had lost favor at court. His marriage was disastrous, and he was already suffering from pneumonia, the disease that would kill him. The author-actor played Harpagon, and much stage business is made of his coughing. After Frosine, the go-between, flatters the old man on his good health, he complains that he has "a touch of phlegm that catches at me now and then." "But you cough beautifully," Frosine replies. Molière uses the bouts of coughing to comic effect, but knowing how close death was, the laughter takes on a cruel edge.

The oedipal rivalry between father and son is ferocious in this play. Molière had a difficult relationship with his father, and in no other work does this bitterness come out so strongly. The fights between Harpagon and his son, Cléante, are funny but with a bitter undertone.

Harpagon is paranoid, and the more money he has, the more he worries. The more he has, the more he has to lose. A thief can break in and steal his treasure. A fire can burn down his house. As long as his sense of security depends solely on material goods, he will always live in paranoia. We all fall into the trap that our worries will cease if we achieve an illusory sense of financial security. Rather than laughing at Harpagon from a moral distance, I hope the audience will recognize a familiar symptom they can identify with. The atmosphere of the play reminds me of Kafka and Beckett, authors who, like Molière, are comic but with a tragic twist.

And Harpagon is not the only character whose sense of reality is shaped by money. Mariane's mother is willing to sell her daughter to an old man for money, and Mariane—even though she would prefer the son because he's young and sexy—goes along with the deal. Cléante's love for Mariane is measured by the amount of money he can give her. Valère, instead of eloping with Élise, decides to use Machiavellian techniques to squeeze money from her father Harpagon. Everywhere you look in the play, money controls relationships, especially love relationships. The play is unrelenting in its dramatization of how money molds people's feelings. And when the plot gets so complicated that no happy end seems possible, along comes a *deus ex machina* in the form of a sugar daddy who makes everyone happy by handing out checks.

Molière's happy ending is a bitter satire on a world where God is absent. It is reminiscent of the ancient legend of Midas, who sacrificed everything for gold. The end of the play should be linked with a mythological image that devours, suffocates, takes away life. The Golden Calf. The strange dance in the night.

Jack Willis (Lopakhin), Claire Bloom (Ranevskaya), Alvin Epstein (Firs), and Jeremy Geidt (Gayev) in *The Cherry Orchard* (1993–1994).

Calderón Comes to Cambridge
by Carlos Fuentes

1. In this, the greatest dream-play ever written, Calderón de la Barca follows a mathematical sequence. First, Prince Segismundo is in his cell in a tower, dressed in hides and with no worldly contact except his old preceptor, Clotado. This is, for him, his natural state. He knows no other. The cell is, for him, "cradle and grave."

Segismundo is neither Rousseau's "natural man" nor Truffaut's "*enfant sauvage*." He is educated and sensible, but he has no time. Cradle and grave are indeed the same to him. The intrusion of Rosaura brings in the outside world. But Rosaura is a woman dressed as a man. When the world breaks in, it is as appearance, not as reality. But that appearance is presented by Calderón (and the final scenes will heighten this feeling) as a homoerotic, androgynous, ambiguous temptation.

There is a force beyond erotic temptation, nevertheless, that will propel Segismundo out of his cell. It is the same force that put him there: his father, the King Basil (a tautology if there ever was one—Basil is Basileus, the Greek name for king; the father is thus Basil-Basil or King-King, a double authority, a double speech). Basil's authority over Segismundo is total, akin to a right over life and death. Before the child was born, his mother, the queen, dreamt repeatedly that she would give forth a monster in human form, who would tear at her guts and bathe her in blood. So it was: the queen died and the king was convinced that if his son ever reached the throne, he would be the cruelest, most vicious prince who ever misruled Poland. King Basil gave credit to augury, announced that the boy had died along with his mother, and sent him to live in the tower.

Yet the king—such is his authority—has now decided to break the chain of fatality and give freedom a chance. He brings poor Segismundo from the jail where he has been trapped since birth and gives him a tacit choice. If the Prince rules wisely, fatality will be given the lie, and the people will have gotten a just ruler. If, on the contrary, he lives up to the evil omen and proves himself to be cruel and arrogant, then the king, the father, Basil, will send him back to his prison.

From the natural fatality of his dungeon, Segismundo is taken to the summit of both freedom and fatality. He acts out the latter. The augury is fulfilled; he is cruel and murderous. Having risen to the top he is once more sent to the bottom and made to believe that whatever he did or saw or felt or understood while acting out the princely role was but a dream. He is back in his cell, dressed as an animal.

2. Pedro Calderón de la Barca was born in 1600 and died in 1681. His life thus covers most of Spain's so-called Golden Age: the age of the novelist Cervantes, the painters Velázquez and Murillo, the poets Góngora and Quevedo, the dramatists Lope de Vega and Tirso de Molina. The Golden Age, nevertheless, is an Age of Janus. It faces backward, toward the rise of the Spanish Empire and the extraordinary feats of the discovery, exploration, conquest, and colonization of the New World: the Spain of the Catholic Kings; Ferdinand and Isabella; and the Hapsburg monarchs, Charles V and Philip II, on whose dominions the sun never set. Calderón lives the Spanish decadence of Philip IV and his imbecile, impotent son, Charles the Bewitched. The Armada has been defeated by Elizabeth I; powerful Spain will not rule unchallenged in Europe or abroad; her energies are drained by her self-assigned role as defender of the Catholic faith against the Reformation; her resources diminished by interminable dynastic wars that devour the vast treasures of the Aztec and the Inca. The age looks forward to the final loss of the empire.

But Spain has always compensated for historical defeat with artistic genius. Calderón faces both duties: he is a great dramatist; he is also a Spaniard and a Catholic. Soldier and priest, he is the greatest author of religious plays, the famous *autos sacramentales* in which the dogma of the presence of Christ in the Eucharist is defended against Lutheran and Calvinist impiety. A poet of Christian symbolism second only, said the great historian of Spanish literature, Menéndez Pelayo, to Dante, Calderón goes beyond mere proselytizing. His *auto, The Great Theater of the World*, where vices and virtues are represented and rewarded or condemned, offers one of the great baroque visions of eroticism disguised as mystic yearning, the world upside down, the world as public place of crumbling glories and passing vanities, and the world as *horror vacui*, the horror of emptiness that animates baroque movement, fills it with action and excess, and converts it, perhaps, into the grand concession to the senses of the rigid world of the Counter-Reformation—much as music was Protestantism's sensual concession to its naked, imageless religious austerity.

Detested by the Enlightenment (much as Shakespeare was, too), Calderón was exalted by the Romantics (again, along with Shakespeare), became a permanent icon of German culture, and generated the most extraordinary brood of dream-plays, from Kleist to Strindberg to Pirandello (and even some popular spinoffs in Buster Keaton and Woody Allen). Life is a dream. But neither *The Prince of Homburg* nor *The Ghost Sonata* nor *Enrico IV* are sacramental, religious plays, and *Life Is a Dream*, in spite of its radical modernity, must be understood as a Catholic play, in which the whole process is that of moving from nature, where man is fallen, to history, where he has a choice but can therefore choose incorrectly, to a second fall which is finally redeemed through suffering, faith, and virtue.

3. From natural dream to fatality to fall to freedom. Calderón's play is written right in the middle of the dispute between the Jesuits, who stressed free will and human intelligence, and the Dominicans, who faulted the Jesuits for their liberalism and underlined, instead, the omnipotence of divine justice. Calderón the Catholic is not unresponsive to this classic debate of Christianity; but he is also responsive to artistic and philosophical demands. His time and its problems, precisely, put forward the great theme of the nature of reality, what is it, where is it, how can we define it, how can we ever know, where do we come from, where are we going to? A literature that does not pose these problems may be entertaining, but it can also "amuse us to death." It is empty; it is absent. No dramatist, in this sense, is more present, and more fulsome (the baroque horror of the void!) than Calderón. In an age demanding that dogma be defended, he uses art to cast an immense shadow on the possibilities of truth, reality, freedom, and predestination. He makes a problem out of any certainty. He is a dramatist: he understands that only out of conflict and doubt can concord and certainty arise. And what greater conflict than that between individuals and the world, nature and civilization, dream and reality?

The dramatic force of *Life Is a Dream* rests on two famous monologues by Segismundo. Already the name is a divided one: Segis-Mundo, Segis and the World. I and You, Myself and the Other. The first monologue tests the division between nature and man. Segismundo says that his only sin is to have been born, and compares himself to nature, which, having less soul than he, is freer. Bird, fish, or stream, soulless, are better equipped with liberty than he is. Montaigne wrote that nature has universally embraced all of its creatures and given them all "the necessary means to conserve their being." But other creatures are given claws, teeth, furs, and quickly begin to walk, run, sing, or fly. Man seems prepared only to cry. He must learn everything, only to die, forget it all, and be forgotten. But first he must be born. And Segismundo's complaint against nature is that he has more soul and less freedom. This absence of freedom is felt as a radical diminution, a not being totally born, a need to finish the act of birth in history, in relation to others, that is not imposed on animals. Yet, is it a greater crime not to have been born at all? This, writes the Spanish philosopher María Zambrano, is the sin of Oedipus: he was never totally born, he remained stuck in his mother's placenta. So did, in a way, Calderón's hero. He killed his mother when he was born; he dragged her to death and was condemned by his father to coincide with his predestination. So was Oedipus. But the Greek king was condemned to act, killing his father and wedding his mother. Segismundo is condemned to dream: this is his reality.

4. But what kind of reality is "dream"? This is the question of Segismundo's second monologue. If we all come from dream and only open our eyes because we were gestated in dream, then perhaps dream is the norm and wakefulness the exception. Understood on its own terms, as its own reality, dream is timeless. It can be eternal. Or it only began five seconds ago. But then, so did "reality." Being timeless, dream is one, undivided, and every instant in it coexists with all other possible instants. Yet nothing can be touched and had in dream. Tantalus is the Lord of the Dream: fruits flee from his fingers, water from his mouth. Kafka's nightmare is the name of contemporary dreams.

Calderón gives us this anguish of dream in the frightening sequence of Segismundo's displacement from a natural state, from which he is wrested only to be offered a "reality" that is then described to him as a "dream." How can he now believe that the "reality" to which he is returned—the prison—is not a dream as well? Calderón's play echoes the ancient lines by the Latin poet Pindarus: "We are but dreams of a shadow." But the reality of the dream is that it must then become the dream of a dream, incessantly, infinitely. Borges gives this reality to dreams in his great short story "The Circular Ruins," in which the dreamer finally understands that someone else is dreaming him.

In Calderón's play, a climax of sorts is reached when Rosaura, the temptress, in herself the dream of ambiguity (male-female-soldier, calling herself "a monster of all species" as Segismundo calls himself "a monster in a labyrinth"), confronts the man with the monstrosity of reality, narrating to him what he believes only happened in a dream, yet she asserts happened in reality: his all-too-brief, and cruel, reign. What happens, indeed, when a real person has shared your dreams, or lived it for you?

What happens is this great play, *Life Is a Dream*. The play is a dream that finally becomes visible. Calderón finds the most perfect unity between what he is trying to say and the way he says it. He organizes the dream on stage. And by doing so, he gives both the dream and the dreamer a chance. And this is the chance of fulfilling the requirements of nature and fatality, of disenchantment and death, and yet, by going through this ordeal, by organizing his two lives—dream and reality—theatrically, Segismundo is given a second chance; Segismundo, because he has accepted all the facets of reality, all the proofs and pains of human frailty and human power, conquers his own freedom. No longer natural, no longer fatal, he is, at the end of the play, free.

Calderón has been faithful to his religious convictions. But he has been even more faithful to his artistic convictions. It is rare indeed to see such a perfect crystal fixing, on a stage, the greatest quandaries of humankind, without sacrificing any of their dimensions to facility or dogma, blithe amusement, novelty or convention.

Calderón proves that creation rests on the continuity of tradition, but that tradition withers without a new creation. I am grateful, even thrilled, that this great, traditional Spanish author is now on the creative stage of the American Repertory Theatre.

Anne Bogart: Splintering the Mirror of Calderón
by Elizabeth C. Ramírez

Q: Why did you want to do *Life Is a Dream*?

ANNE BOGART: It's a play that fascinates but also frightens me. Its theatricality attracted me. Also its mystery, its poetry, and its philosopohy.

Q: Some critics speak of the difficulty of translating such an intensely poetic work. How are you dealing with this?

AB: The problem of translation is a real one. Theoretically it fascinates me that Calderón would spend a great deal of effort designing a text that would never speak directly about its real concern. For example, in the first passage, Calderón avoids using the word *horse*. He'll describe a horse in every way he can, using every sort of baroque metaphor. The play is packed with metaphors that force you to another level of understanding. It begins with a woman dressed as a man in midair, falling off a horse. From then on, layers of metaphors keep revealing themselves, keep opening up to new meanings. The metaphors are in language, and it's my job to translate those into theatrical metaphors.

Like a mirror that splinters and breaks into many pieces, Calderón uses shattered reflections, circling around a particular idea. There's always a tension between what is said and what is not said. Now that's very difficult to translate. What it makes me want to do is try to find a way to stage the play true to Calderón's interest in language and the relationship between language and reality.

Q: What approach are you using to capture the lyricism of Calderón's language?

AB: Giorgio Strehler says that when he stages a play, he's writing an essay on the play, and his essay is created in his language, the languages of the stage. Rather than writing an essay on a play with words, he's writing it with actors, light, movement, sound. It's my intention to translate my understanding of Calderón into the languages of the stage.

I chose the Edwin Honig translation because it's the clearest, but for me the text is only one part of the whole experience. As a director, it's a mistake to think only of the text. The original intentions of the Spanish text should be translated into the way the movement works, the way light falls, the way timing occurs, and the juxtaposition of all these things.

Q: How did you use the student workshop at the A.R.T. Institute?

AB: One of the limitations of resident theatre is the shortness of rehearsal time. I find it absolutely necessary—especially with a play that has a production history to it—to have time to meet the play in a nonproducing situation, not creating staging but exploring the themes and the movement of the play without being concerned with staging it.

The workshop in December allowed me and the Institute actors the luxury of swimming in the themes, the problems, the characters of the play. I got to ask questions like: What does it mean to act a dream? How is that different from acting in a Terrence McNally play? How are events put together in a dream differently than they are put together in waking life? We looked at books like Plato's allegory of the cave in *The Republic*, which is an important part of Calderón's thinking. What does it mean to see life as a reflection of the real thing? The workshop gave us time to meet the play without the pressure of turning that meeting into a result.

Q: Would you discuss the meaning of the play? How are you going to physicalize that meaning in terms of the stage?

AB: There are two things happening in the play. First, a story is being told. Second, a very complex philosophy is being evoked—and evoked in a very theatrical way. What I want to do is play the linear story off against the universal philosophy of the play. I want to create an event where the theatre is an echoing chamber. You go through the story, but you're always aware of past, future, present. The cave is the theatre, and all of the particles of the story are constantly swirling around the story itself.

Q: What is the role of women in the play?

AB: Every object, every character on stage has its opposite inside it, which is why I find it so modern. Both Rosaura and Segismundo are half woman and half man. I think Rosaura is one of the most wonderful female characters in literature because of her constant confrontation with the world as a woman and how she adapts to it by changing into a man and adapts to it again by being a woman. She's a chameleon. For a female actress, this is an extraordinary challenge.

At first glance, Segismundo seems like a cliché Tarzan. But if you look closer, you feel there's a strong feminine thread running through him. He's very vulnerable. I find Calderón plays with the contradictions inherent in each gender stereotype, which is something I agree with philosophically, politically, and personally. I find truth in gender contradictions.

Q: How would you describe Calderón's worldview?

AB: To me his theatre world is completely postmodern because of its shattered refraction of reality and its self-referentiality. The contemporary French philopsopher Baudrillard states that whatever you're looking at is only as real as its image. This approaches Calderón's worldview of reality as a palace of mirrors. In Calderón, human beings are a little off-center in their environment.

Q: What is the role of the audience?

AB: I'd like for the audience to feel as though they are in Plato's cave and that they're in the process of turning around to look at the light. I keep thinking of this word *cave* because it means that sounds and images are bouncing off the walls and reverberating against each other.

There needs to be a sense of intimacy and distance at the same time. At first the audience should feel as though they're going through an art gallery from a distant past, and little by little it gets closer and closer until it feels as if it's inside you. At first it will feel foreign, but it will become more and more understandable.

Q: Would you comment on the designs and costumes?

AB: I'm interested in Calderón's fascination with the artificial as opposed to the natural. I wanted the costumes, sets, lights, and the physicality of the production to embrace the contradiction between an artificial order, represented by the court, and natural chaos.

The designs are a meeting of those two worlds with influences from Spanish culture from many different periods, including Calderón's. It should look like little fragments of history that have reinvented themselves into a world that we know but don't quite know, that is familiar yet we've never seen anything quite like it, that has remnants and artifacts from a number of places in history but also reeks of the play.

Q: Music has been a significant part of your performances. What part will music play in this production?

AB: Several composers wrote music based on the play. We're using a collage of their work. The production will be a journey for the senses, for the ears.

Q: What are the universal qualities of *Life Is a Dream*?

AB: When I think of *Life Is a Dream*, I keep going back to an episode of *Twilight Zone* with Rod Serling. The guy wakes up from a dream. Something's happening to him, but he realizes he's in a dream. He tries to wake up, and he finally does, and yet he's in another dream. Then he's living this other life, and he's in another dream. It goes on and on to infinity. The play speaks directly to every human being struggling with consciousness and waking up. I want to do it in a way that people will not only hear but see and feel.

TWELFTH NIGHT

Notes on Twelfth Night
by Andrei Serban

Twelfth Night was a play I never wanted to direct. All the productions I had seen did not convince me, and I thought maybe this is a bourgeois comedy with no other implication than a good laugh.

But when Brustein persuaded me to read the play in a new way, I started to discover elements of darkness and ambiguity that I was not aware of, and now after having directed it, I am convinced it is a sophisticated comedy with an uneasy look at the human condition. With the shipwreck that throws Viola on Illyria, we enter unsafe territory that challenges and surprises us at every turn.

The first scene is a room in the palace of a Borgia or a Medici. The Duke has his Michelangelos sculpting and his Raphaels painting all around him, like a gathering of the elite searching for artificial purity and refinement: "If music be the food of love, play on."

The second scene takes us to a very different atmosphere—a wild seacoast with rough winds, a shipwreck, and near-death. The third—an absurd domestic quarrel between an older couple talking nonsense about sex.

Each scene is a miniature play in itself, and the universe is shifting: light and subtle at first, mysterious and yearning (Viola comes

Cherry Jones (Viola) and Diane Lane (Olivia) in *Twelfth Night*.

from the sea, lost but craving for love), and then we are plunged down to familiar trivia. What Shakespeare does is make us observe the movement, the flow of images of life as a reflection of a reality that is always shifting. Nothing is what it seems.

The play makes us question what we think we know about love, sexuality, relationships, gender—it gives us a sense of humility and recognition that we are celebrating, on stage, forces that we know very little about. Like the characters caught in a net, we wonder what is missing in our experience of love. Physical love, spiritual love, tyrannical or compassionate love, love between friends—the tornado of forces, the cravings, fears are a manifestation of our divided beings longing for unity.

The actors' opportunity is to display their technique joyfully with such great and colorful parts and to reveal through acting something else that the audience doesn't encounter in daily life—the dreamlike quality of illusion, which tells us that everything we experience is a dream, that we live in a dream and take the dream for reality.

When an actor asks: "How can one act the quality of illusion?" "How can I communicate the experience of a dream?" the best I can answer is "I don't know." Most directors are afraid to acknowledge how little we know and how often we make actors do what we don't know ourselves. Still, "I don't know" is the best answer. It's the only key to discovery.

I remember a Persian tale of a man who comes upon another man who has lost his wife and is digging holes in the sand in an effort to find her. "Why are you looking in the sand?" asks the first man. "I don't know where she is," replies the second, "I know she is somewhere, so I'm looking everywhere." This is our task with Shakespeare—to look everywhere.

THE FATHER

Robert Brustein: The Lava Beneath the Surface
Interview by Robert Scanlan

Q: What do you want to do with this play?

ROBERT BRUSTEIN: Two things. First, to find a theatrical way of communicating the pathology of the play and its author. When Strindberg wrote this play, he was in the grip of a profound paranoia, which dogged him for years until he had a nervous breakdown, something close to madness. He spent a little time in an institution. At the peak of this crisis (which Strindberg himself called his "Inferno crisis"), he felt that he was being pursued by furies and by women who were trying to electrocute him through the walls of his room. After he recovered from this madness, he changed the whole direction of his playwriting career, as well as his religious thinking, political thinking, and attitude toward women. I want to show that there was an incipient feminism in his anti-feminism. I would suggest that the reason he was so enraged about the women's movement in the 1880s was that he feared the female qualities in his own nature. Before his nervous breakdown, he exaggerated his opposition to the female principle.

But after his Inferno crisis, when he stopped resisting his own feminine aspects, he completely transformed his style as a dramatist and his stance on feminism. So the second major objective of my production is to create, if possible, some balance in what is essentially an unbalanced play.

Q: What drew you to the play?

RB: Its incredible energy and power. No one can match Strindberg in his own time for the ferocity of the emotions he puts on stage. His work is Shakespearean in that regard. The title character in *The Father* is an Othello, an Agamemnon, a Hercules, and he's clearly identified with those figures in Strindberg's mind. All of these heroes were done in by women: Agamemnon by Clytemnestra, Othello by Desdemona (or so he thought), and Hercules by Omphale, who took away his club—an obvious metaphor for emasculation—and set him to do women's tasks at the distaff. References to Omphale stud the play.

Q: Does Strindberg still have anything to say to us? Many women think of him as an outdated misogynist.

RB: He was certainly virulent, but the issues he raises are not outdated, only muted in our time. Today most men have been persuaded by the power and eloquence of the feminist movement. There was a time when there was more resistance to feminist ideas, and there was a genuine worry, expressed by Strindberg, that feminism would emasculate men. That's what this play is about—the fears of emasculation, loss of potency, sexual as well as political. It's about loss of control. It isn't a question of sharing power; either one sex has it or the other has it. Strindberg could not envision equality of power between the sexes.

Q: Was Strindberg, when he wrote *The Father*, joining the debate already engaged by Ibsen?

RB: Ibsen wasn't really involved in the feminist debate. Ibsen is often thought of as an early feminist, but he was quite clear when he responded to a women's rights society that wanted to honor him for *A Doll's House*, which they took to be a contribution to their movement. He thanked them for the honor but said he was not sure what women's rights were—or how they differed from the rights of humanity. And that's really what he was interested in: the rights of humanity. By contrast, Strindberg really was interested in what women are, what they do, what the consequences of a shift in power between men and women might be.

Q: There's a clear biographical connection between the Captain and Strindberg. Do you think it's complete identification?

RB: Yes. Strindberg himself said so. After completing the play, he wrote: "I don't know if my life has been so, or if this is a fiction or whether I will soon crash into madness from agony of conscience." He did crash into that intense agony of conscience. He was reflecting in the play his relationship with his first wife, Siri von Essen, whom he accused of doing everything he accuses Laura of doing in the play. He went even further in real life: he thought she was a lesbian and said so publicly, and he was convinced that she didn't keep honest or accurate accounts, one of the worst things he could have accused her of—bad housekeeping. She also made him doubt the paternity of his own children, which is a serious matter, of course. He struck back with so many accusations that she felt herself libeled. He wrote, in addition to *The Father, A Madman's Defense*, an autobiographical exposé of his marriage that was considered libelous. So were many stories in a collection called *Marriage*. Eventually a lawsuit was leveled against Strindberg, and he was forced to leave the country. This precipitated his mental breakdown.

Q: *The Father* gives strong expression to the male view of things, and, obviously, at the time Strindberg felt this point of view was losing its voice. Are there other sources in Strindberg where the female side of things is dealt with in a way that is relevant to your production?

RB: All of Strindberg's plays after the Inferno crisis represent the female side. You'll notice he no longer has heroes in his plays, he has heroines. The Daughter of Indra in *A Dream Play*, Swan White in *Swan White*, Eleanora in *Easter*, the Milk Maid in *Ghost Sonata*—these are highly spiritual beings who rebuke the male characters in the earlier plays and who, I think, express Strindberg's opening up of his female nature. What is also striking is a complete change in his dramatic technique. The pretense of naturalism breaks down entirely, and what we have instead is the dream-play, a new form that is episodic and not necessarily sequential. One scene melts into another in a formless flux, much like the formlessness he found in women's rhythms.

Q: Rhythms of thinking?

RB: Rhythms of being. Cyclical rather than sequential. Lunar rather than terrestrial.

Q: What's the source of your design concepts?

RB: This is not a realistic play. Strindberg may have thought that it was. He sent it to Zola as an example of the then-fashionable naturalism, but Zola sent it back, complaining that it wasn't naturalism, and he was right. Ultimately my ideas for this staging stem from the first production I saw of this play—a production in which I played the part of Njod in 1949 at the Provincetown Playhouse in Greenwich Village. I remember Ward Costello, who played the Father, slamming the door so hard that all the flats began to shake, and I thought: that's what this play is *really* about—a force so powerful that doors and walls can't hold it in. It's ridiculous to put this inside the three walls of a naturalistic set. One has to have the feeling that the forces and the furies that have been set free in this play are so powerful they can knock down walls, that they could even change the contours of the room. Especially when the room is perceived through the increasingly enraged and maddened eyes of the protagonist. We want to turn this room increasingly into a prison, increasingly into a set from *The Cabinet of Dr. Caligari*, which represents reality seen through the eyes of a madman.

Q: Looking at your work as a director, there's a constant exploration of plays from the era characterized as the birth of modern drama. What about these plays attracts you?

RB: There is a quote from Red Smith, the famous sportswriter, which would not be out of place emblazoned on our programs and over our box office. He wrote it after Bobby Thomson's pennant-winning home run in 1951. It really is the motto of our theatre—of contemporary theatre as a whole.

Q: Red Smith was inspired to write the motto for all of contemporary theatre by a home run?

RB: Well, it was Bobby Thomson's famous World Series home run. It came in the ninth inning with two outs, and it seemed like the most implausible thing in the world. It shouldn't have been possible, but it happened. And after it happened, then nothing incredible could ever happen again. Red Smith wrote: "The art of fiction is dead. Reality has strangled invention. Only the utterly impossible, the inexpressibly fantastic, can ever be plausible again."

No literary critic could have expressed it better. It stands behind everything we do at the A.R.T. Reality, or realism, is not possible any more in the face of the implausibility of the contemporary world. All the great dramatists, even the ones usually considered realists like Ibsen, and in this phase of his career, Strindberg, were sitting on furies, on tumultuous lava underneath that flat, apparently realistic surface. And that lava was continually threatening to break out. I have always thought it was my job as a director—as it has been my job as a critic when writing about them—to point out the phantasmagoric, hallucinatory aspect of these works still dominating us.

Q: Realism—especially in the theatre—represents a set of narrow conventions. In the broader perspective of theatre history, realism is turning out to have had a heyday of a very short duration—less than a century, really, with countercurrents appearing at the very beginning of the style.

RB: Yet it still functions as the mainstream of American drama. Few plays get to a mainstream boulevard without being realistic. Realism is still the basic style you find in the resident theatres. It's still the most famous type of acting training.

Q: Why has it had such persistence?

RB: It's not threatening. It's consoling. It's highly concise. It commits itself to causal, linear anecdotes. It creates characters who are recognizable to people from their day-to-day experience. In no way does it provoke or challenge. Instead it confirms common notions of reality. But while this has been going on in the theatres of this country, all of modern science has been undermining our notions of a fixed and comforting reality. Just as Red Smith had to find some way to account for Bobby Thomson's home run, we have to find some way to reflect the enormous complexities of our contemporary world in our art.

THE FATHER

Strindberg's "Invention"
by Richard Gilman

In the winter of 1887, August Strindberg, a man never afflicted with false modesty, wrote to a friend that he had invented a new dramatic genre, which he called "the battle of the brains." His latest play, *The Father*, was, he said, "the realization of modern drama and as such [was] very curious . . . because the struggle takes place between souls." By a cultural coincidence Henry James, who does not seem to

Christopher Lloyd
(The Captain) in
The Father.

have read Strindberg, would later use almost the same words about the plays of Henrik Ibsen, Strindberg's older Scandinavian contemporary and *bête noire*. Ibsen's dramas, James wrote, dealt with "the Ego against the Ego, the Soul against the Soul," and went on to call these actions, in a memorable phrase, "thinkable things."

That these "things," these actions of human life, were thinkable is what made Ibsen and Strindberg, in their different yet related ways, pioneers, revolutionaries of the drama. For there had been very little to think about, for the mind to engage, in the theatre of the nineteenth century (the main exceptions were the plays of Georg Büchner and Heinrich von Kleist, written more than fifty years earlier and scarcely known) or for a long time before that.

Indeed, Strindberg had given up writing for the theatre during the three or four years before *The Father*—his previous dramatic work had been mostly romantic tragedies—on the ground that the theatre was "reprehensible" in its resistance to new consciousness, to changes in sensibility. The new play, his daring "invention," was therefore an adversary act against the seeming immutability of the theatre, one whose consequences for the future course of dramatic art were on the same profound level as Ibsen's somewhat earlier *A Doll's House* and *Ghosts*. *The Father*, whose chief characters and basic situations were to be incorporated fifteen years later into a much longer and complex play, *The Dance of Death*, marked the beginning of Strindberg's popular and even scholarly reputation as an extreme misogynist. The evidence for such a view is of course abundant, yet nothing is simple about Strindberg's attitude toward women; certainly no uncomplicated, comfortable theory of anti-female bias will do much to uncover the psychological or, still more, the aesthetic substance and structures of his work.

In regard to the psychological aspect, Strindberg once said that his hostility to women was "the reverse side of my fearful attraction towards the opposite sex," and everything in his life and work supports the avowal. This may not be much comfort to ardent feminists, but is has to be squarely taken into account in any sound critical perspective. For this condition of violent ambivalence, or emotional polarity, is crucial to an understanding not of Strindberg's misogyny but of *what he did with it* as a writer.

A year or so before the letter I've quoted, Strindberg finished an autobiographical novel, a thinly disguised account of his first marriage to Siri von Essen, which he called *A Madman's Defense*. It was a savage book about marital conflict in which he portrayed himself as a victim in much the same way as the Captain is the victim of his wife in *The Father*; of particular interest is the fact that Strindberg carried over into the play a number of lines and speeches from the novel. Fiction, autobiography, drama: the interweavings, the mesh of connection, are intricate and greatly revealing.

The point for us in encountering *The Father* is, to put it simply, that Strindberg, whatever the pathology of his psychic disposition, used his experience and relation with women within the "sanities" of art, as fictional and then dramatic energies, food for imagination. He turned the domestic scene into an arena where certain battles embodying the marital and sexual (but deeper, or at any rate, wider in nature) could be fought out and—in the case of *The Father* and other plays—shown in the essential theatrical action.

That *The Father* moves past specific sexual tensions and enmities to enter a more general dominion of psychic turbulence and spiritual anguish becomes clear almost from the start. The Captain and his wife are struggling ferociously for mastery in the home, with their daughter as the not-so-secret prize. Laura's chief tactic is to throw doubt on the girl's paternity, but even though this is seemingly what drives the Captain wild, the issues are more profound. "It isn't enough for me to have given the child life," Adolph said in one of his more confident moods, "I want to give it my soul, too." In other words, he wants an extension of himself beyond biology; he wants, the play keeps telling us, to be validated in his own identity.

This is what drives him past sanity, for what validation can there be for any of us? At the deepest level of psychic and dramatic action, the Captain, like his creator, suffers from a metaphysical torment, a stricken recognition of the uncertainty of existence, of human self-division and of the unknowability of others, of whom, for men, women are the central strangers, as men are for them. He is driven mad, really, by the abstractness of the issues, his inability to grasp what is happening. In a speech extraordinarily reminiscent of one in Büchner's *Danton's Death*, that great *Hamlet*-like play about abstractions and reality, the Captain says of the struggle that "it's like fighting with air, a mock battle with blank cartridges . . . my thoughts dissolve, my brain grinds emptiness."

He swims in a sea of doubtfulness, having posed to himself unanswerable questions. This is what gives the play its tragic status, bringing it much closer to Greek theatre than to the prevailing drama of the time. For if anything can be said to characterize conventional nineteenth-century theatre, it's that all things are in fact knowable, all problems can be solved. Now, there are no such things as tragedies, neither as facts nor as Platonic essences; there is only a cast of mind, a way of approaching fate, we have called tragic because it takes us to the edge and holds steady in the dizzying perspective. *The Father* does this, a little uncertainly, a bit erratically, for Strindberg is only at the outset of his full dramatic powers. Yet what Ibsen himself called the overwhelming "force" of Strindberg's vision compels us into assent and admiration.

Brecht and the Law: An Interview with Harvard Law Professor Martha Minow
by Sean Abbott

The Caucasian Chalk Circle asks profound questions about the nature of law and its claims to legitimacy. It is a major dramatic work viewed with equal interest by theatre artists and legal scholars, such as Martha Minow, who teaches *The Caucasian Chalk Circle* in one of her classes at the Harvard Law School. The A.R.T. spoke to Professor Minow about her reading of the play and some of the larger issues of law and the theatre today.

Q: Why have you put *The Caucasian Chalk Circle* on the syllabus at Harvard Law School?

MARTHA MINOW: I teach it in the context of a family law class in which we sometimes discuss the perceived irrationality of the legal system. It's shocking for my students in their clinical work to find that judges can be irascible as well as irrational, unresponsive, or perverse when they do respond. I ask them if Azdak the Judge is a familiar figure and to consider Azdak's origins: he is a scurrilous vagabond who becomes a judge through outrageous circumstances.

But while *The Caucasian Chalk Circle* views the law as irrational, at the same time it proposes an idea of judgment, a kind of test that a judge can perform to get at the truth: a literal tug of war between two women claiming to be the true mother of a child. Most of the time this is not what judges do. Judges hear competing versions of the truth and make selections, but they do not arrive at the Truth.

Q: How does Azdak's test compare with present-day child-custody decisions?

MM: In most states the courts consider "the best interests of the child," a standard that emerged to replace the old common-law tradition that fathers held custody of children and to acknowledge that mothers more typically provide care and nurture. This is the idea Azdak is working with. It is not based on biological claims and certainly not on the parents' rights in an ownership sense; the question is, who cares for the child in the way most likely to help and least likely to harm? A mother who would sooner tear the child to pieces

Members of the company in *The Good Woman of Setzuan* (see essay on page 97).

than lose him to another claimant is obviously not advancing the child's interests.

Q: What else does the play have to say to a contemporary audience about how the justice system works or doesn't work?

MM: We have developed a rationale for our legal system as something distinct from politics, indeed defined in opposition to politics, but one thing this play makes clear is that there are political implications to what judges do as well as political sources for who becomes a judge and how a judge decides. In addition, we tend to deny the important contributions made by luck and chance in our legal system. We suggest that who the judge is and who's on the jury are not significant features, yet they are.

This play explores the gap between the idealized, objectified legal system and the reality: that a judge, in Azdak's view, is someone who may scratch himself and reveal that he is naked beneath his robe. These are things that people don't like to think about and yet could make them more sober in their relationship to the court.

At the same time, one of the reasons *The Caucasian Chalk Circle* intrigues and endures is that in the midst of all its lunacy, Azdak hands down some respectable decisions. Still, what role does Azdak play? The role is important beyond the result in a particular case and beyond the person who is in the role.

Q: In his book *The Promise of American Law*, the legal scholar Milner S. Ball discusses the importance of role and argues that "the courts are not so much in the business of producing decisions . . . as they are of giving a performance," which he says provides not just the catharsis that's missing in contemporary theatre—and certainly in Brecht's theatre—but "an image of legitimate society." *The Caucasian Chalk Circle* asks at one point, what if this "legitimate society" is the society of the governor's wife, who can come in with her team of expensive lawyers and stand a good chance of reclaiming the child? Isn't this just empty role-playing?

MM: This is why we must be critical, like Azdak. And this is why I believe that the great strength of our society lies in the multiplicity of sources of authority, which creates more channels for critique. It's better to live in a society where law and theatre and religion aren't all performed in the same place, as they were with the Greeks, who invented the idea of catharsis.

Q: But why does Milner Ball want to costume the court and call it theatre?

MM: Scholars like Milner Ball are looking to the humanities with the hope of providing the law with a source of criticism and an angle of vision and also to challenge incursions on the law coming from economics or other disciplines.

The legal system is constantly in search of legitimacy. Sometimes courts enable the search by affording opportunities to challenge prevailing practices. Yet the more that courts are arenas where people challenge the structures of society, the more some fear a rupture in the old premises. Whatever answers are available to the big issues of our day, they won't come from legal doctrine alone but from sources of insight and community dialogue that are not themselves engendered by the courtroom. Discussions about the theatre can offer such a source.

Q: By making Grusha and Azdak (despite his perversity) characters with whom we can sympathize and with whom we may wish to identify, is Brecht omitting the more complex dimensions of human nature that the courts are asked to deal with?

MM: Brecht is an advocate. It's not always clear what he's advocating overall, but his characters are advocates just as lawyers are.

Both try to frame claims in one-dimensional terms, portraying "my client, The Good Man" or "my character, The Virtuous Woman." But this schematic quality still permits complexity in the clash between competing simplicities. That seems true to legal reality as well.

Q: Somewhat like the "empirical" test of the chalk circle?

MM: Yes. If your goal is to convince people "this is what happened, this is what's right, and this is what's wrong," it's inevitably and invariably an effort to simplify and indeed, as some current legal scholars argue, to tap into stock stories—the stereotyped narratives that fit your client's claim snugly.

Q: But isn't this molding of precedents limiting? Both for a more abstract sense of justice as well as for some basic sense of human satisfaction, for catharsis, if you wish? Or is that problem for the theatre to worry about and for the law to ignore?

MM: I often say lawyers deal with the same issues that philosophers, historians, social scientists, and artists have dealt with forever and ever. What's good? What's evil? What's right? What's wrong? What's truth? And yet lawyers come up with answers. Now it can't be that lawyers reach answers because they're smarter. Lawyers reach answers because it's their job.

As for this issue of catharsis in the courtroom, the structure of the lawsuit carries with it catharsis simply in the announcement of a verdict. I think that, at the very least, we will have even more law-based dramas. It's a ready-made structure that provides a sense of crisis, trauma, and then resolution. It's an established route to catharsis.

Q: The Marxist critic Darko Suvin calls the play "a seduction to goodness . . . and to justice." But are we really seduced by *The Caucasian Chalk Circle*, or does it leave us skeptical and unsatisfied? Does its happy ending strike us as false because it lacks the seething irony of, say, the "happy ending" of Brecht's *The Threepenny Opera* or the outrageous verdict that ends his *The Exception and the Rule*?

MM: This is a story of chances and crudeness. Its happy ending is no more to be trusted than a tragic or outrageous one. What we are missing in this play is a capacity for justice that adheres to the form as well as to the outcome. This play, at least in its court scenes, reduces the form to the bare minimum and subtracts even from that. The form of justice is gone: it's mimicked and ridiculed, and if the result is nonetheless just, that hardly compensates for a loss of meaning.

Q: Because we need rituals within the courtroom experience? The judge coming in, all rise, the bang of the gavel?

MM: Yes. And the rules being followed and the sense that justice will be done not just in this case but in the next case—and that this is continuity with the past and the future. Grusha's goodness may not be in doubt, but Azdak's version of justice is unreliable.

Q: By ridiculing the prescribed patterns, is Brecht saying the route to justice should be one of discovery and creativity and that these formal trappings only get in the way of justice?

MM: There's another concept I think we need to introduce, and that is "consent" or "participation." One idea is that the form gains its legitimacy because of an underlying *consent* to the process and because of its predictable application over time. Consent then grows, which is the source of the law's legitimacy. And while its creativity may be curbed, something greater is purchased. *The Caucasian Chalk Circle* is an excellent play for juxtaposing the alternative—the alternative to legitimacy is war or anarchy. It's this struggle to define legitimacy that drives the play, and it's an enormously important struggle. In *The Caucasian Chalk Circle*, as in our own experiences of the law today, let's understand that what's at stake is how we constitute ourselves as a human community.

WHEN WE DEAD AWAKEN

Henrik Ibsen and Robert Wilson: New Weapons and New Armor
by Robert Brustein

I had just completed a lecture on Ibsen's *When We Dead Awaken* in my Modern Drama class at Harvard when one of my students suggested that this rarely produced play might make an ideal project for Robert Wilson. The suggestion was not only apt but timely since Bob and I had been looking for something to do together ever since *Quartet* in 1988. Earlier that year, Bob had expressed his desire to do a version of *The Waste Land*, but T. S. Eliot's widow wouldn't release the rights. He subsequently proposed *Our Town*. The rights to this work were also tied up at the time, in preparation for a musical

The cast of *When We Dead Awaken.*

called *Grover's Corners.* When I described Ibsen's last play to Bob over a crackling long-distance line to Germany, he immediately agreed to direct it, though he hadn't yet read it. I was delighted but not entirely surprised. Wilson's realization of *Alcestis* in 1986, with its imposing mountains and rivers, had led us to believe that Ibsen's haunting tale of an aging artist who finds his apotheosis on a mount of aspiration would hold great appeal for Wilson's mystical sense of the stage.

On the other hand, the play was full of words, and Wilson's way with words was notoriously unorthodox. Recognizing that some translators might not be entirely happy with the way this director liked to rearrange a text, I volunteered to do the English version myself, promising Bob freedom to treat it any way he wished with the hope that my own vanity wouldn't be offended. On the basis of that understanding, and some initial cuts by Bob, I set about rendering Ibsen's strange, occasionally verbose play into the kind of suggestive English I hoped might spark Wilson's imagistic imagination. The major task was to cut away everything extraneous, repetitive, or explanatory—everything, that is, that could not be rendered through the symbology of the stage. I ended up with a text about half the length of the original without, I believe, excising anything vital to the action, the characters, or the theme.

Bob had originally requested language that evolved from modern to archaic as Irene and Rubek gradually ascend the mountain, but I thought this might confuse audiences—if, indeed, I was even capable of rendering it. We finally agreed on a terse, clipped style of speech— contemporary without being idiomatic—for Ulfheim and Maya and a more formal language for Rubek and Irene that would sit comfortably in the mouths of actors. When we went into workshop with the adaptation, it underwent further alteration. Wilson decided to restore a passage I had cut as a taped refrain running through the play. Other speeches were transposed. Our literary director, Robert Scanlan, helped shorten others still more as Wilson—inspired by the casting of Charles "Honi" Coles in the part of the Hotel Manager—began to introduce "knee plays" (Wilson's word for interludes) between the scenes, including some of Mr. Cole's own songs.

When We Dead Awaken is such a radical departure from Ibsen's more realistic plays that such prose-minded admirers as William Archer and H. L. Mencken believed the playwright to have lost his sanity. But the play is a visionary and prophetic glimpse into radically new forms. Often considered his last will and testament, it actually shows Ibsen poised and ready for new battle, "with new weapons and new armor," as he puts it. Had Ibsen lived he might have anticipated Strindberg in writing dream-plays and investigating expressionism. He has certainly inspired one of the finest theatrical artists of the postmodern period to take on new weapons and new armor in pursuit of a similar vision.

WHEN WE DEAD AWAKEN

The Disease of Art: Ibsen's When We Dead Awaken
by Arthur Holmberg

Is art a disease? Does it infect not only the artist but everyone he touches? Does art kill life? To create, must an artist wreak havoc on the lives of the people he loves? Or is an artist incapable of love, preferring imagination to flesh, lavishing attention on figments of the mind while neglecting real people? Was old prune-faced Plato right? Should poets be banned from the Republic? Ibsen toys with these questions in his last play, *When We Dead Awaken* (1899).

In contrast to this interrogation of art, when Ibsen's play appeared, the sacralization of art—the cult of art as religion—was raging through Europe like an epidemic. The poet as seer, as prophet, as priest—the zealots of aestheticism coined many litanies to swathe the artist in a divine nimbus. Bayreuth, holiest shrine of the new faith, drew hosts of pious pilgrims, and Ibsen in Act II makes references to *Lohengrin* that mock this hocus-pocus mysticism.

The dead in *When We Dead Awaken* are the living, and art is the agent of their destruction: opium for the soul. Watching a great artist like Ibsen question the value of art at the end of his life unsettles. But it was never Ibsen's intention to let the unjust sleep, and in this play, artists are the unjust. "My plays," he said, "make people uncomfortable because when they see them they have to think, and most people want to be effortlessly entertained, not to be told unpleasant truths."

Ibsen poses the problem in blunt sexual terms. What is the connection between eros and art? Does artistic creation require sexual repression? Was Freud right? Is art a sublimation of instinct, a consolation for the lost paradise of gratification? Ibsen bodies forth the life/art dichotomy in a quartet of characters who square off in a battle of the sexes that calls into question both idealism and realism, asceticism and sensuality. All his life, Ibsen searched for a "third kingdom" that would heal the wound between flesh and spirit.

But what does Robert Wilson, the high priest of postmodernism, have up his sleeve? Why is he casting his cool eye on Ibsen, the grandfather of realism, whom even Henry James stigmatized as "bottomlessly bourgeois"?

Wilson and Ibsen. What strange bedfellows. The coupling of the wizard of stage images with the windbag of the drawing room does not naturally present itself to the cultivated imagination. It took the percipience of a Robert Brustein to sense that it was precisely the stage magic of Wilson that *When We Dead Awaken* needs to reveal it for what it is: the last masterpiece of the first genius of the modern stage. The play—seldom read, less seldom produced—has never earned the place it deserves in the Ibsen canon.

"I don't like most of Ibsen's plays," Robert Wilson said in recent conversation. "Ibsen usually explains too much. But *When We Dead Awaken* is different. It's so mysterious. Nothing is as beautiful as mystery. I like this play because I don't understand it. The minute you think you understand a work of art, it's dead. It no longer lives in you. This play lives on in the mind like a hallucination. It's Ibsen's dream-play."

Mystery, dream, hallucination. These are Wilson's stock in trade. They are also the best way to describe the atmosphere of *When We Dead Awaken*. Ibsen subtitled the play "A dramatic epilogue." The seventy-one-year-old author was not planning to quit the boards, but he wanted to mark the end of a period in his career, a period that included the great realistic plays that ushered in modern drama. He explained:

> All I meant by "epilogue" was that the play forms an epilogue to the series of plays which began with *A Doll's House* and which now ends with *When We Dead Awaken*. . . . It completes the cycle, and makes of it an entity, and now I am finished with it. If I write anything more, it will be in another context; perhaps, too, in another form. . . . If it be granted to me to retain the strength of body and spirit which I still enjoy, I shall not be able to absent myself long from the old battlefields. But if I return, I shall come forward with new weapons, and with new equipment.

What these "new weapons" might have been, we need not guess. *When We Dead Awaken* indicates where Ibsen wanted to go. In this work he is less interested in exterior action than interior mood. He explores a borderland of the mind where memory and desire forge a new reality. T. S. Eliot observed:

> It seems to me, that beyond the nameable, classifiable emotions and motives of our conscious life when directed towards action—the part of life which prose drama is wholly adequate to express—there is a fringe of indefinite extent, of feeling which we can only detect, so to speak, out of the corner of the eye and can never completely focus. . . .There are great prose dramatists—such as Ibsen and Chekhov—who have at times done things of which I would not otherwise have supposed prose to be capable, but who seem to me, in spite of their success, to have been hampered in expression by writing in prose. This peculiar range of sensibility can be expressed by

dramatic poetry, at its moments of great intensity. At such moments, we touch the border of those feelings which only music can express.

In *When We Dead Awaken*, Ibsen struggles to break free of the straitjacket of prose and create a new poetry of the stage. He no longer relies on the conventions of plot, character, and dialogue to translate the inner world. What he tries to express—a mystical longing that blesses life at the same time it transcends it—cannot, finally, be put into language, and Ibsen is thinking less and less in terms of rational discourse and more and more in terms of visual metaphors. The play starts realistically enough. It might be a boulevard comedy that begins in an elegant spa with a lusty young wife saddled with a decrepit, world-weary husband. This plot has been spun a thousand and one times. We know the end. But soon Ibsen switches gear and undermines our sense of reality. With the entrance of Irene and her sweetly sadistic double-self, we leave realism down in the valley and begin to scale the heights of a mythopoetic vision of human love filled with tenderness and brutality. "I can only speak freely through the mouths of characters in a play," Ibsen said. And in his last play he speaks freely of the crimes he committed in the name of art. Nowhere else has Ibsen sounded so elegiac. Nowhere else has he confessed so freely his guilt. And Grandfather Ibsen had much to confess, especially about the shabby way he had treated the women to whom he owed his triumphs, including his wife Suzannah, who gave him the will to fight for a career, and Laura Kieler, who by serving as the principal model for Nora in *A Doll's House* assured Ibsen his first *succès de scandale*. In his biography, Michael Meyer recounts how Kieler's husband divorced her and received from the courts sole custody of their children. When Laura as a result suffered a nervous breakdown, her husband put her in a mental institution. Distressed by the notoriety Ibsen's play burdened her with, Laura asked the author to state publicly that she was not Nora. Ibsen refused, and Paul Johnson in *Intellectuals* denominates Ibsen's behavior "human larceny." "This was characteristic," Johnson continues, "not only of the way in which Ibsen pitched real people into his fictional brews but of his cruel disregard for their feelings in carelessly exposing them."

If Laura Kieler's strange, eventful life provided Ibsen with material for his first great heroine, she also came back in the guise of Irene to haunt his last masterpiece, dressed exactly like Laura when Ibsen saw her last. "How is it," Ibsen asked, "that we hurt those we love although we know that remorse will follow?" How? For the sake of art, which in the eyes of an artist exonerates every sin.

Ibsen loved women but neither wisely nor too well, and he rivals Shakespeare in the portrait gallery of complex female characters he created. Irene may not be the most complex, but she enjoys the virtue of being the most bizarre. She is demented, and everyone recognizes this fact except Rubek. Exploiting her innocence, Rubek had created the masterwork *Resurrection Day* that made his name by raping Irene spiritually. Driven to debauchery by his unwillingness to consummate their passion except through art, Irene—a character more at home in Gothic romance than on a realistic stage—claims to have died many years ago and refers to herself as a corpse. With a dagger always concealed somewhere about her lovely person, she has come to kill Rubek; she claims responsibility for the deaths of at least two former husbands and all her children. She blames Rubek for not having taken her sexually. "But I couldn't," Rubek blurts out in self-defense, "I was an artist."

Around the time Ibsen was writing this play, he said: I still have "various bits of madness in store." Delirium, Artaud reminds us, is desirable not only on stage but in life. Irene comes to a young Rubek as the muse who sets fire to his genius. She returns to an old Rubek to rekindle the idealism that life has slowly corroded. That the muse is demented, that she leads to death, leaves ample room for speculation. Is art neurosis or is it spiritual transcendence? Ibsen turns to madness to explore mental processes buried deep in the psyche, safely hidden from the conscious and beyond the control of reason. With Irene, Ibsen leaves realism behind to explore a symbolic world in which the will to live and the will to die, the desire to create and the desire to destroy, battle for possession of the soul. The name "Irene" means peace, and peace is what she offers Rubek—a peace beyond understanding that begins when life ends. In her madness, he finds wisdom; in her insanity, salvation.

If Irene steps from the pages of a penny dreadful, Ulfheim—the name in Norwegian suggests wolfman—steps from the stage of a knock-'em-down farce. With what loving care did Ibsen create this beast. While Rubek and Maya sip champagne from long-stemmed flutes, he chugs aquavit from a hip flask. On being introduced to the young wife, he tells her he likes to hunt reindeer and women—"fresh and full-bodied." Wolfman likes to eat hearty and drink deep. He believes that the weak and sick should be put out of their misery. He takes Maya for a walk and tries to rape her. He calls it "sport." Is man, as Zola insisted, nothing but the sum of his appetites? Simple and brutal, and (so Maya believes) a healthy antidote to art, Ulfheim repulses and excites her. She accuses Rubek of duping her into a cage by promising "all the glory of the world." In Ulfheim's arms she hopes to find freedom, but one suspects his embrace will form another cage. As Rubek and Irene lose themselves in the heights, Ulfheim and Maya turn to each other for whatever pleasure the body can give.

Is art a palsy of the flesh or balm in Gilead for the aridity of life? Must we, as Yeats pondered, "choose perfection of the life, or of the work"? Are we, as Unamuno claimed, sick animals, and does art exacerbate the disease? With his motley quartet of lovers, Ibsen sets whirling a carnival of so many different moods, tones, genres, and points of view that the spectator is left in a state of undecidability. This play may be an epilogue, but it is an epilogue in the interrogative mode. It concludes nothing. And it is this state of undecidability that appeals so strongly to the postmodern temper. Mikhail Bakhtin—one of the guiding spirits of contemporary literary theory—defines the spirit of carnival as a celebration of change and renewal, a festive acceptance of the relativity of truth—a celebration that "frees human consciousness, thought, and imagination for new possibilities." With a sense of transition and rebirth, Ibsen bids farewell to the nineteenth century and his career.

A young James Joyce, reviewing the published play in 1900, prized it as one of "the greatest of the author's work—if, indeed, it be not the greatest." Ibsen referred to it as "the best and biggest I have written." If posterity has failed to concur with these two titans, perhaps the fault lies not so much with the play as with the productions it has received. By approaching it as realistic claptrap, most performances swindle the play of its grandeur. And now Robert Wilson, by blowing the dust off this masterpiece, will show it—to use Rubek's phrase—in all its glory.

Trinidadian Pastiche
by Thomas C. Holt

"For as I see it," writes the African-American novelist and music critic Ralph Ellison in *Shadow and Act* (1964), "from the days of their introduction into the colonies, Negroes have taken, with the ruthlessness of those without articulate investments in cultural styles, whatever they could of European music, making of it that which would, when blended with the cultural tendencies inherited from Africa, express their own sense of life—while rejecting the rest. Perhaps this is only another way of saying that whatever the degree of injustice and inequality sustained by the slaves, American culture was, even before the official founding of the nation, pluralistic; and it was the African's origin in cultures in which art was highly functional which gave him an edge in shaping the music and dance of this nation."

Ellison's striking insight into the reality and ultimate strength of the cultural pastiche that is African-American music suggests a frame of reference for considering Derek Walcott's *Steel*. Fundamentally Walcott's play dramatizes a special process of cultural creativity and survival: the creation of cultural forms out of "nothing"—from the leavings, quite literally the garbage, of the Euro-American world. The plot of Walcott's play turns on the criminalization of that creative process, the stealing of a steel (the homonym appears deliberate) oil drum to make a uniquely Afro-Trinidadian musical instrument. But not only are the panmen stealing the means of their musical production from the American oil companies, they incorporate bits of American culture into their creations. In the nineteenth century, characters from American minstrel shows were incorporated into Trinidad's Carnival parades. In the twentieth century, steel bands were often named after American movies; and figures from American movies—cowboys and gangsters especially—found their way into calypso themes and Carnival masquerades.

In unfolding his plot, however, Walcott also suggests a larger and more subtle social process, wherein there is a refashioning of identities—personal and national—in a (neo)colonized society. Thus a society maligned (much like its Caribbean neighbors) as politically fragmented, economically dependent, culturally imitative, and (un)viable outside an imperialist womb struggles to know and become itself. It is a play, then, about colonialism, specifically British colonialism, and about the neocolonial American world order of the postwar era. Through culture, therefore, *Steel* addresses issues of identity and purpose that are broadly social, political, and economic. Through Trinidad, the play speaks truth about all Africans in the Americas.

But thematically transcendent though it may be, the particular acts of cultural creation and identity-fashioning to which *Steel* refers were grounded in a specific history. The play is set in the late 1960s, the decade in which Britain sloughed off most of what remained of its colonial empire. Along with Jamaica, Trinidad gained its independence in 1962. By this time, however, Britain's Caribbean colonies had become economic satellites to their northern neighbors, the United States and Canada. That new dependency had its origins in the late nineteenth century when the United States had become the main purchaser of the Caribbean's staple exports, sugar and fruit, and the main supplier of its food and manufactures. During the twentieth century, American, Canadian, and European multinationals had invested in the extraction of mineral deposits—oil in Trinidad, bauxite in Jamaica and Guyana.

The stage for this decolonization-recolonization process had been set in the period of the Great Depression and World War II. The depression unleashed labor rebellions throughout the British colonial empire, culminating with strikes by oilfield workers in Trinidad in 1937 and by sugar and dock workers in Jamaica in 1938. These upheavals set in motion discussions and reactions that would eventually lead to decolonization two decades hence. During the late 1940s Trinidad's steel bands were becoming better organized, and its government was being reorganized to allow more democratic procedures and structures. Universal suffrage was inaugurated in 1946, and a government analogous to a parliamentary system replaced direct rule from England. These decolonization initiatives were consciously linked, however, to a policy of economic development designed to encourage greater foreign investment in and control over the economy. It was a strategy that produced tremendous growth over the next decades but did not improve the lot of poor West Indians like those in Port of Spain's Laventille, the setting for *Steel*. For example, the foreign-owned oil industry was soon supplying 75 percent of Trinidad's exports, but it hardly dented the nation's growing unemployment. And in some areas the sales of vast tracts of land to multinational corporations complicated efforts at land reform and redistribution.

Like many other ex-colonials, Trinidadians also confronted the formidable task of social reconstruction after centuries of dependence on Great Britain. The voracious appetite of plantations for cheap and docile labor had brought into being a multi-ethnic population, a veritable cultural mosaic of Africans, Asians, and northern and southern Europeans. After slavery was abolished in the British West Indies in 1838, British planters had been exasperated by the new limitations on their ability to control and exploit the freed workers. So they turned to Africa, India, and China for indentured workers, bringing nearly half a million into the West Indies by 1924, when the practice was ended. Ten thousand Africans and 145,000 East Indians had been brought to Trinidad alone. By this action, planters created a classically segmented workforce, which reinforced their hegemony over an ostensibly free society. Efforts by blacks to organize and resist could be weakened by the planters' access to an indentured labor force legally obligated to work when, where, and at the price they dictated. On the other hand, the Chinese, East Indians, and Portuguese were sometimes victimized by explosions of violence from the frustrated black majority. These developments structured a social order in which ethnic and racial tensions would continue well into the twentieth century.

Out of this seemingly fragmented pluralism, new nations had to be created. In many places, particularly Trinidad, that process is not yet complete, as recent episodes of violence have demonstrated. But arguably, the official slogan of cultural pastiche—*"e pluribus unum"* in the United States or "out of many, one" in Jamaica—has achieved more reality in some Caribbean societies than in those of their northern neighbors. Perhaps it is a necessary consequence of their manifest plurality that such societies must face the problem of identity—which taxes us all in the postmodern world—with fewer illusions, knowing that always and everywhere it is not given but must be created.

Beryl McBurnie, a pioneer in Caribbean dance performance, once said of Trinidad: "The basic rhythm of our culture is syncopated, a calypso rhythm. . . .The whole spirit of the country is calypso." Indeed, the power of calypso historically has been its ability to draw disparate cultural elements into a harmonious whole, much as the panman tunes a steel drum by welding its different planes into musical consonance. Similarly, art, music, dance, and theatre may well prove the most important solvents of cultural difference, and the creation of national identity, the most striking act of cultural creativity.

KING LEAR

The Demand for Love
by Stephen Greenblatt

"Which of you shall we say doth love us most?" (*King Lear* I.i.51).

This question initiates the great unraveling, the love test that leads in the end to the destruction of Lear's kingdom, the death of his three daughters, the collapse of his identity. The question Lear asks his children is not "Which of you doth love us most?" but "Which of you shall we say doth love us most?" The focus turns back from the daughters to the all-powerful father, the king whose sole and unchallenged word will determine the disposition of his lands and his power. Lear evidently knows the answer to his question ahead of time; he has a favorite, "our joy / Although our last and least." His preference for his youngest daughter Cordelia is no secret—"He always lov'd our sister most," Goneril says matter-of-factly to her sister Regan—and he has already in fact settled the division of the kingdom. The map marking the precise boundaries has been scrutinized well before the love test takes place. Why then does Lear ask the fatal question? Why does he insist on staging a performance whose outcome is already known?

In the early seventeenth century you did not have to know Shakespeare's play to know about Lear's question and its consequences. The story was told repeatedly—in folk tales, chronicle histories, sermons, narrative poems, and at least one other surviving stage play. But rarely if ever in these constant retellings is the meaning or purpose or legitimacy of Lear's question at issue. It is like the unexamined premise of a fairy tale or, alternatively, like a question so familiar that no one takes notice of it. What is inevitably at issue in the Lear story is not the unbearable demands of parents but the ingratitude of

F. Murray Abraham (King Lear) and Stephanie Roth (Cordelia) in
King Lear.

children; Lear's fate is rehearsed as an admonition about family life, a
warning to fathers not to put too much trust in their children. "Remember what happened to old Lear."

Everywhere in this patriarchal society there were reassuring
signs of deference, formal exhibitions of the supposedly natural love
of children for their parents—children were expected at the appropriate moments to stand up, curtsy, bow down, uncover the head, kneel,
and ask for blessing. These public rituals enacted respect not only for
parents but for a whole interlocking system of authority: for wealth,
caste, power, and, at virtually every level of society, age. Jacobean England told itself that, by the will of God and the natural order of
things, authority belonged to the old, and it contrived to ensure that

this proper, sanctified arrangement of society be formally observed. But the Lear story insists that parents cannot, must not, trust these signs. "Fathers fear," wrote the seventeenth-century French philosopher Pascal, "that the natural love of their children can be erased. What kind of nature is this, that can thus be erased?" This is precisely the question that haunts Shakespeare's *King Lear*.

"Is there any cause in nature," the tormented Lear asks about his evil daughters, "that makes these hard hearts?" It would be more bearable if the cause were manifestly supernatural—a demonic agent, a ghost demanding revenge, a coven of witches on the heath dancing to Hecate. But there were no cloven hoofs in this play, no magic charms, and no weird sisters. Edgar pretends that he is possessed by devils, but he is not; he is only trying to save himself from the punitive powers of the state, powers unleashed by his all-too-human father and stepbrother. And though Albany at one point calls his wife Goneril a "devil" and a "fiend," she and her sister Regan stand before us not as monsters but as daughters.

The anxiety that wells up in Shakespeare's version of the Lear story is not simply that there are horrible individuals bustling about in the world and that some of these might turn out to be your children but that there is something about your society, your family, yourself that is disposed to generate such individuals. Of course, Lear vehemently denies any responsibility for the horrors that are visited upon him. "I gave you all," he tells Goneril and Regan; while in the great scene of torment and insight on the heath, he cries, "I am a man/More sinn'd against than sinning." But the Fool—the half-crazed and sublimely loyal Fool—continually reminds Lear that he bears at least partial responsibility for what has befallen him and his kingdom. And that responsibility merges with the social organization that as king he embodies. A family system based upon absolute patriarchal authority and the public performance of filial love will tend to produce flattery and hypocrisy; a system of inheritance that sets one child against another will tend to produce rivalry and hatred; a system of governance that vests all power in the old will tend to produce conspiracy among the young.

All the innate tensions of such a system reach the point of crisis at the moment of retirement. On the Continent, the emperor Charles V had abdicated and retreated to a monastery, but the act was almost inconceivable for an English monarch. Retirement, always discouraged, occurred most frequently in Shakespeare's own class of origin, that is, among artisans and small landowners who might be forced in their old age to transfer a workshop or farm to the young. Those facing retirement showed remarkably little confidence in the supposedly inherent or customary rights of parents; they turned instead to the law, commonly obtaining contracts or maintenance agreements by which, in return for the transfer of the family property, children undertook to provide food, clothing, shelter. The extent of parental anxiety may be gauged by the great specificity of the requirements—so many yards of woolen cloth, pounds of coal, or bushels of grain—and by the pervasive fear of being turned out of the house in the wake of a quarrel.

King Lear is very far from the social world of yeomen and artisans, but his fate in Shakespeare's play powerfully registers the concerns of the humble makers of these contracts: the terror of being turned out of doors or of becoming a stranger in one's own house, the humiliating loss of dignity, the dread of being supplanted by the young, the misery of dependence upon one's children. "Thou mad'st thy daughters thy mothers," the bitter Fool tells Lear.

How can the authority of the generation that is, as Lear puts it, crawling toward death survive the alienation of the property, and hence the power, upon which this authority rested? And what happens to patriarchal authority when there is no male heir, when the goods of the father cannot be conferred upon the eldest son? The aging Lear attempts to meet his crisis by dividing his kingdom among his daughters, but this attempt is a disastrous failure. Partible inheritance solves nothing. It was possible to take Lear's fate as a cautionary tale in favor of primogeniture: find a male, the oldest son-in-law if absolutely necessary, and confer all your property on him. Possible, but not for the audience of Shakespeare's play. Shakespeare's brilliant stroke of weaving Lear's story together with Gloucester's subverts the lesson, for the story of Gloucester and his sons highlights the murderous resentment spawned by the systematic, customary impoverishment of younger brothers and illegitimate children.

The wicked Edmund attributes to his brother Edgar sentiments that the fathers in this play fear lie just beneath the surface of deference. "I begin to find an idle and fond bondage in the oppression of aged tyranny, who sways, not as it hath power, but as it is suffer'd." Why should children put up with the absurd, confining power of unjust custom? Why should they reiterate the lies that sustain an impotent social order? "Aged tyranny"—the words reflect away from gullible old Gloucester and back to the scene that we have just witnessed, a scene in which everyone, except Kent, has tamely allowed an irascible old tyrant to banish his daughter. Edmund's cunning libel prepares us to glimpse the hidden intentions that underlie Goneril and Regan's flatteries, to glimpse as well the fears that Lear himself is trying desperately to ward off by demanding from his children a public declaration of their love.

In his initial stipulation that he be attended by a train of one hundred knights, Lear seems to make a gesture toward contractual protection of his right to retain his royal dignities, but there has been and can be no real contract. A king is not a poor yeoman who could go to court to demand his rights; a king, wrote King James, is "a little God." Lear speaks at the play's opening as if he were the master of existence: "Better thou/ Had'st not been born," he tells Cordelia, "than not t'have pleas'd me better." Such a man can brook no maintenance agreement with his children, for any contractual obligation would undermine the absolute sovereignty upon which his identity as king is founded. How can a "little God" retire? For that matter, how can any self-respecting father admit that only a legal contract with his own flesh and blood assures him of his survival?

Lear, who has, as he thinks, given all to his daughters, demands all from them. Like the Calvinist God—and like an increasing number of fathers in this period—he does not traffic in contracts and mutual obligations and reciprocal good works; he expects absolute love. He wants, that is, not only the formal marks of deference that publicly acknowledge his position but also the inward and unqualified tribute of the heart.

But as the play's tragic logic reveals, Lear cannot have both the public deference and the inward love of his children. The public deference is only as good as the legal and communal constraints that Lear's absolute power paradoxically deprives him of, and the inward love, as his favorite daughter immediately grasps, cannot be authentically performed in social discourse, enacted as in a court or theater. It is only the terrifying Goneril and Regan who can mime the absolute devotion that Lear craves, while Cordelia understands that there is something either hypocritical or obscene about the attempt to satisfy the craving: "Why have my sisters husbands, if they say/ They love you all?" And if, in the end, Lear does in fact glimpse this unconditional, boundless love—in his youngest daughter's return and forgiveness—it is at an unbearable, unredeemable cost. "Thou'lt come no more, / Never, never, never, never, never."

HAMLET

What Should the Ghost Look Like?
by Jan Kott

Shakespeare scholars have always been uneasy with the Ghost in *Hamlet*. They have never been sure whether it came from hell or purgatory or according to what system of theology, Protestant or Catholic, or how much the student of philosophy, just back from Wittenberg, could trust it. But directors have ever-greater troubles with the Ghost. The dramatic function of the Ghost is important, but even more important is the question: what should the Ghost look like? The Ghost of the dead king is not only supposed to frighten Horatio and the sentinels on the battlements, but it should also arouse a feeling of dread in the audience (at the very least it should not provoke laughter). A Ghost in rusted armor that clinks at every step cannot be taken seriously. But how else can it be presented?

In Peter Hall's production of *Hamlet* some twenty years ago, the actor playing the ghost sat on the shoulders of a hidden extra who rode a bicycle. This gave the impression that the Ghost was swimming silently through space. The *onnagata* playing the roles of the geisha in the Japanese kabuki theatre glides in a similar fashion. But after a few moments the audience caught on to Hall's trick, and laughter accompanied the bicycle-riding Ghost to the end of the scene. Of course, there are other ways of doing it. I have seen a Ghost on stilts and an Italian Ghost created by projecting Hamlet's enlarged shadow, lighted from underneath, onto a screen at the back of the stage. But even this shadow, which spoke with an amplified voice, did little to make the Ghost convincing to me.

So perhaps the Ghost does not have to look like a ghost at all. Perhaps it should appear as the dead do in our dreams. That was how it was presented more than ten years ago when Jonathan Miller showed his *Hamlet* in New York, cast with students from Oxford and

Royal Miller (Fortinbras), Gus Johnson (Marcellus), and Mark Rylance (Hamlet) in *Hamlet*.

Cambridge. It was in no way amateur theatre but one of the most penetrating, analytical productions of *Hamlet* I have ever seen. The actors looked as though they had just stepped out of a court painting by Velázquez. They all wore the same black costumes with enormous white ruffs, as did Hamlet. And the Ghost appeared in the same black outfit, with a white ruff and a black peaked hat with a broad brim. There was a small bench by the proscenium on which the Ghost sat with Hamlet and conversed with him as father with son. The Ghost put his arm around Hamlet's shoulder and explained everything, very considerately, as though it were an ordinary conversation. And the ordinariness of the conversation with the Ghost was deeply moving.

In his never-realized production of *Hamlet*, Konrad Swinarski had intended to return to the traditional, armor-plated image of the Ghost. We know how the Ghost was supposed to look from a conversation with the set designers, Lidia and Jerzy Skarzynski, which was faithfully recorded by Jozef Opalski in *The Conversations with Swinarski* (1988). The Ghost was not only to have been encased in armor, but beneath this armor his body was to have been visible, "putrefying, with pulsating abscesses." "A cheap trick on the part of the old Ghost," the Skarzynskis say, undoubtedly repeating Swinarski's own words, "designed to affect his naive, young son and incite him to vengeance."

In this conception, if we are to believe *The Conversations with Swinarski*, the Ghost was to have been the embodiment of the feudal wars of plunder waged by old Hamlet, which the cautious Claudius, following a new policy of pragmatic diplomacy, has abandoned, *Pace!* We need not always have blind faith in the theorizing of even the most brilliant director. But Swinarski had an astonishing and penetrating intuition about another role for the Ghost: the Ghost as an evocation of the past, as an appeal that it never be forgotten.

Something like that happened about ten years ago. I saw a production of *Hamlet* in Dubrovnik. It was August, and Dubrovnik was baked white by the sun. The old town is surrounded by walls that shut out the sea at almost every point. The small, rocky beaches are located outside the town, and inside the walls one has menacing feelings of claustrophobia, as though there is no place to escape to. One continually meets the same faces, and hears the same voices, even in the evenings, when, once the relentless heat has abated, the white walls of the houses still radiate the feverish heat. Well into the early hours of the morning, the narrow streets resound with broken cries in assorted languages.

In Dubrovnik, right outside the old town, sits an old castle in ruins. Every summer *Hamlet* is presented in this castle. Often, given the surroundings, these productions are quite extraordinary. I particularly remember one such *Hamlet* that I saw some ten years ago. The performances began late in the evening in the courtyard of the castle, where wooden benches were set up in front of a simple platform made of planks. When the royal court appeared on the platform, it seemed for a moment as if the spectators had left their benches and gone up on the stage. Gertrude and Claudius wore brightly colored coats, a cross between beach and evening wear, and looked as if they had just stepped into one of the innumerable Dubrovnik *gostinica* (restaurants) for the local specialty: grilled *reznici* and a bottle of red wine. Ophelia was barefoot in the then-fashionable red bikini, her small round breasts almost completely exposed. The ladies in waiting and courtiers looked as though they had been unexpectedly transported from a Venetian carnival to Dubrovnik in the middle of summer.

When the stage grew empty, the Ghost appeared at the top of a flight of crumbling stairs in a niche in the wall. He was wearing a striped concentration camp uniform. His farewell to Hamlet, "Adieu, adieu, adieu. Remember me," echoed throughout the ruins of the castle. Yet his cry remained suspended in the void. The Ghost in the striped uniform, bathed in the spotlights, seemed to be a specter from the past—from the past that everyone in Dubrovnik/Elsinore wanted to forget forever.

But the Ghost was not the only guest who arrived at the castle on the third day after the marriage of the new king to his elder brother's freshly made widow. Hamlet was likewise a stranger in this new court of magnificent European holiday festivities. In his black cape, Hamlet too appeared to be an anachronistic specter of dead ideologies amidst the spectators and actors, who even at that late hour in the evening seemed equally heated by the midday sun and by the wine. The sarcastic remarks of that lean and long-haired dissident from Wittenberg sounded hopelessly out of place, and his complaints that the time was out of joint and that he was born to set it right seemed uncalled-for arrogance. There were not Hamlets in the audience in Dubrovnik.

In Jonathan Miller's production and in Swinarski's *Hamlet*, which had reached the final rehearsals, one actor played both the Ghost and Fortinbras. For me the reasons for such doubling in casting were neither clear nor convincing. But with the passing of time, I have learned to trust directors more than Shakespeare scholars. Since the time of young Goethe and then of the German and French romantics, through the naturalists, modernists, and decadents both early and later, Hamlet has not only been the central character in drama but also always someone contemporary. In Hamlet, directors discover their own traits, their own hopes, defeats, and despair. All the other characters in the tragedy are not only secondary, they are purely historical. But in the last decade, and maybe even somewhat earlier, directors have been paying closer and closer attention to the significance of the Ghost and Fortinbras. And perhaps not only because in the logic of action and structure the tragedy at Elsinore begins with the arrival of the Ghost and ends with the departure of Fortinbras. With increasing urgency, the Ghost and Fortinbras appear as signs of history, and not only the history of Elsinore but the history that has already happened and could happen again.

A few years after seeing the Dubrovnik Ghost in the striped concentration camp uniform, I saw a *Hamlet* at the Royal National Theatre in London, with the Ghost in a long World War I trench coat coming down to the ground, riddled with bullet holes, and in another *Hamlet*, also British, Fortinbras's bodyguard wore armbands with swastikas. For the contemporary director, the Ghost and Fortinbras are once again ante portas.

Bergman's Swedish *Hamlet*, shown briefly in New York a few years back, ends in a glare of lights and the buzzing of television sets. Fortinbras's soldiers pile the corpses one on top of the other and count them, methodically, as if they were clearing a battlefield. Everyone has forgotten about Hamlet. And no one bears off his body. In *Hamlet*, as planned by Swinarski, troops were to gather on Szczepanski Square in front of the Stary Theatre before the performance. And then in the last scene they were to invade not only the stage but also the windows facing the square, and descend on ropes from the balconies onto the heads of the spectators.

"The rest is silence." The end is not Hamlet's silence, but the deafening drums of Fortinbras's troops.

Translated by Jadwiga Kosicka.

HEDDA GABLER

Shakespeare's Envy: Ibsen's Hedda
by Harold Bloom

Ibsen, by a universal consent that transcends even the Western world, is acknowledged to be without rival among dramatists since Shakespeare. His precise relation to Shakespeare is not easy to determine, for reasons that go beyond the treacheries of translation. If the reader should turn to the admirable anthology Oswald LeWinter's *Shakespeare in Europe* (1963), she will find Voltaire and Goethe, Hegel and Stendhal, Manzoni and Pushkin, Hugo and

Turgenev, Tolstoy (being totally outrageous) and many others, but no writing on Shakespeare by Ibsen, his principal European heir. Ibsen anxiously pretended that he was unaware of Shakespeare precisely because he had learned from Shakespeare everything that mattered most in his dramatic art. To evade one's prime precursor is almost the first principle of poetic influence, but to get behind such evasion is the hope of the critic of poetic influence. Ibsen was as shy, cunning, and exuberant as his own Peer Gynt and also as willful, stubborn, and turned-against-the-self as his own Hedda Gabler. No one is going to get utterly behind Ibsen's subtle mastery of evasion, and I am not an Ibsen scholar, so I will attempt only a speculation here.

The central puzzle of Ibsen's half-century career as a playwright (1850–1899) was its transition, halfway through, from verse drama to prose drama and from a High Romantic aesthetic individualism to what only superficially seems a naturalistic kind of social theatre. I would speculate that the design of that transition was to become less overtly Shakespearean while inwardly becoming more Shakespearean than before. *Hedda Gabler* seems to me more Shakespearean than *Brand* or *Peer Gynt*, while *When We Dead Awaken* is precisely what a late Shakespearean romance had to turn into as the nineteenth century edged into the twentieth. Ibsen would be the most original and influential Western dramatist since Euripides were it not for Shakespeare. The overwhelming facility of Shakespeare has diluted Ibsen's influence, and a side-by-side reading of Shakespeare and Ibsen certainly diminishes our sense of Ibsen's originality. Ibsenite representation simply is Shakespearean representation brought more or less up-to-date with regard to history yet considerably less advanced as psychology than Shakespeare's map of the mind. Here Ibsen shrinks exactly as Freud shrinks, though the nature of this curtailment is hardly to the particuliar discredit either of Ibsen or of Freud.

Michael Meyer, Ibsen's accomplished biographer and translator, notes that Ibsen's starting point for his first poetic drama, *Catiline* (1849), was Shakespeare's *Julius Caesar*:

When in his later years Ibsen was asked what books he had read in his youth and what authors had influenced him, he tended to shy away from the question almost psychologically. But *Catiline*—written mainly at night, when the twenty-one-year-old Ibsen was working as an apothecary's apprentice—owes an obvious debt to Shakespeare. Catiline himself has much in common with Brutus in *Julius Caesar*, and the scenes between Catiline and his fellow conspirators, and his final suicide after his defeat in battle, seem plainly indebted to the same play.

St. John's Night (1851), a kind of version of *A Midsummer Night's Dream*, was abandoned by Ibsen because its Shakespearean debt was too plain. *Brand* (1865) was not written to be acted and yet is clearly Ibsen's first great dramatic triumph. Though founded explicitly on Kierkegaard, *Brand* nevertheless echoes the even more illustrious Dane, Hamlet, and in some sense is Hamlet gone mad in the mists of northern theology. Northern mythology, a more natural mode for Ibsen, gave him *Peer Gynt*, my own favorite among his plays, at once his most original and least Shakespearean work, though Peer has more than a touch of the Falstaffian gusto in him.

George Bernard Shaw, who asserted his preference for Ibsen over Shakespeare (how Shaw wished Shakespeare had written in Norwegian!), ventured even to remark that "Shakespeare survives by what he has in common with Ibsen." Reversing the observation, we have the truth, which remains implicit in Shaw even at his most deliciously outrageous:

> As to the deaths in Ibsen's last acts, they are a sweeping up of the remains of dramatically finished people. Solness's fall from the tower is as obviously symbolic as Phaeton's fall from the chariot of the sun. Ibsen's dead bodies are those of the exhausted or destroyed; he does not kill Hilda, for instance, as Shakespeare killed Juliet. He is ruthless enough with Hedvig and Eyolf because he wants to use their deaths to expose their parents; but if he had written *Hamlet* nobody would have been killed in the last act except perhaps Horatio, whose correct nullity might have provoked Fortinbras to let some of the moral sawdust out of him with his sword. For Shakespearean deaths in Ibsen you must go back to Lady Inger and the plays of his nonage, with which this book is not concerned.

The drama was born of old from the union of our desires: the desire to have a dance and the desire to hear a story. The dance became a rant; the story became a situation. And it was held that the stranger the situation, the better the play. Ibsen saw that, on the contrary, the more familiar the situation, the more interesting the play. Shakespeare had put ourselves on the stage but not our situations. Our uncles seldom murder our fathers, and cannot legally marry our mothers; we do not meet witches; our kings are not as a rule stabbed and succeeded by their stabbers; and when we raise money by bills we do not promise to pay pounds of our flesh. Ibsen supplies the want left by Shakespeare. He gives us not only ourselves, but ourselves in our own situations. The things that happen to his stage figures are things that happen to us. One consequence is that his plays are much more important to us than Shakespeare's. Another is that they are capable both of hurting us cruelly and of filling us with excited hopes of escape from idealistic tyrannies, and with visions of intenser life in the future.

Shakespeare, grand dramatic pragmatist as he is, sometimes does sweep away a protagonist or two in order to clear the stage, as it were, but then so does Ibsen, despite Shaw's assertions. Much more interesting is Shaw's best observation: "Shakespeare had put ourselves on the stage but not our situations." Shakespeare's representation of character, personality, and cognition—of ethos, pathos, and logos—is thereby conceded as permanently subsuming every Ibsenite (and Shavian) representation. To represent "things that happen to us" indeed remains Ibsen's originality and continued influence, but that is a relatively limited achievement and does not diminish whatsoever the long Shakespearean shadow that stretches across every one of Ibsen's dramas.

If we do well not to inflate Ibsen's stature beyond all reasonable measure, we must reflect also that no dramatist since Ibsen has matched him, not even Chekhov, Beckett, Brecht, let alone Strindberg, Shaw, Pirandello. His dramatic peers are few: Aeschylus, Sophocles, Euripides, Aristophanes, Calderón, Lope de Vega, Racine, Molière, and of these only Molière can compete with Shakespeare and Ibsen for a universal audience, at least since the ancients. Shaw, shrewd heir of Ibsen as he was, may have mislocated the center of Ibsen's power over and for us. Eric Bentley came closer to it by seeing its relation not to our situation in general or particular but to our disabilities. "No playwright has managed to project into his scenes more of the pressure of modern life, its special anxiety, strain, and stress." We are still, in the early 1990s, in the era of Freud, even as Proust is its novelist. The shadow of the Norwegian master may not prove to be as long as the Shakespearean shadow, but it flickers over us still.

Hedda Gabler, written in 1890 in Munich, is the masterpiece of the Aesthetic Age. I myself have never recovered from seeing Peggy Ashcroft playing Hedda in London in 1954, so that rereading the play now, a third of a century later, I hear Ashcroft throughout. Strong and perverse as Hedda doubtless is, Ashcroft may have been too strong for the part, or else the others on stage just were not capable of playing against her. I need to keep reminding myself that Hedda is not Pater's *Mona Lisa*, older than the rocks among which she sits. Critics tend to agree that Hedda is Ibsen—Brand and Peer combined in the body of a single woman, who is at once as passionate and as repressed as Ibsen himself. Like Ibsen, Hedda is the ultimate bad news, a reductionist of genius, a rage for the abyss. No major female figure in Western drama since Euripides matches Hedda in negativity; she has turned her wounded narcissism against her own self, and she incarnates her death drive, beyond the pleasure principle.

The inward meaning of *Hedda Gabler* may be Ibsen's sexual impotence, or fear of impotence, since Hedda's implied frigidity is a dominant element in the play. To term Hedda "neurotic" is an absurd litotes; she is the most dangerous of neurotics, with her self-frustrated sexuality fiercely expressed in her sadism and in her incessant reductionism. She is also immensely attractive; no other woman in Ibsen carries about her so intense and seductive an aura. Henry James, who was jealous of Ibsen, if only because James failed perpetually in writing for the theatre, yielded partly to that aura:

> What material, indeed, the dissentient spirit may explain, and what "use," worthy of the sacred name, is to be made of a wicked, diseased, disagreeable woman? That is just what Ibsen attempts to gauge, and from the moment such an attempt is resolute the case ceases to be so simple. The "use" of Hedda Gabler is that she acts on others and that even her most disagreeable qualities have the privilege, thoroughly undeserved doubtless, but equally irresistible, of becoming a part of the history of others. And then one isn't so sure she is wicked, and by no means sure (especially when she is represented by an actress who makes the point ambiguous) that she is disagreeable. She is various and sinuous and graceful, complicated and natural; she suffers, she struggles, she is human, and by that fact exposed to a dozen interpretations, to the importunity of one suspense.

Christopher Walken (Astrov) and Lindsay Crouse (Yelena) in *Uncle Vanya* (1987–1988).

If you substitute "Ibsen" for "Hedda Gabler" in the Jamesian passage, then you have an apt general critical estimate of the Norwegian dramatist and his privilege of becoming a part of our history. You could not make the same substitution in Shaw's harsh, really rather mean description of Hedda:

Hedda Gabler has no ethical ideals at all, only romantic ones. She is a typical nineteenth-century figure, falling into the abyss between the ideals which do not impose on her and the realities she has not yet discovered. The result is that though she has imagination, and an intense appetite for beauty, she has no conscience, no conviction, with plenty of cleverness, energy, and personal fascination that remains mean, envious, insolent, cruel, in protest against others' happiness, fiendish in her dislike of inartistic people and things, a bully in reaction from her own cowardice.

Shaw's Hedda is the foremother of our contemporary School of Resentment, but I do not recognize Shaw's Hedda when I attend or read the play. Paradoxically, her trollish aspect, barely repressed, is far more savage than the cruelty and bullying that Shaw attributes to her. She is as diseased and various as Henry James found her to be.

Her sexual satisfactions apparently are either vicarious or sado-masochistic, and her most characteristic gestures are in handing Lovborg a pistol and asking him to kill himself "beautifully," and in burning Lovborg's manuscript while whispering, "I'm burning your child, Thea! You with your beautiful wavy hair!" We remember that at the end, when she runs her hands gently through Thea's hair, shortly before killing herself "beautifully" with the other pistol. If Hedda has any desire for anyone except herself, it is for Thea, but even that desire is antithetical in the extreme.

That Hedda is a phantasmagoric self-parody on Ibsen's part is palpable to us now, but that appears to be also one of the major modes of the imagination, except probably in Shakespeare, that picnic of selves who may have parodied his contemporary rivals precisely because they represented some of his potential selves. There are elements of wily Christopher Marlowe in Edmund and in Shylock and strong traces of burly Ben Jonson in Malvolio. Ibsen also parodies his contemporaries, but his Gyntian and Brandian selves had to be his principal resources for representation. Both selves have gone very bad in Hedda, but they combined to make her a powerful and inescapable presence, replete with charismatic negativity, or sexuality gone dank. Walt Whitman's line—"From pent-up, aching rivers"—is a splendid description of Hedda as outwardly composed but inwardly turbulent source.

Hedda, who dreads farce and possible ill repute, provokes both. She accepts every convention that she despises and is a perfect embodiment of William Blake's Proverb of Hell, that whosoever curbs desire breeds pestilence, a sickness-unto-action. Ibsen's own definition of Hedda's trollishness is unsurpassed: "The demon in Hedda is that she wants to influence another human being, but once that has happened, she despises him." Insofar as Ibsen has influenced us, he certainly would despise us, and Hedda was his vision of what he most feared he might become. That makes her the greatest of Ibsen's apotropaic gestures, the most advanced of his theatrical tropes for warding off the dilemmas of his own nature. But she is also one of his handful of astonishing successes at representation. Shakespeare himself might have envied Ibsen her creation and might have wished to build a problematic or dark comedy around her. For Ibsen, her drama was a tragedy: his own.

Hedda Gabler: A Feminist Debate
Two Leading Feminist Writers Assess Ibsen's Most Famous Female

PRO by Molly Haskell

I read *Hedda Gabler* in a college drama course and was immediately enthralled by this demonic Nietzschean anti-heroine whose withering contempt for marriage seemed more radical at the time than Nora's slamming the door on an obtuse husband.

This was the early sixties. I was at an all-female college, with many daughters of the still-Victorian Old South. Marriage was much on everyone's minds, and at almost every Monday lunch someone would announce her engagement, followed by a ceremony in which the diamond ring was passed around for all to see, admire, and appraise. I had no desire to marry but no sense of a multitude of options either.

Thus the appeal of Hedda Gabler, a woman of ambition and intelligence, who goes overnight from being a spirited and independent horsewoman, admired by all, a "figure" in the community, to Mrs. Tesman, with a house to run, unwanted relatives, a child on the way, and her husband's prospects as a scholar growing dimmer by the minute.

It's not as if she envisions a beautiful alternative. Only the urge to manipulate relieves her boredom. Her rage is often mean-spirited, and the objects of her scorn and contempt are not weak-minded people at all but women who are both more courageous and, in the traditional mold, more selfless than she. But there was and still is something majestic, exhilarating, and darkly comical in her rudeness, her derision of all that is domestic, boxed-in, cheap.

With her fondness for guns and her avid curiosity about men's doings—faithfully satisfied first by Lovborg, then by Judge Brack—one can't escape the sense that this daughter of a military man, with whom she obviously identifies, is a man trapped in a woman's body. Her interest in Lovborg was comradely rather than sexual (and turned murderous when he became romantic), and there are homoerotic overtones in her dealings with Thea Elvsted, tellingly expressed in her ambivalent fixation on her rival's blond tresses. She knows she lacks courage, but even her vision of courage and "manliness" is a shallow and loveless thing, the avoidance of dependency rather than a heroic act.

And yet, with all her malignancy, what is astonishing is that we continue to be fascinated and engaged, even charmed, by Hedda. She seems to defy a double standard that allows male protagonists to behave in socially unacceptable ways and still retain our sympathy as charming murderers and philandering rogues, whereas a comparable female is despised as unwomanly, a bitch.

It is a measure of Ibsen's skill and ambiguous empathy that Hedda is one of the few thoroughly destructive women who is not unwomanned, who retains her sex appeal even as her monstrousness is revealed. Is this despite—or because—there is a large quotient of masculinity in her character makeup?

Finally she shoots herself, a method of suicide rarely chosen by women, and joins her father in death.

CON *by Anne Roiphe*

Hedda Gabler—cruel, narcissistic, hysterical, romantic, evil, destructive, self-glorifying, materialistic, snobbish, vengeful, jealous, and petty—is mythic in her repulsiveness. She conveys all too accurately the male idea of witchhood, of the calculating, manipulating, woman beyond control, conscience-lacking, all-devouring female. A male nightmare if I ever heard one. If we ask Freud's question of Hedda Gabler, we get an unambiguous answer. She wants political power. She wants wealth. She wants brilliance—if not her own, another's will do. She wants beauty. Where does she see beauty? In the well-placed bullet, of course, in the body destroyed heroically. Freud made the mistake of thinking female ethical capacity slightly damaged. In Hedda the damage is more than slight. She is cruel to her husband's aunt. She is deceptive, manipulative, vicious. She destroys the manuscript that represents the love of another woman for the man she had wanted. She destroys the man's life, leading him to self-destruction, arranging his extinction, first through liquor, then by handing him a pistol. She eats the weak and despises those who play by the rules, including servants. She is certainly the Lady Macbeth of Norway.

Yes, she is limited by the social possibilities for women in her historical moment. Of course it's a pity she wasn't given more money, more power, more education. Naturally we should have sympathy for her because her sexual life was expected to be confined within inflexible, bourgeois rules. She is no feminist heroine, however, and let's not confuse her self-aggrandizement with any true reach for social freedoms for women. In speaking of motherhood, she says she will not accept any claim on her person. She will not be beholden to another. She will not create another. She will not care for another. This denial of the nurturing functions, the biologically creative functions, leaves her with only herself to love. Her unwillingness to care for another is the warning sign of her crippled, distorted humanity. By contrast, Miss Tesman, the long-suffering aunt who is martyred to the sick, is presented as a woman who tends to others to the point of absurdity. Miss Tesman sacrifices her own life for others in such an extreme manner that we can hardly have sympathy for her. We can hardly admire her. But the opposite flaw—a hardness and self-absorption, an unwillingness to care for another, an incapacity to nurture or create—this is anti-life, anti-female, anti-male, a gross parody of the human condition.

Her death is not tragic as much as disgusting. Among the feelings that trigger her suicide is her rage that Lovborg has not shot himself "beautifully." In effect she kills herself because she sees that she cannot control everything, that she herself will fail, has failed, and is not destined for greatness. This hysteria, romanticism, emotion in place of thought, is hardly a compliment to the female, is hardly a reflection on the society that issued her. I think what we have here is misogyny of the worst order. The good Mrs. Elvsted is a sweet dope. The good Miss Tesman is a Christian parody. The fantastic Hedda is the stuff of nightmares. Let her get on her broom and with her creator fly off into the night of oblivion.

OLEANNA

The Language of Misunderstanding
by Arthur Holmberg

David Mamet's new play, *Oleanna*, is an urgent, upsetting examination of sexual harassment, a subject that has gripped America since the Clarence Thomas hearings. During the play's world premiere at the A.R.T., Mamet was attacked by people on both sides of the sexual battlefront. "Your play is politically irresponsible," one female student challenged the playwright. "You don't take a position. Your political statement is wrong."

What has Mamet wrought? Is he just another macho playwright lashing out at guerrilla feminists? Or does his play legitimately explore the gender gap? Or is it about two human beings who misread each other, tragically? "As a playwright," Mamet answered the student, "I have no political responsibility. I'm an artist. I write plays, not political propaganda. If you want easy solutions, turn on the boob tube. Social and political issues on TV are cartoons; the good guy wears a white hat, the bad guy a black hat. Cartoons don't interest me. We are living through a time of deep transition, so everyone is unsettled. I'm as angry, scared, and confused as the rest of you. I don't have answers."

If Mamet believes an artist has no political responsibility, what then is the function of theatre in society? In his collection of essays, *Writing in Restaurants*, Mamet provides an answer: "In dreams we do not seek answers to those questions which our conscious (rational) mind is capable of supplying, we seek answers to those questions which the conscious mind is incompetent to deal with. So with the drama, if the question posed is one which can be answered rationally, e.g., how does one fix a car, should white people be nice to black people, are the physically handicapped entitled to our respect, our enjoyment of the drama is incomplete—we feel diverted but not fulfilled. Only if the question posed is one whose complexity and depth renders it unsusceptible to rational examination does the dramatic treatment seem to us appropriate, and the dramatic solution become enlightening."

Oleanna, which featured Rebecca Pidgeon and William H. Macy in the A.R.T. and New York productions, focuses on a female student who accuses an older male professor of sexual harassment. Although the play's polarized subject matter might lead one to expect an overtly polemical approach, Mamet's use of language gives the play rich texture. Speaking past each other and often at cross-purposes, the two characters get trapped in a tragic comedy of errors in which misunderstanding piled on misunderstanding builds a labyrinth of ambiguity.

Formalized, repetitive, hypnotic, Mamet's language is both real and surreal. In his hands, it ceases to be a transparent medium of communication, translating thoughts and feelings clearly and un-equivocally from one mind to another. Instead language spins its wheels and gets nowhere. Sentences refuse to complete themselves; they run on, loop back, start over, peter out, or suspend flight midair as the other character butts in. This stop-and-go creates a hallucinatory rhythm, a litany of broken sentences.

Rhythm gives Mamet's dialogue its undeniable theatrical punch. When asked about the difference between dialogue in novel and dialogue on stage, Mamet answered: "I grappled with this problem when I was adapting *The Postman Always Rings Twice* for the screen. Once you take dialogue out of a novel and delete the descriptions and the 'he said' 'she said,' once you put pictures with this dialogue, it collapses. The rhythm is wrong. The rhythm of a line of prose on a page is not the rhythm of a line of dialogue on a stage. If you break the rhythm, you break the meaning. Rhythm conveys meaning. It's puzzling. I can't explain it. But my ear hears it. Each medium has its own rules."

The rhythm of the language translates directly into the rhythm of the scene in performance. During a rehearsal, Mamet talks the actors through the final, violent moments of the play. "Filming *Homicide*, I learned the traditional bang-bang-bang way is wrong. It's too fast. Do it like a slow dance. Let the audience take it in. Be gentle with the violence. Then it terrifies. Then drive, drive, drive to the end. The blood-sugar level is a little low. Let me hear those words full voice. This play is a protest. Protest from the bottom of your balls and the bottom of your ovaries. The last ninety seconds are the most important part of the play. Wrap it up, but don't tell the audience something they already know."

"To act is to do," Mamet says later, casting himself as the Hemingway of directors. "The difference between what is actable and what is not is physical. Emotions are not important in acting. An actor can't act angry. But a reprimand can be acted, and the reprimand will convey anger to the audience. You get at the inner thread of a play by what a character does. If you write a play correctly, you don't need stage directions. Let the script do the work. A director brings the actor in line with the text. And the director must always remember that on stage, as Stanislavsky found out, real palm trees from Yalta look fake. The purpose of theatre is to express, not duplicate."

On an archetypal level, Mamet's play—a sexual minuet of violence—deals with the unending struggle for power between male and female. Deep within, men and women mistrust each other, and the relationship between them can never be easy due to primal fears: the male fear of castration and the female fear of male force and rape. The play unsettles spectators because it taps deep into the collective unconscious, where these instinctive fears lurk just beneath waking life. This archetypal level gives *Oleanna* its muscle. "The moment this mythological situation reappears," writes Jung, "is always characterized by a peculiar emotional intensity. It is as though forces whose existence we never suspected were unloosed." With his back to the wall, the professor discovers brutality within him he never knew existed.

Mamet sums up his play with questions, not answers. "My play is about two people looking for answers and torturing each other. Both characters are in a state of flux. In this play the unthinkable, the unbelievable become real. The point of the play is, at the end, to ask, 'How did we get here?' The professor adores his students and prides himself on being a good teacher. How did he wind up thrashing a student?"

BLACK SNOW

Diary of a Dead Man or The Theatre Novel
by Anatoly Smelyansky

Mikhail Bulgakov first started thinking about writing a book about the theatre, centered on a playwright's destiny, in 1929, a year Stalin called "the year of the great fracture." The dictator was right in a sense: the country named Russia had had its spine broken that year. In the spring of 1929, all Bulgakov's plays were condemned, and the playwright was brought to the verge of poverty and of a physical and emotional breakdown. He was then saved by an unpredictable fate: he did not end up committing suicide, he was neither annihilated nor assimilated by the regime, and he was not expatriated. Bulgakov was given a different choice: Stalin himself arranged an appointment for him at the Moscow Art Theatre. This was the same great theatre where the author and his play *The White Guard* had received their joint theatrical baptism in 1926, the same great theatre that, in the thirties, was converted into the first official stage of the empire.

Bulgakov served at the theatre for almost six years. In the fall of 1936 he left following the banning from the theatre's repertory of his play *Molière*, which had received only seven performances. To put it more precisely, Bulgakov was forcibly outcast from Stanislavsky's company. For him this eviction was a catastrophe, and he always regarded the theatre's attitude as a betrayal. Soon after his pullout he decided to get back to his old idea for a novel about the theatre. This work, given the title *The Theatre Novel* in its original edition in 1965 (it is known as *Black Snow* in English) was called *Diary of a Dead Man* in Bulgakov's manuscript. His title introduces a bitter image. The world of the theatre seems to be observed by a person who has ceased to exist. What began as a personal account of the author's relations with the Moscow Art Theatre was broadened by Bulgakov into a universal story about the fate of the artist.

Laughter in the novel serves as a borderland: it is laughter on the edge of nowhere. Through the laughter we see the theatre from the edge of a vanishing life. The author's powers of prediction were uncanny. *The Theatre Novel* has become a book about our lives; to a certain extent it is also Bulgakov's theatrical last will and testament.

To get the book's meaning, one needs to recognize the correlation between its imaginary world and the actual Moscow Art Theatre. Those Moscow Art actors who heard chapters of the unfinished manuscript read aloud at Bulgakov's, took the novel as an in-house joke. Some of them nagged the author to show "parts about me." Some enjoyed the playwright's ridicule of Stanislavsky's system as well as the irreverent spoofs of the powerful, dictatorial directors of the Moscow Art. But it was decades before anyone could see the book's higher purposes and its deeper social critique.

The question of who is whom in the novel is not an idle one. Pavel Markov, then a legendary Moscow Art dramaturg and prototype for Misha Panin, the master of the "Analytical Office," drew up a key to the book's cast of characters in the form of a theatre program. The author's widow, Elena Bulgakova, impatient with such primitive interpretations, also gathered materials for eventual reviewers of the novel. In addition to confirming several obvious equivalencies (Ivan Vasilievich = Stanislavsky; Aristarkh Platonovich = Nemirovich-Danchenko), she prepared some important notes on correlations between the novel and the artistic and theatrical environment to which Bulgakov belonged, but in which he was regarded as an enemy.

It is important to know the prototypes, but I'll risk going farther by confirming important similarities between the Moscow Art Theatre as it existed in the thirties and the fictional theatre we encounter in the *Diary of a Dead Man*. Both the celebrated theatre and its satirical counterpart are correctly characterized by a stone deafness to what was going on outside the institutional walls. The animosity between its two leaders was also real enough, and at the actual Moscow Art their rivalry took ugly and grotesque forms. The satirical and real theatre had both lost touch with real life, and this is accurately portrayed by an Ivan Vasilievich, locked in the comfortable prison of his mansion. Behind all these images we see clearly the destiny of the Russian theatre. In the end, Bulgakov's ironically named Independent Theatre, utterly dependent despite its name, represents everything institutional in the Soviet Union. The backstage atmosphere, so perfectly captured by Bulgakov, is as poisoned as the historical moment: fear and desperation are everywhere in the new empire, and the theatre of Ivan Vasilievich and Aristarkh Platonovich was destined to serve as a decorative façade for the Soviet empire.

Diary of a Dead Man is a book about assassinated laughter, about an unborn, new theatre residing in the playwright's soul. The biographical explanation of the story, reflecting the author's break with Stanislavsky during rehearsals of *Molière*, can be extended from his personal experience to the portrayal of a fate common to all. Bulgakov's unfinished novel was about the man and the artist who sensed the truth but could not expose it to the people: ". . . and meanwhile I saw, I realized, that the play would then cease to exist. But it must not cease to exist, because I knew it carried the truth." This passage begins the development of a major conflict. The truth that was apparent to the author could not be forced on the world by his efforts alone. In *The Theatre Novel* Maksudov takes his play to the Independent Theatre, an institution that, while exhibiting the usual follies inherent in any theatre, also represents all the characteristic features of a totalitarian society.

The author's attitude toward his fellow theatre people is tragic affection. The truth cannot be expressed without these people, regardless of what they are beyond the glare of the spotlight. No truth can find expression without the laughter and tears of a thousand audience members filling the house. "I returned to the theatre, without which I couldn't live, much as a morphine addict returns to morphine." Elsewhere, Maksudov says: "Exhausted by my affection for the Independent Theatre, pinned to it like a beetle to a cork, I continued to go see its performances at night." The latter of these two merciless metaphors marks the end of the manuscript.

In the autumn of 1937, Bulgakov stopped working on the novel. We will never hear Maksudov's final objection to Ivan Vasilievich's theory on an actor's transformation. We will never read about the opening night of *Black Snow*, if there was one. Whatever happiness Bulgakov was able to experience in life and express in his art remained unknown for the hero of *Diary of a Dead Man*. Neither Maksudov nor Bulgakov was given a chance to make it to the opening night. Neither saw his truthful visions come into the world.

THOSE THE RIVER KEEPS

David Rabe: From Hurlyburly to Those the River Keeps
Interview by David Edelstein

Asked about an incident to which the characters in his new drama, *Those the River Keeps*, refer, David Rabe shrugs and quotes the characters themselves. "That's all they say about it," he adds in his soft, uninflected voice, "so I assume that's all there is." When reminded that he wrote the play and crafted those characters' lines, he seems puzzled. Yes, he replies, he wrote it, but that doesn't mean he knows more about his characters' lives than they do.

If Rabe were any other kind of playwright, you might think his response a goofy, Pirandellian affectation. But a look at his plays— among them *The Basic Training of Pavlo Hummel, Sticks and Bones, Streamers,* and *Hurlyburly*—suggests that this, indeed, is how he creates: Rabe sets up a dramatic situation and then allows his characters to take him over—groping and staggering and cursing their way to a volcanic finale.

You believe his response because of how his characters talk— run-on sentences that pile clause upon clause, then double back on themselves like an amusement park head-scrambler. Much of the thrill is that everything seems unpremeditated.

"The language is an instinctive thing that I trust," says Rabe. "I don't quite know what I'm doing. It comes and I welcome it, and I try to learn from it. I guess anybody who writes knows that your unconscious has to furnish a lot."

Those the River Keeps, like all Rabe's forays into his own unconscious, evolved gradually and mysteriously. A.R.T. literary director Robert Scanlan has noted that the first drafts of Rabe plays seem like "huge spiral nebulae of material that only slowly cluster into gravitational fields." Once the play arrives on *terra firma*, Rabe studies what he has and then explains what it's about to himself. "It's as though I look at the play and do a kind of think piece about how I interpret it," he says.

The rumblings of the unconscious are, in fact, the subject of *Those the River Keeps*. The odd title refers to victims of gangland hits. Before a corpse is tossed into the river, the belly is slit open so that gases won't bloat the corpse and send it floating to the surface. But the title also hints at the inner life of Phil, the gangster-turned-character-actor whose attempt to repress his violent past and make a new life in Hollywood with his young wife, Suzy, is shattered by a visit from Sal, a former East Coast pal and fellow belly-slitter.

"In order to live," says Rabe, Phil has "forgotten" his past: "He struggles to find a way to say, 'I didn't do it: my circumstance did it, my doppelganger did it.' I think all of us separate ourselves from our past crimes—lesser crimes or even worse crimes. Hidden away in Phil's unconscious are emotions that are quaking and shaking and starting to break open about what he did.

"That's how all of us live, with this whole unconscious government of our lives, large chunks being directed by something we've completely forgotten. And what this play is about is an incredible, unconscious displacement and struggle and then finally an acceptance."

Phil began life as a character in Rabe's *Hurlyburly*, a Hollywood tale of anomie and drug abuse that many consider Rabe's masterpiece. Yet there were problems with director Mike Nichols's 1984 Broadway production, despite an all-star cast that included William Hurt, Christopher Walken, Harvey Keitel, and Sigourney Weaver. Rabe has made no secret that he detested the production—that it drove him, in fact, to directing his plays himself. "In order to understand how what had happened happened," he says, "I sat and sort of deconstructed the production for months. I was in agony. It was a humiliating experience, and the fact that there were thousands of people coming in to see it only made it worse. That made it worse. . . ."

Rabe adds that, for what it was, the Broadway production was skillfully done. But it reversed his intentions. In Rabe's script, the protagonist, Eddie, is flanked by two chums, Phil and Mickey. Phil is a chaotic blowhard who behaves with passionate intensity; Mickey is a smart-aleck cynic who has made peace with Hollywood and disapproves of Eddie's affection for Phil. Although Rabe doesn't exactly endorse Phil's whacked-out and abusive behavior, he clearly prefers the ex-gangster to Mickey, who represents the ultimate corruption.

But in the Broadway production, with much of Phil's part cut and Eddie an addled, coked-out mess, Mickey emerged as the *raisonneur*. "It took a very bourgeois, middle-class point-of-view," says Rabe, "in which this kind of behavior is automatically to be condemned no matter what the circumstances. The drugs, the whatever—there's no context for it. It eliminated the context, it made the play about the kind of crippled soul that sometimes compels people to that behavior. It took Mickey, who is in my view Iago, and made him the voice of reason. There's no drama, there's no action—it's dead."

Rabe reworked and then directed the play, to considerable acclaim, in Los Angeles in 1998, with a cast that included Sean Penn and, as Phil, Danny Aiello. He wanted to sketch out what happened before and between the scenes of *Hurlyburly*.

Rabe disagrees with those who say a playwright should never direct his own work. "There's always people who say you can't learn how to cut or structure your own play," he says. "But you can. You need another person there, you need a very good dramaturg or assistant, you have to have someone to talk to. But the pressure—that's another question. There is a moment when as the playwright you simply want to flee, and as the director, you can't. It doesn't matter how well it's going, you just want out."

Rabe talks of someday thinking a play through before he writes it—premeditating it. But one doubts he'd be happy with so safe a way of working. He still talks about the last act of *Hurlyburly*, in which, after Phil was gone, the other characters began to babble and free-associate and explain their friend's destiny in terms of anagrams.

"I had no idea what they were going to come up with, it was just amazing," Rabe says. "That kind of stuff I thrive on as a writer. The moment in the work when something comes up that I never would have dreamed of."

Henry IV
by David Bevington

Why today do we find the story of a fourteenth- and fifteenth-century prince of England so gripping? Surely not because of the history itself, however much we may have been taught in school about the kings of England. The issues of royal succession and of loyalty to the monarchy seem distant to us in our democratic world. And yet *Henry IV, Parts I and 2*, are great plays. A good part of their appeal has to do with fathers and sons, with generational conflict, with the rival claims of the public and private spheres, and with civil war.

This A.R.T. production, directed by Ron Daniels, makes its point about generational conflict and civil strife by contrasting two familiar worlds: the American Civil War of the mid-nineteenth century and our current world of punk rock and Los Angeles riots. One (expressing the world of the aging king, Henry IV) is an older, more traditional society of stern authoritarianism and a nation divided against itself; the other (that of young Prince Hal) is a mad world of youthful rebellion, drugs, sexual permissiveness, and the exploration of pluralistic values. These contrasting theatrical fictions are technically distant from the immediacies of Shakespeare's history, but they capture what Shakespeare does so well: they see into the universality of his depiction of generational and civil strife and allow us as audience to place these conflicts in the context of our own recent experience as a nation.

Shakespeare's text gives us many signals of his interest in generational difference. At the start of the play, Henry IV is an old and even frightened man. He has seized the English throne from his first cousin, Richard II, in an act that violated the English (unwritten) constitution, thereby fueling divided loyalties between Henry's followers and those still loyal to the dead Richard's memory. But his doing so was at first a popular coup. Richard had governed so

Bill Camp (Prince Hal) and Jeremy Geidt (Falstaff) in *Henry IV, Part I*.

irresponsibly that his people, and especially his nobles, could put up with no more, so they backed his rival cousin. Yet now, as *Henry IV, Part I* gets under way, King Henry IV is caught in open-ended war—a guerrilla war, really. The Scots attack Henry in the north, and the Welsh, led by the charismatic bandit Glendower, attack him in the west. Worst of all, Lord Mortimer, assigned the task of fighting the Welsh, has been captured and has married Glendower's daughter.

We stand at the beginning of a century of civil war between two Lancastrians, Henry's faction and the Yorkists. Mortimer, by descent and marriage, is King Henry's rival claimant. He is related by marriage, moreover, to Henry Percy, the "Hotspur" of *Henry IV, Part I*, and thus to the formidable Percy clan that originally sided with Henry against Richard II but has now turned against him.

What is Henry to do? He resents and suspects the Percys, most of all the Duke of Worcester. Mortimer's marriage to Glendower's daughter confirms his worst fears. But does not Henry's harsh way of attempting to put down the insurrection, by banishing Worcester and refusing to discuss the matter, escalate rather than soothe animosities? Hotspur, the wonderfully outspoken young warrior with whom Henry quarrels over the ransoming of prisoners of war, quickly learns from his family that King Henry is not to be trusted. The Percys have their reasons to fear that Henry is banishing them from political influence and that all they did to help him to the throne will lead to nothing, or worse than nothing.

Shakespeare's sympathies in this civil tug-of-war are wonderfully balanced. As we see in this A.R.T. production, there are no "good guys" and "bad guys" but a vastly more interesting and convincing portrayal of political difference in which both sides, considering first and foremost their own political interests, have some truth on their side and also bear some responsibility for a breakdown in negotiations. The stalemate leads to a civil war that no one really wants and that will be immensely costly in lives and material goods, but which no one seems able to stop.

Meantime, King Henry also has huge problems with his son, Prince Hal. This young man has developed a reputation as a wastrel, a prodigal son. He idles with an old, fat rogue named Falstaff, a man so irresponsible that he is perennially one step ahead of the sheriff. He does in fact rob, and his friends are accomplished highwaymen. What is Hal doing in his company? Hal is persuaded to go on one of Falstaff's robbing expeditions, and gold is taken, even if Hal then turns the escapade into a practical joke by robbing Falstaff of the stolen gold and returning it to its rightful owner.

Once again, however, Shakespeare's presentation is complex and multidimensional in its sympathies. Falstaff is a robber, a moocher, a breaker of promises, and a liar on an epic scale, but he also possesses a *joie de vivre* that Hal can find nowhere but at the tavern. In every way Falstaff is the opposite of Hal's father: irresponsible, childish, ebullient, infectiously funny, outrageous. Falstaff is also the antithesis of Hotspur, Hal's opposite number, the Percy leader whose fanaticism and belief in family honor contrast at every turn with Falstaff's laid-back irony and skeptical notion about honor. ("What is honor? A word. What is the word 'honor'? What is that 'honor'? Air.") Hal, brooding over his role as heir to the English throne, finds Falstaff's company wonderfully useful and congenial, not just as release from the constraints of court formality and a joyless father-son relationship but as a means of trying out various roles. As king-to-be, he needs to know how to be all things to all people. It is no coincidence that he and Falstaff love play-acting, for Hal is trying on various identities to see what kind of king he might eventually be.

The second play, *Henry IV, Part 2*, turns to darker values on both personal and political fronts. The rebellion continues, but in a dispiriting way. The ending is a triumph of Realpolitik—neither an unambiguously good thing nor a bad thing but a fact of history often repeated. "The old order changeth, yielding place to new" (As Tennyson put it), and part of the new order is to value practical self-interest over more traditional claims of honor. As the English nation struggles to know itself through civil conflict, it moves inevitably toward the pragmatic, the matter of fact, and away from the chivalric. Falstaff too grows darker as a figure, less in Hal's company, more of a political liability, more of an embarrassment. The once and future king discovers finally what he must have known all along, that being monarch is not compatible with rousting in the tavern or on the highways near Gad's Hill. Falstaff is expendable, a painful loss to Hal. In the conflict of generations, young men grow up to replace their fathers only to discover that older responsibilities bring new demands of role-playing. At the end of *Henry IV, Part 2*, Hal stands ready to be king of England.

SHLEMIEL THE FIRST

The Journey of Shlemiel the First: "All Roads Lead to Chelm"
by Heather Lindsley

The Origin of Shlemiel the First

In the course of a long and distinguished career, Isaac Bashevis Singer (1904–1991) wrote many tales for children featuring Shlemiel and the fools of Chelm. One of the earliest, "The First Shlemiel," appeared in Singer's 1966 collection, *Zlateh the Goat and Other Stories*. When Robert Brustein commissioned Singer in

1974 to write a play for the Yale Repertory Theatre, Singer built the world of *Shlemiel the First* around his fictions, filling in the basic plot of "When Shlemiel Went to Warsaw" (1968) with vividly drawn characters from his 1973 collection, *The Fools of Chelm and Their History.*

In the spring of 1993, while attending a concert of the Klezmer Conservatory Band, Brustein conceived of adapting Singer's various Shlemiel materials—both the stories and the play—into a musical featuring traditional klezmer music. The subsequent creative collaboration of Brustein, who fashioned Singer's several texts into a musical book; Hankus Netsky, who adapted traditional klezmer tunes and composed new ones wherever needed; Arnold Weinstein, who wrote the lyrics; director David Gordon, who helped guide and shape the story and the songs; and conductor Zalmen Mlotek, who helped develop the music, gradually brought *Shlemiel the First*, the musical, into being. The wedding of Isaac Bashevis Singer's rich folk material with the infectious energy of klezmer music brought together two powerful Jewish folkloric traditions.

As Hankus Netsky explained: "The music that is now known as klezmer is traditional Jewish Eastern European wedding music. The word *klezmer* is taken from the Hebrew words *kle* and *zomer*, meaning vessels of song, which is a biblical description of musicians. The term *klezmer* came into Yiddish when Jews in Western Europe started having their own troubadours in the Middle Ages to play dance music for Jewish celebrations. Most of the music in *Shlemiel the First* is Yiddish folk songs. I. B. Singer himself knew and liked klezmer. He wrote liner notes for a klezmer album in which he said that this music brought him back to his youth in Poland when *klezmorim* (or musicians) played at every celebration."

The Origin of Chelm

"There was no agreement among the scholars of Chelm on how the town came into existence. The pious believed that God said, 'Let there be Chelm.' And there was Chelm. But many scholars insisted that the town happened as the result of an eruption."

—*The Fools of Chelm and Their History*

At one time, there were at least three villages in Eastern Europe called Chelm (one about twenty miles west of the Ukrainian border

Members of the company in *Shlemiel the First*.

can still be found on a map of Poland today), but there is no conclusive evidence to connect any one of them with the Chelm of folklore.

The origin of Chelm in Yiddish folklore is equally difficult to pinpoint: stories about the fools of Chelm have been around for centuries, and in that time quite an array of stories and versions of stories have accumulated: some short and simple, others elaborate. All share the same theme—the foolishness of the inhabitants of Chelm. One story found in *A Treasury of Yiddish Stories* describes the origin of Chelm's foolishness this way:

> After God had created the universe and had proceeded to people its regions,
> He sent off an angel with two sacks filled with souls: one of them
> Held the souls of the wise, the other those of the slow-witted.
> Soaring thus over the terrestrial globe, the angel sowed the
> Souls in equal proportion: a handful of the wise, another of the
> Foolish. Thus did he distribute the souls, half and half, so that no
> Community might be given too many souls of one kind.
> But as the angel hovered over the region now known as

Chelm he suffered a mishap—one of his sacks caught on the very
Tip of a hill, spilling the souls it held into the place whose very name
Was to become a proverb.

Singer's tales of Chelm draw on the traditional stories but also differ from them. While most Chelm anecdotes focus on the activity of "a certain Chelmite" or "a citizen of Chelm," Singer's stories give us full characters with detailed lives. His Chelm is not populated with homogeneous fools but with specifically drawn individuals who managed to evoke both derision and compassion in their foolishness and innocence.

Singer's Magic

As with most enduring folktales and fairy tales, Singer's stories for children contain elements of darkness: demons, witches, rascals, war, poverty. Singer, however, departs from more traditional tales that contrast good and evil. He never assures us whether good or evil will dominate. As he said in 1963, "I make no rules: evil doesn't always triumph and it isn't always defeated. Once you establish a rule, it's against literature and against life."

In his use of good and evil, folklore, magic, and the world of fantasy, Singer reminds us that the world of children and the world of adults, though overlapping, are not the same. In his remarks in 1978 when he received the Nobel Prize for Literature, Singer gave several reasons why he writes for children. Among them:

Children read books, not reviews.

They love interesting stories, not commentary, guides, or footnotes.

When a book is boring, they yawn openly, without any shame or fear of authority.

They don't expect their beloved writer to redeem humanity. Young as they are, they know it is not in his power. Only adults have such childish illusions.

Adults, too, have their own world, which in many of Singer's works is created by closing doors and speaking in whispers. But in Singer's Chelm, we see adults with the naiveté of children and children with the wisdom of adults. Magic is in the air, and grim realities are just around the corner. Chelm lies at the intersection of fantasy and reality. And in Singer's geography—the geography of the imagination—all roads lead to Chelm.

Coming into the Light
by Robert Scanlan

Samuel Beckett wrote *Waiting for Godot* in Paris during the winter of 1948–1949. The play came to him in a rush of inspiration after he had completed the second of three novels on which he had been working since 1947. The great prose trilogy *Molloy, Malone Dies*, and the still-unwritten *The Unnameable* were destined to revolutionize prose fiction as completely as *Godot* transformed the theatre, and the writing of these voluminous novels took a great deal out of their author. Beckett, born and raised in Ireland, was writing exclusively in French in this important phase of his career, and when he turned his hand to the composition of stage dialogue, after hundreds and hundreds of handwritten pages of arduous prose, he experienced—as he put it himself—a great sense of relief. "I didn't choose to write a play, it just happened like that. I was in search of respite from the wasteland of prose. I wrote *Godot* to come into the light. I needed a habitable space, and I found it on the stage."

Waiting for Godot is indeed, a "relaxation," and, as such, a very playful work. Conceived from the beginning as a metaphysical clown show, *Waiting for Godot* was inspired by Beckett's memories of the great clowns of silent film—in particular Charlie Chaplin, Buster Keaton, and the mismatched pair Laurel and Hardy. But the clowning in Beckett's play is performed on a ground of despair, and this aspect of the play directly reflects its origins in the catastrophic upheavals of the Second World War.

Although much has been written over the years about the metaphysical overtones of *Waiting for Godot*, there are much closer parallels in the play to Beckett's war experiences than has generally been realized. Beckett was deeply involved in the French Resistance during the German Occupation, and the constant tension and coping strategies of hunted underground operatives is never far below the surface of the play. Beckett belonged to a Resistance cell in Paris that gathered military intelligence; transcribed, translated, and microfilmed this data; then smuggled it out of German-occupied areas for delivery by courier to the Allied command in England. This was extremely dangerous work, and the Nazi SS was on high alert to stem this flow of damaging intelligence. Whenever they caught Resistance

John Bottoms (Estragon) and Mark Linn-Baker (Vladimir) in *Waiting for Godot* (1982–1983).

workers, the Nazis tortured them relentlessly to obtain the names needed to crack their cells, then swiftly hunted down their victims' associates before they had time to change cover.

These circumstances led to a constant game of coded identities, mysterious drop-point rendezvous, and elaborate charades of evasion and escape. In *Waiting for Godot*, Vladimir and Estragon are under mysterious compulsion to wait by a lone tree until a certain Godot appears. They do not know him, cannot remember him clearly, and have no idea what will happen when he does appear, yet they have no other choice but to keep this appointment. So they wait, passing the time and relieving their anxiety as best they can.

In Beckett's case, the worst finally happened. In the summer of 1942 his Resistance cell (code-named Gloria) was betrayed to the Germans, and one of the arrested members broke down under torture and named names, among them Beckett's and that of his companion (later his wife) Suzanne Deschevaux-Dumesnil. Hunted now in earnest, but tipped off in the nick of time, they walked away from their apartment, taking nothing with them. They would not return until after the war, three years later. After a month spent hiding in Paris, they obtained forged papers and took a train to Lyons. From there they worked their way to the tiny Provençal village of Roussillon, traveling the last 150 miles of their journey mostly on foot, hiding during the daytime in barns, haystacks, or the woods and walking all night through open fields and along back roads. The country on Beckett's mind when he wrote *Waiting for Godot* is that that led him and Suzanne, exhausted by night after night of weary tramping, to Roussillon. It is not hard to imagine them tired, hungry, unbathed, catching only fitful daytime sleeps in makeshift shelters, and never free of the fear of being arrested. Of the eighty Resistance fighters in Gloria, only thirty made it through the war alive.

Once in Roussillon, Beckett lay low during the day, but at night he became involved again with the local *Maquisards*, clandestine French Resistance operatives who harassed German patrols, sabotaged transportation and communication links, and circulated military intelligence. On several occasions during these years, Beckett delivered documents to prearranged drop points, and it is not hard to correlate Vladimir and Estragon's enigmatic appointment in *Waiting for Godot* to Beckett's wartime rendezvous with code-named *Marquisards* along isolated country roads in the Vaucluse region, which is repeatedly alluded to in the play. Beckett characterized these efforts years later as "Boy Scout stuff," and no doubt he was conscious of the vast disparity between such scattered rearguard actions and the massive combat achievements and casualties among those who really fought the war. Nevertheless he was awarded a *Croix de Guerre* after the war in recognition of his courageous loyalty.

Waiting for Godot does not represent these experiences in any literal sense, but its imagery—and, more important, the states of mind it suggests—derive from these experiences. All those who endured the war in Europe emerged transformed, and they had great difficulty expressing the magnitude of their inner tumult. When Beckett stumbled onto the inspiration to write this play, he released some of the pent-up energies of his generation. In so doing he expressed permanent insights into the human condition *in extremis*.

The first wave of critical response to the play associated it with the postwar Parisian intellectual movement loosely labeled existentialism. In the 1950s the play was seen as a parable of man's fate in an absurd and godless universe, where the void surrounding human destiny left individual actions without moral reference and therefore with no fixed meaning. Jean-Paul Sartre and Albert Camus were the leading figures of this movement, but despite the speculations of early critics, Beckett had nothing to do with them. In fact, Beckett was never comfortable with any association of his work with existentialism (or any other movement, political or aesthetic). He frustrated his critics by refusing to discuss the play and by giving no hint of any hidden or allegorical meanings.

This silence left critics free to speculate wildly about the play, and learned exegetes knocked themselves out trying to interpret the significance of Godot. Was it an allusion to God? Or did Beckett have the famous bicycle racer Godeau in mind? There was, after all, an amusing story about a crowd of bicycle-race enthusiasts who, having missed their champion when he went by, stood waiting expectantly along a country road long after the race was finished. When someone asked them what they were waiting for, they replied, *"On attend Godeau."* ("We are waiting for Godeau.") Beckett laughed when he first heard this story, but it was long after he had written the play.

Another critic was certain he had cracked the code when he discovered a character named Godeau in the play *Mercadet* by Balzac. Godeau was central to this 1838 melodrama, but, though his arrival was eagerly anticipated by all the characters in the play (he owed them all money), he never actually appeared onstage. Again, Beckett had no knowledge of this antecedent when he wrote *Waiting for Godot*, and he urged those who badgered him with questions not to search too far afield for recondite explanations of his play. He told Alan Schneider (the first American director), "If I knew who Godot was, I would have said so in the play."

Still, it is significant for Americans to know that Beckett always pronounced the name "Godot" in the Irish fashion, as "God-oh," such that it sounded like a diminutive or derisive version of "God," and he went further in referring several of us who discussed the play with him to the seventeenth-century Catholic philosopher Arnold Geulincx. The scholar Martha Fehsenfeld followed up these leads, and she discovered in the Latin works of the obscure Belgian theologian (in particular his treatise *Ethica*) passages that are deeply in tune with *Waiting for Godot* and have nothing to do with the existentialism of the 1950s.

The first line of *Waiting for Godot* foreshadows the whole action of the play: "Nothing to be done." It is also a significant echo of a passage near the beginning of Geulincx's *Ethica*, which Beckett greatly admired and frequently quoted in Latin: *"Ubi nihil vales. . . ."*

Jeremy Geidt
(Vladimir) and Alvin
Epstein (Estragon)
in *Waiting for Godot*
(1994–1995).

Here is Professor Ronald Begley's translation of this sentence and succeeding passage in Geulincx:

> Where you can do nothing, there wish nothing . . . or in other words, nothing is to be done for naught . . . it follows that if nothing ought to be done in vain, one ought not to struggle against God's calling us and releasing us from the human condition . . . this is the first obligation: to accept death and make no effort to elude it. One ought also not to struggle against God's bidding us still to live, detaining us in the human condition . . . this is the second obligation: to accept life and make no effort to escape from it.

Geulincx goes on to specify seven ethical obligations, all of them far more germane to the action of *Waiting for Godot* than any existentialist maxims about being and nothingness. Each of Geulincx's seven obligations is meticulously enacted by Vladimir and Estragon in some passage of the play, and the overall action of waiting, of fulfilling the obligation to be there, at the appointed place, at the appointed time, as specified by the unanswerable Godot, is analogous to the two obligations expressed above. In another passage in the *Ethica*, Geulincx is even more explicit about the nature of mankind's fundamental obligation to God: "My second obligation is not to go unless called and not to leave my station—my post in life—without a summons from the highest Commander."

Martha Fehsenfeld, in her book *Beckett in the Theatre*, juxtaposes this passage to the trademark exchange between Beckett's Didi and Gogo:

GOGO: Let's go
DIDI: We can't
GOGO: Why not?
DIDI: We're waiting for Godot.
GOGO: Ah!

Beckett, of course, is devastatingly ironic, skeptical, and disbelieving where Geulincx is devout. Godot is so obviously an allusion to God that he felt it unseemly to elaborate it further. At a famous point in Act II, Vladimir says (again in a deflating, ironic context) ". . . at this place, at this moment of time, all mankind is us." And a large proportion of mankind in Beckett's time has found itself deeply mirrored by this endlessly disappointed waiting. Godot can stand for any light we choose to imagine at the end of the tunnel.

As they help each other wait, Vladimir and Estragon witness the awful spectacle of Pozzo and Lucky, a master/slave pair who present a very different image of human relations. Didi and Gogo care intensely for each other, in classical biblical fashion: each is his brother's keeper. But Posso has brutally enslaved the hapless Lucky, and this most abject of stage creatures (played in the first Broadway production in 1956 by Alvin Epstein) is famous for his delivery of one of the longest (and hardest to memorize) speeches in the theatre. Lucky's tirade is barely comprehensible in performance, but its apparent gibberish, when stripped of all its stutterings, digressions, nonsense citations, and groping repetitions, is a single stark sentence that leaves little doubt about Beckett's vision in the play: "Given the existence of a personal God who loves us dearly and suffers with those who are plunged in torment, it is established beyond all doubt that man wastes and pines, wastes and pines . . . the skull fading fading fading."

To build a comedy on such a vision is a *tour de force* indeed, and therein lies the perennial appeal and challenge of this play. The spectacle of "all mankind's" capacity to endure, to meet with courage, humility, and humor the awful obligations of existence, is indeed a "coming into the light."

Body and Soul: Naomi Wallace's Slaughter City
by Gideon Lester

He is a beef-boner, and that is a dangerous trade, especially when you are on piecework and trying to earn a bride. Your hands are slippery, and your knife is slippery, and you are toiling like mad, when somebody happens to speak to you, or you strike a bone. Then your hand slips up on the blade, and there is a fearful gash. And that would not be so bad, only for the deadly contagion. The cut may heal, but you never can tell. There are learned people who can tell you out of the statistics that beef-boners make forty cents an hour, but, perhaps these people have never looked into a beef-boner's hands.

—Upton Sinclair, *The Jungle*

Upton Sinclair's novel of the slaughterhouse, *The Jungle*, was first published ninety years ago. We like to believe that our enlightened age yields little shelter for the "moral, spiritual and physical degradation" that Sinclair sought to expose, but as recently as three years ago, conditions as bad as anything described in *The Jungle* were discovered in a reputable meat-processing plant in Louisville, Kentucky. A young worker had died after inhaling ammonia fumes, and the employees of Fischer's Packing Company decided to blow the whistle on the inhuman environment in which they were forced to work. In *Slaughter City*, poet and playwright Naomi Wallace vividly brings to life the story of their struggles, both public and personal.

Ms. Wallace talked to Fischer's employees as they stood on strike outside the factory near her father's Kentucky home. "I drove past the picket lines every day," she recalls, "and started to wonder what kind of lives those people must lead, working with knives all day, blood up to their ankles." Their eyewitness accounts of life inside the slaughterhouses form the basis for almost all the episodes in the play. "I told the strikers that I was interested in their stories," says Wallace, "and they let me interview them. For a long while I had been interested in the violence such an industry inflicts on the human body. Meatpacking is now even more dangerous than coal mining; the longer people work there, the more their bodies are broken by the labor. I asked the striking workers whether any of them had been hurt on the job, and each of them showed me a cut on their hands, a missing finger, or the scar from an operation."

Wallace regards the relationship between organized labor and the individual body as the central subject of *Slaughter City*. "We live in an economic system that uses up the body and throws it away," she says. "We work with our bodies, but we also live, love, have sex in them. There are still few protections for these vessels we live our lives in. We tend to see the workplace as disconnected from our intimate lives, but if you lose your fingers or develop carpal tunnel syndrome, that affects the way you touch your lover or hold your children. I wanted to make those connections between our daily lives and lovings."

This tension between the two spheres of existence in *Slaughter City* first drew director Ron Daniels to Wallace's work. "It's a public play set in a public place," he says, "which at the same time allows the individual's fantasy life to express itself. These two struggles, public and private, make it Shakespearean." The play derives great power, Daniels believes, from the tenacity of its political stance. "In an age when the left has been demoralized by the traumas of Hungary, Czechoslovakia, Berlin, and finally the Soviet Union, it's refreshing to have Naomi embracing the search for justice and struggle for the poor, the helpless, the maimed."

Wallace spent considerable time researching the historical and social background of *Slaughter City*, as she does with all her plays. "I need to know the history of the period I'm dramatizing," she says. "I couldn't write about the meat-packing industry before I'd studied it from the nineteenth century onward; I've even included a bibliography with the published text of *Slaughter City*." According to Daniels, who directed the American premiere of *Slaughter City* for A.R.T., descriptions of Packingtown in *The Jungle* formed an important source for Wallace. "The images are violent, and Naomi wanted to create a world that is a hell." Wallace also cites as inspirational the work of Peter Rachleff, author of *Hard-Pressed in the Heartland: The Hormel Strike and the Future of the Labor Movement*. Rachleff himself regards Wallace as "one of the most important playwrights at work today," and finds in the play an original approach to labor history. "For Wallace," he says, "personal liberation and social liberation are indissoluble, and it's in the quest for them that utopian possibility becomes imaginable—and attainable—by a working class that has been historically divided by race, gender, and sexual orientation."

Ron Daniels first directed *Slaughter City* for the Royal Shakespeare Company. The London critics were struck by the energy of Wallace's play and praised the delicate counterpoint it traces between public and private events: the social disturbances in the factory and the increasingly tender relationships of the four central characters. In *The Guardian*, Michael Billington wrote, "The play has passion, poetry, and a wild strangeness. Running through it is the Whitmanesque idea that sexual and economic liberation are inseparable. And Ron Daniels's production is astonishingly successful at welding them together."

Like Wallace's other plays, *In the Heart of America* and *One Flea Spare, Slaughter City* tests the limits of dramatic structure and form. It was only when he reached the rehearsal room that Daniels recognized the innovations of Wallace's style. "The play begins in a Brechtian, epic mold," he says, "then suddenly skids in different directions. It seems to veer away from itself. It's not written by someone who is interested in linear development but by a poet. Naomi is interested in textures, in the fabric of human life, with its contradictions, surprises, and obstacles."

Wallace sees in her work a dialogue with the classical paradigm of dramatic structure. "I used to believe that the Aristotelian arc was a reactionary form. I disliked the notion of *catharsis*, that at the end of the evening we could all go home and feel much better. By now, I've seen so many plays with radical form that are as reactionary as they come that I no longer believe that radical structure alone can give voice to radical politics. I now like to work both with and against the form of Aristotelian drama."

As a poet who writes for the theatre, Wallace sees as her greatest challenge the development of "a language so visual that it becomes a physical being on stage." "Today," she says, "we're always told that theatre should show rather than tell. Theatre is such a visual medium that it's easy to forget the importance of language on stage. Somewhere in each of my plays you'll find a monstrous monologue that you think should never work, but once it's spoken through the actor it takes on a dramatic life of its own."

The violence and horror of Wallace's work are usually associated with naturalistic playwriting, but *Slaughter City* never strays far from the realms of metaphor and symbolism. Anticipating the films of Quentin Tarentino by almost a century, Sinclair argued in *The Jungle* that violence and poetry are fundamentally related: "It was like some horrible crime committed in a dungeon, all unseen and unheeded, buried out of sight and of memory. One could not stand and watch very long without becoming philosophical, without beginning to deal in symbols and similes, and to hear the hog squeal of the universe."

THE NAKED EYE

Shock Art
by Paul Rudnick

The Naked Eye was inspired by my attendance at the opening of a Mapplethorpe exhibit of highly erotic art at a Manhattan gallery a few years back. Upper East Side socialites mingled with downtown, black-clad *artistes*, amid a feverishly blasé assortment of editors, critics, art dealers, and cabernet-clutching wannabees. Everyone gossiped and nibbled canapés in the most sophisticated fashion, all the while standing in front of enormous photographs of erect penises, heavily pierced S&M couples, and extreme close-ups of some exhaustively imaginative sex acts. This combination of social behavior, shock art, and the specter of censorship struck me as a ripe field for rambunctious satire.

My idols have always been Oscar Wilde, for his perversely elegant wit, and Charles Ludlam, the founder of the Ridiculous Theatre Company, for his deliciously low comedy, his triumphant embrace of gender-crazed burlesque. In *The Naked Eye* I have tried to blend, or perhaps collide, social commentary with all-out farce. The story focuses on Nan Bemiss, the well-bred, Chanel-wearing wife of a Republican presidential nominee. The candidate is set to appear at the high-profile opening-night gala of a museum retrospective, featuring the work of the notorious photographer Alex Del Flavio. Nan is dispatched to Alex's studio to persuade him to remove three of the exhibit's most extreme pictures, including the fearsome *Number 15*. When Alex asks Nan to describe this portrait, she says, "It's a composition in light and dark. It's a powerful statement on American repression. It's a witty essay in erotica. It's a penis, it's a big, huge black penis!"

Needless to say, Alex [the protagonist of *The Naked Eye*] resists all attempts at censoring his work, not so much out of noble artistic integrity as from glorious careerism. He tells Nan that he lusts for "an uptown event with downtown cachet," complete with "5,000 trumpet lilies fresh today from the Philippines" and a platinum guest list. Nan and Alex do battle, augmented by Alex's assistant Mumbali, a hard-core lesbian activist with a pathological aversion to bad French, and Nan's daughter Sissy, a post-deb fretting over the plight of "the second homeless—where's their place at the beach?" The play's second act takes place at the gala, at the grandly postmodern Civil Central Museum, and includes the arrival of Nan's husband Pete, giddy from a primary landslide, and Pete's mistress Lynette, a *Playboy* centerfold with an addiction to aging, powerful men.

The Naked Eye explores the power and value of shock in art and elsewhere; as Alex commands a heartsick Nan, "Do something you can never take back. Shock your life." I have tried to find both the comic flaws and the surprising virtues in all the characters; I desperately wanted to avoid writing a partisan tract, a do-goody liberal ode to art and freedom. Artists can be every ounce as venal and ambitious as Republicans, and Republicans can, at the very least, mix a decent cocktail. At one point in the action, Nan confronts Alex: "Excuse me! Do you think there's some sort of cosmic trade-off? Do you think that God says to all Republicans, yes, I'll give you wealth and power in exchange for your libido? Do you think that homosexuals and minorities have a monopoly on the orgasm?" To which Alex replies, "Of course. It's our golf."

I wanted to see if I could write a comedy that was no holds barred. I didn't want any character or special-interest group to be sacred because I think political correctness is an enemy of comedy. I believe if there is a political platform that can be destroyed by humor, then it wasn't very strong to begin with. I'm interested in celebrating absurdity. Comedy is my personal God.

Mr. Rudnick's comments have been excerpted from an A.R.T. News *interview by Shawn René Graham.*

David Mamet: It's Never Easy to Go Back
Interview by Arthur Holmberg

Q: The copyrights on the three plays in *The Old Neighborhood* are seven years apart. "The Disappearance of the Jews" is copyrighted 1982, and the other two, "Jolly" and "D.," are copyrighted 1989. What is it about the character of Bobby Gould that after seven years you wanted to go back and explore him again?

DAVID MAMET: I have no idea. I just came across it, and I don't really know anything more than that.

Q: You came across "The Disappearance of the Jews," and you decided to explore further Bobby's attempt to return home?

DM: That's right.

Q: And you put the three plays together in one evening because they established a dialogue among one another?

DM: I think so.

Q: You have said many times in many different contexts that drama is the quest of the protagonist for a single goal. What is Bobby Gould's goal in *The Old Neighborhood*?

DM: He's attempting to close out some unfinished business.

Q: What would that unfinished business be?

DM: Well, if I tell you, then you're going to tell the subscribers, and then they're not going to come to the theatre.

Q: Although they both try, neither Bob Gold in *Homicide* nor Bobby Gould in *The Old Neighborhood* seems to be able to find a meaningful way to be Jewish in the United States. Why do they fail?

DM: Because they're Jewish in the United States.

Q: You're saying it's impossible to be Jewish in the United States?

DM: No, it's not impossible to be Jewish, but it's difficult to be Jewish and come to grips with it. This problem is explored in the plays.

Q: You said once, and this is a direct quote, that theatre is a place of recognition; it's where we show ethical exchange. What would you say is the recognition, the ethical exchange, in *The Old Neighborhood*?

DM: Well, it's something very gentle, perhaps on the order of one can't go home again, or perhaps not. I don't know. I hope the audience enjoys it. It's an unusual form. It would be too grand to call it a trilogy, but it's something trilological. Three explorations of the same theme, which make the evening partake of the dramatic, I hope, and also of the epic. Other than that, I just hope the audience has a good time.

Q: I'm surprised by the word "epic."

DM: I am too, but I think that's what it is.

Q: Epic because there's more at stake than just this one character, because there is a whole social and historical panorama sketched in behind him?

DM: Yes, there is certainly that dynamic in the play. The guy went away and came back, and everyone else has stayed.

Q: Like Orestes, who comes home after being in exile for many years. You've been writing plays since your last year in college—for almost thirty years now. What evolution do you see in your career as a playwright?

DM: I've started writing tragedies. The last couple of plays that I did at the A.R.T., *The Cryptogram* and *Oleanna*, were tragedies—classically structured tragedies, which I'd written a couple of before, and they're much, much more challenging, and much more rewarding to write.

Q: What were the tragedies before *The Cryptogram* and *Oleanna*?

DM: *American Buffalo* and *The Woods*.

Q: Why do you find them more challenging and more rewarding? And how would you classify the other plays you've written?

DM: Some of the others were gang comedies.

Q: *Glengarry Glen Ross*?

DM: Yes.

Q: You call that a gang comedy?

DM: Yes, or a gang drama.

Q: And *The Old Neighborhood*, what would you call that?

DM: I don't know what it is. What would you call it?

Q: Like *The Cryptogram* it differs from most of your earlier work with the exception of *Reunion*. *Reunion* explores the same territory. First, they're about families and the search for a family and a home. Also, the tone is gentler and more nostalgic and yearning. The issues they explore are also more personal. But to get back to your career. You've had an astonishing career in theatre and film. What has surprised you the most about your career?

DM: That it all went so quickly.

Q: In "D.," the third segment of *The Old Neighborhood*, there is a wonderful passage in which the woman says, "Oh, yes. (Pause) I never knew what you wanted. (Pause) I thought I knew. (Pause) I thought that I knew. (Pause) Finally. (Pause) And I said, they say there's going to be a frost." It's a beautifully written passage. There are many such pauses throughout *The Old Neighborhood*. Like Pinter and Beckett, you use pauses to great dramatic purpose. But your pauses are different than Pinter's and Beckett's, and I wondered if you could say something about how and why you use pauses and silence.

DM: It's just a rhythmic device. It's like a rest. You know, if you take a rest out of any composer's work, the work's going to sound very different.

Q: One of the great tragedies of American theatre is that playwrights, after they write one or two good plays, often go to Hollywood, on the one hand, or simply fail to develop. It's sad to see young playwrights who don't sustain a career in the theatre. You have managed for almost thirty years not only to write good plays but to develop as a playwright and constantly add colors to your palette. Why have you been able to sustain a creative output in theatre for thirty years?

DM: For the first ten years I was writing, I was represented by the William Morris Agency in New York. They couldn't get me a job. So I kept on writing, and it got to be a habit.

Q: But you can get jobs now, and you still continue to write.

DM: Well, it's a habit, you know.

Q: And not only do you write plays, but you write novels, you write film scripts, you write poetry, you write essays. Could you say something about how the use of language differs when you write these different genres?

DM: I probably could, but not unless I'd had a couple more hours of sleep.

Q: You once defined technique as the breaking down of barriers between the unconscious and the conscious mind.

DM: No, I said that the *purpose* of technique is to break down the barriers between the conscious and the unconscious mind.

Q: Could you tell me exactly what you mean by "technique"?

DM: The purpose of any technique, the purpose of any skill that is learned through cognition and repetition in the arts or in sports for that matter, is to break down the barriers between the conscious

David Mamet during a rehearsal of his play *The Old Neighborhood*, with Jack Willis and Brooke Adams.

and the unconscious mind so that you don't have to think about what you're doing. You can only be free if your unconscious is unfettered. There are a lot of people who don't have technique but whose unconscious is unfettered: children, psychotics, some artists. But for most of us, we need a technique to enable us to get out of our own way.

Q: Could you give me an example, so that I know exactly what you mean by a writing technique?

DM: No. But I could give you an example of a sports technique. You practice putting. You practice it over and over.

Q: So in terms of a playwright, it would mean that you write over and over, so that the techniques of what makes a good line, what makes a good rhythm, what makes a good scene is so automatic that it frees you to be able to let the unconscious seep into the sentence, the rhythm, the scene?

DM: I think so. Somebody intelligent said, and it might have been Bob Brustein as a matter of fact, that the way you write a good play is that you write a lot of plays.

Q: In a very beautiful essay on Tennessee Williams, you said that he had an impact on you but only very late in your career. What kind of impact?

DM: A wonderful, wonderful writer. He's a lyric poet. He was such a good structuralist that his plays sustained the poetry. The poetry and the drama give life to each other.

Q: How did being raised in Chicago affect your writing? Do people in Chicago talk differently from people in, say, New York?

DM: Yes.

Q: How would you define that difference?

DM: I don't know if I could define it.

Q: But you hear it.

DM: I was just on the West Coast, and I was hanging around with Joey Mantegna, whom I hadn't seen for a while, and just to hear the rhythms and cadences of the old speech, of the old country, it made me smile. It was wonderful to hear that.

Q: You frequently mention Beckett and Pinter as influences. How did they influence you in terms of dramatic technique?

DM: Well they're great. They're stunning geniuses. I mean, the revelations of one and then the other, and Pinter, of course, as a writer in his own and also as an inheritor of Beckett. That's the revelation of twentieth-century drama. You can apply the Aristotelian unities to a microcosm, to a very, very small human interchange. You can take it apart. It didn't have to be about conquering France. It can be about who did or did not turn on the gas on the stove.

Q: You often talk about novelists like Willa Cather and Dreiser, who influenced you. You never mention Dostoevsky.

DM: It's very difficult to read Dostoevsky because of all those characters; their names are too long. Some of their names are so long that just to read their names you have to start early in the morning and pack a lunch. That being the case, when I was a kid, I would kind of mmm-mmm-mmm over them in my mind, but then one day I had an English teacher who said that it was wrong to do that, that you actually had to say the name. That ruined Dostoevsky for me.

Q: One of my favorite Mamet plays is *The Duck Variations*. The speech patterns of the two old men reflect the influence of Yiddish. You've said that one of the old men is based on your grandfather. Which of the two?

DM: Perhaps both of them.

Q: Your maternal or paternal grandfather?

DM: My maternal grandfather.

Q: Was he from Russia?

DM: He was from Warsaw. Poland.

Q: Could you tell me something about him?

DM: He was a traveling salesman. He traveled in the Midwest, and he was in clothing, just like Willy Loman. He came home one day a week. He was also a great storyteller.

Q: Did you spend a lot of time with him?

DM: I spent a pretty good amount of time with him.

Q: Is there anything else you'd like to say about *The Old Neighborhood*?

DM: I'm real glad A.R.T. is doing it. I'm very grateful to Bob Brustein. It's been terrific working over at A.R.T. with my two last plays, *Oleanna* and *The Cryptogram*. I was and remain thrilled by the way they were done, and I'm grateful for everybody's support over there.

THE BACCHAE

François Rochaix and Jean-Claude Maret: Geneva Convention
by Doug Kirshen

Q: You have directed many plays by Aeschylus.

FRANÇOIS ROCHAIX: Three times *The Oresteia*. Plus the workshop with the A.R.T. Institute in 1994.

Q: Euripides is different.

FR: Very different. When Aeschylus was born, Athens was still a dictatorship, and the Athenians still had a unified vision of the world where natural forces are closely related to humans. But during the life of Aeschylus the whole world breaks apart and changes, becoming modern with the introduction of democracy. You see this change in *The Oresteia*. When you go from *Agamemnon*, the first play of the trilogy, to *The Eumenides*, the third play, you see how the structure of society is changing the plays. They become much freer. *Agamemnon* is a classical tragedy. *The Eumenides* is the start of melodrama. Euripides is already on the other side. There is more distance in his way of considering things, more irony. There is even collage sometimes in his techniques. Somebody said that Euripides invented the archetype of the TV melodrama. Aeschylus is still related to Homer and all that is the old world. In Euripides there is more distance from this old world. I feel this difference in style.

Q: There is more humor in Euripides.

FR: More humor, yes. Also in a lot of plays Euripides takes a position for women, in *Alcestis* and *Medea* for example.

Q: *Ion?*

FR: Absolutely, *Ion*, and also in *The Phoenician Women* and *The Madness of Heracles*, which I did in workshop with the Institute students last spring. There is sympathy for Antigone and Jocasta. The feminine side is more important, and in *The Bacchae* also, the feminine side of Dionysos, in contradiction to the macho character Pentheus.

Q: In *The Bacchae*, a whole generation of men seems to be missing. We don't know what happened to Pentheus's father and why the rule had to pass to the son. Do you see Pentheus as very young?

FR: Yes. I mean, these ages in myth . . . it's like when you read the Bible, Noah died at I don't remember, three hundred years old. But of course, if I proposed the part of Kadmos to Alvin Epstein and the part of Pentheus to Ben Evett, it's also to show two generations between them. That is, to make it easier for the audience to see that somewhere there should have been a father.

Q: The play in part is about Pentheus's inability to mature into an adult. He's stuck in adolescence.

FR: Yes. You know I have mixed feelings about *The Bacchae*. Pentheus is totally stubborn, totally macho, totally as you say, stuck, blocked. He has no feminine side, no intuition, no balance. On the other hand, Dionysos is terrible. He is vengeful, violent. I'm saying this because in the sixties this play was often performed as the play of liberation, of sex, of theatre. It's one aspect, but something that was totally underestimated was the violent and repressive side of what Dionysos does.

Q: It's like a bad acid trip. The play has incredible contradictions, a god who is both violent and beneficial.

FR: Exactly, and of course Agave, the sister of Dionysos's mother, cast doubt about the god's birth and his divine origins, but the punishment is like something out of the Old Testament. It's out of proportion, and don't forget that. He is the attractive god of theatre, but he can also be violent and repressive.

[Jean-Claude Maret joins the interview.]

Q: François, when you think about directing a play, do you think visually?

FR: When you read scripts, some call out for space. These in general are the better scripts. There are also scripts in which there is just dialogue and no third dimension. You could do them on radio, and it would be better. But sometimes there are interesting texts that don't call immediately for a space, and you have to find it. Especially in the last twenty or thirty years, the new scripts have been much too traditional and old-fashioned. I was fed up, so I started looking into monologues and poems. I was more interested in finding theatricality behind these texts than in interpreting texts that were just clichés. But with *The Bacchae* we are dealing with a great theatrical author.

Q: So you look into the text and see what is there.

FR: Looking into the text of *The Bacchae* is not so simple, because we had the problem of translations. It's not possible to do all these Greek plays in an absolutely word-for-word poetical translation without any cuts. It's not possible because they're loaded with images and a whole mythology we do not know well enough.

So the question of translation and adaptation comes up. Obviously, it has to be in the language of today. But then do we work with anachronisms, or is it better to work with the original Greek images? These questions are important. In the different languages I speak, I have access to at least fifteen or twenty translations of *The Bacchae*, and I always begin with a word-by-word translation to know what is really in the original material. Then comes the question of the adaptation, and here I made a choice different from the one I made for Robert Auletta's *The Oresteia*. For *The Oresteia*, I was looking for both a poet and a man who translates everything into pictures of today, who works with anachronisms, sometimes in a provocative way. For *The Bacchae*, I again wanted something in the language of today, yet close to the original structure. Paul Schmidt's approach does not use anachronistic imagery, but the result is equally modern.

Q: And that choice helps you discover what the production looks like?

JEAN-CLAUDE MARET: Yes, because I do the same. The images I build on stage are related to the real Greece. But it has to communicate straightforwardly to the audience, so it has to include some everyday images as well.

Q: Let's look at the set overall. It's completely black except for this white palace in a classical style. There is another structure on the left. What is that?

FR: The palace of Semele, the mother of Dionysos, and her tomb, which was destroyed by Zeus's lightning. This is Dionysos, his black side.

JM: The whole set is black. Everything is black because it is polluted by ashes from Semele's tomb. Yet the new king is trying to keep a white house. Whether he wants it or not, Pentheus has to deal with the past. The past is there and it is disturbing, even more disturbing than he thought.

FR: And if he doesn't deal with it, the past will deal with him.

JM: Exactly! But I present the set as something where the past takes place. You can see on the ground plan there is a competition. Pentheus would prefer his white palace to be in the center, but this old thing—Semele's tomb—is still there.

FR: And in this tomb there is something living—the vine Dionysos planted.

JM: Something lives in the ashes, as opposed to the whiteness of Pentheus's palace, which is quite dead. On Semele's side you have ashes but also a sign of life, the grapevine, which grows and grows green. We have one color there; the rest of the set is black and white. Dionysos is intervening.

FR: The grape is Dionysos's signature. When you don't take care of the grape it becomes a monster.

JM: It will grow ten meters in one year! The grape is a magic plant. Wine is the best and the worst. It depends on how you use it. We know it can destroy people, but we also know how it brings ecstasy.

THE TAMING OF THE SHREW

Symposium Excerpts

The A.R.T. organizes symposia for almost all of its mainstage plays. Eminent scholars as well as the artists who created the production participate. The symposium on The Taming of the Shrew *took place on February 9, 1998. Robert Brustein moderated, Arthur Holmberg pre-*

sented a slide lecture on the production history of the play, Professors Marjorie Garber and Stephen Greenblatt of Harvard responded to the production, and Andrei Serban responded to the other panelists and to questions from the audience.

ANDREI SERBAN: The whole play builds to the resolution of Kate's final monologue, and that moment is the key to my production. Every performance I have attended, including opening night, after she delivers this speech, a long silence arises from the audience, accompanying her gesture of surrender. [In Mr. Serban's production, Kate ritualistically kneels and slowly places her outstretched hand on the floor in the middle of the stage, waiting for Petruchio to put his foot on it.] Everybody wonders what Petruchio will do. And then he mirrors exactly what she does; he kneels next to her in equal submission. The silence of the audience, witnessing their surrender, is total. You can cut it with a knife.

For me, *The Taming of the Shrew* is not at all about the battle of the sexes, about who's on top, who's the victim, or love used as a desire for power and control. Kate grew up trapped by the complex of being dependent on her father, and she wanted to get out. Petruchio arrived to help her make the critical transition into adulthood. He plays the old role of the catalyst or, in recent times, a psychoanalyst. There are many of us who, like Kate, need to come into contact with someone who knows more than we do, who is more developed than we are. Through the play's difficult journey, Kate discovers who she is. The old medieval tradition inspired the young Shakespeare. The feminine consciousness had to do with love as receiving, surrendering to one's own destiny. In the symbolism of the Middle Ages, a man's body is also feminine, all matter is feminine. This has nothing to do with gender; our problem today is that we can view our world only through gender issues, and we have a great resistance when it comes to surrender. Kate's gesture of obeying at the end communicates to me what *The Taming of the Shrew* is about. It's about letting go and finding oneself in the process. So our production acknowledges that we are here to obey and to serve something higher and larger than ourselves.

The actress who plays Kate [Kristin Flanders] is a modern woman, and it's hard for her to believe what Kate says: "I am ashamed that women are so simple/To offer war where they should kneel for peace,/Or seek for rule, supremacy, and sway/Where they

Don Reilly (Petruchio) and Kristin Flanders (Kate) in *The Taming of the Shrew.*

are bound to serve, love, and obey." It's also physically difficult for any actress to wend her way through this monologue. It requires enormous vocal prowess. It goes on for almost two pages. Often this monologue is drastically cut. We kept it intact.

The wink tradition that started with Mary Pickford, who played Kate in a movie version, is to undercut the speech to let the women know that they should tell the men what the men want to hear and go about their business of manipulating their husbands. For me this is not the right answer, because then the play should be called *The Untaming of the Shrew*. I wanted to honor the title *The Taming of the Shrew*. There must be a shrew, and the action in the play is to tame her.

But every Shakespeare play works on several levels. On a politically correct level, today this is a problem play. As Shaw pointed out: "No man with any decency of feeling can sit it out in the company of a woman without being extremely ashamed of the lord-of-creation moral implied in the wager and the speech put into the woman's own mouth. Therefore the play, though still worthy of a complete and efficient representation, would need, even at that, some apology."

For me, though, the play works as a metaphor on a metaphysical level. If we talk about *The Taming of the Shrew* from that perspective, then Katharina is Everyman and Everywoman, mankind, womankind, me, anybody. There is a shrew naturally growing inside us that needs taming.

In the old tradition, it must be understood that one is free only by submitting to something higher. During her monologue, when she says the word "Lord," the actress pauses and looks up. The lord is no longer Petruchio; for a moment there is another relationship—a vertical connection is established. We all must obey something higher than ourselves. Some of us who are believers can call it God. Others might say love. Or art. At the end, Kate and Petruchio are united in a ceremonial gesture. But they're serving something. The idea of service is totally out of focus in our time, which explains why so many relationships fail. Everything in American culture is, what do I get out of this? Everything in American culture is self-expression. I want what I want, when I want it, the way I want it, and blast off. [audience laughter] America is a culture of shrews, and we are part of it.

Today, on my way to La Guardia to fly here, I passed a grocery store on Broadway, and outside a dog on a leash was looking inside intently, concentrating totally on his master, who was shopping. Nothing, but nothing could take this focus away. I thought, if actors could see this, they would understand what concentration and attention mean. [audience laughs] The loving attention of a dog, it's unbelievable. I was deeply touched to see that he was just waiting for his master, and nothing would take his eyes away from that.

MARJORIE GARBER: Remember, Petruchio has a dog he calls Troilus, and it's a spaniel. In Shakespeare, spaniels are often images of unthinking fidelity. I think that what we're defining here is an achieved fidelity as opposed to the word "obey" in the marriage ceremony, which is glibly used.

AS: Which is a mechanical and misunderstood obedience. You are free to obey only if you make the decision. Kate made the decision to obey freely.

ROBERT BRUSTEIN: Shakespeare didn't like dogs very much, to judge by a number of his references to dogs, because he thought that in their excessive affection they were symbols of abasement.

MG: Only certain kinds, Bob, only certain kinds. [audience laughs] Shakespeare is very conscious of different kinds of dogs. In *Macbeth*: You think you're dogs, but actually you're curs. There's the wonderful dog in *The Two Gentlemen of Verona*, Crab, the beloved.

There's Tray, Blanch, and Sweetheart, the dogs that shun him like the daughters in *King Lear*. But to go back to this other point, isn't it a matter of Kate's having to find some space to disobey in order to come back to obeying? What she can't do is be handed by the father to the suitor. She needs to have a space in which she can choose to obey because that's where obedience comes to mean something.

AS: Exactly. It's choosing; it's being free to choose. No one should force you to do it. That's the real obedience.

STEPHEN GREENBLATT: But there is force and compulsion in the play. There's lots of force and compulsion. This is not simply a play about free choice and the will to choose to submit. It's about mastery and submission; it's about keeping Kate from eating, keeping her from sleeping. It's about manipulating public perception so that when you say no, everyone else perceives it as saying yes.

AS: On a realistic level, you're absolutely right. If you talk that way, I cannot answer. But on another level, you miss it totally. In a Zen monastery, people deprive themselves, not sleeping, not eating, to reach something higher, and after all, Kate is not asked to face death, just skip a meal and sacrifice a nap.

SG: That's an admirable vision, but it's a monastery that Kate doesn't exactly choose to enter.

AS: But later it proves to be a valuable journey. At the end of the play, she's happier. Nobody forces her to speak the words of the monologue.

SG: But you could justify lots of nasty regimes—domestic regimes, political regimes—on this logic. I had a cousin who owned a shoe factory in Brazil years ago, and I said to him, in a 1960s way, "But they torture people in Brazil!" And he said, "Well, they don't torture them too much." [laughter] What's the right amount of physical discomfort that Katharina should feel to enable her to love Petruchio?

AS: Charles Morowitz, the famous British-American director, did a production a few years ago in Los Angeles, which was exactly what you just said. He mounted an unbelievably grim, funny, nasty Strindberg dream-play of *The Taming of the Shrew*. In the end, Kate appeared in a straightjacket in an asylum, and her last speech was redone as a coercion. He, like any other director, is entitled to his version, but that's certainly not what Shakespeare had in mind.

SG: I'm not sure I would have liked it, exactly, but in the middle of the seventeenth century Hobbes says in *Leviathan*, the sovereign can compel you not to show in either word or action that you don't believe everything he says, but he can't compel you to think things that he wants you to think. The good news is that your thoughts are free. The bad news is that it doesn't matter that your thoughts are free or not; what matters is whether you submit. It's a little difficult to say that everyone is happy in this situation.

AS: To me, the quality of Kate's submission is different from the disgruntled and seditious subjects of a king. Her submission speech is joyful, and I feel in the language of this speech a sense of transcendence. If the quality of her final submission had been grotesquely cynical, I wouldn't have done *The Taming of the Shrew*. I would have done a different play. But for me, the play ends in a harmonious way. Kate didn't die of starvation, she doesn't die of sleep deprivation. Yes, she's hungry for a moment, but that passes, and in the end she's much better off than in the beginning. Petruchio won't let her die. He's there, and he's in control just like in any voodoo ritual where there is a priest who knows what the danger is and who watches that the trance should not get out of hand. The hidden meaning of *The Taming of the Shrew* is about transformation and transcendence. Only by transcending yourself can you become yourself; this is, I confess, my subjective interpretation.

THE IMAGINARY INVALID

Andrei Belgrader and Shelley Berc: The Mischievous Duo
Interview by Michelle Powell

Q: Mr. Belgrader, Molière's plays demand a lot from an actor physically. How will you rehearse the actors for this type of comic theatre?

ANDREI BELGRADER: I never really know how I will work with actors because the assembly of artists differs for every show. For first rehearsals I need to be a silent observer, watching to see how the actor/director relationship might work. I discover each actor's unique ability, whether it be voice, acrobatics, or farcical gestures. I never know what I will discover, and that is part of the excitement of working in the theatre: you can never predict the outcome. Typically I begin with improvisational exercises. I find that is the best way to familiarize the actors with each other and, most important, with the text. Molière was a superb comic actor, influenced by the Italian *commedia dell'arte* tradition that uses slapstick and word games. For American actors who are often trained in a more psychological and not a physical method, it is important that first rehearsals focus on the actors' spatial relationship to each other, to the rehearsal space, and to the imaginary world that Molière creates for them. Getting the actors to move around as Molière's characters is my primary concern for the first two weeks.

Q: How will you encourage the actors to move in certain ways?

AB: Every text dictates a certain rehearsal as well as performance style. For *The Imaginary Invalid*, I will familiarize the actors with the comic routines of artists like Charlie Chaplin, Laurel and Hardy, and the Three Stooges. These comedians, who owe their talent to the *commedia* tradition, inspire the actors to use their bodies as comic tools.

Q: Ms. Berc, how did you approach *The Imaginary Invalid*?

SHELLEY BERC: I am not a straight translator who finds an equivalent for every one of Molière's original words. That type of translation is lifeless. I come to adaptation as a novelist, so I'm aware that a play needs to tell a story as well as entertain. It's always difficult to adapt a comedy. First I ask, "What is funny about Molière's plays?" For me, the sound and speed of the language, its overall rhythm, is where the real humor lies; liars speak quickly and colorfully, as if they are trying to distract the listener from what is actually being said. In order to be faithful to the original text, I retain the essence of the play: aphorism, comedy, and spirit—which is all in the timing. Then I transpose the jokes into a comparable American idiom that evokes the same feeling.

Molière provides the observer with a wonderful cast of players. His plays are perfect for the "me" generation. Some of his characters are absolutely shameless, self-centered, and paranoid. Yet they all possess a grain of wisdom despite how silly and foolish they first appear. This wisdom is Molière's, which he ingeniously weaves into his dramas.

Q: Mr. Belgrader, how do you feel about your return to the A.R.T.?

AB: I love Cambridge. A director meets a different breed of audience there. It's the combination of intelligence and awareness about the theatre that challenges any artist.

Thomas Derrah (Dr. Diaforus), Will LeBow (Argan), and Remo Airaldi (Thomas Diaforus) in *The Imaginary Invalid*.

Q: And what would you hope to create for them?

AB: The fantastic world Molière imagined. Molière created his magic with an ensemble of gifted actors. How lucky artists are to work consistently with the same people—a luxury rarely found in today's theatre. In an ensemble, the players strive together for excellence. This is the reason Molière was faithful to the idea of ensemble. It was a family that spoke as one unit to the audience about their dreams.

SB: I agree. You could say my job is made wonderfully simple because I am adapting famous recipes for the A.R.T. group of spices. Like Molière, who wrote his plays with certain performers in mind, I know when I write for the A.R.T., I'm writing for gifted comedians like Will LeBow, Tommy Derrah, and Jeremy Geidt. Understanding their acting strengths allows me to tailor roles to them. I can't imagine a better way to capitalize on a performer's strong points, and, overall, I believe the audience receives the best possible experience.

NOBODY DIES ON FRIDAY

Robert Brustein: The Price of Fame
Interview by Arthur Holmberg

Q: How many plays have you written?

ROBERT BRUSTEIN: Three plays and eleven adaptations, not counting *Shlemiel the First*. *Nobody Dies on Friday* is my first wholly original play, although it's based on existing material.

Q: Why does the theme of celebrity interest you? In your production of Pirandello's *Right You Are*, celebrity was also a theme, with the flash bulbs of the press going off.

RB: I've grappled personally with the idea of celebrity. If Jacob were to wrestle with the angel today, the angel's name would be Celebrity.

Q: Why do you see it as a pitfall?

RB: It kills your privacy. The prying reporter, the gossip monger, the yellow journalist—all conspire to invade the privacy of individuals and make everything public. Whom the gods would destroy they first make famous.

Q: So the dynamics of celebrity played a part in the genesis of your third play, *Nobody Dies on Friday*.

RB: Yes. I'd been investigating Lee Strasberg for a long time, trying to understand what it was about his Method that made his actors all end up in the movies, why he ended up in movies himself, starting with *The Godfather*, and how symbolic it was that he died after dancing in the celebrity chorus line of a TV program called "Night of a Thousand Stars." Then I read John Strasberg's bitter writings about his father. And I started thinking about Strasberg's acting company and how quickly it disintegrated because of his own ethical blindness. Under Strasberg, the Studio became a celebrity factory, a symbol for me of how people abandon their calling to seek fame in the movies. And Strasberg's Method was essentially a technique designed for the movies, not for the stage.

Q: Is there anything inherently wrong about acting in the movies?

RB: No, there's nothing morally wrong with acting in the movies. But a true actor's first allegiance is to the stage.

Q: Why?

RB: The stage is an actor's medium, the movies a director's. The film actor has little control over his or her performance. The director edits it, cuts it, shapes it, lip-synchs it, reworks it. The actor is virtually powerless in that medium. True, he gets paid a lot and has a shot at mass appeal. But the only convincing argument I've heard in favor of movies is that you have your evenings to yourself. The theatre is a much more monastic profession than the movies. It demands discipline, stamina, and moral commitment. Stanislavsky wrote eloquently about this. He didn't just offer a method to actors, like Strasberg, he also spoke of the ethical obligations of the actor to the profession.

Q: What are they?

RB: As Stanislavsky famously said, "To love the art in yourself, not yourself in art." Talent is a God-given gift. The actor has an obligation to cultivate that talent for the purpose of performing great roles, not for the sake of careerism.

Q: So you were interested in writing about Strasberg because you find Strasberg emblematic of a corruption that has plagued American theatre, sacrificing the ideals of art to pursue fame and fortune through movies.

RB: I was looking for the moment when things changed, and everything kept coming back to him. But you know, I wasn't simply trying to expose Strasberg, though I find him a highly overrated cultural icon. He also struck me as a tragic figure, considering the kind of pulls that were made on him. So I looked at the progress of his life as tragic.

Q: Tragic because he destroyed what he had of value to contribute to American culture?

RB: Yes.

Q: Do you think he made any contribution to American theatre?

RB: His greatest contribution to American theatre was his intensification of proletarian naturalism, a style best represented by the acting in plays like *A Hatful of Rain*, movies like *On the Waterfront*, and a variety of works from that period no one remembers. But the performers in them are remembered. People like Ben Gazzara, Shelley Winters—performers capable of creating a believable reality. Those plays and that kind of acting don't hold much interest for me.

Q: Did you know Strasberg?

RB: No, never met him.

Q: So the appeal of the subject for you was you felt that it's an important turning point in American theatre history.

RB: Yes. But I think the concept of celebrity has a larger reference than the theatre or the movies. It touches every American.

Q: Every American?

RB: Most of us either are celebrities or worship celebrities.

Q: You see this as a peculiarly American phenomenon?

RB: Yes.

Q: Why are Americans so mesmerized by the cult of celebrity?

RB: The country is essentially rootless. It never really developed its own traditions—no royalty, no church, no heritage. We have to satisfy our hunger for icons through rock singers and movies stars.

Q: But today the icons don't last. Joan Crawford and Bette Davis, John Wayne and Katherine Hepburn had careers that spanned over thirty years.

RB: Even the English nobility has less staying power these days. Princess Di, Prince Philip, Fergie, they're all grist for the tabloid press. This is a brand-new phenomenon. For us, too. Roosevelt's mistress wasn't identified until thirty years after the event. Nor was Eisenhower's. Now we know every motion of Clinton's private life, even the shape of his private parts.

Q: You're writing about Lee Strasberg, who is now a historical figure. Sometimes the desire to be historically accurate and the desire to create great theatre can clash because theatre demands dramatic power. How do you negotiate these antagonistic demands, trying to tell the truth about somebody's life and at the same time writing a compelling play?

RB: It's hard. I compressed a lot of events. The play takes place in one day. It observes the Aristotelian unities: place, time, and action. But I've had to import some events that took place a few months later and a few months earlier and pretend they all happened on this one day. It's not quite as crowded a day as in Corneille's *The Cid*, where the events of many years are compressed into twenty-four hours. But

I took some liberties with history. For example, Marilyn Monroe's breakup with Arthur Miller did not happen on New Year's Eve, 1959. It happened a few months later, though it was already in the works. So I have tinkered with when things happened, though rarely with what things happened. I've had to imagine a few scenes in Lee Strasberg's early life from my own father's early life, which was probably not too different. They lived in the same neighborhood around the same time.

Q: Why was it important to sketch in Lee Strasberg's early life?

RB: To see where he came from, what turned him into what he became. Why he felt he had to protect himself as much as he did, why he lost his emotional ties with his family. His son continually accuses him of not being able to feel toward his family, yet he stressed feeling above all things in his acting training. He also stressed believability and truth, but he wasn't always capable of acknowledging the truth.

Q: In terms of *Nobody Dies on Friday* and the destiny of the Strasbergs, why is the day your play takes place different from all other days?

RB: A crisis occurs in everybody's life on this particular day. Monroe's divorce from Arthur Miller. John Strasberg's decision to leave home. Paula's recognition that Lee is more devoted to Marilyn than to her or the children. And Susan's acknowledgment that her father will never love her or nourish her as much as he does Marilyn.

Q: So each character arrives at a moment of recognition. How does your play dramatize the relationship between Paula and her husband?

RB: Such a strange relationship. Both of them are battening on Marilyn for the sake of their careers. Paula is her acting coach—Marilyn can't say a line without her. Lee is her mentor as to what roles she takes, and he's teaching her how to act. They're both exploiting the woman, but at the same time Paula is recognizing that by participating in this she's losing Lee. Lee is getting more and more absorbed into Marilyn's world. Paula retains her love for her family and her need to protect them. She realizes that Lee is pulling away as a result of this obsession with Marilyn.

Q: You used the word "exploit." That's a very harsh word.

RB: That's pretty much what they were doing. They were both concerned about Marilyn, but she was their bread and butter.

Q: So you think that Lee Strasberg had no illusions about Monroe's talent and ability.

RB: I think he talked himself into believing that she was a great actress.

Q: So he was self-deceived.

RB: Yes. That's part of the interest of the character, that he is believed to be one of the great teachers of acting and one of the great critics of acting. And yet he has deluded himself into thinking that a woman with a modest comic talent could play all the great tragic roles: Grushenka in *The Brothers Karamazov*, Lady Macbeth, Ophelia. It was a delusion, one that John Strasberg saw through immediately.

Q: How does Marilyn figure into your play?

RB: She's a presence hovering in the wings. Rather like the Greek concept of Fate. You never see her. She's just a voice and a bell. She's a suffering monster, similar to Tennessee Williams's Southern belles. You have great sympathy for her, but part of her capacity to stimulate your sympathy comes from her incredible emotional needs.

Q: She had nothing but contempt for herself.

RB: Well, when you consider how she got to the top, you can see why. She was the sex toy of hundreds of powerful men.

Q: Why do you see her as a Tennessee Williams character?

RB: Because she's in a state of disintegration. From the first moment you hear her voice, she's in a spiral of self-destruction like Blanche DuBois. Blanche drank to escape reality, Marilyn drank and popped pills for the same reason. She was a walking pharmacy, a perambulating liquor store. Which is what ultimately killed her. So there's foreboding in the play about her eventual overdose.

Q: Why did you make the decision to have her offstage all the time?

RB: I've never seen a persuasive representation of Marilyn on stage. It always seems like an impersonation. So I thought this device would create more tension and suspense than actually showing her in the flesh.

Q: How would you describe the style of the play?

RB: The style is an odd choice for me, because I'm generally assumed to be opposed to realism, but the play is essentially a traditional Jewish family play with roots in Yiddish theatre. The Yiddish audiences loved Shakespeare plays about wronged parents like *King Lear* and *The Merchant of Venice*, especially if they ended in reconciliation. Clifford Odets and Arthur Miller come out of that tradition. Remember the ending of *Death of a Salesman*? Willy realizes that his estranged son Biff actually loves him. And Linda replies, "He always loved you." That's a perfect Yiddish theatre moment. My play comes out of the same tradition.

Q: Some critics attack American theatre as never looking outside the living room. But I find in your play and the plays of Miller, Odets, and Mamet a virulent indictment of America. I don't see them as just family dramas.

RB: Miller works hard to make that family a microcosm for what he considers both the strengths and weaknesses of American society. And so does Odets. Their plays always have a social and sometimes a metaphysical dimension, beyond the family. But it is typical of American playwrights to work from the family. O'Neill's great plays are family plays, even *The Iceman Cometh*. When I created Lee, I heard the voice of my father in my ear. I gave Lee some past events that happened to my father, particularly his involvement with the Yiddish theatre. My father used to tell me those stories over and over. I loved hearing them.

Q: Why?

RB: I felt closer to him when he talked about his childhood.

Q: Why did he want to talk about his childhood?

RB: He had a success story to tell. He grew from a poor East Side immigrant into a successful self-made businessman.

Q: What has surprised you most about the evolution of American theatre?

RB: That it has evolved from a frivolous entertainment into a serious, world-class expression. When I was a kid there was little around but light entertainment. But think of the quality of our theatre over the last forty years!

Q: What is the most difficult thing about writing a play?

RB: The most difficult thing about writing a play is letting the action carry the theme and not the author's didactic voice. To let what happens happen more through character and action than through reflections and pronouncements about what the audience ought to think. The best playwrights do that. Strindberg does that. Chekhov does that. Ibsen does that. And so does David Mamet. I'm trying to learn that mystery, walking humbly in their lengthening footsteps.

Paula Vogel: Through the Eyes of Lolita
Interview by Arthur Holmberg

Q: Your plays frequently deal with taboos. If I had to explain your theatrical signature to someone unfamiliar with your work, I would say that you trespass into forbidden territory with a smile on your face. You disturb the bones of forbidden topics, then make the audience laugh. What is the function of humor in your vision?

PAULA VOGEL: I actually describe *Drive* as a comedy. Of course it's not, but the first half very much functions as comedy. At some elemental level, it is who I am. My family had the most inappropriate moments of humor at funerals. Maybe it's a survival strategy. Some people say that this comes from Jewish genes. At the beginning of *The Baltimore Waltz* [a play about her brother's death from AIDS], I used a real letter my brother wrote me with instructions for his funeral that included directions on how to lay him out in the coffin in drag. For me, combining sadness and comedy heightens both. The collision of tones makes both more extreme. One of my favorite movies is Roman Polanski's *The Fearless Vampire Killers*. I've seen it sixteen times, and the reason I watch it so often is the combination of terror and comedy. You're scared to the point of screaming, then he cracks a joke. It doesn't defuse the terror, it defuses the guarding against the terror. We don't want to be taken by surprise, so we keep our guard up. Comedy defuses that vigilance, so in the next moment we are unprepared for the explosion. I'll give you an example. There is a little Jewish hotel keeper who lusts after voluptuous young women in the village, but his wife keeps him on a tight leash. One night he stays out too late, and vampires kill him. In the grave he is finally beyond his wife's reach. So he comes back that night to get a buxom virgin. She screams and screams, and it's a horrifying moment. He starts to attack, she reaches for a cross, and he says, "Boy, have you got the wrong vampire," then lunges for the kill. The comedy dismantles any protective covering. Hitchcock uses comedy and terror the same way. So that's why I think I do it.

Q: Humor is also a form of seduction. In one of the play's funniest speeches, "A Mother's Guide to Social Drinking," an older woman tells a young girl how not to get drunk. She advises her never to touch a drink with a sexual position in the name, like Dead Man Screw or the Missionary, and to learn to drink like a man: straight up. The speech makes the audience laugh, but then you hit hard with an emotionally devastating scene.

PV: Li'l Bit's drunk and can't defend herself.

Q: A double seduction, Li'l Bit and the audience.

PV: Comedy is complicity. If you make an audience laugh . . .

Q: They are your friends.

PV: Not only your friends but also in alliance with the play world. They're on the side of the play now because they laughed.

Q: Many of your plays deal with families. European critics often say American drama does not achieve greatness because our playwrights, obsessed by petty family melodramas, never look through the living room window to see the larger world and the problems outside.

PV: Rubbish. The Greeks dealt with the family. Aristotle describes domestic violence among kings as tragedy. British critics often throw that complaint at me, but Pinter and David Hare also deal with families. It's important that the family be put in its social context, that there is a world beyond. The family remains the structure at the heart of most drama because the family, after all, reflects its community's values and the politics of their time.

Q: *King Lear* and *The Oresteia* are family dramas.

PV: So are *Hamlet* and *Mother Courage*. The great American playwrights, like the great European playwrights, like the great global playwrights, deal with the family as a unit within a greater body politic.

Q: So how do you see *Drive* as political?

PV: A lot of people are trying to turn this into a drama about an individual family. To me it is not. It is a way of looking on a microcosmic level at how this culture sexualizes children. How we are taught at an extremely early age to look at female bodies. One of the tag lines I had in my head when I was writing this play was, it takes a whole village to molest a child. JonBenet Ramsey was not a fluke. When we Americans saw the videotape of her at the beauty contest when she was five, a chill went up our collective spines. At what age are we sexualizing our children in a consumer culture to sell blue jeans and underwear? So children's bodies are sexualized all the way down from Madison Avenue to the wealthy suburb of Denver where

Debra Winger (Li'l Bit) and Arliss Howard (Peck) in *How I Learned to Drive*.

the Ramseys lived. I would call that political and not specifically the psychopathology of an individual family. I would say that's culture. And now we are starting to see a sexualized gaze toward young boys. Leonardo DiCaprio enjoys cult status because he looks prepubescent. Whenever there is confusion or double, triple, and quadruple standards, that is the realm of theatre. Drama lives in paradoxes and contradictions. If you look at the structure of my play, all I'm doing is asking how do you feel about this? We see a girl of seventeen and an older man in a car seat. You think you know how you feel about this relationship? All right, fine. Now, let's go back a year earlier. Do you still think you know what you feel about this situation? Great. Now let's change the situation a little bit more. He's married to her aunt.

How do you feel about that? The play allows me this kind of slippage because we have these contradictory feelings about the sexuality of boys and girls. So I tease out those contradictions. The play is a reverse syllogism. It constantly pulls the rug out from under our emotional responses by going back earlier and earlier in time. The play moves in reverse.

Q: Earlier you said we are starting to see a sexual gaze toward young boys. *Drive* eroticizes the male. It eroticizes the female as well but in different ways. Whereas you eroticize the male verbally in "Recipe for a Southern Boy," you eroticize the female visually.

PV: Yes, Li'l Bit is eroticized through the photo shoots, through the visual presentation of the body. When I was doing research for *Hot 'n' Throbbing* [a play about female pornography that premiered at the A.R.T.], I discovered that women tend to eroticize through words and narration as much or more than through the eyes. So for me, "Recipe for a Southern Boy" was the way to really present the desiring female subject and the desired male object.

Q: *Drive* dramatizes in a disturbing way how we receive great harm from the people who love us.

PV: I would reverse that. I would say that we can receive great love from the people who harm us.

Q: Why is it significant to reverse it?

PV: We are now living in a culture of victimization, and great harm can be inflicted by well-intentioned therapists, social workers, and talk-show hosts who encourage people to dwell in their identity as victim. Without denying or forgetting the original pain, I wanted to write about the great gifts that can also be inside that box of abuse. My play dramatizes the gifts we receive from the people who hurt us.

Q: So what does Li'l Bit receive?

PV: She received the gift of how to survive.

Q: From her uncle?

PV: Absolutely. I'm going to teach you to drive like a man, he says. He becomes her mentor and shows her a way of thinking ahead ten steps down the road before anyone else to figure out what the other guy is going to do before he does it. That not only enables her to survive but actually enables her, I think, to reject him and destroy him.

Q: And she does destroy him.

PV: He gives her the gifts to do that. He gives her the training. He gives her the ego formation. You, he says, you've got a fire in the head. He gives her gifts in just about every scene. He teaches her the importance of herself as an individual and the ability to strategize to protect that. It's all there in the driving lessons. It's abuse simultaneously with a kind of affirmation and reassurance.

Q: In *Drive*, Li'l Bit looks at her painful memories, processes the experiences, and then moves on. Why is it important to forgive the harm?

PV: Many people stay rooted in anger against transgressions that occurred in childhood, and this rage will be directed to other people in their adult lives and toward themselves. Whether we call it forgiveness or understanding, there comes a moment when the past has to be processed, and we have to find some control. There are two forgivenesses in the play. One forgiveness for Peck, but the most crucial forgiveness would be Li'l Bit's forgiving Li'l Bit. Li'l Bit as an adult looking at and understanding her complicity . . .

Q: Her destructiveness. You once said that it was important to give the audience a catharsis.

PV: Catharsis purges the pity and the terror and enables the audience to transcend them. So you have her memories of the final confrontation with Peck in the hotel room and afterward the flashback to the first driving lesson. And then the last scene, which brings us up to the present. This is a movement forward. For me, purgation means a forward movement.

Q: In *Drive*, as in many of your plays, music is a crucial element.

PV: Music contains a subliminal message that I will never be able to accomplish with words, because words always involve the cognitive. Music speaks directly to the emotions. So for me as a playwright, music is an important ally. It is also important as a way of saying this was gender in 1960.

Q: Gender? You gender music?

PV: Yes. It has messages about being a man and being a woman. When you listen to the Beach Boys, what comes back is a code of the 1960s. Just like disco music brings back the entire culture of the seventies. So I used music to get to the culture of the sixties. Music is a time capsule.

Q: You're a feminist, but some critics have called your plays misogynistic.

PV: In the seventies, a lot of people at the Women's Project [a theatre company in New York] thought I was misogynistic. And Julia Miles always commented that my work was so negative about women, that it was so dark and distressing. For me, being a feminist does not mean showing a positive image of women. For me, being a feminist means looking at things that disturb me, looking at things that hurt me as a woman. We live in a misogynist world, and I want to see why. And I want to look and see why not just men are the enemy but how I as a woman participate in the system. To say that men are the enemy is patronizing. It makes me a victim, and I am not comfortable as a victim. It's a mistake to attribute goodness, pure abstract goodness, to either sex. I don't recognize that, so maybe I'm not extremely feminist. To me a play doesn't need to make me feel good. It can be a view of the world that is so upsetting that when I leave the theatre, I want to say no to that play, I will not allow that to happen in my life.

Q: *Desdemona* [a play in which Vogel explores the secret lives of the women in Shakespeare's tragedy] may not have positive female role models, but it most certainly is a feminist play.

PV: *Desdemona* shows how women participate in a social system that does not allow them to bond. We bond with our husbands and our class structure rather than with each other. I don't know how you can get more feminist than that. Does it make me feel good? No. Does it worry me? Yes. Does it call on me to act? Absolutely. At the moment, we women are colluding with the patriarchal system and with the class structure. You can't deport the enemy, the enemy is inside us. The really dangerous enemy is that we have internalized misogyny and homophobia. There were a lot of headlines, "Lesbian wins Pulitzer, blah, blah, blah. . . ." I am the first person to say, hey wait, I'm not here to make everyone else feel homophobic, I'm homophobic. I was brought up in this country. I was taught to hate gays. I was taught to hate women. What we are taught to hate unifies us as a society. Our communal bond is that we are all racist, not just whites. Blacks are racist, Latinos are racist. We're taught racism the way we're taught homophobia and misogyny. It's all internalized. So it's not clear-cut to me, here is the good guy and here is the bad guy. I understand Strindberg. Strindberg is an extremely powerful ally for me as a woman dramatist because in his plays there is a fear and a power of woman not approached by any other dramatist. In grad school I steeped myself in Strindberg. He is a remarkable dramatist. But in the sixties and seventies, feminist theatre did not produce plays of negative empathy. Like Hollywood, they only wanted positive role models—feel-good role models. There is nothing wrong with that. It's necessary, and I am finally about to write my first play with a positive role model. It takes place on the last Christmas Eve of the Civil War in Washington, D.C. The kids in my family—my nephews and godchildren—keep asking, "When can we see one of your plays," and I go, "Oh, maybe in another ten years when you're old enough." So now I'm writing a Christmas play with positive role models for the kids.

THE MARRIAGE OF BETTE AND BOO

Christopher Durang: Family Survival
Interview by Arthur Holmberg

Q: Of all your plays, *Bette and Boo* is your favorite. Why?

CHRISTOPHER DURANG: Since it's based on my parents, it's emotionally closer to me than some of my more surreal plays. And then I like the balance of comic and sad. It should play as funny, but you should care about the characters and feel sad for them. My family argued a lot. One of my impulses in writing is to take people's crazy behavior and try to make order of what sometimes feels chaotic in the past.

Q: You once said writing plays was a way of taming the past. What do you mean?

CD: When you're in the midst of a specific incident in your family, it's upsetting. By putting it into a play, you clarify it. All this convoluted interaction between people is taken out of my brain and put into an understandable form on the stage. I feel like it's out of my brain and handled.

Q: Like Stephen Daedalus in *A Portrait of the Artist as a Young Man*, looking for *integritas, consonantia, claritas*.

CD: Yeah, seeing connections between things.

Q: In another interview, you said that laughter is a healing process. Please explain.

CD: Usually you can't laugh if you are in a bad mood or in the throes of the most serious problem in the world. My father was an alcoholic, and my mother fought with him when he was drunk, which was not necessarily the best way to confront the problem. Late in the play, Bette finally gets a divorce from Boo. She drags out all her calendars on which throughout the years of their marriage she had marked on certain days "DD" for dead drunk and "HD" for half drunk. She was refreshing her memory for the divorce proceedings. I was with her, and she was saying, oh look at this, he was dead drunk here and half drunk here, and then I looked at her funny, and we both laughed at the craziness of putting "DD" and "HD" on the calendar for years at a time. It was the beginning of perspective. When she was doing it, she had no perspective. She was just angry. But as the years passed, suddenly it struck her as foolish and futile. It meant a new understanding that nagging my father was not the best way to help him. Laughter can bring a new perspective. Sometimes people are offended by my plays. They say no, no this is serious, there is no laughter here. But I like to mix the serious with laughter. It's a way of admitting that the stories we're all involved in are crazy.

Q: Do audiences find your mixture of comic and serious disconcerting?

CD: In *Bette and Boo*, Bette loses three children to stillbirth.

Q: Three? I thought four.

CD: You're right, it is four. In life my mother lost three. I added one for . . .

Q: Comic effect . . .

CD: For dramatic effect. I present the babies' deaths by having the doctor come out saying the baby is dead and then dropping the baby on the ground. When done properly, it's funny. I also thought that it's obviously so sad that to have a realistic scene in which someone comes out and says your baby's dead takes you into the realm of a TV movie. I wasn't writing a realist play about how to deal with the death of a baby. But there was something about the way I wrote that play that the audience got that I meant them to feel sympathy for Bette, even though I presented it somewhat surrealistically. So I became more aware of wanting to cue the audience in about where there was genuine emotion.

Q: Can you give me an example of a cue in *Bette and Boo*?

CD: It isn't in the element of the babies; it's how Bette is treated other places, for instance, the scene in which Bette talks on the phone in the middle of the night to her friend Bonnie. There's a bit of humor in that scene, but basically it isn't funny. It communicates how sad Bette feels about the deaths of the children. And so, I think the audience absolutely knows that they are meant to feel empathy for her. You don't know during the first scene when the baby is dropped, and now I'm getting to the nitty gritty of it. The first time this happens, it's Skippy, who goes on to live. So the first time you're shocked, and you laugh, and you're let off the hook because it isn't a real death, it's a misunderstanding. Now I did not do this consciously, I just wrote it. The second time, you think, oh God, they're doing it again. But it turns out this baby's really dead. And in the next scene, Emily has a breakdown and Bette goes into catatonia. Again, the scene that follows communicates sympathy, that we are not just finding these people funny. That's what I mean by cueing the audience, making the shift in tones clear.

Q: In exasperation, the priest exclaims, "Why did God make people so stupid, why don't they think before they get married?"

CD: My parents didn't really know one another. My father knew the charming side of my mother, and my mother thought that he was attentive and pleasant and was an architect, which was a respectable profession, but I don't think that they actually got to know one another deeply. So Father Donnally makes a point when he says people come to me with problems when it's too late, once you're already married and have children. So that is a frustration I let him express. What can you say to these couples who are in such a mess? Because even if you could recommend divorce, if young children are involved that is not a cure-all. But divorce can sometimes be the better thing to do. When my parents separated, I was very grateful.

Q: Grateful?

CD: Oh, God, yes. They argued too much. It was hellish being around them. I never knew when they were going to explode into screaming.

Q: You have frequently stated that you're against authoritarian dogmas. Bette and Boo got married in the late forties, and both of them accept the fascistic gender roles their culture promulgates. But neither fits easily into those rigid stereotypes. For instance, Boo neither can nor wants to play the brutal patriarch we see in his father, yet the wife communicates to him in a destructive way how disappointed she is that he's not omnipotent and not successful enough for her. And she doesn't get what she wants out of the marriage: emotional intimacy and a big brood. She cannot be the happy homemaker. When their marriage doesn't conform to their expectations, neither one can deal with the reality of their relationship.

CD: Those questions are very complicated. Let me try to address

Kristin Flanders, Karen MacDonald, Caroline Hall (seated), Thomas Derrah, and Sophia Fox-Long in *The Marriage of Bette and Boo*.

them. I do not view this play as an attack on marriage or the nuclear family. In Chekhov everyone falls in love with the wrong person, yet I don't think Chekhov is saying let's do away with love. He's saying, isn't this sad . . . this is the way things are.

Q: And funny.

CD: Yeah, theoretically funny. So my play is about the pain that exists in the nuclear family, but I am mostly writing about psychology. I am actually very drawn to the way you described Bette and Boo, talking about their gender roles. I thought it was a very accurate description of the play, but I'm not a writer who sits down and says, okay, now I'm going to write about gender roles. I think, oh, I'm going to write a story about these characters, and they do this and talk this way. The way you described Bette's disappointment that Boo isn't more of a patriarch is very interesting. What you say about gender roles in the play is apt, but I picked it up unconsciously. I wasn't making a generalized comment about marriage beyond saying that when people are bound together and have large incompatibilities, it makes for a great deal of unhappiness. But when I was growing up, I really didn't know any marriages that seemed to be happy.

Q: You once said that the women in your family were very strong, and to have a disagreement with one of them was like arm wrestling. How do you see the women in this play as strong?

CD: When I say strong, I partially mean obstinate. Also, the women were very vibrant; they were lively but also had a strong force of will. My mother and aunt are the most talkative females I have ever met. If you tried to argue with them, they would bury you with words. I am quite verbal too, so I was a stronger match for my mother than my father was. My father would get overwhelmed and disappear.

Q: We get to know the women in this play much better than the men. Skippy, the son, doesn't have any positive male role models. His father doesn't know how to talk to him and withdraws. The maternal grandfather has been reduced by a stroke to a blathering idiot; the paternal grandfather is a militant misogynist, constantly putting women down. Although you show us the absurd side of Bette, you also go to great lengths to humanize her so that we feel sorry for her. Emotionally, the play puts us on the side of the females, who are fleshed out with more psychological details than the men.

CD: I knew my father less well than I knew my mother, so the details I ended up giving came more naturally about Bette than Boo. I don't know what else to say.

Q: Doesn't Boo say at one point to Bette, I don't want any more kids?

CD: Yeah, and, truthfully, I always envisioned it as a sad thing to say. He goes on to say that kids wake you up in the middle of the night dead. Obviously, that is a way of saying he feels sad that we've had all these children who have died. In the last several years I have gotten to know some of my father's family more than I did. I was thirteen when my parents separated, and we actually stopped dealing with that side of the family. I do regret that I didn't get to know my father. For instance, he fought in World War II and was part of the D-Day invasion on Normandy Beach. But it wasn't something he talked much about. Now that he is dead, I am so regretful that my mother and I looked at him not as a human being but as this problem and how do we get this problem to stop drinking. So I never really had a conversation, saying what did you do in the war, Daddy. And I regret that. One of his sisters sent me a letter that he had written to his father shortly after the D-Day invasion. He was actually articulate in the letter. It sounded scary, it would be scary, and it was an interesting view into him. There were a couple of paragraphs crossed out by the government about, I guess, troop movements and military stuff like that. So it was kind of odd, but I wondered what he had written in those crossed-out paragraphs. That part of my father I am sorry I did not know, so I think that element of not knowing my father is what you are picking up in the play.

Q: I saw the original production at the Public Theater with Joan Allen, Mercedes Ruehl, and Olympia Dukakis. The last scene caught me completely off guard. I was not prepared for such an emotional reaction when the father and son visit the mother in the hospital. Your play moves toward a powerful catharsis—they finally talk to each other and seem to enjoy each other's company. It's fun seeing the family reunited again.

CD: When we rehearsed it with Jerry Zaks, who directed it, he said in this scene Bette and Boo finally speak to each other with an ease they have not shown before. It's very nice, but it's also sad. Why couldn't they have found that earlier? But maybe now Bette, having been divorced, was no longer committed to changing him and actually accepted him and his flaws. In many of the other scenes, she keeps saying you've got to do this, you've got to do that, you've got to change. My parents actually did love one another on some level and cared for one another, too. Jerry told us not to play sadness.

Q: It's a happy scene but also sad because you realize they could have succeeded in their marriage.

CD: That's true.

Q: And when your father turns to you and says, we are so glad we had you, Skippy, it detonates like Mary Tyrone's "I fell in love with James Tyrone and was so happy for a time."

CD: Plays can be mysterious. Olympia Dukakis played Soot, and once, late in rehearsals, she said this is a very forgiving play. And I remember thinking that that sounded right. I had not thought it because as you're sitting through the play . . .

Q: It's so unrelenting. . . .

CD: Yeah . . . you don't feel like this is all about forgiveness, so it's something surprising about this scene. I acted the part of Skippy at the Public. In the first preview I was startled by how much emotion I felt at the end of the play. I hadn't felt it in rehearsal, and I was thrown by it. That happened often in the last scene. The play never sent me home depressed. I actually left with a nice feeling about Bette and Boo.

PHAEDRA

Liz Diamond: Facing the Monster
Interview by Jennifer Kiger

Q: Why *Phaedra*?

LIZ DIAMOND: When Bob Brustein approached me about doing *Phaedra*, I reread the play. As I did, I felt the oxygen draining out of the room. Phaedra's choking on her frustrated passion terrified me. Theseus's murderous rage appalled me. Our inability to master our destructive emotions is portrayed here with clinical clarity. The possibility that we will not, when seized in its grip, be able to release ourselves from a violent passion is deeply frightening. But, of course, what frightens me is also what draws me to the play.

Q: How would you define Racine's tragic vision?

LD: In *Phaedra*, Racine's conviction is that our reason is ultimately impotent in the face of our most monstrous passions. Monster is the image that recurs in the play. Phaedra, half-sister to the Minotaur, is besieged by a monstrous desire, a lust for her own stepson. At every step Phaedra knows that not to suppress this desire will be fatal, but she cannot, because in suppressing it, she is devoured from the inside. She speaks, unleashing in her husband Theseus a passion so monstrous that it devours his son.

What makes this play so modern is that there is a hideous noninevitability to the tragedy. The gods cannot be blamed. Responsibility for the tragedy rests in the hands of human beings. Their fallibility is their own. In the play, Phaedra is given every opportunity to call back her lies; Theseus his curses. They squander every one.

Q: How does language function in the tragedy?

LD: Spoken words are responsible for the tragedy. Confessions,

Randy Danson (Phaedra) and Karen MacDonald (Enone) in *Phaedra*.

lies, and curses unleash the havoc. The alexandrine line in Racine—its formal, rigid cadence—contains Phaedra's tumult like a vice. The more she speaks of how fatal it will be to speak, the more impossible it becomes for the vice to contain her. Her poetry finally gives way to action—the grabbing of Hippolytus's sword. This gesture becomes catastrophic.

Paul Schmidt's translation in blank verse has a similar pulse and tension. He renders her speech in a modern, American English, free of self-conscious anachronisms or colloquialisms. He creates a rare thing, a translation that illuminates both Racine's world and our own.

Q: You've been described as having a formalist approach to staging.

LD: The plays I've loved working on share one common element: language that is dense, layered, and complicated, however simple the surface may appear. The metaphors unfold like onion skin; the word-play and image-play seem to go forever. The plays of Suzan-Lori Parks, Molière, Brecht, Beckett, Sophocles, and Heaney all have this in common. I want a play on stage to operate like a poem—to have a sense of form carrying meaning, image giving way to image. But I am not just interested in form from an aesthetic point of view. For me, the principal challenge and pleasure of directing, and sometimes the agony, is to try to make every plastic element in the production—clothes, gesture, movement, space, light, and sound—embody the emotions contained in the text. It's fantastic when you watch and listen in the theatre, and suddenly you witness the alchemical transubstantiation spoken of by Artaud, where the invisible is made visible, where the abstract is made concrete. You feel you have understood something viscerally for the first time.

Q: How did you approach bringing the poetry of *Phaedra* to life through design?

LD: What I kept returning to in the play is the image of the labyrinth. I wanted to create a maddeningly logical, rational interior where Phaedra will be trapped. The interior needs to be monolithic, endless, relentless, airless. There is no place in the social world of the court for what Phaedra desires, which is an anarchic, passionate, taboo-blasting sexuality. So, with Riccardo Hernandez, the set designer (with whom I've enjoyed some of my happiest collaborations, precisely in terms of visual poetry), I spoke of wanting Phaedra's fleshy, earthly sensuality and violent passion to crash against the walls, so to speak.

Architectural form always betrays the dominant forms of culture, and in looking at the neoclassical architecture of Racine's own period, we were struck by the rationality of spaces. It opened up another way of responding to the play. It became possible to see *Phaedra* not only as I have described above, as a kind of warning against succumbing to the "humors," but at the same time as a critique of the kind of social order that demands a total suppression of such anarchic sensation. We went on to look at images of tombs and prisons. Riccardo brought in ground plans of elevations of the great Egyptian tombs and of Third Reich architecture—that apotheosis of rational planning—and gradually the design emerged. Catherine Zuber's stunning costumes vividly contrast that reality. Phaedra's garments, for example, are in layers—the outer being a vast, pyramid-shaped robe that weighs her down. She walks out of it, and beneath, her gowns are flowing, sensual silks in deep reds. There is something frightfully vulnerable about seeing this soft, fleshy figure trapped inside this hard, unforgiving space.

Q: What are your fears going into rehearsal?

LD: Fears? They're always the same. Death by theatre for us and the audience. Blind alleys. Lame ideas. Other than those, none. [laughter] Or, maybe also, veering into camp. Great tragedies always flirt with camp. I can imagine *Phaedra* as a really fabulous, lurid psychological horror movie. But camp is metatheatrical, and *Phaedra* is not. It is vast, elemental, reverberant. I can't wait.

THE MERCHANT OF VENICE

Andrei Serban: In Search of Understanding
Interview by Gideon Lester

After the first three weeks of rehearsals for The Merchant of Venice, *director Andrei Serban discussed his production with A.R.T. resident dramaturg Gideon Lester.*

Q: At the end of the twentieth century, is it still possible to stage *The Merchant of Venice* as a comedy?

ANDREI SERBAN: We've certainly been laughing a lot in rehearsals, though why this is I'm not sure. We're discovering Shylock to be a dangerously intelligent man, a Jewish vaudevillian who makes a cabaret of his life to entertain the Christians out of self-defense, because he wants to appear to assimilate. Richard Burbage, who was probably the first Shylock, seems to have played him comically, but in the eighteenth and nineteenth century such actors as Charles Macklin, Edmund Kean, and Henry Irving turned him into a noble, heroic gentleman. Laurence Olivier, supposedly the best Shylock of our times, continued this tradition and played him as a dignified, tragic figure who won the audience's sympathy. That may appear to work well after the events of the twentieth century, but it's not the play Shakespeare wrote.

Q: You spend a great deal of time researching the production history of each play you direct.

AS: Yes. It allows me to steal good ideas from the best productions and turn them into a ratatouille of my own. At the first rehearsal I know everyone else's productions by heart, but I have no idea what mine will be. By understanding the habits and clichés of performance, I can question them and make the play look as fresh as possible.

Q: If you begin rehearsing a play without knowing what form your production will take, how do you manage to design a set in advance?

AS: For me, the best designs are not conceptual sets but scenic components that I can experiment with. The designers working with me on *Merchant*, Christine Jones and Marielle Bancou, have created elements that playfully signify Venice—poles, bridges, benches—and colored screens that suggest the paradise of Belmont, the passions of Venice, and so on. I use these elements freely in rehearsal, like a child playing with Lego bricks. If a director and designer decide on a set too early, they are often stuck with an intellectual concept that cannot encompass the discoveries made with the actors in rehearsal. The improvisational quality of the *Merchant* set allows us to embrace the complexity of Shakespeare's play. I'm not suggesting the scenic design should be a chaotic mess but that its final shape should reflect in a disciplined way whatever understanding of the play we have evolved by opening night.

Q: So you regard rehearsals as a path toward an understanding of Shakespeare's text?

AS: Of the text but also of myself and of my colleagues, the actors, and designers.

Q: In other words, you cannot know what your production will be until you begin to work with your cast.

AS: Exactly.

Q: Does this mean that if, for example, Will LeBow were not playing Shylock, you would understand the part differently?

AS: Rather than forcing the actors to perform my concept of a play, I try to meet whatever the actors can do best and use their talents to explore what the play is telling us. The danger of imposing my own interpretation on the cast is that the production would be governed by the head rather than evolving naturally out of our experience.

Q: You've spent much of the past fifteen years directing opera. Has this changed the way you approach theatre?

AS: I'm more sensitive to the rhythm and musicality of a scene. Modern, naturalistic acting techniques that work so well in cinema tend to flatten a performance; actors today talk in a soft, monotonous voice and understand only the small-scale psychology of a moment. On the contrary, an opera like La Bohème may be telling a realistic story, but the people in it can only express themselves by singing. Their feelings are simple but they have to sing the lines, and the experience is incredibly rich. Theatre used to be like that, but it's become weak and bland because actors no longer sing. Great performances require a state of high inner charge, and the voice takes on another dimension, as if speaking actors are singing and their bodies dancing. We should sing and dance our parts; that I learned from opera.

Q: Your favorite playwrights—Shakespeare, Brecht, Gozzi, Chekhov, the Greeks—all wrote for nonrealistic, heightened, operatic styles of theatre.

AS: What interests me in their work is the contradiction, the paradox, the quality of surprise. Theatre needs to surprise us at every second, otherwise it becomes lifeless and we lose interest.

Q: What Peter Brook refers to as "deadly theatre."

AS: "Deadly" because only a miracle can save it from death!

Q: You studied under Brook for several years. Did you observe rehearsals for any of his Shakespeare productions?

AS: For *Timon of Athens* and part of *A Midsummer Night's Dream*. I learned how to analyze a Shakespearean text by watching him. He takes every line and studies it deeply, extracting as many meanings as possible from the language.

Q: While rehearsing *Merchant*, you often spoke of the play's complex structure. Could you explain what you meant?

AS: It never takes more than three pages for the situation of a Shakespeare play to change completely, as if another play has entered and interrupted the action. A play by Racine or Corneille establishes a single mood that continues for two hours, but Shakespeare gives us a kaleidoscope of moods, presenting many shifting aspects of life and the human condition. The third act of *Merchant* opens with a Shylock scene that we're staging in the style of the Grand Guignol, as an unbelievably witty, imaginative, intelligent cabaret. The next scene, in Belmont, is as mystical and ritualistic as Japanese Noh theatre, as Bassanio attempts to find the right casket and Portia confesses the nature of her soul. That tempo is broken by the arrival of the Venetians; Salerio, the gossip columnist, invades the temple, and we're hurled into a play of small talk and intrigue. Moments later we enter the formality of the trial, and the theatrical style has changed once again. The play shifts from ritual to the trivia of the street in seconds; one moment we're watching a romantic comedy, the next a solemn courtroom drama. Shakespeare allows us to question the way we perform; it's impossible to present the play in a single acting style.

Q: You've said in the past that you regard Shakespeare as an allegorical playwright. Is *The Merchant of Venice* an allegory?

AS: There are certainly allegorical layers within it, and aspects of the play that can only be understood symbolically. Take Portia's relationship with Bassanio. A group of students asked me recently how such a wise and mature woman could love so unsteady a man. The answer, I think, is that Portia understands her goal is to help Bassanio grow spiritually. Portia, like Petruchio in *The Taming of the Shrew* and Imogen in *Cymbeline*, begins the play as a mature and complete human being. She has longings and desires, but she doesn't need to grow. She is, in allegorical terms, the anima, and Bassanio the animus that she must train so that the two can live together harmoniously. Portia sets him a series of tests to teach him the lessons he needs. Bassanio begins the play as a spendthrift, in a state of sexual and emotional confusion. He journeys to Belmont in part because he is attracted by Portia's wealth but also because he longs for something higher, something that enables him to speak such extraordinary poetry as he faces the caskets. Like Bassanio, we all wish to be better than we are; we seek the salvation that Portia can provide.

Q: Bassanio moves from Venice to Belmont, but so do Lancelot, Jessica, Lorenzo, and even Antonio.

AS: Gratiano, too. Belmont functions as a kind of Arcadia, a place of escape from the world of Shylock, from the schemings of the material mind. But Bassanio cannot stay long—even though he has passed the first test and won Portia's hand, he is not yet ready to enter Belmont fully. Portia knows this and sets him a second test. She warns him to behave nobly as she hands him her ring, but he fails the test and gives it away. Only when he finally leaves Venice and his old life can she forgive him and offer him a second chance. The play's fifth act is, according to this interpretation, wonderfully hopeful, because Bassanio really has a chance to start over. Salvation is always possible, provided we are able to discover our own Arcadia.

Q: Does Portia also teach Shylock?

AS: She tries to. It's often said that after praising "the quality of mercy" she shows little mercy herself, but if she had allowed him to leave the trial and keep his money, he would simply have gone home to his old, manipulative habits. There would be no change, no transformation. Shylock must be transformed, because in symbolic terms a man who has no heart, who is unable to exercise mercy, is equated with the devil. Today, Shylock's enforced conversion to Christianity seems unacceptable. But if we understand Portia's actions from an allegorical point of view, she is teaching him humility by example. He appears to have been destroyed, but who really knows what happens to Shylock? When he leaves the trial, is he going to kill himself or change? Rather than give a dogmatic answer, Shakespeare prefers to leave the question mysteriously open.

THE MERCHANT OF VENICE

The Jew in the Spotlight
by Gideon Lester

The Merchant of Venice has been performed more than any of Shakespeare's plays except *Hamlet*. It has also been the most reviled and reinvented, thanks in no small part to its portrayal of a certain Jewish moneylender. Shylock has swollen in our imaginations to become the star of a show in which he was written as a relatively small part. But beneath four hundred years of hatred and bravura lies a more elusive, delicately crafted play than the rough-and-tumble of the "Jewish question" will ever allow.

In 1981, when PBS announced plans to broadcast Jonathan Miller's BBC production of *The Merchant of Venice*, the Anti-Defamation League sought an injunction to prevent the transmission on the grounds that the play might incite racial hatred against Jewish Americans. Their action was not without precedent. Nineteen years earlier, the New York Board of Rabbis successfully prevented the national televising of Joseph Papp's production of *Merchant* with George C. Scott as Shylock, which had already been lambasted by critics and religious leaders when it opened in Central Park. "Many of the lines were embarrassing, vicious and infectious," wrote Guy Savino in the *Newark Evening News*. Rabbi Louis Newman of Congregation Rodeph Shalom on the Upper West Side denounced the play as "hate-provoking" and "obnoxious" and preached a sermon entitled "Shylock in Central Park—A Municipal and Cultural Mistake." After much public debate and lengthy, angry correspondence in the *New York Times*, Papp and the television executives agreed to abandon the proposed national broadcast and air the program on New York stations alone.

It is no surprise that in the decades since World War II, *The Merchant of Venice* has suffered an equivocal critical reception. While the Anti-Defamation League was attempting to halt broadcast of the BBC production, the British playwright Arnold Wesker wrote an article in the *Guardian* describing the play as "a hateful, ignorant portrayal" that "confirms and feeds those whose anti-Semitism is dormant." It has become common for directors approaching *Merchant* to recontextualize the play's perceived bigotry by invoking images of Nazi persecution: in Bill Alexander's production for the Royal Shakespeare Company in 1987, a lynch mob hurtled through the streets of Venice spraying swastikas on walls and chanting anti-Jewish slogans, while in 1989 Peter Hall surrounded Shylock with a spitting, cursing bevy of Christians who provoked Dustin Hoffman's temperate moneylender to a justifiable fury.

The irony of such revisionist productions is that, in seeking to recast *The Merchant of Venice* in an ideologically acceptable form, they are compelled to focus their attention on those parts of the text that today seem most problematic. Shylock, who appears in just five of the play's twenty scenes, is, as we shall see, a subsidiary figure in *Merchant*; to judge from the reviews of major postwar productions, he might have been the only character on stage. The most notorious of all Shakespeare's creations, Shylock carries on his shoulders a grim significiance for millions who have neither seen nor read the play. Many of the world's finest actors have tackled the role— Laurence Olivier and Morris Carnovsky, Warren Mitchell and Antony

Sher—but we remember nothing of the actors who played their Bassanios, Antonios, and Portias, the parts that, by virtue of their length alone, might ordinarily receive top billing.

As if to prove the maxim that we are most fascinated by that which most disgusts us, Arnold Wesker himself wrote a play about Shylock, first produced in Stockholm in 1976. The history of *The Merchant of Venice* is filled with such contradictions. There is, for instance, a strong tradition of Hebrew and Yiddish productions that portray Shylock as a misunderstood victim of anti-Semitic persecution. One of the finest actors of the Yiddish theatre in New York, Jacob Adler, played Shylock as a noble patriarch, a man "who is rooted in life and has grown strong in it."

In 1903 Adler performed Shylock on Broadway, speaking Yiddish while the rest of his cast spoke English. Less than four decades later, the role had become a significant weapon in the armory of Nazi propaganda. A review of one Viennese production of the play described Shylock as "a pathological image of the East European Jewish type, expressing all its inner and outer uncleanliness, emphasizing danger through humor."

World War II may have refocused our interest in *The Merchant of Venice*, but the tradition of a Shylock-centered production began long before the Holocaust. Actors from Edwin Booth in London to Ira Aldridge in New York used the role as a star turn, frequently cutting the fifth act of the play from which Shylock is absent and inserting additional scenes to heighten the impact of their performance. The most famous Shylock of the nineteenth century was the British actor Henry Irving, who, according to one observer, played the part as "the only gentleman in the play, and most ill-used." George Bernard Shaw was less than enthusiastic about Irving's interpretation, remarking famously that his "huge and enduring success as Shylock was due to his absolutely refusing to allow Shylock to be the discomforted villain of the piece. *The Merchant of Venice* became 'The Martyrdom of Irving,' which was, it must be confessed, far finer than 'The Tricking of Shylock.'"

But to what extent does a performance of Shylock that heightens the character's tragic nobility require the suppression of Shakespeare's text? Although the Jewish moneylender was clearly born of a medieval comic tradition akin to the Italian *commedia dell'arte*, we know little about early performances of the role. It is not even certain which of Shakespeare's actors first created the part; conflicting traditions assign the honor to Richard Burbage, the tragedian who performed Othello and King Lear, and to Will Kemp, the company buffoon. The earliest surviving account of a production of the play suggests that Shylock has long been seen as a psychologically ambiguous character. Nicholas Rowe, Shakespeare's first editor and biographer, watched the role performed by Thomas Doggett, a celebrated clown, and later wrote:

> Though we have seen that play received and acted as a comedy, and the part of the Jew performed by an excellent comedian, yet I cannot but think it was designed tragically by the author. There appears in it such a deadly spirit of revenge, such a savage fierceness and fellness, and such a bloody designation of cruelty and mischief, as cannot agree either with the style or characters of comedy.

Is *The Merchant of Venice* a comedy or a tragedy? Is Shylock, in Jacob Adler's words, a man of "high intellect and proud convictions" or an embodiment of pure evil, a savage spirit of darkness and revenge? The anxiety experienced by Rowe is not an uncommon reaction among audiences, for *Merchant* defies easy categorization. The play appears to embrace every dramatic genre—comedy and tragedy, romance and melodrama—a balancing act that suggests the operation of narrative strategies more complex than might be implied by the heavy-handed approach of recent Shylock-centered productions.

The structure of *The Merchant of Venice* incorporates two primary narratives: the Antonio plot, in which a merchant, thinking he has lost all his wealth at sea, discovers that his ships have miraculously been saved, and the Bassanio/Portia plot, where a young nobleman, having squandered his inheritance, seeks to marry a wealthy heiress.

The exposition, development, and resolution of these two narratives, neither of which directly concerns the character of Shylock, provide the essential structure of the text. Woven into, and frequently interrupting, this structure is a matrix of classical and medieval narrative motifs. The play contains at least eleven of these subsidiary fables, among them the casket plot, in which Portia's father demands that his daughter marry the suitor who correctly answers a riddle; the flesh bond stipulated by Shylock as security against his loan to Antonio; the fable of the servant who flees his cantankerous master to seek employment from a young nobleman; the recognition plot, where the blind Old Gobbo is finally reunited with his son Lancelot (a motif Shakespeare employs to greater effect in *King Lear*); the disguise plot, in which Portia dresses up as a young lawyer in order to rescue her husband's "dearest friend"; the ring trick that forms most of the play's fifth act; and the revenge plot, in which a wronged man, his daughter and riches stolen from him and his faith reviled, seeks a terrible revenge on his aggressors. All these fables are familiar stocks-in-trade from medieval romance and classical mythology, and all, incidentally, are in some manner concerned with the transforming, corrupting power of wealth so central to *The Merchant of Venice*.

In this matrix of interdependent narrative motifs, the principal characters of *Merchant* play many parts. Shylock is not only the intractable, bloodthirsty usurer of the flesh-bond fable but also the abandoned father in the revenge plot and a Jewish businessman forced to compromise his beliefs and his fortune. Portia may be the passive trophy of the casket plot, but she serves more active character functions as the male impersonator in the disguise plot, the artful wife in the fable of the ring trick, and the bearer of extraordinary news who reveals to Antonio that his ships have been saved.

These simple narrative motifs establish patterns of anticipation in an audience; the protagonist of a revenge tragedy is expected to behave in one way, a suitor to the hand of a young princess quite another. As Dudley Andrews remarks in *Concepts in Film Theory* (1984), viewers of a play or film are adept at synthesizing expectation based on their *a priori* knowledge of the genre they are watching. Andrews defines genres as "specific networks of formulas which deliver a certified product to the waiting customer." When the formula changes, as it does frequently in *The Merchant of Venice*, audience members are required to amend their expectations of the narrative and character structures unfolding before them.

Such protean characterization, where one character can exist in several narrative planes simultaneously, gives rise to a subjective model of dramatic psychology that is strikingly modern. Shylock's scene with Tubal at the opening of Act III is a case in point. Virtually every line in this remarkable dialogue switches Shylock's role from antagonist to protagonist and back again as he plays first the malevolent usurer, cackling with pleasure as he plans to "plague" and "torture" Antonio, then the wretched, broken old man, abandoned by his daughter and utterly alone in a bigoted, hostile world. An audience is hard-pressed to keep up with this theatrical sleight of hand in which

Shylock is essentially fulfilling two dramatic functions in a single scene: the tragic figure of loss and despair so brilliantly captured by Henry Irving and the odious caricature of a grasping mercenary that feeds claims of the play's anti-Semitism.

These frequent recontextualizations, and the shifts in emotional allegience that result, yield great dramatic dividends. The scene that immediately follows Shylock's dialogue with Tubal takes place at Belmont, where Bassanio correctly solves the riddle of the caskets. No sooner have he and Portia, Nerissa and Gratiano sworn "to solemnize/The bargain of [their] faith" than Salerio enters with news from Antonio "That steals the colour from Bassanio's cheek" and suspends the action of the scene. One of the play's principal narratives is, without warning, obtruding on the other, forestalling resolution and forcing Bassanio (and eventually Portia and Nerissa) to adopt quite different character functions. Only after the fable of the flesh bond has been concluded can we return to the Bassanio/Portia narrative— a salient reminder that Antonio, as well as Portia, requires Bassanio's emotional and practical support.

The shifting layers of narrative that permeate the structure of *The Merchant of Venice* not only subvert traditional categories of genre, they also refuse to coalesce into a tidy unity of plot. The play's final act may provide closure to the two principal narratives—Bassanio and Portia are united, Antonio's wealth is safe—but for several of the subordinate fables there can be no such comic resolution. Shylock has lost his daughter, his riches, and his dignity; the ring trick has demonstrated how little Portia may trust the flighty Bassanio; the Christians of Venice have employed tactics that bear no trace of the "quality of mercy" to punish Shylock; Antonio, the merchant whose overwhelming melancholy frames the play, remains an isolated figure, wealthy but quite alone.

These suspensions in the narrative substructure deflate the comic *élan* of the final scene and conclude the play with a dying fall. Nicholas Rowe's careful anxiety is well placed; *The Merchant of Venice*, elusive to the last, is not a single, simple story with an easily digestible moral. To stage it as an ideological parable is to risk swamping its fine-tuned mechanism that so carefully refrains from the judgment of closure. After four hundred years in the spotlight, it's time for Shylock to take a few measured paces upstage.

Reflections
by Rob Orchard

Twenty seasons seems like a long time. We've produced 139 new works (60 percent of which were American or world premieres) and toured to 20 international festivals in 15 countries on 4 continents, as well as to 63 cities across the United States. The pace is relentless; little is predictable. It can be frustrating at times, but it's never boring. Time flies.

I thought I'd reflect on the past twenty seasons by attempting to answer some of the questions I'm most often asked: How do we select our plays? Why a resident company? Why rotating repertory? Why at a university? Why are we not-for-profit?

I'll start with the last question because the answer informs all the others. It began with a challenge. In February 1979, after the basic arrangements had been made to bring our company from Yale to Harvard, Anne Hawley, the dynamic executive director of the Massachusetts Cultural Council (now head of the Isabella Stewart Gardner Museum), promised us a grant—with a hitch. By law, Council funds were awarded only to separately incorporated, federally designated not-for-profit entities. The grant deadline was March 31. Generally it takes a minimum of six months (not six weeks) to secure official nonprofit 501(c) status. But happily we did it, and the result was a grant of $50,000. The most we had received from the state of Connecticut during thirteen years at Yale was $15,000. It was the first signal that we were playing on a bigger field.

But why not-for-profit? The question lingers behind the voices of corporate officers, audiences, and even loyal volunteers and friends. Why can't we balance the budget with income from ticket sales alone? They do on Broadway. Not-for-profit corporations, however, are responsible for a more complex mission than one measured strictly by the bottom line. Notice I use the term *not-for-profit* rather than *nonprofit*. Although technically the same, there's an important perceptual distinction. Nonprofit suggests an effort that, regrettably, didn't make money, not-*for*-profit one that doesn't have to.

Moreover, not-for-profit entities don't pay taxes. And as public charities they receive contributions from foundations, corporations, and individuals, who in turn enjoy additional tax breaks for their gifts. Why? Because the government has determined that official not-for-profit corporations are performing an essential public service—one that could not be delivered if the organization were structured solely for the purpose of making a profit. We readily acknowledge these efforts in three other areas of public not-for-profit service—education, health, and religion. But not necessarily in culture.

Theatres in America are relatively new to the not-for-profit world. Before the 1950s, most professional theatre in the United States was for-profit work traveling to or from New York. Every city had at least one Broadway-style "road house" (standard proscenium, minimum of twelve hundred seats) to host these productions. Indeed, earlier in this century traveling professional troupes out of New York performed Shakespeare's plays throughout the country without the need for subsidy. The works of Shakespeare have always been popular with the public. At that time, box office income was sufficient to cover costs and provide for a reasonable profit.

Eventually, however, market forces made this increasingly difficult. Transportation, advertising, and personnel costs went up, and competition from other leisure-time activities emerged. Because they relied exclusively on the box office, the operators of these for-profit companies were forced to increase ticket prices in an attempt to cover costs. Gradually, increased costs resulted in higher ticket prices and produced smaller audiences. Shakespeare, although universally admired, had become too expensive, and the number and variety of productions available declined. As a result, communities began to explore alternatives to the New York–centric system for access to serious professional theatre.

One obvious alternative was to try to do it more efficiently. Eighty percent of production costs, however, involve people. To do *Hamlet* as written takes thirty-one actors. It can be adapted and performed with fewer, but not many fewer than twenty. And by today's for-profit

Members of the company in *Henry V* (1994–1995).

standards you can't justify a commercial production of Neil Simon with twenty actors, much less William Shakespeare. The average cast size for a Broadway drama (as opposed to a musical) is fewer than ten.

In the end, I think few would argue against the idea that great works deserve to be produced regardless of size. And such plays demand the talent of the most highly skilled actors. But we know from experience that if we relied exclusively on the marketplace, live professional productions of Shakespeare's plays (as well as those by Chekhov, Pirandello, Ibsen, Brecht, Shaw, Euripides, Aristophanes, Racine, Pinter, Ionesco, Beckett, and others) throughout America would cease. This isn't theory; it's fact.

So, to those who question the necessity of not-for-profit theatre, I say, look to the past. Experience proves without doubt that we need alternatives to the commercial model to give the public access to important works of art. Moreover, if we relied only on the marketplace, young, untested talent and new forms of expression would suffer. There is little if any basic research and development in the commercial theatre. And the status quo that results from a lack of experimentation is the enemy of creativity.

The ultimate solution to this dilemma was the establishment of ongoing, not-for-profit theatres, based in and supported by local communities, producing a range of recognized and neglected classics along with new work at affordable prices, connecting with young people, and encouraging a process of experimentation and discovery in partnership with attentive audiences. Along with the commercial "road houses" serving the financial interests of Broadway musicals, there are now hundreds of resident theatre organizations in the United States based in virtually every major city and serving the interests of artists, audiences, and the community at large. The theatre has taken its place alongside the local symphony, ballet, opera, and fine arts museum as a defining part of the municipal landscape.

Our not-for-profit structure may have been conceived as an expedient administrative mechanism to receive a grant, but it has functioned over these past twenty seasons in many more profound and deeply felt ways to serve the public and the art form we revere.

Why Are We Based at a University?

Theatre engages the mind and the heart simultaneously. When the basic elements of great writing, acting, design, and staging are present, the resulting experience should be intellectually and emotionally transforming. These moments often have their greatest impact on us when our imaginations are exercised and our minds hospitable to experiences for their own sake—before the practical concerns of careers and family dominate. In a university, the elemental power of theatre benefits from a young, inquiring, receptive audience. It's the perfect environment for progressive work.

Theatregoing is also enriched when the issues addressed stimulate debate. Universities generally respect alternative points of view and encourage their expression. Our audience listens carefully and argues forcefully. After almost every performance, people cluster in small groups for animated discussion.

So, as a base for the ideal audience, free expression, debate, experimentation, intellectual inquiry, and aesthetic exploration, the university would seem to be the right environment for theatre. There is, however, frequently tension between the academic and artistic worlds. In the university as in society at large, the arts are often considered frills. We've had to contend with these forces, and it's been more of a challenge at Harvard than it was at Yale.

Yale is distinguished by preeminent graduate schools of music, drama, art, and architecture. It has adjunct professorships to engage and embrace artists. Their creativity occupies a valued place alongside the scholarship of academic colleagues.

When we arrived at Harvard in 1979, there wasn't a school of drama or even a department for that matter. Indeed, there wasn't even a credit course in the art and practice of theatre. Students could study theatre literature and playwriting for credit, but not acting, directing, or design. Artistic expression was largely extracurricular. The studio and performing arts have historically been viewed at Harvard as a diversion for enlightened amateurs, not a central course of activity with academic respectability. It has, therefore, been more difficult in Cambridge to sustain an artistic community and penetrate the life of the university.

To me, the condition at Harvard seemed ripe. We were, after all, a teaching organization. Bob Brustein presided over the birth of the Yale Repertory Theatre for the express purpose of providing a professional laboratory for the students and faculty in the School of Drama of which he was dean and I was managing director. The company has always been populated by dedicated teachers, many of whom joined us in Cambridge.

Over time we've been able to introduce credit courses in theatre practice at Harvard College (and the Harvard Extension and Summer Schools), and we established the Institute for Advanced Theatre Training—a small, intensive, graduate-level, two-year professional training conservatory now operating in an exclusive association with the Moscow Art Theatre School. Progress has been made.

Harvard is also currently engaged in an admirable attempt to encourage more interaction between and among its various schools, departments, centers, projects, and institutes. The arts have something to contribute to this effort. The culture may change. We're also hoping to increase our endowment sufficiently to lessen the pressures on annual fund-raising and thus provide time to participate more actively in this process.

But the ideal of the university as incubator and facilitator of artistic expression has yet to be realized. And our theatre must continue to explore mutually beneficial connections with the students and faculty to demonstrate the value of this ideal. As Chekhov implores, "We must work."

Why a Resident Company? Why Rotating Repertory?

The repertory system is a pattern of production commonly used outside the United States. It's a method of work in which our productions are rehearsed and performed in groups of two or three, presented in daily rotation, and cast largely from a pool of actors engaged for the entire season. Ten to twelve actors are part of the ongoing company each year. We supplement this core group as needed with additional actors for the season and for each repertory sequence. And to this we add talented students from our advanced training program as well as undergraduates on occasion. Since we've been an active producing and teaching organization for decades, it's not surprising that the vast majority of actors in the company are people we've trained or worked with extensively.

For the actors, the value of this system can probably be best understood by analogy to sports. We refer to this as an artistic ensemble: people working together on multiple projects over extended periods. As a result, the players (actors) and coaches (directors) know how best to utilize individual talent in support of the greater needs of the team (production). It makes for a winning effort.

Most theatre projects in America are produced by hiring a different group of actors for each play. Actors are brought together for the first time at the beginning of rehearsals and continue until the last performance, after which they disperse. This is not necessarily a bad way of working. Indeed, some would argue that this method allows each production to engage only those actors who are ideally suited for each role. The pool of available actors is obviously larger than that of a resident company.

There is, however, value to a well-drilled ensemble, value to a company whose talent has been honed by months and years of careful coaching, individual development, and group experience. Moreover, if the acting company is in residence full-time, you also have the advantage of developing plays over an extended period—the best way to evolve new and progressive work.

In addition, good actors respond to the challenges of working on multiple projects simultaneously. It stretches their acting "muscles." In a repertory system, actors may be rehearsing and/or performing up to four roles each week—perhaps a large part in one work and supporting roles in others. Variety breeds spontaneity. Actors aren't shackled to a single character for eight weeks.

Our system combines the benefits of both approaches. We add actors to the core group to accommodate the idiosyncratic needs of specific productions but place them in the company of a well-developed, mature, mutually supportive ensemble.

From a business perspective, this system also has its advantages. Normally in the United States, when a production ends a standard four-week run (in time for the next work to take the stage) the actors head to the airport and the sets to the dump. The months of planning, rehearsing, and performing cease. What other industry would throw away an investment of $400,000 (the average cost of developing an A.R.T. production) after only four weeks "on the market" when there's still a demand for the "product"?

The repertory system provides an alternative. When a theatre employs a resident company and produces in rotating repertory, every investment can be more fully exploited. Initially each new production has a standard run of thirty to thirty-five performances. If the work has found an audience, it can be easily extended. Each repertory sequence has predetermined "open dates" into which additional performances of the more popular works can be scheduled because the actors are still in residence and the sets are portable. In this way, productions that are successful at the box office support those that are not. This liberates artistic choices by surrounding riskier productions with those more likely to catch on with the public.

Moreover, following the initial repertory sequence, a production can be easily brought back in later years. Our warehouse is stocked with works ready for revival at any time anywhere in the world. We currently have productions in our repertory (such as *The King Stag* and *Six Characters in Search of an Author*) that have been active for more than fifteen years and have been performed hundreds of times in dozens of countries.

Is maintaining a resident acting company working in repertory more expensive than hiring a separate company of actors rehearsing and performing one production at a time? In our current season, the number of actor weeks (one actor for one week equals one actor week) would be roughly the same under either system. But there are considerable savings in transportation and living costs with a resident company.

Building and shifting the sets, however, is more expensive because of the engineering, construction, and labor costs associated with changing them over and making them capable of breakdown into transportable and storable units. This additional cost (a factor of roughly 10 percent) is an investment in being able to extend, revive, and tour successful works. Over twenty years, the additional income from being able to extend works within each season has alone far surpassed the increased expense. When you add to this the net income from revivals and tours in subsequent seasons, the value of the investment is clear.

Still, theatre is the most evanescent of all the arts. Not every production is saved. Guest directors and designers depart after opening night and rarely return to see the production's true rhythms after a few weeks of performances. Actors go on to other projects, leaving behind every word, move, and gesture.

In the visual arts, the work doesn't change. A painting or sculpture exists as created for centuries. In the collaborative performing arts, a standard repertory in ballet, opera, and music is often repeated (and reinterpreted). But on Broadway, as soon as a production starts losing money it closes. And in regional theatre, although a production may transfer or extend, it does so usually only if it's a huge success and only immediately after it was initially scheduled to close. The resident repertory system provides an alternative. An artistic community has the satisfaction of knowing that a production, like a good book, can be plucked off the shelf, put back on stage, and enjoyed by artists and audiences for years.

How Do We Select Our Plays?

This most common question is also the most elusive.

We once made a list of the various factors taken into account when selecting a season. They are available artists (resident actors, directors, designers), audience trends/interest (season-ticket holders, single-ticket buyers), marketing (can we sell it), fund-raising (will it attract/turn off contributors), balance (new plays versus classics, better known versus less well known, comedy versus tragedy), scale (number of characters, scenic locations, costumes), opportunities for students, touring/residency potential, corporate underwriting possibilities, cosponsorship prospects, and so forth. The list goes on.

The primary choice for each project, however, is usually rooted in one core artistic area. One person or group emerges as the initial reason for the selection. For instance, in 1984 *The King Stag* was produced primarily as a vehicle for the designs and choreography of Julie Taymor and the directorial vision of Andrei Serban. When David Mamet, Paula Vogel, or Don DeLillo, among others, sends us a new play, or Philip Glass a chamber opera, we do it—such is our respect and working relationship with these distinguished artists.

At various times we have been committed to developing multiple projects with particular directors: Andrei Serban, Ron Daniels, Anne

Bogart, Andrei Belgrader, François Rochaix, Robert Brustein, Richard Foreman, JoAnne Akalaitis, Marcus Stern, Scott Zigler, David Wheeler, and Robert Wilson, to name a few.

In addition, more often than not projects are driven by our desire to cast certain members of the company: *Heartbreak House* for Jeremy Geidt; *Tartuffe* for Alvin Epstein; *The Wild Duck* for Will LeBow, Karen MacDonald, and Steve Rowe; *Phaedra* for Randy Danson and Ben Evett; *The Taming of the Shrew* for Kristin Flanders and Don Riley; *The Servant of Two Masters* and *Woyzeck* for Tommy Derrah; *Long Day's Journey into Night* for Claire Bloom and Bill Camp; *The Caretaker* for Jack Willis and Jeremy Geidt; and the ensemble of Epstein, Geidt, Evett, and Remo Airaldi for the 1994 *Waiting for Godot*—to name just a few examples from recent members of the company. None of the plays would have been selected at the time if these leading actors had not been available.

Other examples over time include *Hamlet* for Mark Rylance; *King Lear* for F. Murray Abraham; *Godot* in 1983 for Mark Linn-Baker, John Bottoms, and Tony Shalhoub; *The Serpent Woman* for Cherry Jones; *Uncle Vanya* for Christopher Walken, Dan Von Bargen, and Lindsay Crouse; and *How I Learned to Drive* for Arliss Howard and Debra Winger.

At the heart of all this, of course, is Robert Brustein. His taste and wide-ranging talent inform every artistic choice. Bob not only guides and oversees this process, he also participates as director, playwright, translator/adaptor, and, on occasion, actor.

From the management side it has been important to provide an environment where artistic choices are made with enthusiasm rather than reluctance. Decisions made for reasons other than artistic possibility are usually wrong. My favorite phantom five-play season made for plausible but distinctly wrong reasons includes a small-cast first play (because the weekly payroll must be kept to a minimum until box office income starts coming in) with broad appeal (because season tickets are still being sold) opening in October (because no one goes to serious theatre until after Labor Day), followed by something calculated to appeal to families (because it runs during the holidays), leading to a farce or comedy (because people are depressed after the holidays), leaving the fourth slot entirely up to the artistic director (because it's February and whatever risks this entails are diminished by the likelihood that all major donors are headed south for the month), and finally ending with a perky spring musical (because it's important to please the greatest number of people when season tickets are being renewed). Disproportionate dependence on choices like these, however logical from a purely business point of view, mitigate against artistic achievement.

When administrative calculations dominate artistic choices (rather than the other way around), there's trouble. Artists, managers, and technicians are at their best when they share a genuine enthusiasm for the work. That enthusiasm translates onto the stage, and audiences sense it immediately. When decisions are made for other than core artistic purposes, the production process becomes mechanical, turning out widgets rather than works of art.

I'll end with an example that speaks to many if not all these issues. In May 1983 I was in my office interviewing a prospective employee. Through the glass door I could see Bob Brustein heading my way. He burst into the office shaking a script in his hand. For a brief moment one of the most articulate men on the planet was speechless. He waved the script over his head until the words "I've just read the most powerful new play" stumbled out.

We had chosen a play. It was Marsha Norman's newest work, *'Night, Mother*, a ninety-minute dialogue between a mother and daughter in which the daughter announces in the opening moment that she's going to commit suicide. As Bob went on to describe this profoundly moving play, he began to caution that the subject matter might not appeal to vast audiences. In the final moments the daughter does the deed she threatens.

We had to reconfigure the upcoming season (which had already been chosen) to include *'Night, Mother*. The then little-known Kathy Bates played the suicidal daughter and Anne Pitoniak the mother. For a variety of complex reasons, it could only be slotted into repertory over the holidays. Not exactly a Christmas confection. But after the first week the run instantly sold out—a testament to a talented playwright's power to tell a compelling story; to the determination and commitment of an artistic director; and to our audience and local critics, who instantly recognized the play's distinction. *'Night, Mother* went on to win the Pulitzer Prize (the first time the prize was awarded to a play based on a production outside of New York) and to a successful run on Broadway and finally a film. It's a success story, but at the time it gave us a case of nerves.

Often, however, the riskiest works turn out to be the most rewarding. The public is usually more accommodating to innovation

Terry Alexander (Founding Father) and Royal Miller (Brazil) in *The America Play* (1993–1994).

than we think. We had the same trepidation before the opening of our first production with Robert Wilson, *the CIVIL warS*. Wilson's work can't be explained. He has a nonlinear, highly abstract artistic sensibility. You can't "read" a Wilson play; you can only experience it. During the initial preview performances, half the subscribers left in the first act. In fairness, despite extensive advance newsletter material and feature coverage, the general audience didn't have a clue what it was getting into. By the time *the CIVIL warS* opened officially in the second week, word was out that this was a "difficult" production. Subscribers stayed away. They stopped walking out because they didn't walk in.

Then something thrilling happened. A new, largely younger audience instantly emerged. Single tickets sold out. And since we still had empty seats because subscribers didn't show, we sold vast quantities of standing room, confident that standees could easily slip into empty "no show" seats.

Eventually, by the final weeks, not only were we completely sold out, but the subscriber "no shows" ceased, and people who walked out during previews or didn't show during the earlier part of the run came back demanding to be seated.

This and other experiences like it confirm the power of the theatre to renew and engage an audience. They're also a tribute to our audience, a tenacious, intellectually and aesthetically curious one. And even when we experience a decline in season-ticket renewals after presenting works like *the CIVIL warS,* it's often offset by new subscribers drawn to the theatre by the same production that turned others away. It's a fascinating dialogue.

Not every risky artistic venture, of course, was a success. And just because we bring our collective enthusiasm and commitment to a work doesn't mean that the critics or the public will approve. Conversely, productions we've been disappointed in have sometimes been praised by the press and popular with the public. Nothing is wholly predictable.

In the end, the ultimate challenge and the most likely road to distinction is to ensure that in selecting plays we are guided primarily by the anarchic, idiosyncratic, surprising, confounding, creative character of the individual artist. And to do so, every theatre needs a strong, animated, evolving artistic center. In Cambridge for these twenty seasons, we've been blessed with the determination and intelligence of Robert Brustein. He's made twenty seasons seem like twenty seconds.

The trial scene from *The Merchant of Venice.*

Biographical Notes

JoAnne Akalaitis is currently co-chair of the Directing Program at Juilliard's Drama Division and professor of theatre at Bard College. Former artistic director of the New York Shakespeare Festival/Public Theater, she has received five Obie awards for direction and production, the Drama Desk Award, the NEA award for Sustained Artistic Achievement, a Guggenheim Fellowship, and the National Theatre Residency Grant at the Court Theatre in Chicago. Ms. Akalaitis has directed at such theatres as the A.R.T., the Guthrie, the Goodman, Arena Stage, and Lincoln Center. She was the co-founder and co-artistic director of Mabou Mines, where she directed several productions.

Director **Andrei Belgrader** arrived in the United States from his native Romania in 1978. Since then he has directed three off-Broadway productions: *Woyzeck, Troilus and Cressida,* and his recent *Waiting for Godot.* He has also worked at several regional theatres, including the A.R.T., Yale Repertory Theatre, and the Goodman. At the A.R.T. he received the Boston Circle Critics Awards for Best Play and Best Director for his production of *Waiting for Godot* in the 1982–1983 season. He has also worked at the West Bank Café, and his production of *The Bit Player* there was later performed at the Edinburgh Festival and then moved to two London theatres. Mr. Belgrader has also directed several episodes of the TV show "Coach" for MCA Universal.

Playwright, translator, and adaptor **Shelley Berc**'s plays and essays have been published in the *Drama Review, Performing Arts Journal*, and *Theatre Magazine*. She has collaborated with Andrei Belgrader on such pieces as *Rameau's Nephew, The Servant of Two Masters, Ubu Rock*, and *The Imaginary Invalid* at the A.R.T. and is now working with him on a new musical adaptation of Molière's *Scapin* for the Yale Repertory Theatre. Her plays include *Dual Heads, Burn Out, Shooting Shiva*, and *A Girl's Guide to the Divine Comedy*. Ms. Berc is a professor in the International Writing Program at the University of Iowa and the recipient of several grants and awards, including two Lila Wallace Readers Digest "New Young Audiences" commissions and an NEA Opera/Music Librettist fellowship. She is also the author of two novels: *The Shape of Wilderness* and *Light and Its Shadow*.

David Bevington, the Phyllis Fay Horton Professor in the Humanities at the University of Chicago, is the editor of the *Bantam Shakespeare* and *The Complete Works of Shakespeare* published by Longman, as well as the author of numerous books on medieval, Tudor, and Stuart theatre, including *From "Mankind" to Marlowe* (1962), *Tudor Drama and Politics* (1968), and *Action Is Eloquence: Shakespeare's Language of Gesture* (1984). He has co-edited, with Peter Holbrook, *The Politics of the Stuart Court Masque* (1998). Mr. Bevington is twice past-president of the Shakespeare Association of America.

Sterling Professor of the Humanities at Yale and Berg Professor of English at New York University, **Harold Bloom** has written more than twenty books of literary and religious criticism as well as hundreds of articles and reviews. His books include *The Visionary Company* (1961), *The Anxiety of Influence* (1973), *The Western Canon* (1994), and, most recently, *Shakespeare* (1998). Mr. Bloom has received a Guggenheim Fellowship, the Melville Cane Award, and the Morton Dauwen Zabel Award.

Anne Bogart is artistic director of the Saratoga International Theater Institute (SITI), which she founded with Japanese director Tadashi Suzuki in 1992. Recent works with the SITI company included *Culture of Desire*, a piece combining Andy Warhol and the Velvet Underground with Dante's *Inferno*, and *Bob*, a one-man performance about Robert Wilson. Ms. Bogart has directed at the A.R.T., Alley Theatre, Trinity Repertory Company, En Garde Arts, and Circle Repertory Company, among many other theatres. She has received two Obie awards for Best Direction and a Bessie Award. She was also the recipient of an NEA Artistic Associate Grant in association with Music-Theatre Group. Ms. Bogart was president of Theatre Communications Group from 1991 to 1993 and artistic director of Trinity Repertory Company from 1989 to 1990. She is now an associate professor at Columbia University.

Romanian-born actor, director, and designer **Liviu Ciulei** holds degrees in architecture and theatre. Mr. Ciulei served as artistic director of the Bulandra Theatre in Romania for nine years (1963–1972) and has introduced Romanian audiences to many American works, including Paul Foster's *Elizabeth I*. Mr. Ciulei came to the United States in 1974 when he was invited to the Arena Stage, where he directed and designed *Leonce and Lena*. He returned to Arena Stage in 1997 and made his New York debut that year with *Spring Awakening* at Juilliard and the Public Theater. Mr. Ciulei served as artistic director of the Guthrie Theater from 1980 to 1986, and his stage credits there include *Peer Gynt, Three Sisters*, and *A Midsummer Night's Dream*. He has directed theatre, opera, and film throughout the United States and the world. Mr. Ciulei is now a visiting artist at the University of Tennessee, Knoxville.

Don DeLillo was born in New York and attended Fordham University. Since 1971 he has published eleven novels. They include *Americana, End Zone, Great Jones Street, Ratner's Star, Players, Running Dog, White Noise, Libra, Mao II*, and the recently published and highly acclaimed *Underworld*. *Libra* was adapted by John Malkovich and produced as a play by Steppenwolf Theatre in 1994. Mr. DeLillo's previous play, *The Day Room*, was premiered by the American Repertory Theatre in 1987 and was published by Knopf.

Liz Diamond is resident director of the Yale Repertory Theatre, where her productions have included Seamus Heaney's *The Cure at Troy, Mrs. Warren's Profession*, and the world premiere of *The America Play* by Suzan-Lori Parks, which she also directed at the New York Public Theater. Her productions have won several Obie and Connecticut Critics Circle awards. Ms. Diamond has served as resident director of New Dramatists in New York and teaches directing at the Yale School of Drama.

Christopher Durang is the author of *The Marriage of Bette and Boo, Baby with the Bathwater*, and *Media Amok*, all of which have been presented at the A.R.T., as well as *Laughing Wild, Durang/Durang* (an evening of six plays), and *Sex and Longing*. His new play, *Betty's Summer Vacation*, will premiere at Playwrights Horizons in 1999. In cabaret he has performed *Das Lusitania Songspiel* with Sigourney Weaver and in *Chris Durang and Dawne* (which received the 1995 Bistro Award). He has acted in films and in the Sondheim evening *Putting It Together* with Julie Andrews. For four years he and Marsha Norman have co-chaired the playwriting program at the Juilliard School.

Donald Fanger, the Harry Levin Research Professor of Literature at Harvard, is the author of *Dostoevsky and Romantic Realism: A Study of Dostoevsky in Relation to Balzac, Dickens, and Gogol* (1965; 1998). Other works include "Solzhenitsyn: Art and Foreign Matter" (1975) and *The Creation of Nikolai Gogol* (1979), which won the Christian Gauss Award of Phi Beta Kappa. Professor Fanger writes on modern Russian literature for the *Times Literary Supplement*, the *New Republic*, and other journals.

Jules Feiffer, author of a weekly comic strip, "Feiffer," has been called by Kenneth Tynan "not only the best cartoonist writing, but the best writer cartooning." His honors include a Pulitzer Prize, an Academy Award, and a Library of Congress exhibition of his cartoons and manuscripts. He draws a monthly op-ed cartoon for the *New York Times*, the first cartoonist to be commissioned to do so. Mr. Feiffer has been awarded an Obie and two Outer Critics Circle awards for his plays, which include *Little Murders, Knock Knock, GrownUps*, and *Carnal Knowledge*, for which he wrote the screenplay. More recently he has devoted himself to writing and illustrating books for young readers: *The Man in the Ceiling* and *I Lost My Bear* (an American Library Association Notable Selection). His latest, *Bark, George*, is a Children's Book-of-the-Month Club choice. His latest work for the theatre is a revue, *Jules' Blues*.

Dramatist, actor, director, political activist, satirist, painter, designer, TV comedian, and itinerant clown, **Dario Fo** began his theatrical career in small cabarets and theatres and on Italian television and radio. In collaboration with his wife, actress Franca Rame, he has founded three theatre companies—Compagnia Dario Fo, Nuova Scena, and La Commune. He has written over seventy plays, including *He Had Two Pistols with White and Black*

Eyes; Knock, Knock—Who's There?—The Police!; Accidental Death of an Anarchist; We Won't Play, We Won't Pay; Almost by Accident a Woman: Elizabeth; Female Parts (with Franca Rame); and *Open Couple* (with Franca Rame). In addition to producing more than thirty of his own plays with Ms. Rame and their theatres, he has also directed operas and other theatre works throughout Europe. Mr. Fo made his American acting debut in his internationally celebrated signature piece *Mistero Buffo* at the A.R.T. He and Ms. Rame received an Obie Award for distinguished achievements in theatre, and he was the recipient of the Nobel Prize for literature in 1997.

Playwright, director (theatre, opera, and television), and designer, **Richard Foreman** founded the Ontological-Hysteric Theatre in 1968. He has written, directed, and designed more than thirty of his own plays in the United States and abroad, which have often been co-produced with such groups as the New York Shakespeare Festival, LaMama, the Wooster Group, and Festival d'Automne in Paris. Five of Mr. Foreman's plays have received Obie Awards as best play of the year, and he has been awarded four additional Obie Awards for direction and sustained achievement. In 1995 he was given a MacArthur Award for his "original vision and helping to shape American avant-garde theater." He received the annual literature award from the American Academy and Institute of Arts and Letters in 1992, and in 1991 he was one of the first recipients of the NEA's Lifetime Achievement in the Theater Award. He is also the recipient of a Guggenheim Fellowship, a Rockefeller Foundation Playwright's Award, an NEA Playwright's Fellowship, and a Ford Foundation New American Plays Award.

Carlos Fuentes has written novels, short stories, plays, and essays on both literary and political topics. His novels include *Where the Air Is Clear* (1960), *Aura* (1962), *The Death of Artemio Cruz* (1962), *Terra Nostra* (1975), and *The Old Gringo* (1985). He has received the Rubén Dario Prize (1988); the Miguel de Cervantes Literary Prize from the Spanish Ministry of Culture (1987); the Medal of Honor for Literature, National Arts Club, New York (1988); the Order of Merit (1992, Chile); the French Legion of Honor (1992); the Menéndez Pelayo International Award, University of Santander (1992); the Picasso Medal (1994, UNESCO); and the Príncipe de Asturias Prize (1994). In addition to his literary career, Mr. Fuentes served as Mexico's ambassador to France and has taught at several major universities, including in the Department of Comparative Literature at Harvard.

Marjorie Garber is William R. Kenan, Jr., Professor of English and director of the Center for Literary and Cultural Studies at Harvard University. A cultural critic, she has published three books on Shakespeare: *Dream in Shakespeare* (1974), *Coming of Age in Shakespeare* (1981), and *Shakespeare's Ghost Writers* (1987), and has written general books on the history of the analysis of culture, including *Vested Interests: Cross Dressing and Cultural Anxiety* (1992), *Vice Versa: Bisexuality and the Eroticism of Everyday Life* (1995), and *Symptoms of Culture* (1998). She has also edited *Media Spectacles* (1993); *Secret Agents: The Rosenberg Case, McCarthyism, and Fifties America* (1995); and *Field Work: Sites in Literary and Cultural Studies*. Her academic honors include fellowships from the American Council of

Learned Societies and the Stanford Humanities Center. She is a trustee of the English Institute and a former trustee of the Shakespeare Association of America.

One of the country's foremost comedy writers, **Larry Gelbart** has written for radio, television, film, and stage. He received a Tony Award for co-authoring the stage musical *A Funny Thing Happened on the Way to the Forum*. Other stage credits include *Sly Fox* and *City of Angels*. For the television series "M*A*S*H" he received an Emmy Award. He also wrote for "The Red Buttons Show," "Caesar's Hour," and "The Danny Kaye Show." His screenplay for the 1982 film *Tootsie* received the Los Angeles and New York Film Critics Awards.

A professor at the Yale School of Drama and a critic of the theatre, **Richard Gilman** is the author of *Common and Uncommon Masks: Writings on Theatre* (1961), *The Confusion of Realms* (1969), *The Making of Modern Drama* (1974), *Decadence: The Strange Life of an Epithet* (1979), and *Chekhov's Plays: An Opening into Eternity* (1995). Professor Gilman received the George Jean Nathan Award for Dramatic Criticism in 1971.

Philip Glass has composed work that ranges from opera to film scores to symphonic works and string quartets, as well as writing for dance and theatre pieces. He has composed music for the theatre company Mabou Mines (which he co-founded) and for his own performing group, the Philip Glass Ensemble, and has been a frequent collaborator with director Robert Wilson. Mr. Glass received a Los Angeles Film Critics Award, as well as Oscar and Golden Globe nominations for Best Original Score for the film *Kundun*, and he was made a Chevalier de l'Ordre des Arts et des Lettres by the French government in 1995. He is at work on a new choral symphony that was commissioned by the Salzburg Festival and is scheduled for world premiere in 1999.

Elliot Goldenthal—whose music has been heard at the A.R.T. in Andrei Serban's productions of *The King Stag* (1984) and *The Serpent Woman* (1988)—studied composition with Aaron Copland and John Corigliano. In addition to his theatre music, he has composed for ballets; an oratorio commemorating the end of the Vietnam War; and numerous scores for television and film, including Andy Warhol's *Cocaine Cowboys* (1979), *Drug Store Cowboy* (1989), *Alien 3* (1992), *Interview with the Vampire* (1994), and *Batman Forever* (1995). The American Ballet Theater commissioned the music for a full-length ballet, *Othello*, in 1997. Mr. Goldenthal collaborated with Julie Taymor, the director, puppeteer, and designer, on *Juan Darién*, which won an Obie Award in 1988 and was revived on Broadway in 1996.

Stephen Greenblatt is Harry Levin Professor of Literature at Harvard University. His books include *Marvelous Possessions: The Wonder of the New World; Learning to Curse: Essays in Early Modern Culture; Shakespearean Negotiations: The Circulation of Social Energy in Renaissance England;* and *Renaissance Self-Fashioning: From More to Shakespeare*. He is general editor of *The Norton Shakespeare* and of *The New Historicism: Studies in Cultural*

Poetics and the founding editor and co-chair of *Representations*. He is a Fellow of the American Academy of Arts and Sciences and has been awarded two Guggenheim Fellowships along with other grants and prizes.

Molly Haskell, author and critic, was a longtime staff writer for the *Village Voice, New York Magazine*, and *Vogue*. She has covered films for the feminist quarterly *On the Issues* and does a monthly column for the *New York Observer*. She has written for many publications, including the *New York Times Book Review, Mirabella, Esquire*, the *Nation*, and the *New York Review of Books*. Ms. Haskell has served as artistic director of the Sarasota French Film Festival, on the selection committee of the New York Film Festival, and as adjunct professor of film at Columbia University. Her books include *From Reverence to Rape: The Treatment of Women in the Movies* (1973; revised and reissued in 1989); a memoir, *Love and Other Infectious Diseases* (1990); and a collection of essays and interviews, *Holding My Own in No Man's Land: Women and Men and Films and Feminists* (1997).

In addition to plays, **William Hauptman** has written fiction and scripts for both film and television. His play *Domino Courts* won an Obie Award for distinguished playwriting in 1978, and *Big River* won a Tony Award for Best Book of a Musical (1985). *Gillette*, which had its world premiere at the American Repertory Theatre in 1985, went on to win a Los Angeles Drama Logue Award for distinguished playwriting in 1986. His teleplay *Denmark Vesey's Rebellion* won an Emmy Award nomination, an NAACP award, and a Freedom Foundation award. Mr. Hauptman has contributed short stories and articles to such publications as the *Atlantic Monthly* and the *New York Times*.

Arthur Holmberg, literary director of the A.R.T., heads the playwriting program at Brandeis, where he also teaches dramatic literature and theories of performance. In 1996 Cambridge University Press published his book *The Theatre of Robert Wilson*, the first comprehensive study of this innovative director's work. Mr. Holmberg served on the editorial board of *The World Encyclopedia of Contemporary Theatre* (1996). His writings on theatre, film, and opera have appeared in the *International Herald Tribune, Los Angeles Times, New York Times, Washington Post*, and *Opera News*. Mr. Holmberg is now writing *The Vision of David Mamet* for Cambridge University Press.

Polish-born writer and scholar **Jan Kott** is the author of *Shakespeare Our Contemporary* (1967), a book of criticism that encouraged directors to break with tradition and explore Shakespeare's plays as metaphor and image. It influenced many major theatre directors—Peter Brook, Ariane Mnouchkine, Andrei Serban, and Georgio Strehler, among others. Mr. Kott's other books include *Eating the Gods: An Interpretation of Greek Tragedy* (1973), *The Theater of Essence* (1984), *The Bottom Translation* (1987), and *The Gender of Rosalind* (1992).

Born in Czechoslovakia, **Milan Kundera** established his international reputation with *Laughable Loves* (1974), a collection of short stories, and the novel *The Unbearable Lightness of Being* (Los Angeles Times Book Prize for Fiction, 1984). *Jacques and His Master* (1985) is his only play. Other novels include *The Joke* (Czechoslovak Writers Union Prize, 1968), *Life Is Elsewhere* (Prix Medicis, 1973), *The Farewell Party* (1976, Premio Letterario Mondello, 1978), and *The Book of Laughter and Forgetting* (1980). He has received the Commonwealth Award for distinguished service in literature (1981), the Prix Europa for literature (1982), the Jerusalem Prize (1985), the Académie Française Critics Prize (1987), and the Independent Award for Foreign Fiction (1991).

Gideon Lester has worked as the American Repertory Theatre's resident dramaturg since 1997. His translations include Georg Büchner's *Woyzeck*, directed by Marcus Stern at A.R.T., and Michel Vinaver's *King and Overboard*, produced at the Orange Tree Theatre in London and published by Methuen. He has written for *Theater*, the *Sunday Times*, and the *Boston Globe*. *Enter the Actress*, a one-woman show that he wrote with Claire Bloom, has been performed by Ms. Bloom at theatres throughout this country and abroad. Mr. Lester was educated at Westminster School, Oxford University, and the A.R.T. Institute for Advanced Theatre Training, where he was a Fulbright and Frank Knox scholar.

David Leveaux has directed for both theatre and opera. His Broadway credits include *Electra*, *Anna Christie* with Liam Neeson and Natasha Richardson (which won a Tony Award for Best Revival), and *A Moon for the Misbegotten* (which received a Tony nomination for Outstanding Direction). Mr. Leveaux has directed for the Royal Shakespeare Theatre, the Royal National Theatre, and the Scottish Opera. Since 1993 he has been artistic director of Theatre Project Tokyo, Japan.

For many years **Harry Levin** (now deceased) was Irving Babbitt Professor of Comparative Literature and chair of the Department of Comparative Literature at Harvard. His numerous books include *James Joyce* (1949), *The Overreacher: A Study of Christopher Marlowe* (1952), *The Question of Hamlet* (1959), *The Gates of Horn: Five French Realists* (1963), *The Myth of the Golden Age in the Renaissance* (1969), *Grounds for Comparison* (1972), *Shakespeare and the Revolution of the Times* (1976), and *Playboys and Killjoys: An Essay on the Theory and Practice of Comedy* (1987). In 1953 Mr. Levin was named Chevalier of the Legion of Honor, and in 1962 he received the prize for Distinguished Scholarship in the Humanities from the American Council of Learned Societies.

David Mamet is the award-winning author of such plays as *The Cryptogram* (1995 Obie Award), *The Old Neighborhood*, *Oleanna*, *Sexual Perversity in Chicago* (Obie Award), *American Buffalo* (Obie Award, New York Drama Critics Circle Award), *Edmond* (Obie Award), *Glengarry Glen Ross* (1984 Pulitzer Prize, New York Drama Critics Award), *Speed-the-Plow*, and *The Duck Variations*. His translations and adaptations include *The Cherry Orchard*, *Three Sisters*, and *Uncle Vanya*. Mr. Mamet's screenplays include *The Postman Always Rings Twice*, *The Verdict*, *The Untouchables*, *Wag the Dog*, and *The Rock*, and he wrote and directed the films *The Spanish Prisoner*, *House of Games*, *Things Change*, *Homicide*, and *Oleanna*. His books include *The Village*, *The Old Religion*, *True and False: Heresy and Common*

Sense for the Actor, and *Three Uses of the Knife*, as well as the children's books *Warm and Cold* and *The Duck and the Goat*.

Set designer **Jean-Claude Maret** lives and works in Geneva. His numerous collaborations with Françoise Rochaix include plays and operas in Switzerland, Norway, England, and France. He has also designed for ballet and film, and is the designer of *La Fête des Vignerons 1999* in Vevey, Switzerland.

Jonathan Marks is associate professor and head of directing at Texas Tech University. As literary manager at Yale Repertory Theatre and literary director of the A.R.T., he was the company's chief dramaturg for a dozen years and acted in a number of the company's productions, including *Sganarelle* at both theatres and on tours. He has also worked at the American Conservatory Theater, San Francisco State, Stanford, the Magic Theatre, and Berkeley Repertory Theatre. A Fulbright Fellow in France, he holds a D.F.A. from Yale.

Two-time Tony Award–winning director **Des MacAnuff** co-founded the Dodger Theatre Company and directed its first production, *Gimme Shelter*, in 1978. For several years he served as artistic director of La Jolla Playhouse. During that time he directed four shows that he eventually brought to Broadway: *Big River* (1985), for which he received the Tony Award for Best Director of a Musical; *A Walk in the Woods* (1988); *The Who's "Tommy"* (1993), for which he received an Outer Critics Circle Award, a Drama Desk Award, and a Tony Award for Best Director of a Musical; and the revival of *How to Succeed in Business Without Really Trying* (1995). He made his feature directorial debut with *Cousin Bette*; he is now producing the animated *Iron Giant*.

After training as a physician at Cambridge, **Jonathan Miller**—doctor, director, professor, and philosopher—co-authored and performed in the comedy review *Beyond the Fringe* with Peter Cook, Dudley Moore, and Alan Bennett. His television series for the BBC on the history of medicine, *The Body in Question*, was shown in Britain and America, as were the twelve plays he produced for the BBC's Shakespeare series. Dr. Miller's productions include *The Merchant of Venice* with Laurence Olivier and Joan Plowright at the Royal National Theatre and operas at Covent Garden, the English National Opera, La Scala, and the Metropolitan Opera. His books include *Subsequent Performances*, *Darwin for Beginners*, and biographies of Freud and Marshall McLuhan. In 1998 Dr. Miller curated *On Reflection*, an exhibition combining cognitive science, perceptual theory, and art history, at the National Gallery in London.

Composer and recording artist **Roger Miller** (now deceased) began his career in Nashville writing music for many country music stars. His songs have also been recorded by Neil Diamond, Ringo Starr, and Barbra Streisand. He performed his own songs and won eleven Grammy Awards and six Gold Records. *Big River* was Mr. Miller's first score for the theatre.

Director and playwright **Heiner Müller** (now deceased) is one of the most-produced playwrights in Europe today. Although his works were banned by the German government in the early 1960s, he was awarded the GDR National Prize in 1986. Mr. Müller wrote more than twenty works for the stage, often appropriations and reworkings of Greek tragedy, Shakespeare, Kleist, and Wagner. His plays include *The Scab* (1956), *Philoctetes* (1964), *Germania Death in Berlin* (1971), *Grundling's Life Frederick of Prussia Lessing's Sleep Dream Scream* (1976), *Hamletmachine* (1977), *The Mission* (1979), *Quartet* (1980), and *Despoiled Shore Medeamaterial Landscape with Argonauts* (1982). He received the Heinrich Mann Prize (1959), the Lessing Prize (1975), the Kleist Prize (1990), and the European Theater Prize (1991).

Playwright **Marsha Norman** is co-chair of the playwriting program at the Juilliard School. Her play *'Night, Mother* was awarded the 1983 Pulitzer Prize, the Susan Smith Blackburn Prize, and Hull-Warriner and Drama Desk awards. *The Secret Garden* won a Tony Award and Drama Desk awards, and *Getting Out* received the John Gassner Medallion, the *Newsday* Oppenheimer Award, and the American Theatre Critics Association Citation. She has also written for television and film, including *Face of a Stranger*, starring Gena Rowlands and Tyne Daley, and is the author of a novel, *The Fortune Teller*. Ms. Norman has received grants and awards from the National Endowment for the Arts, the Rockefeller Foundation, and the American Academy and Institute of Arts and Letters.

Playwright **David Rabe**'s first play in New York, *The Basic Training of Pavlo Hummel*, was produced by Joseph Papp at the Public Theater in 1971. His plays have since been produced at such theatres as the A.R.T., Long Wharf, Lincoln Center, and the New York Theatre Workshop, among others. They include *The Orphan*, *In the Boom Boom Room*, *Streamers*, *Goose and Tom Tom*, *Hurlyburly*, *Those the River Keeps*, and *A Question of Mercy*. His work has been honored with numerous Tony nominations and Obie awards, as well as by the Outer Critics Circle. He won a Tony in 1972 for *Sticks and Bones* and has three times received the Hull Warriner Award for playwriting. He has also written several screenplays: *I'm Dancing as Fast as I Can*, *Streamers, Casualties of War*, and *Hurlyburly*. His novel, *Recital of the Dog*, was published in 1993.

Swiss theatre and opera director **François Rochaix** is associate director of the A.R.T. and director of the A.R.T./MXAT Institute for Advanced Theatre Training. He has worked extensively in theatres and opera houses throughout Europe and the United States, including the Scottish Opera, Opera North, and the Seattle Opera, where he directed Wagner's *Ring*. He founded the Théâtre de l'Atelier in Geneva and served as general director of the Théâtre de Carouge. Mr. Rochaix is artistic director of *La Fête des Vignerons 1999*.

Anne Roiphe is the author of seven novels, including *Generation Without a Memory: A Jewish Journey in Christian America* (1981), *A Season for Healing: Reflections on the Holocaust* (1988), *Fruitful: A Real Mother in the*

Modern World (1996), and *Up the Sandbox*. She writes a biweekly column for the *New York Observer*, and her reviews and articles have appeared in such publications as the *New York Times, Washington Post*, and *Glamour*, among others.

Paul Rudnick's plays include *The Most Fabulous Story Ever Told; Jeffrey; Mr. Charles, Currently of Palm Beach; The Naked Eye*; and *I Hate Hamlet*. His novels include *Social Disease* and *I'll Take It*, and his articles and essays have appeared in *Vanity Fair, Vogue, Esquire*, the *New Yorker, Spy*, and the *New York Times*. He is rumored to be quite close to *Premiere* magazine's film critic, Libby Gelman-Waxner, whose collected columns have been published under the title *If You Ask Me*. His screenplays include *Addams Family Values*, the screen adaptation of *Jeffrey*, and *In & Out*.

Robert Scanlan was literary director of the A.R.T. and a lecturer on dramatic arts at Harvard University from 1989 to 1997. He directs frequently in the United States and abroad and has specialized throughout his career in the works of Samuel Beckett. Recent directing assignments include the trio of Beckett plays *Eh Joe, Ghost Trio*, and *Nacht und Träume*, which were presented at the A.R.T. and at the 1996 Beckett Festival in Strasbourg, France; the Polish language premiere of *Speed-the-Plow* at the Stary Theatre in Cracow; the world premiere of *The Hamster Wheel* in Belfast; the Chinese-language premiere of *Crimes of the Heart* in the People's Republic of China; and the world premiere of Derek Walcott and Galt MacDermot's Caribbean musical *Steel* at the A.R.T. (co-directed with Mr. Walcott). Mr. Scanlan received the 1995 Boston Theatre Award for Outstanding Director.

Peter Sellars, director of opera, theatre, and film, made his professional debut directing on the Loeb Mainstage at the A.R.T. He has since served as artistic director of the Los Angeles Festival (1988–1996), the American National Theatre at the Kennedy Center, the Boston Shakespeare Company, and the Elitch Theatre for Children in Denver. Mr. Sellars has won numerous honors, including a MacArthur Fellowship and an Emmy Award. His past teaching positions include a visiting professorship in the Center for Theatre Arts at the University of California, Berkeley. Mr. Sellars is a professor in the Department of World Arts and Cultures at the University of California, Los Angeles.

Associated with Robert Brustein's theatre company for more than twenty years, at the A.R.T. **Andrei Serban** has directed *The King Stag, Sganarelle, Three Sisters, The Juniper Tree, The Miser, Twelfth Night, Sweet Table at the Richelieu, The Taming of the Shrew*, and *The Merchant of Venice*. At the Yale Repertory Theatre he directed *Sganarelle, Ghost Sonata*, and *Mad Dog Blues*. In New York, for Ellen Stewart's LaMama, he conceived, together with Elizabeth Swados, *Fragments of a Trilogy (Medea, Electra, The Trojan Women), As You Like It, The Good Woman of Setzuan*, and *Uncle Vanya*. For Joseph Papp's New York Shakespeare Festival, he directed *The Cherry Orchard, Agamemnon, Master and Margarita, The Umbrellas of Cherbourg, The Seagull*, and most recently *Cymbeline* in Central Park. He teaches at Columbia University, where he is director of the Oscar Hammerstein II Center for Theatre Studies and the acting program.

Anatoly Smelyansky, leading Russian theatre writer, scholar, and critic, is the associate artistic director of the Moscow Art Theatre, dean of the Moscow Art Theatre School for Academic Studies, and associate director of the Institute for Advanced Theatre Training at Harvard. His books, published in Russia, the United States, and Great Britain, include *Our Collocutors: Russian Classics on Stage, Is Comrade Bulgakov Dead?* (Bulgakov and the Moscow Art Theatre), and *The Russian Theatre After Stalin*. Dr. Smelyansky is also the editor of new ten-volume *Complete Works by Stanislavsky* and *Moscow Art Theatre: One Hundred Years* encyclopedia.

Susan Sontag has published three novels: *The Benefactor, Death Kit*, and *The Volcano Lover*; a collection of short stories; a story with etchings by Howard Hodgkin; and six books of essays, including *Illness as Metaphor, Under the Sign of Saturn*, and *AIDS and Its Metaphors*. Her *On Photography* won the National Book Critics Award for criticism. Her books have been translated into twenty-three languages. Ms. Sontag has written and directed four feature-length films and has directed plays in the United States and Europe. A member of the American Academy of Arts and Letters, she was president of PEN American Center from 1987 to 1989 and was a MacArthur Fellow from 1990 to 1995. Ms. Sontag's play, *Alice in Bed*, was presented as part of the A.R.T.'s 1995–1996 New Stages Series.

Playwright **Paula Vogel**'s work has been performed at such theatres as the A.R.T., the Lortel Theatre and Circle Repertory in New York, the Goodman, the Intiman Theatre, the Magic Theatre, Center Stage, the Trinity Repertory Company, Berkeley Repertory Theatre, and the Alley Theatre, as well as throughout Canada, England, Brazil, and Chile. Her play *The Baltimore Waltz* received an Obie Award in 1992, and *How I Learned to Drive* won the 1997 Obie Award and the Lucille Lortel Award for Best Play, as well as awards from Drama Desk, Outer Critics Circle, the New York Drama Critics, and the Pulitzer Prize. Ms. Vogel has been on the faculty at Brown University since 1984.

Poet and playwright **Naomi Wallace** was born in Kentucky and now lives in Yorkshire, England. Her plays, which combine poetry and politics in a framework of magic realism, include *In the Fields of Aceldama, The War Boys, One Flea Spare, Slaughter City, The Trestle at Pope Lick Creek*, and *In the Heart of America*, which was awarded the Susan Smith Blackburn Prize. Her first poetry collection, *To Dance a Stony Field*, was published in 1995. In 1993 Ms. Wallace received the National Poetry Competition Award.

Robert Wilson is the author, designer, and director of more than one hundred theatre, opera, dance, film, and video works. He is known for such creations as *Einstein on the Beach*, his 1976 opera with composer Philip Glass; *Death Destruction & Detroit* (1979, German Critics Award); and *the CIVIL warS: a tree is best measured when it is down*, an opera written and designed in collaboration with an internationally diverse group of artists. Mr. Wilson has toured his works throughout the world. He has received a Drama

Desk Award; an Obie Award; the German Theatre Critics Award; the Golden Lion Award in Sculpture at the Venice Biennale; a Best Director Award, International Widescreen Festival, Amsterdam; the Dorothy and Lillian Gish Prize; Brandeis University's Award for Creative Arts for Alternative and Multidiscipline Art Forms; and the Harvard Excellence and Design Award from Harvard University's Graduate School of Design. He has also received two Guggenheim Fellowships and two Rockefeller Foundation Grants in Playwriting. The Boston Museum of Fine Arts presented a retrospective of his work in 1991. The Harvard Graduate School of Design exhibited his work in 1998.

A Complete Listing of A.R.T. Productions, 1980–1999

Season One: 1980 (March–August)

Loeb Stage

A Midsummer Night's Dream
by William Shakespeare
with the music of Henry Purcell's
The Fairy Queen
Directed by Alvin Epstein
Musical direction by Daniel Stepner
Choreography by Carmen de
  Lavallade
Selected musical adaptations by
  Otto Werner Mueller
Sets by Tony Straiges
Costumes by Zach Brown
Lighting by Paul Gallo
March 20, 1980

Terry by Terry (*World Premiere*)
by Mark Lieb
Directed by John Madden
Sets by Andrew Jackness
Costumes by Nan Cibula
Lighting by Paul Gallo
April 3, 1980

Happy End
Lyrics by Bertolt Brecht
Music by Kurt Weill
Original German play by Elisabeth
  Hauptmann
American adaptation and lyrics by
  Michael Feingold
Directed by Walton Jones

Music directed and conducted by
  Gary Fagin
Sets by Michael H. Yeargan
Costumes by William Ivey Long
Lighting by William Armstrong
April 26, 1980

The Inspector General
by Nikolai Gogol
A new translation by Sam
  Guckenhelmer and
  Peter Sellars
Directed by Peter Sellars
Sets by Adrianne Lobel
Costumes by Dunya Ramicova
Lighting by Paul Gallo
May 22, 1980

Season Two: 1980–1981

Loeb Stage

As You Like It
by William Shakespeare
Directed by Andrei Belgrader
Sets by Tom Lynch
Costumes by Adrianne Lobel
Lighting by William Armstrong
Music composed and orchestrated
  by Paul Schierhorn
Music directed by Stephen Drury
September 13, 1980
Also performed as part of Jubilee 350
  Celebration at City Hall Plaza,
  Boston, and at the Loeb Drama
  Center.

The Berlin Requiem and The Seven Deadly Sins
Text by Bertolt Brecht
Music by Kurt Weill
The Berlin Requiem directed by Travis Preston
The Seven Deadly Sins directed by Alvin Epstein
Choreographic Associate: Carmen de Lavallade
Translated by Michael Feingold
Sets by Michael H. Yeargan
Costumes by Dunya Ramicova
Lighting by James F. Ingalls
Music directed by Gary Fagin
November 23, 1980

Lulu
by Frank Wedekind
A new translation and adaptation of *Earth Spirit* and *Pandora's Box* by Michael Feingold
Directed by Lee Breuer
Production design by Adrianne Lobel
Costumes by Rita Ryack
Lighting by Paul Gallo
December 11, 1980

Has "Washington" Legs? (*American Premiere*)
by Charles Wood
Directed by Michael Kustow
Sets by Michael H. Yeargan
Costumes by Nancy Thun
Lighting by James F. Ingalls
Sound collages composed by Tim Mukherjee
"Washington" sequence directed by Midge McKenzie
January 22, 1981

The Marriage of Figaro
by Pierre-Augustin Caron de Beaumarchais
A new translation and adaptation by Mark Lieb
Directed by Alvin Epstein
Set by Kate Edmunds
Costumes by Rita Ryack
Lighting by James F. Ingalls
Music composed and directed by Stephen Drury
May 7, 1981

Grownups (*World Premiere*)
by Jules Feiffer
Directed by John Madden
Sets by Andrew Jackness
Costumes by Dunya Ramicova
Lighting by James F. Ingalls
May 24, 1981

At the Wilbur Theatre in Boston, October 1980, the A.R.T. revived its production of **A Midsummer Night's Dream**

Season Three: 1981–1982

Fall Festival Guest Series

They All Want to Play *Hamlet*, a production by TheatreWorks of Boston
Mummenschanz
An Evening with Luise Rainer, in a performance of Alfred Lord Tennyson's poem *Enoch Arden* (*Premiere*)
Epstein and Schlamme Sing Blitzstein and Bernstein (*Premiere*)

Loeb Stage

Sganarelle—An evening of Molière Farces (**The Flying Doctor, The Forced Marriage, Sganarelle,** and **A Dumb Show**)
Directed by Andrei Serban
Translations by Albert Bermel
Sets by Michael H. Yeargan
Costumes by Dunya Ramicova
Lighting by James F. Ingalls
Music arranged and directed by Stephen Drury
Adaptation and translation of **A Dumb Show** by Sandra Boynton, Andrei Serban, Elizabeth Swados, and members of the **Sganarelle** acting company
December 1, 1981

Orlando (*American Stage Premiere*)
by George Frideric Handel
Libretto by Grazio Braccioli, after *Orlando Furioso* by Ariosto
Directed by Peter Sellars
Music directed by Craig Smith
Sets by Elaine Spatz-Rabinowitz

Costumes by Rita Ryack
Lighting by James F. Ingalls
December 8, 1981

The Journey of the Fifth Horse
by Ronald Ribman
Directed by Adrian Hall
Sets by Kevin Rupnik
Costumes by Rita Ryack
Lighting by James F. Ingalls
Based in part on the story *Diary of a Superfluous Man* by Ivan Turgenev
January 22, 1982

Ghosts
by Henrik Ibsen
Adapted and directed by Robert Brustein
Sets by Tony Straiges
Costumes by Rita Ryack
Lighting by James F. Ingalls
May 14, 1982

Orchids in the Moonlight (*World Premiere*)
by Carlos Fuentes
Directed by Joanne Green
Sets by Elaine Spatz-Rabinowitz
Costumes by Nan Cibula
Lighting by James F. Ingalls
June 4, 1982

1982 New Stages Series

True West
by Sam Shepard
Directed by David Wheeler
Sets by Kate Edmunds
Costumes by Nancy Thun
Lighting by James F. Ingalls
April 7, 1982

Rundown (*World Premiere*)
by Robert Auleta
Directed by William Foeller
Sets by Kate Edmunds
Costumes by Nancy Thun
Lighting by James F. Ingalls
Sound by Stephen Drury
April 15, 1982

TOURS:
FALL 1981: FIRST TOUR OF NORTHEASTERN STATES, including communities in seven states (Maine, New Hampshire, Vermont, Massachusetts, Connecticut, Rhode Island, and New York)
Performing Molière's **Sganarelle.**

RESIDENCY, GOODMAN THEATRE, CHICAGO, May–June 1982, performing **Sganarelle**

SUMMER 1982: FIRST TOUR OF EUROPE AND MIDDLE EAST, including major festivals in Asti; Avignon; the Netherlands (Rotterdam and Amsterdam); Edinburgh; Israel (Tel Aviv, Haifa, and Jerusalem); BITEG (Belgrade and Ljubjana); and London, where **Sganarelle** was filmed by Britain's Channel 4 for television airing. The four productions performed in repertory on tour were **Sganarelle, Lulu, Rundown,** and **True West.** (July–September)

Season Four: 1982–1983

Loeb Stage

Three Sisters
by Anton Chekhov
A new translation by Jean-Claude van Itallie
Directed by Andrei Serban
Sets, costumes, and lighting by Beni Montressor
Original music by Richard Peaslee
November 26, 1982

'Night, Mother (*World Premiere*)
by Marsha Norman
Directed by Tom Moore
Sets and costumes by Heidi Landesman
Lighting by James F. Ingalls
December 10, 1982

Waiting for Godot
by Samuel Beckett
Directed by Andrei Belgrader
Sets by Tony Straiges

Costumes by Kevin Rupnik
Lighting by James F. Ingalls
January 14, 1983

Boys from Syracuse
Music by Richard Rodgers
Lyrics by Lorenz Hart
Book by George Abbott
Based on William Shakespeare's **The Comedy of Errors**
Directed by Alvin Epstein
Music arranged and directed by Paul Schierhorn
Conducted by Tom Gilligan
Choreography by Kathryn Posin
Sets by Tom Lynch
Costumes by Nancy Thun
Lighting by James F. Ingalls
February 18, 1983

The School for Scandal
by Richard Brinsley Sheridan
Directed by Jonathan Miller
Sets by Patrick Robertson
Costumes by Rosemary Vercoe
Lighting by Jennifer Tipton
May 12, 1983

1983 New Stages Series

Footfalls and **Rockaby**
by Samuel Beckett
Directed by John Grant-Phillips
Sets by Don Soulé
Costumes by Lynn Jeffery
Lighting by Thom Palm
Sound by Randolph Head
April 15, 1983

Baby with the Bathwater (*World Premiere*)
by Christopher Durang
Directed by Mark Linn-Baker
Sets by Don Soulé
Costumes by Elizabeth Perlman
Lighting by Thom Palm
Sound by Randolph Head
March 31, 1983

Hughie
by Eugene O'Neill
Directed by Bill Foeller
Sets by Don Soulé
Costumes by Lynn Jeffery
Lighting by Thom Palm
Sound by Randolph Head
April 7, 1983

PRIZES:
Marsha Norman's **'Night, Mother** received *Pulitzer Prize for Drama;* first time in history of prize that the award was given to a play based on a production outside New York City.

Season Five: 1983–1984

Fall Festival

Philippe Genty Company

Loeb Stage

Measure for Measure
by William Shakespeare
Directed by Andrei Belgrader
Sets by Douglas Stein
Costumes by Kurt Wilhelm
Lighting by Jennifer Tipton
Music composed and directed by William Uttley
November 25, 1983

A Moon for the Misbegotten
by Eugene O'Neill
Directed by David Leveaux
Sets and costumes by Brien Vahey
Lighting by Donald Edmund Thomas
Original Music by Stephen Endelman
December 9, 1983

Traveler in the Dark (*World Premiere*)
by Marsha Norman
Directed by Tom Moore
Sets by Heidi Landesman
Costumes by Robert Blackman
Lighting by James F. Ingalls
February 3, 1984

Big River: The Adventures of Huckleberry Finn
(*World Premiere*)
Music and lyrics by Roger Miller
Book by William Hauptman
Directed by Des McAnuff
Sets by Heidi Landesman
Costumes by Patricia McGourty
Lighting by James F. Ingalls
Sound by Randolph Head
Orchestrations, vocal arrangements,

and musical direction by Michael
S. Roth
February 17, 1984

**Six Characters in Search of an
Author**
by Luigi Pirandello
A new adaptation by Robert Brustein
and the Company
Directed by Robert Brustein
Sets and costumes by Michael H.
Yeargan
Lighting by Jennifer Tipton
May 11, 1984

1984 New Stages Series

Angel City
by Sam Shepard
Directed by David Wheeler
Sets by Kate Edmunds
Costumes by Lynn Jeffery and
Elizabeth Perlman
Lighting by Thom Palm
April 2, 1984

Strokes (*World Premiere*)
by Leslie Glass
Directed by Philip Cates
Sets by Kate Edmunds
Costumes by Elizabeth Perlman and
Lynn Jeffery
Lighting by Thom Palm
April 11, 1984

Holy Wars—*Morroco* and ***The
Road to Jerusalem***
(*World Premiere*)
by Allan Havis
Directed by Gerald Chapman
Sets by Kate Edmunds
Costumes by Lynn Jeffery and
Elizabeth Perlman
Lighting by Thom Palm
April 5, 1984

TOURS:
*SECOND SEVEN-STATE TOUR
OF NORTHEAST*
(Massachusetts, Rhode Island,
New Hampshire, Vermont, New
York, Pennsylvania, Connecticut),
performing **The School for
Scandal** (October 1983)

*INTERNATIONAL FORTNIGHT
OF THEATRE, QUEBEC*:
Performed **The School for
Scandal** and **Sganarelle** in
repertory (June 1984)

*1984 OLYMPIC ARTS FESTIVAL
IN LOS ANGELES*: Performed
The School for Scandal and
Sganarelle in repertory (June/July
1984)

Season Six: 1984–1985

Fall Festival

**Six Characters in Search of an
Author**
by Luigi Pirandello
A new adaptation by Robert Brustein
and the Company
Directed by Robert Brustein
Sets and costumes by Michael H.
Yeargan
Lighting by Jennifer Tipton
October 2, 1984

Loeb Stage

The King Stag
by Carlo Gozzi
English version by Albert Bermel
Directed by Andrei Serban
Sets by Michael H. Yeargan
Costumes, masks, and puppetry by
Julie Taymor
Lighting by Jennifer Tipton
Original music by Elliot Goldenthal
November 23, 1984

Endgame
by Samuel Beckett
Directed by JoAnne Akalaitis
Set by Douglas Stein
Costumes by Kurt Wilhelm
Lighting by Jennifer Tipton
Prelude to **Endgame** and incidental
music by Philip Glass
Music produced by Kurt Munkacsi
December 7, 1984

Jacques and His Master (*American
Premiere*)
by Milan Kundera
English translation by Michael
Henry Heim
Directed by Susan Sontag

Set by Douglas Stein
Costumes by Jane Greenwood
Lighting by Jennifer Tipton
Original music by Elizabeth Swados
January 11, 1985

**the CIVIL warS: a tree is best
measured when it is down**
(*American Premiere*)
Act III, Scene E by Robert Wilson
Act IV, Scene A and **Epilogue** by
Robert Wilson and Heiner Müller
English translation of **Act IV, Scene
A** and **Epilogue** by Christopher
Martin and Daniel Woker
Directed by Robert Wilson
Sets by Robert Wilson and Tom
Kamm
Costumes by Yoshio Yabara
Lighting by Jennifer Tipton and
Robert Wilson
Compositions and Sound by Hans
Peter Kuhn
Assistant Director: Ann-Christin
Rommen
February 22, 1985
*Produced in association with Boston's
Institute of Contemporary Art*

Love's Labour's Lost
by William Shakespeare
Directed by Jerome Kilty
Set by Michael H. Yeargan
Costumes by Constance R. Wexler
Lighting by Spencer Mosse
Music by Conrad Susa
May 10, 1985

1985 New Stages Series

Gillette (*World Premiere*)
by William Hauptman
Directed by David Wheeler
Sets by Karen Schultz
Costumes by Lynn Jeffery
Lighting by Thom Palm
Sound by Randolph Head
March 27, 1985

Claptrap
by Ken Friedman
Directed by Robert Drivas
Set by Karen Schultz
Costumes by Karen Eister
Lighting by Thom Palm
Sound by Randolph Head
April 3, 1985

TOURS:
NATIONAL TOUR: Month-long,
ten-state (Maine, New
Hampshire, Pennsylvania,
Nebraska, Iowa, Missouri,
Oklahoma, Minnesota, Wisconsin,
and Ohio) tour, performing
Sganarelle and **Six Characters in
Search of an Author**
(September–October 1984)

*RESIDENCY, GOODMAN
THEATRE, CHICAGO:*
June–July 1985, performing **Six
Characters in Search of an
Author.**

PRIZES:
A.R.T. American premiere
production of a section of Robert
Wilson's **the CIVIL warS**
unanimous choice of Pulitzer
Prize Jury.

Season Seven: 1985–1986
Fall Festival

The King Stag
by Carlo Gozzi
English version by Albert Bermel
Directed by Andrei Serban
Sets by Michael H. Yeargan
Costumes, masks, and puppetry by
Julie Taymor
Lighting by Jennifer Tipton
Original music by Elliot Goldenthal
September 6, 1985

**Six Characters in Search of an
Author**
by Luigi Pirandello
A new adaptation by Robert Brustein
and the Company
Directed by Robert Brustein
Sets and costumes by Michael H.
Yeargan
Lighting by Jennifer Tipton
September 12, 1985

The Garden of Earthly Delights
(*not developed at A.R.T.*)
A Dance Piece by Martha Clarke
based on a painting by Bosch,
produced by the Music Theatre
Group/Lenox Arts Center
September 25, 1985

Loeb Stage

The Changeling
by Thomas Middleton
Directed by Robert Brustein
Sets and costumes by Michael H.
    Yeargan
Lighting by Richard Riddell
November 22, 1985

The Juniper Tree (*World Premiere*)
An opera by Philip Glass and Robert
    Moran
Libretto by Arthur Yorinks
Based on a tale by the Brothers
    Grimm
Directed by Andrei Serban
Sets and costumes by Michael H.
    Yeargan
Lighting by Jennifer Tipton
December 6, 1985

The Balcony
by Jean Genet
A new translation by Jean-Claude
    van Itallie
Directed by JoAnne Akalaitis
Sets by George Tsypin
Costumes by Kristi Zea
Lighting by Jennifer Tipton
Music by Rubén Blades
Choreography by Johanna Boyce
Sound by Peter Michael Sullivan
Wigs and makeup by Bobby Miller
Assistant Director: Peter Confalone
January 15, 1986

Alcestis
Adapted by Robert Wilson from a
    play by Euripides as translated by
    Dudley Fitts and Robert Fitzgerald
    with additional text by Heiner
    Müller
Description of a Picture translated
    by Carl Weber
Epilogue, Japanese Kyogen
The Birdcatcher in Hell, translated
    by Mark Oshima
Music by Laurie Anderson
Conceived, directed, and designed
    by Robert Wilson
Sets by Tom Kamm and Robert
    Wilson
Costumes by John Conklin

Lighting by Jennifer Tipton and
    Robert Wilson
Movement by Suzushi Hanayagi
Audio environment by Hans Peter
    Kuhn
Assistant Director: Ann-Christin
    Rommen
March 7, 1986

Olympian Games
Based on Ovid's *Metamorphosis*
Book and lyrics by Kenneth
    Cavander and Barbara Damashek
Directed by Barbara Damashek
Music composed by Barbara
    Damashek
Sets and costumes by Alexander
    Okun
Lighting by Spencer Mosse
May 9, 1986

1986 New Stages Series

The Day Room (*World Premiere*)
by Don DeLillo
Directed by Michael Bloom
Sets by Loy Arcenas
Costumes by Karen Eister
Lighting by Richard Riddell
April 8, 1986

**Tutta Casa, Letto, E Chiesa (It's
    all bed, board, and church)** (*not
    developed at A.R.T.*)
Written by Dario Fo and Franca
    Rame
Directed by Dario Fo
Performed by Franca Rame
Onstage translator for Ms. Rame:
    Maria Consagra
Set and lighting by Lino Avolio
May 2, 1986

Mistero Buffo (a comic mystery)
(*American Premiere*) (*not developed
    at A.R.T.*)
Written, staged, and performed by
    Dario Fo
English Supertitle translation by
    Stuart Hodd, Ron Jenkins, and
    Walter Valeri
Onstage Translator for Mr. Fo: Ron
    Jenkins
Set and lighting by Lino Avolio
May 11, 1986

TOURS:
VENICE BIENNALE: Performed
The King Stag, Sept./Oct. 1985,
at the Theatre Malibran, Venice

PRIZES:
1985 JUJAMCYN PRIZE for
outstanding contribution to the
development of creative talent for
the theatre.

Season Eight: 1986–1987

Fall Festival

The King Stag
by Carlo Gozzi
English version by Albert Bermel
Directed by Andrei Serban
Sets by Michael H. Yeargan
Costumes, masks, and puppetry by
Julie Taymor
Lighting by Jennifer Tipton
Original music by Elliot Goldenthal
August 29, 1986

the Knee Plays (*not developed at
A.R.T.*)
A section of Robert Wilson's **the
CIVIL warS,** with music by David
Byrne
September 23, 1986

Loeb Stage

Tonight We Improvise
by Luigi Pirandello
Adapted and directed by Robert
Brustein
Video sequences directed by
Frederick Wiseman
Sets and costumes by Michael H.
Yeargan
Lighting by Stephen Strawbridge
November 28, 1986

**End of the World (with
Symposium to Follow)**
by Arthur Kopit
Directed by Richard Foreman
Sets by Michael H. Yeargan
Costumes by Lindsay W. Davis
Lighting by Stephen Strawbridge
December 12, 1986

Sweet Table at the Richelieu
(*World Premiere*)
by Ronald Ribman

Directed by Andrei Serban
Sets and costumes by John Conklin
Lighting by Howell Binkley
February 6, 1987

The Day Room
by Don DeLillo
Originally directed by Michael
Bloom for the *1985–1986 New
Stages Series*
Restaged by David Wheeler
Sets by Loy Arcenas
Costumes by Karen Eister
Lighting by Richard Riddell
February 18, 1987

The Good Woman of Setzuan
by Bertolt Brecht
Translated by Eric Bentley
Directed by Andrei Serban
Music by Elizabeth Swados
Sets by Jeff Muskovin
Costumes by Catherine Zuber
Lighting by Howell Binkley
Movement by Thom Molinaro
Associate Director: Charles Otte
May 15, 1987

Archangels Don't Play Pinball
(*American Premiere*)
by Dario Fo
Translated by Ron Jenkins
Directed by Dario Fo and Franca
Rame
Sets and Costumes by Dario Fo
Lighting by Robert M. Wierzel
Music by Fiorenzo Carpi
Sound by Stephen Santomenna
Associate Director: Arturo Corso
Assistant Director: Ron Jenkins
June 5, 1987

1987 New Stages Series

**The Cannibal Masque
(The Cannibal Masque
and A Serpent's Egg)** (*World
Premiere*)
by Ronald Ribman
Directed by David Wheeler
Sets by Loy Arcenas
Costumes by Christine Joly de
Lotbinière
Lighting by Frank Butler
Sound by Stephen D. Santomenna
April 5, 1987

Mrs. Sorkin Presents . . . ("Ubu Lear" and Other Peerless Classics) (*World Premiere*)
by Christopher Durang
Directed by R. J. Cutler and Wesley Savick
Sets by Loy Arcenas
Costumes by Karen Eister
Lighting by Frank Butler
Sound by Stephen D. Santomenna
Music by Richard Peaslee
Music directed by Paul Brusiloff
April 8, 1987

Late Night Cabaret

The Case of the Danish Prince
by Miles Kington
Directed by Wesley Savick
Lighting by Frank Butler
Sound by Stephen D. Santomenna
April 17, 1987

The Skinhead Hamlet
by Richard Curtis
Directed by Wesley Savick
Lighting by Frank Butler
Sound by Stephen D. Santomenna

TOURS:
FESTIVAL D'AUTOMNE, PARIS: Performed Robert Wilson's **Alcestis,** September 1986.
WEST COAST: Three-week, four-city tour of California (University of California at Davis; The Doolittle Theatre, Los Angeles; La Jolla Playhouse, University of California at San Diego; and Memorial Auditorium, Stanford University, Palo Alto), performing **The King Stag** and **The Day Room,** *October 3–18*

PRIZES:
1986 Antoinette Perry "Tony" Award for continued excellence in resident theatre.
Best in France for 1986
A.R.T. production of Robert Wilson's **Alcestis** voted Best Foreign Work seen in France by French Drama Critics Association.

Season Nine: 1987–1988

Fall Festival

Le Cirque Imaginaire (*not developed at A.R.T.*)
Conceived and performed by Jean-Baptiste Thierrée and Victoria Chaplin
September 8, 1987

Six Characters in Search of an Author
by Luigi Pirandello
Adapted and directed by Robert Brustein and the Company
Directed by Robert Brustein
Sets and costumes by Michael H. Yeargan
Lighting by Jennifer Tipton
September 26, 1987

The Good Woman of Setzuan
by Bertolt Brecht
Translated by Eric Bentley
Directed by Andrei Serban
Music by Elizabeth Swados
Sets by Jeff Muskovin
Costumes by Catherine Zuber
Lighting by Howell Binkley
Movement by Thom Molinaro
October 2, 1987

Loeb Stage

Gillette
by William Hauptman
Directed by David Wheeler
Sets by Loy Arcenas
Costumes by Catherine Zuber
Lighting by Howell Binkley
Sound Design by Stephen D. Santomenna
November 27, 1987

Right You Are (If You Think You Are)
by Luigi Pirandello
Adapted and directed by Robert Brustein
Sets by Michael H. Yeargan
Costumes by Christine Joly de Lotbinière
Lighting by Richard Riddell
December 11, 1987

Quartet
by Heiner Müller
Translated by Carl Weber
Based on *Les Liaisons dangereuses*
  by Choderlos de Laclos
Directed by Robert Wilson
Music composed and adapted by
  Martin Pearlman
Sets by Robert Wilson
Costumes by Frida Parmegianni
Lighting by Howell Binkley and
  Robert Wilson
Sound by Stephen D. Santomenna
Assistant Director: Jane Perry
February 5, 1988

The Fall of the House of Usher
  (*World Premiere*)
Music by Philip Glass
Libretto by Arthur Yorinks
Based on a tale by Edgar Allan Poe
Music directed and conducted by
  Richard Pittman
Directed by Richard Foreman
Set design by Richard Foreman
Costumes by Patricia Zipprodt
Lighting by Richard Riddell
Sound by Stephen D. Santomenna
May 13, 1988
In association with Kentucky Opera

'Tis Pity She's a Whore
by John Ford
Directed by Michael Kahn
Sets by Derek McLane
Costumes by Catherine Zuber
Lighting by Frances Aronson
Sound by Stephen D. Santomenna
Fights directed by David S. Leong
May 27, 1988

Spring Festival

Two by Pirandello:
Six Characters in Search of an
  Author
Right You Are (If You Think You
  Are)
March 17, 1988

Two Works in Progress:
City of Amateurs
Written and directed by Richard
  Foreman with members of the
  A.R.T. Institute for Advanced
  Theatre Training at Harvard

Sueños
Adapted and directed by Ruth
  Maleczech
Produced by Mabou Mines and
  Boston Musica Viva
March 30, 1988

Life and Fate
Based on a chapter in the novel by
  Vasily Grossman
Directed by Frederick Wiseman with
  Ruth Maleczech
May 10, 1988

1988 New Stages Series

Big Time: Scenes from a Service
  Economy
by Keith Reddin
Directed by Steven Schachter
Sets by Bill Clarke
Costumes by Ellen McCarmey
Lighting by Thom Palm
Sound by Stephen D. Santomenna
April 6, 1988

Uncle Vanya
by Anton Chekhov
Translated by Vlada Chernomordik
Adapted by David Mamet
Directed by David Wheeler
Sets by Bill Clarke
Costumes by Catherine Zuber
Lighting by Thom Palm
April 13, 1988

TOURS:
THE FIRST NEW YORK
  INTERNATIONAL FESTIVAL
  FOR THE ARTS: (July 1–30)
Six Characters in Search of an
  Author and **Big Time: Scenes**
  from a Service Economy

TEATRO ESPAÑOL, MADRID:
Six Characters in Search of an
  Author and **The King Stag**

Season Ten: 1988–1989

Fall Festival

The King Stag
September 15, 1988

Alec McCowen, Shakespeare, Cole, & Co. (*World Premiere*)
September 20, 1988

Satirical Subversives, A Festival of Election Year Comedy, Culture, and Politics
September 29, 1988

Mort Sahl In Concert
Paul Zaloom in *The House of Horror*
Eric Bogosian in *Sex, Drugs & Rock 'n Roll*

Loeb Stage

The Serpent Woman
by Carlo Gozzi
Translated by Albert Bermel
Directed by Andrei Serban
Sets, costumes, masks, and puppets by Setsu Asakura
Lighting by Victor En Yu Tan
November 26, 1988

Platonov
by Anton Chekhov
Adapted and directed by Liviu Ciulei
Translated by Mark Leib
Sets by Liviu Ciulei
Costumes by Smaranda Branescu
Lighting by Richard Riddell
December 16, 1988

Mastergate (*World Premiere*)
by Larry Gelbart
Directed by Michael Engler
Sets by Philipp Jung
Costumes by Candice Donnelly
Lighting by James F. Ingalls
February 3, 1989

The Miser
by Molière
Directed by Andrei Serban
Translated by Albert Bermel
Sets by Derek McLane
Costumes by Judith Anne Dolan
Lighting by Howell Binkley
Sound by Stephen D. Santomenna
Movement Coach: Thom Molinaro
May 12, 1989

Life Is a Dream
by Pedro Calderón de la Barca
Directed by Anne Bogart

Translated by Edwin Honig
Sets by Loy Arcenas
Costumes by Catherine Zuber
Lighting by Richard Riddell
Music composed by Matthias Gohl
Sound by Stephen D. Santomenna and Matthias Gohl
May 28, 1989

1989 New Stages Series

In Twilight: Tales from Chekhov
by Anton Chekhov
Directed and adapted for the stage by Tina Landau
Sets by Derek McLane
Costumes by Christine Joly de Lotbinière
Lighting by John R. Malinowski
Original music composed and performed by Scott Frankel
March 29, 1989

Two by Korder: Fun and **Nobody**
by Howard Korder
Directed by David Wheeler
Sets by Derek McLane
Costumes by Karen Eister
Lighting by Peter West
Sound by Stephen D. Santomenna
April 12, 1989

Summer 1989

The Boys Next Door
by Tom Griffin
Directed by David Wheeler
Sets by Robert D. Soulé
Costumes by Bill Lane
Lighting by John F. Custer
July 12, 1989

TOURS:
SERIOUS FUN! FESTIVAL: Lincoln Center, New York (July 14–August 3)
The Fall of the House of Usher

Season Eleven: 1989–1990

Fall Festival

The Boys Next Door
by Tom Griffin
Directed by David Wheeler
Sets by Robert D. Soulé
Costumes by Bill Lane

Lighting by John F. Custer
August 24, 1989

Tru
An American Comedy
Written and directed by Jay Presson
  Allen from the words and works of
  Truman Capote
Sets by David Mitchell
Costumes by Sarah Edwards
Lighting by Ken Billington and Jason
  Kantrowitz
Sound by Otts Munderloh
September 6, 1989

1000 Airplanes on the Roof
by David Henry Hwang
Directed and composed by Philip
  Glass
Sets and projections by Jerome
  Sirlin
Lighting by Robert Wierzel
Sound by Kurt Munkacsi
September 18, 1989

More Sex, Drugs, Rock & Roll
Written and performed by Eric
  Bogosian
Directed by Jo Bonney
October 6, 1989

Loeb Stage

The Bald Soprano and **The Chairs**
by Eugene Ionesco
Translated by Donald Watson
Directed by Andrei Belgrader
Sets by Anita Stewart
Costumes by Candice Donnelly
Lighting by Stephen Strawbridge
Sound by Maribeth Back
November 24, 1989

Twelfth Night
by William Shakespeare
Directed by Andrei Serban
Music Composed by Mel Marvin
Sets by Derek McLane
Costumes by Catherine Zuber
Lighting by Howell Binkley
Sound by Maribeth Back
December 8, 1989

Major Barbara
by George Bernard Shaw
Directed by Michael Engler
Sets by Philipp Jung

Costumes by Catherine Zuber
Lighting by James Ingalls
Sound by Maribeth Back
January 26, 1990

The Father
by August Strindberg
Adapted and directed by Robert
  Brustein
Sets by Derek McLane
Costumes by Dunya Ramicova
Lighting by Richard Riddell
Sound by Maribeth Back
February 9, 1990

The Caucasian Chalk Circle
by Bertolt Brecht
Translated by Ralph Manheim
Directed by Slobodan Unkovski
Music by Mel Marvin
Sets by Meta Hocevar
Costumes by Catherine Zuber
Lighting by Richard Riddell
Sound by Maribeth Back
May 11, 1990

1990 New Stages Series

Road to Nirvana
by Arthur Kopit
Directed by Michael Bloom
Sets by Scott Bradley
Costumes by Ellen McCartney
Lighting by Peter West
Sound by Maribeth Back
March 28, 1990

The Lost Boys
by Allan Knee
Directed by Jerome Kilty
Sets by Scott Bradley
Costumes by Karen Eister
Lighting by John Ambrosone
Sound by Maribeth Back
April 5, 1990

Summer 1990

The Moscow Taganka Theatre
  production of **Phaedra**
by Marina Tsvetaeva
Scenic adaption and direction by
  Roman Viktyuk
Choreography by Valentin Gneushev
Design by Vladimir Boer
Music by Edison Denisov
June 16, 1990

Le Cirque Imaginaire
Created and performed by Victoria
   Chaplin and Jean Baptiste
   Thierrée
June 26, 1990

The Island of Anyplace
by Charles Marz
Directed by Thomas Derrah
Music by Barry Rocklin
Sets and costumes by Scott Bradley
Lighting by John Ambrosone
July 29, 1990

TOURS:
*MITSUI FESTIVAL, TOKYO: (June
   8–10)* **The King Stag**

Season Twelve: 1990–1991

Fall Festival

The King Stag
by Carlo Gozzi
Directed by Andrei Serban
Sets by Michael H. Yeargan
Costumes by Julie Taymor
Lighting by John Ambrosone
Sound by Maribeth Back
August 23, 1990

We Keep Our Victims Ready
Written, performed, and directed by
   Karen Finley
September 4, 1990

The CSC Repertory production of
   Rameau's Nephew by Denis
   Diderot
Adapted by Shelley Berc and Andrei
   Belgrader
Directed by Andrei Belgrader
Sets by Anita Stewart
Costumes by Candice Donnelly
Lighting by Robert Wierzel
Sound by William Uttley
September 9, 1990

The Island of Anyplace
by Charles Marz
Directed by Thomas Derrah
Music by Barry Rocklin
Sets and costumes by Scott Bradley
Lighting by John Ambrosone
September 22, 1990

Loeb Stage

The Homecoming
by Harold Pinter
Directed by David Wheeler
Sets by Derek McLane
Costumes by Catherine Zuber
Lighting by Frances Aronson
Sound by Maribeth Back
November 23, 1990

Once in a Lifetime
by George S. Kaufman and Moss
   Hart
Directed by Anne Bogart
Sets by Loy Arcenas
Costumes by Catherine Zuber
Lighting by James F. Ingalls
Sound by Maribeth Back
December 7, 1990

When We Dead Awaken
by Henrik Ibsen
English version by Robert Brustein
Adapted and directed by Robert
   Wilson
Sets by Robert Wilson and John
   Conklin
Costumes by John Conklin
Lighting by Stephen Strawbridge
   and Robert Wilson
Sound Environment by Hans Peter
   Kuhn
Songs by Charles "Honi" Coles
Assistant Director: Ann-Christin
   Rommen
February 8, 1991
*In collaboration with the Alley
   Theatre, Houston*

King Lear
by William Shakespeare
Directed by Adrian Hall
Sets by Eugene Lee
Costumes by Catherine Zuber
Lighting by Natasha Katz
Music by Richard Cumming
Fight Choreography by William
   Finlay
May 10, 1991

Power Failure (*World Premiere*)
by Larry Gelbart
Directed by Michael Engler
Sets by Philipp Jung
Costumes by Candice Donnelly
Lighting by Natasha Katz
Sound by Maribeth Back
May 24, 1991

1991 New Stages Series

The Writing Game (*American Premiere*)
by David Lodge
Directed by Michael Bloom
Sets by Bill Clarke
Costumes by Ellen McCartney
Lighting by Richard Riddell
Sound by Maribeth Back
March 14, 1991

Steel (*World Premiere*)
by Derek Walcott
Music and musical direction by Galt MacDermot
Directed by Robert Scanlan and Derek Walcott
Choreography and musical staging by Mary Barnett
Sets by Richard Montgomery
Costumes by Catherine Zuber
Lighting by Richard Riddell
Sound by Maribeth Back
April 3, 1991
In association with the American Music Theater Festival

Summer 1991

The Island of Anyplace
by Charles Marz
Directed by Thomas Derrah
Music by Barry Rocklin
Sets and costumes by Scott Bradley
Lighting by John Ambrosone
July 29, 1991

Le Cirque Invisible
Created and performed by Victoria Chaplin and Jean Baptiste Thierrée, with James Spencer Thierrée
August 13, 1991

TOURS:
RESIDENCY, ALLEY THEATRE, HOUSTON:
The King Stag, September 1–30, 1990

ANNENBERG CENTER, PHILADELPHIA:
The King Stag, October 3–7, 1990

AMERICAN MUSIC THEATER FESTIVAL PHILADELPHIA:
Steel, April 26–May 11, 1991

ALLEY THEATRE, HOUSTON:
When We Dead Awaken,
May 22–26, 1991

Season Thirteen: 1991–1992

Fall Festival

The Mysteries and What's So Funny?
Written and directed by David Gordon
Music by Philip Glass
Visual design by Red Grooms
Lighting by Dan Kotlowitz
Sound by David Meschter
Produced by Jedediah Wheeler
September 4, 1991

A Room of One's Own
Adapted and directed by Patrick Garland with Eileen Atkins as Virginia Woolf
September 24, 1991

Winter 1991

The Island of Anyplace
Written by Charles Marz
Directed by Thomas Derrah
Music by Barry Rocklin
Sets and costumes by Scott Bradley
Lighting by John Ambrosone
December 27–30, 1991

Loeb Stage

Hamlet
by William Shakespeare
Directed by Ron Daniels
Set and costumes by Antony McDonald
Lighting by Frances Aronson

Original music by Claire van
  Kampen
Sound by Maribeth Back
Fight choreography by Alexis
  Denisof
November 22, 1991
In collaboration with Pittsburgh
  Public Theater

Misalliance
by George Bernard Shaw
Directed by David Wheeler
Sets by Derek McLane
Costumes by Catherine Zuber
Lighting by Christopher Ackerlind
Sound by Maribeth Back
January 17, 1992

The Seagull
by Anton Chekhov
Directed by Ron Daniels
Adapted by Robert Brustein from
  George Calderon's translation
Sets by Antony MacDonald
Costumes by Catherine Zuber
Lighting by James Ingalls
Original music by Claire van
  Kampen
Sound by Maribeth Back
February 14, 1992

Hedda Gabler
by Henrik Ibsen
Directed by Adrian Hall
Sets by Derek McLane
Costumes by Catherine Zuber
Lighting by Natasha Katz
Sound by Maribeth Back
May 1, 1992

The Servant of Two Masters
by Carlo Goldoni
Adapted by Shelley Berc and Andrei
  Belgrader
Directed by Andrei Belgrader
Sets by Anita Stewart
Costumes by Catherine Zuber
Lighting by Natasha Katz
Sound by Maribeth Back
May 29, 1992

1992 New Stages Series

Media Amok (*World Premiere*)
by Christopher Durang
Directed by Les Waters

Sets by Bill Clark
Costumes by Christine Joly de
  Lotbinière
Lighting by John Ambrosone
Sound by Maribeth Back
March 26, 1992

Oleanna (*World Premiere*)
A Back Bay Theater Company
  Production
Written and directed by David
  Mamet
Sets by Michael Merritt
Costumes by Harriet Voyt
Lighting by Kevin Rigdon
Sound by Maribeth Back
May 1, 1992

Spring 1992

The Island of Anyplace
Written by Charles Marz
Directed by Thomas Derrah
Music by Barry Rocklin
Sets and costumes by Scott Bradley
Lighting by John Ambrosone
June 10–11, 1992

TOURS:
21st INTERNATIONAL BIENNAL
  OF SAO PAULO, Teatro
  Municipal, Sao Paulo, Brazil:
When We Dead Awaken,
October 4–9, 1991

Season Fourteen: 1992–1993

Fall Festival

Amphigorey: The Musical
Book and lyrics by Edward Gorey
Music by Peter Golub
Scenic design by Edward Gorey
Costumes by Kelly Lamb and James
  Hammer
Original lighting by Roger Morgan
Sound by Theater Sound
August 26, 1992

Dog Show
Written and performed by Eric
  Bogosian
Directed by Jo Bonney
September 9, 1992

Frida: The Story of Frida Kahlo
Book by Hilary Blecher
Monologues and lyrics by Migdalia
  Cruz
Music by Robert Xavier Rodriguez
Scenic design by Andrew Jackness
Costumes by Ann Roth and Robert
  de Mora
Lighting by Robert Wierzel
Sound by Theater Sound
September 16, 1992

**Fires in the Mirror: Crown
  Heights, Brooklyn and Other
  Identities**
Conceived, written, and performed
  by Anna Deavere Smith
Projections by Wendall K.
  Harrington
Original music by Joseph Jarman
Costumes by Candice Donnelly
Lighting by John Ambrosone
September 29, 1992

Loeb Stage

Black Snow (*American Premiere*)
by Keith Dewhurst
Based on the novel by Mikhail
  Bulgakov
Directed by Richard Jones
Set and costumes by Antony
  McDonald
Lighting by Scott Zielinski
Sound by Maribeth Back
November 27, 1992

Heartbreak House
by George Bernard Shaw
Directed by David Wheeler
Sets by Derek McLane
Costumes by Catherine Zuber
Lighting by Howell Binkley
Sound by Maribeth Back
January 2, 1993

Dream of the Red Spider (*World
  Premiere*)
by Ronald Ribman
Directed by Ron Daniels
Sets by Riccardo Hernandez
Costumes by Catherine Zuber
Lighting by Frances Aronson
Sound by Maribeth Back
February 5, 1993

The Caretaker
by Harold Pinter
Directed by David Wheeler
Sets by Derek McLane
Costumes by Catherine Zuber and
  Kenneth Mooney
Lighting by John Ambrosone
Sound by Maribeth Back
March 17, 1993

Orphée (*World Premiere*)
Opera by Philip Glass
Based upon the scenario by Jean
  Cocteau
Adaptation by Philip Glass
Directed by Francesca Zambello
Music director/conductor: Martin
  Goldray
Sets by Robert Israel
Costumes by Catherine Zuber
Lighting by Pat Collins
Sound by Maribeth Back
May 14, 1993
*In association with the Brooklyn
  Academy of Music*

Cakewalk (*World Premiere*)
by Peter Feibleman
Directed by Ron Daniels
Sets by Tony Streiges
Costumes by Catherine Zuber
Lighting by Howell Binkley
Sound by Maribeth Back
Incidental music by Carly Simon
Arranged and produced by Matthias
  Gohl
May 28, 1993

New Stages

Silence, Cunning, Exile (*World
  Premiere*)
by Stuart Greenman
Directed by Ron Daniels
Sets by Christine Jones
Costumes by Karen Eister
Lighting by John Ambrosone
Sound by Maribeth Back
April 1, 1993

The L.A. Plays (*World Premiere*)
by Han Ong
Directed by Steven Maler
Sets by Christine Jones
Costumes by Gail A. Buckley

Lighting by John Ambrosone
Music & sound design by Don
 Dinicola
April 8, 1993

Those the River Keeps
by David Rabe
Directed by David Rabe
Sets by Loren Shemman
Costumes by Gail A. Buckley
Lighting by John Ambrosone
Sound by Chris Walker
May 6, 1993

At Zero Church Street
Performance Space

Macbeth
by William Shakespeare
Directed by Alvin Epstein
Music and sound design by Don
 Dinicola
Costume design and coordination by
 Karen Eister
Lighting by John Ambrosone
June 24, 1993

Summer 1993

The Reduced Shakespeare Company
 in **The Complete Works of
 Shakespeare (Abridged)** and **The
 Complete History of America
 (Abridged)**
Created and performed by Reed
 Martin, Adam Long, and Austin
 Tichenor
July 6, 1993

Season Fifteen: 1993–1994

Fall Festival

Le Cirque Invisible
Created and performed by Victoria
 Chaplin and Jean Baptiste
 Thierrée, with James Spencer
 Thierrée
August 17, 1993

Time on Fire
Written and performed by Evan
 Handler
Directed by Marcia Jean Kurtz
September 7–19, 1993

A Certain Level of Denial
Written, directed, and performed by
 Karen Finley
September 20–21, 1993

**Dog Show: Pounding Nails in the
 Floor with My Forehead**
Written and performed by Eric
 Bogosian
Directed by Jo Bonney
September 22–26, 1993

**The Late Great Ladies of Blues
 and Jazz**
Conceived, written, and performed
 by Sandra Reaves with the All-Star
 Jazz Band
September 28–October 9, 1993

Loeb Stage

Henry IV, Parts 1 and 2
by William Shakespeare
Adapted by Robert Brustein
Directed by Ron Daniels
Sets by John Conklin
Costumes by Gabriel Berry
Lighting by Frances Aronson
Music by Bruce Odland
Fight choreography by Jenny Breen
November 26, 1993

What the Butler Saw
by Joe Orton
Directed by David Wheeler
Sets by Derek McLane
Costumes by Catherine Zuber
Lighting by John Ambrosone
Sound by Christopher Walker
January 7, 1994

The Cherry Orchard
by Anton Chekhov
Directed by Ron Daniels
Sets by George Tsypin
Costumes by Catherine Zuber
Lighting by Frances Aronson
Sound by Christopher Walker
January 21, 1994

A Touch of the Poet
by Eugene O'Neill
Directed by Joe Dowling
Sets by Derek McLane
Costumes by Catherine Zuber
Lighting by Frances Aronson

Sound by Christopher Walker
March 4, 1994

Shlemiel the First (*World Premiere*)
Conceived and adapted by Robert
  Brustein from Isaac Bashevis
  Singer's play
Music composed and adapted by
  Hankus Netsky with additional
  music by Zalmen Mlotek
Lyrics by Arnold Weinstein
Music directed by Zalmen Mlotek
Directed and choreographed by
  David Gordon
Sets by Robert Israel
Costumes by Catherine Zuber
Lighting by Peter Kaczorowski
Sound by Christopher Walker
May 13, 1994
*In association with the American
  Music Theater Festival*

A.R.T. New Stages

The America Play
by Suzan-Lori Parks
Directed by Marcus Stern
Sets by Allison Koturbash
Costumes by Gail Astrid Buckley
Lighting by John Ambrosone
Sound by Christopher Walker
March 31, 1994

Hot 'n' Throbbing (*World Premiere*)
by Paula Vogel
Directed by Anne Bogart
Sets by Christine Jones
Costumes by Jenny Fulton
Lighting by John Ambrosone
Sound by Christopher Walker
April 14, 1994

Picasso at the Lapin Agile
by Steve Martin
Directed by David Wheeler
Sets by Christine Jones
Costumes by Catherine Zuber
Lighting by John Ambrosone
Sound by Christopher Walker
April 28, 1994

Spring 1994

The Island of Anyplace
Written by Charles Marz
Directed by Thomas Derrah
Music by Barry Rocklin

Sets and Costumes by Scott Bradley
Lighting by John Ambrosone
May 31, June 1, 2, 1994

Summer 1994

Ennio Marchetto
Written, directed, and performed by
  Ennio Marchetto
June 14–26, 1994

El Tricicle in *Slastic*
Written, directed, and performed by
  Joan Garcia, Paco Mir, and Carles
  Sans
June 21–July 3, 1994

Mump & Smoot
in *Caged* and *Ferno*
Written, created, and performed by
  Michael Kennard and John Turner
July 7–24, 1994

TOURS:
SERIOUS FUN FESTIVAL,
Lincoln Center (John Jay Theatre),
  New York
Shlemiel the First, July 5–10, 1994

Season Sixteen: 1994–1995

Fall Festival

The Reduced Shakespeare Company
  in **The Complete History of
  America (Abridged)**
Created and performed by Reed
  Martin, Adam Long, and Austin
  Tichenor
August 24–September 3, 1994

Picasso at the Lapin Agile
by Steve Martin
Directed by David Wheeler
Sets by Christine Jones
Costumes by Catherine Zuber
Lighting by John Ambrosone
Sound by Christopher Walker
September 6–17, 1994

Shlemiel the First (*World Premiere*)
Conceived and adapted by Robert
  Brustein from Isaac Bashevis
  Singer's play
Music composed and adapted by
  Hankus Netsky with additional
  music by Zalmen Mlotek
Lyrics by Arnold Weinstein

Music directed by Zalmen Mlotek
Directed and choreographed by
    David Gordon
Sets by Robert Israel
Costumes by Catherine Zuber
Lighting by Peter Kaczorowski
Sound by Christopher Walker
September 21–October 8, 1994

**At Zero Church Street
    Performance Space**

**An Evening of Beckett: Krapp's
    Last Tape, A Piece of
    Monologue, Ohio Impromptu**
by Samuel Beckett
Directed by Robert Scanlan
Sets by Lauren Ariel Bon
Costumes by Karen Eister
Lighting by John Ambrosone
Original music and sound design by
    Christopher Walker
September 21, 1994

Loeb Stage

**The Oresteia: Agamemnon, The
    Libation Bearers, The
    Eumenides**
English version by Robert Auletta
    from the trilogy by Aeschylus
Directed by François Rochaix
Set design by Robert Dahlstrom
Costume design by Catherine Zuber
Lighting design by Mimi Jordan
    Sherin
Sound design by Christopher Walker
November 25, 1994

Waiting for Godot
by Samuel Beckett
Directed by David Wheeler
Set design by Derek McLane
Costume design by Catherine Zuber
Lighting design by John Ambrosone
Sound design by Christopher Walker
January 13, 1995

Henry V
by William Shakespeare
Directed by Ron Daniels
Set design by John Conklin
Costume design by Gabriel Berry
Lighting design by Frances Aronson
Music and sound design by Bruce
    Odland
February 17, 1995

The Threepenny Opera
by Bertolt Brecht
Music by Kurt Weill
Book translated by Michael Feingold
Lyrics translated by Jeremy Sams
Directed by Ron Daniels
Musical direction by Craig Smith
Set design by Michael Yeargan
Costume design by Gabriel Berry
Lighting design by Anne Militello
Sound design by Christopher Walker
May 12, 1995

Ubu Rock (*World Premiere*)
by Shelley Berc and Andrei
    Belgrader
Based on Alfred Jarry's play
Music and lyrics by Rusty Magee
Directed by Andrei Belgrader
Set design by Andrei Both
Costume design by Catherine Zuber
Lighting design by John Ambrosone
Sound design by Christopher Walker
June 2, 1995

*1995 New Stages Series
at the C. Walsh Theatre, Suffolk
    University*

The Cryptogram (*American
    Premiere*)
Written and directed by David
    Mamet
Set design by John Lee Beatty
Costume design by Harriet Voyt
Lighting design by Dennis Parichy
February 2, 1995

The Reduced Shakespeare Company
    in **THE BIBLE: The Complete
    Word of God (abridged)**
April 18, 1995

At the Hasty Pudding Theatre

Demons (*World Stage Premiere*)
by Robert Brustein
Directed by Francesca Zambello
Set design by Allison Koturbash
Costume design by Catherine Zuber
Lighting design by John Ambrosone
Sound design by Christopher Walker
March 30, 1995

Accident (*World Premiere*)
by Carol K. Mack
Directed by Marcus Stern

Set design by Alison Koturbash
Costume design by Gail Buckley
Lighting design by John Ambrosone
Sound design by Christopher Walker
April 6, 1995

Summer 1995

The King Stag
by Carlo Gozzi
Directed by Andrei Serban
Choreography by Julie Taymor
Sets by Michael H. Yeargan
Costumes, masks, and puppetry by
Julie Taymor
Lighting by John Ambrosone
Sound by Christopher Walker
Production restaged by John Grant-
Phillips
July 27, 1995

TOURS:
BOCA RATON, CORAL SPRINGS,
LAKE WORTH, PALM BEACH,
FT. LAUDERDALE (FLORIDA):
Shlemiel the First, January
12–March 12, 1995
AMERICAN MUSIC THEATER
FESTIVAL, Philadelphia:
Shlemiel the First, March 23–April
2, 1995
STAMFORD CENTER FOR THE
ARTS, Stamford, CT:
Shlemiel the First, April 4–16,
1995

THE TAIPEI INTERNATIONAL
ARTS FESTIVAL, Taipei, Taiwan:
Six Characters in Search of an
Author, September 23–25, 1995
The King Stag, September 28–30,
1995

Season Seventeen: 1995–1996

Fall Festival

The Late Great Ladies of Blues
and Jazz
Conceived, written, and performed
by Sandra Reaves with the All-Star
Jazz Band
September 5–10, 1995

The American Chestnut
Created and performed by Karen
Finley
September 12–17, 1995

Citizen Reno
Written and performed by Reno
September 17, 18, 25, 1995

Don't Smoke in Bed!
An Evening of 20th Century Song
Performed by Marianne Faithfull
September 19–October 1, 1995

101 Humiliating Stories
Written and performed by Lisa Kron
September 2, 4, 6, 7, 1995

Lillian
Written and performed by David
Cale
October 3, 5, 6, 7, 1995

At the Loeb Experimental Theatre

Winter Circus
A new Dance–Theatre Work
Choreographed and directed by Amy
Spencer and Richard Colton
September 12–17, 1995

At Zero Church Street Performance
Space

Eh Joe • Ghost Trio • Nacht und
Träume
by Samuel Beckett
Directed by Robert Scanlan
Video production by Glenn Litton
Set design by John Ambrosone
Costume design by Karen Eister
Sound design and original music by
Christopher Walker
September 14–24, 1995

Loeb Stage

The Tempest
by William Shakespeare
Directed by Ron Daniels
Set design by John Conklin
Costume design by Gabriel Berry
Lighting design by Chris Parry
Original music and sound design by
Bruce Odland
Choreography by Amy Spencer and
Richard Colton
November 24, 1995

Buried Child
by Sam Shepard
Directed by Marcus Stern
Set design by Allison Koturbash
Costume design by Catherine Zuber
Lighting design by John Ambrosone
Sound design by Marcus Stern and
  Christopher Walker
January 5, 1996

Tartuffe
by Molière
Modern adaptation by Robert
  Auletta
Directed by François Rochaix
Set design by Robert Israel
Costume design by Catherine Zuber
Lighting design by Mimi Jordan
  Sherin
Sound design by Christopher Walker
February 9, 1996

The Naked Eye
by Paul Rudnick
Directed by Christopher Ashley
Set design by Derek McLane
Costume design by Catherine Zuber
Lighting design by Don Holder
Projections by Wendall K.
  Harrington
Sound design by Christopher Walker
Composer and music coordinator
  Mark Bennett
May 10, 1996

Long Day's Journey into Night
by Eugene O'Neill
Directed by Ron Daniels
Set design by Michael H. Yeargan
Costume design by Catherine Zuber
Lighting design by Frances Aronson
Sound design by Christopher Walker
May 23, 1996

1996 New Stages Series
at the Hasty Pudding Theatre

Slaughter City (*American Premiere*)
by Naomi Wallace
Directed by Ron Daniels
Set and costume design by
  Ashley Martin-Davis
Lighting design by John Ambrosone
Original sound score by Glyn Perrin

Additional sound design by
  Christopher Walker
March 28, 1996

Alice in Bed (*American Premiere*)
by Susan Sontag
Directed by Bob McGrath
Set design by Laurie Olinder and
  Fred Teitz
Film by Bill Morrison
Costume design by Susan Anderson
Lighting design by John Ambrosone
Sound design by Christopher Walker
  with compositions by James
  Farmer
April 11, 1996

Spring 1996

Ubu Rock
by Shelley Berc and Andrei
  Belgrader based on Alfred Jarry's
  play
Music and lyrics by Rusty Magee
Directed by Andrei Belgrader
Set design by Andrei Both
Costume design by Catherine Zuber
Lighting design by John Ambrosone
Sound design by Christopher Walker
March 11–19, 1996

TOURS:
JOURNÉES BECKETT,
Strasbourg, France:
Beckett Trio: Eh Joe, Ghost Trio,
  Nacht und Träume, April 3–4,
  1996
STAMFORD CENTER FOR THE
  ARTS, Stamford, CT:
Long Day's Journey into Night,
  May 7–19, 1996
AMERICAN CONSERVATORY
  THEATRE, San Francisco:
Shlemiel the First,
  September 16–October 13, 1996

Season Eighteen: 1996–1997

Loeb Stage

The Wild Duck
by Henrik Ibsen
Adapted by Robert Brustein
Directed by François Rochaix
Set design by Jean-Claude Maret
Costume design by Catherine Zuber

Lighting design by Michael
Chybowski
Sound design by Christopher Walker
November 22, 1996

**Six Characters in Search of an
Author**
by Luigi Pirandello
Adapted and directed by Robert
Brustein
Set and costume design by Michael
Yeargan
Original lighting adapted by John
Ambrosone
Sound adapted by Christopher
Walker
December 5, 1996

The King Stag
by Carlo Gozzi
Directed by Andrei Serban
Choreography by Julie Taymor
Sets by Michael H. Yeargan
Costumes, masks, and puppetry by
Julie Taymor
Lighting by John Ambrosone
Sound by Christopher Walker
Production restaged by John Grant-
Phillips
December 11, 1996

Woyzeck
by Georg Büchner
New Translation by Gideon Lester
Directed by Marcus Stern
Set design by Allison Koturbash
Costume design by Catherine Zuber
Lighting design by Scott Zielinski
Sound design by Christopher Walker
and Marcus Stern
January 31, 1997

The Cabinet of Dr. Caligari (*World
Premiere*)
by John Moran
Directed by Bob McGrath
Set design by Laurie Olinder and
Fred Tietz
Slide design by Laurie Olinder
Costume design by Catherine Zuber
Lighting design by Howard S. Thies
Films by Anthony Chase
February 21, 1997

Man and Superman
by George Bernard Shaw
Directed by David Wheeler
Set design by Christine Jones
Costume design by Catherine Zuber
Lighting design by John Ambrosone
Sound design by David Remedios
May 9, 1997

1996–1997 New Stages Series

Punch and Judy Get Divorced
(*American Premiere*)
by David Gordon and Ain Gordon
Music by Edward Barnes
Lyrics by Arnold Weinstein, David
Gordon, and Ain Gordon
Directed and choreographed by
David Gordon
Set design by David Gordon
Costume design by Adelle Lutz
Lighting design by Stan Pressner
Sound design by Christopher Walker
Musical direction by Alan Johnson
October 25, 1996
*C. Walsh Theatre at Suffolk
University*

**When the World Was Green
(A Chef's Fable)**
(*World Premiere Production*)
by Joseph Chaikin and Sam Shepard
Directed by Joseph Chaikin
Set design by Christine Jones
Costume design by Mary Brecht
Lighting design by John Ambrosone
Sound design by Christopher Walker
Music composition by Woody Regan
*March 26, 1997, Hasty Pudding
Theatre*

The Old Neighborhood (*World
Premiere*)
by David Mamet
Directed by Scott Zigler
Set design by Kevin Rigdon
Costume design by Harriet Voyt
Lighting design by John Ambrosone
*April 11, 1997, Hasty Pudding
Theatre*

TOURS:
GEFFEN PLAYHOUSE, Los
 Angeles:
Shlemiel the First,
 May 14–June 8, 1997

Season Nineteen: 1997–1998

Fall

Shlemiel the First
Conceived and adapted by Robert
 Brustein from Isaac Bashevis
 Singer's play
Music composed and adapted by
 Hankus Netsky with additional
 music by Zalmen Mlotek
Lyrics by Arnold Weinstein
Music directed by Zalmen Mlotek
Directed and choreographed by
 David Gordon
Sets by Robert Israel
Costumes by Catherine Zuber
Lighting by Peter Kaczorowski
Sound by Christopher Walker
September 9–28, 1997

Loeb Stage

The Bacchae
by Euripides
New translation by Paul Schmidt
Directed by François Rochaix
Set design by Jean-Claude Maret
Costume design by Catherine Zuber
Lighting design by Michael
 Chybowski
Sound design by Christopher Walker
Movement by Amy Spencer and
 Richard Colton
November 21, 1997

Peter Pan and Wendy (*World
 Premiere*)
A play based on the novel by J. M.
 Barrie
Conceived by Marcus Stern and
 Elizabeth Egloff
Written by Elizabeth Egloff
Directed by Marcus Stern
Set design by Allison Koturbash
Costume design by Catherine Zuber
Lighting design by Scott Zielinski
Sound design by Marcus Stern and
 Christopher Walker
December 12, 1997

The Taming of the Shrew
by William Shakespeare
Adapted and directed by Andrei
 Serban
Movement by Amy Spencer and
 Richard Colton
Set design by Christine Jones
Costume design by Catherine Zuber
Lighting design by Michael
 Chybowski
Sound design by Christopher Walker
January 30, 1998

In the Jungle of Cities
by Bertolt Brecht
New translation by Paul Schmidt
Directed by Robert Woodruff
Set design by Robert Pyzocha
Costume design by Catherine Zuber
Lighting design by Michael
 Chybowski
Sound design by Christopher Walker
February 20, 1998

The Imaginary Invalid
by Molière
Translated and adapted by Shelly
 Berc and Andrei Belgrader
Incidental music and lyrics by Rusty
 Magee
Directed by Andrei Belgrader
Movement by Richard Colton
Set design by Anita Stewart
Costume design by Catherine Zuber
Lighting design by Michael
 Chybowski
Sound design by Christopher Walker
May 8, 1998

1997–1998 New Stages Series

2.5 Minute Ride
Written and performed by Lisa Kron
January 6–18, 1998
*C. Walsh Theatre at Suffolk
 University*

Albee's Men
Excerpted from the works of Edward
 Albee
Created by Glyn O'Malley and
 Stephen Rowe
Performed by Stephen Rowe
Directed by Glyn O'Malley
*March 24, 1998, Hasty Pudding
 Theatre*

Nobody Dies on Friday (*World Premiere*)
by Robert Brustein
Directed by David Wheeler
Set design by Michael Griggs
Costume design by Catherine Zuber
Lighting design by John Ambrosone
Sound design by Christopher Walker
April 16, 1998, Hasty Pudding Theatre

TOURS:
CHEKHOV INTERNATIONAL THEATRE FESTIVAL, Chekhov
Moscow Art Theatre, Moscow:
Six Characters in Search of an Author,
March 26–28, 1998
When the World Was Green (A Chef's Fable),
March 28, 29, 1998
The King Stag,
March 31, April 1, 1998
1998 SINGAPORE FESTIVAL OF ARTS
Jubilee Hall, Singapore:
When the World Was Green (A Chef's Fable),
June 5, 6, 7, 1998
Nobody Dies on Friday,
June 9, 10, 11, 1998

Season Twenty: 1998–1999

Fall 1998

How I Learned to Drive
by Paula Vogel
Directed by David Wheeler
Set design by J. Michael Griggs
Costume design by Viola Mackenthun
Lighting design by John Ambrosone
Sound design by David Remedios
September 18, 1998

Nobody Dies on Friday
by Robert Brustein
Directed by David Wheeler
Set design by J. Michael Griggs
Costume design by Catherine Zuber
Lighting deign by John Ambrosone
Sound design by Christopher Walker
September 30, 1998

Loeb Stage

Phaedra
by Jean Racine
Translated and adapted by Paul Schmidt
Directed by Liz Diamond
Set design by Riccardo Hernandez
Costume design by Catherine Zuber
Lighting design by Michael Chybowski
Sound design by Christopher Walker
November 27, 1998

The Merchant of Venice
by William Shakespeare
Directed by Andrei Serban
Original music composed by Elizabeth Swados
Set design by Christine Jones
Screen designs by Marielle Bancou and William Bonnell
Costume design by Catherine Zuber
Lighting design by Michael Chybowski
Sound design by Christopher Walker
Musical direction by Michael Friedman
December 11, 1998

Valparaiso (*World Premiere*)
by Don DeLillo
Directed by David Wheeler
Set design by Karl Eigsti
Costume design by Catherine Zuber
Lighting design by John Ambrosone
Sound design by Christopher Walker
January 31, 1999

The Master Builder
by Henrik Ibsen
New adaptation by Robert Brustein
Directed by Kate Whoriskey and Robert Brustein
Set design by Christine Jones
Costume design by Catherine Zuber
Lighting design by Michael Chybowski
Sound design by Christopher Walker
February 12, 1999

The Cripple of Inishmaan
by Martin McDonagh
Directed by Scott Zigler
Set design by Derek McLane

Costume design by Catherine Zuber
Lighting design by John Ambrosone
Sound design by Christopher Walker
May 14, 1999

**1998–1999 New Stages Series
at the Hasty Pudding Theatre**

The Marriage of Bette and Boo
by Christopher Durang
Directed by Marcus Stern
Set design by Molly Hughes
Costume design by Karen Eister
Lighting design by John Ambrosone
Sound design by John Huntington
October 16, 1998

Charlie in the House of Rue
 (*World Premiere*)
by Robert Coover
Directed by Bob McGrath
Set design by Laurie Olinder
Costume design by Catherine Zuber
Lighting design by John Ambrosone
Sound design by Christopher Walker
Film by Bill Morrison
April 1, 1999

Boston Marriage (*World Premiere*)
Written and directed by David
 Mamet
Set design by Sharon Kaitz and
 J. Michael Griggs
Costume design by Harriet Voyt
Lighting design by John Ambrosone
Sound design by Christopher Walker
June 4, 1999

Over the past twenty years, the
 American Repertory Theatre has
 received major support from:

National Endowment for the Arts,
 National Endowment for the
 Humanities, Massachusetts
 Cultural Council, National Arts
 Stabilization Fund and the
 Greater Boston Arts Fund,
 National Corporate Theatre Fund,
 Fund for the Arts, Fund for New
 American Plays

American Express Company,
 Annenberg Foundation, Arts
 International, AT&T, Billy Rose
 Foundation, Boston Investor
 Services Inc., Capital Cities/ ABC,
 CITICORP/ CITIBANK, Coopers
 & Lybrand, Eleanor Naylor Dana
 Charitable Trust, Exxon
 Corporation, Ford Foundation,
 Hearst Foundation, Hershey
 Family Foundation, Lechmere
 Inc., Joe and Emily Lowe
 Foundation Inc., Andrew W.
 Mellon Foundation, Mobil Oil
 Corporation, Newman's Own Inc.,
 One World Arts Foundation Inc.,
 Overbrook Foundation,
 PaineWebber Group Inc., Amelia
 Peabody Charitable Fund, Pew
 Charitable Trusts/ Theatre
 Communications Group, Philip
 Morris Companies Inc., Princess
 Grace Foundation–USA,
 Rockefeller Foundation, Shubert
 Foundation, Harold and Mimi
 Steinberg Charitable Trust, Trust
 for Mutual Understanding, Lila
 Wallace–Reader's Digest Fund,
 W. Alton Jones Foundation

Mr. and Mrs. Joseph Auerbach,
 James H. Binger, Mr. and Mrs.
 Philip Burling, Paul and Katie
 Buttenwieser, Marianna Collins,*
 Mr. and Mrs. T. J. Coolidge Jr.,
 Charlene B. Engelhard through
 the Charles Engelhard
 Foundation, Alan and Niki
 Friedberg, Lee Day Gillespie,
 Barbara and Steven Grossman,
 Ann and Graham Gund, Susan
 Morse Hilles, Richard and
 Priscilla Hunt and the Hunt
 Foundation, Professor George
 Kelly,* Myra H. and Robert K.
 Kraft, Lizbeth and George Krupp,
 John L.* and Frances L. Loeb,*
 Thomas H. Lee and Ann
 Tenenbaum, Dr. Josephine
 Murray, Alford P. Rudnick,* Mrs.
 Ralph P. Rudnick, Mr. and Mrs.
 Daniel Steiner, Faith K. and
 Joseph W. Tiberio.

*deceased

Finally, the A.R.T. owes special debts of gratitude to Harvard University; members of the Theatre's Advisory Board, National Advisory Committee, Honorary Board, and Visiting Committee for the Loeb Drama Center; the Harvard Division of Continuing Education; and, of course, the A.R.T.'s adventurous and loyal audience.

The A.R.T. Professional Acting Company, 1980–1999

F. Murray Abraham
David Ackroyd
Brooke Adams
P. J. Adamson
Remo Airaldi
Terry Alexander
Michael Allard
Patti Allison
James Andreassi
Barbara Andres
Philip Anglim
Simon Arlidge
Mario Arrambide
Rose Arrick
Linda Atkinson
Dennis Bacigalupi
Michael Balcanoff
Gerry Bamman
Ian Bannen
Kathy Bates
Edwin Louis Battle
Leslie Beatty
Ed Begley, Jr.
John Bellucci
Paul Benedict
Starla Benford
Nina Bernstein
Lewis Black
Larry Block
Claire Bloom
Roberts Blossom

Ron Bobb-Semple
Susan Botti
John Bottoms
Kim Brockington
Robert Brustein
Candy Buckley
Debra Byrd
J. Smith-Cameron
Bill Camp
Rosalind Cash
Marilyn Caskey
Philip Cates
Tom Cayler
Lynn Chausow
Hilary Chaplain
Ken Cheeseman
Lucinda Childs
Charles "Honi" Coles
Robert Colston
Dmetrius Conley-
   Williams
William Converse-
   Roberts
Joseph Costa
Peter Crombie
Hume Cronyn
Lindsay Crouse
Deborah Culpin
Scott Cunningham
Roger Curtis
Elzbieta Czyzewska

Shelton Dane
Randy Danson
Diane D'Aquila
Cynthia Darlow
Robertson Dean
François de la Giroday
Carmen de Lavallade
Thomas Derrah
Bob Dishy
Herb Downer
John S. Drabik
Ursula Drabik
Robert Drivas
Brigette Dunn
Eric Elice
Alvin Epstein
Jonathan Epstein
Christine Estabrook
Benjamin Evett
Janice Felty
Kristin Flanders
Richard Fracker
Elizabeth Franz
Paul Freeman
Jonathan Fried
Elizabeth Futral
Andrew Garman
Jeremy Geidt
Peter Gerety
Daniel Gerroll
Rosalie Gerut

Cheryl Giannini
Margaret Gibson
Pamela Gien
Jessalyn Gilsig
Gail Grate
John Grant-Phillips
Joel Grey
Ellen Greene
Richard Grusin
Vincent Guastaferro
Paul Guilfoyle
Caroline Hall
Georgine Hall
Ben Halley, Jr.
Baxter Harris
Harriet Harris
Jason Harvey
Judith Hawkins
Tom Hewitt
Lisa Hilboldt
Wendy Hill
Joe Hindy
Ellen Holly
Arliss Howard
Ken Howard
Geoff Hoyle
Rodney Scott Hudson
Felicity Huffman
Tresa Hughes
Ras Iginga
Jahneen
Elmore James
Randall Jaynes
Gustave Johnson
Cherry Jones
John Christopher
  Jones
Robert Joy
James Judy
Richard Kavanaugh
Ted Kazanoff
Michael Edo Keane
Jerome Kilty
Jeremiah Kissel
Robert Kropf
Monica Koskey
Adrianne Krstansky
James Lally
Diane Lane

Susan Larson
Linda Lavin
Will LeBow
Justine Lewis
Charles Levin
Christopher Lloyd
Mark Linn-Baker
Marya Lowry
Karen MacDonald
Joan MacIntosh
Neil Maffin
Ruth Maleczech
Mansur
David Margulies
Jonathan Marks
Christopher Martin
George Martin
Larry Marshall
Elizabeth Marvel
Norman Matlock
Nancy Mayans
John McAndrews
Christopher McCann
Brian McCue
Tim McDonough
William McGlinn
Yanna McIntosh
Maureen McVerry
Eric Menyuk
Mark Metcalf
Valois Mickens
Annette Miller
Rima Miller
Royal Miller
Alan Mixon
Thom Molinaro
Dearbhla Molloy
Leon Morenzie
Harry S. Murphy
Andrew Mutnick
Kate Nelligan
Frederick Neumann
Shirley Nemetz-Ress
Elizabeth Norment
Dan O'Herlihy
Barbara Orson
Marianne Owen
Lola Pashalinski
Will Patton

Mary Beth Peil
Miguel Perez
Eugene Perry
Karen Phillips
Rebecca Pidgeon
Anne Pitoniak
Alice Playten
Paula Plum
Paula Prentiss
David Purdham
Amie Quigley
Scott Rabinowitz
James Ramlet
Martin Rayner
Don Reilly
Scott Ripley
Emma Roberts
Laila Robins
Jennifer Rohn
Natacha Roi
Tom Rooney
Mary Lou Rosato
Stephanie Roth
Tisha Roth
Stephen Rowe
Paul Rudd
Michael Rudko
Maggie Rush
Kenneth Ryan
Mark Rylance
Tracy Sallows
Damion Scheller
Paul Schierhorn
Sharon Scruggs
John Seitz
Nestor Serrano
Tony Shalhoub
Sandra Shipley
Sylvia Short
Frances Shrand
Noble Shropshire
Joseph Siravo
Stephen Skybell
Catherine Slade
John Slattery
Lisa Sloane
Derek Smith
Priscilla Smith
Marilyn Sokol

Phyllis Somerville
Ingrid Sonnichsen
David Spielberg
Richard Spore
Robert Stanton
Robert Stattel
Jack Stehlin
Denise Stephenson
Michael Stuhlbarg
Elaine Strich
Cheryl Sutton
Faran Tahir
Margarita Taylor

John Thompson
Lynn Torgove
Francine Torres
Daniel J. Travanti
Eugene Troobnick
Vontress Tyrone
Lisa Vidal
Leroy Villanueva
Daniel Von Bargen
Adam Wade
Christopher Walken
Sam Waterston
Jon David Weigand

Jason Weinberg
Greg Welch
Bronia Stefan Wheeler
Lisa D. White
Kathleen Widdoes
Shirley Wilber
Treat Williams
Jack Willis
Debra Winger
Max Wright
William Young
Mark Zeisler

Index of Names and Plays in the Text

Page numbers in italics refer to photographs.

Scanlan, Robert, 10, 144, 158, 192, 201
Schmidt, Paul, 219, 247
Schneider, Alan, 9, 204
School for Scandal, The, 38–40, *39*
Schrand, Frances, *64*
Schubert, Franz, 62, 115
Scott, George C., 254
Seagull, The, 11, 24
Sellars, Peter, 3, 4, 16, 25
Sendak, Maurice, 78
Serban, Andrei, 7, 8, 11, 21, 31, 51, 52, 71, 76, 78, 89, 97, 121, 124, 125, 132, 142–144, 221–225, 249–253, 266
Serling, Rod, 142
Serpent Woman, The 121–126, *123,* 267
Servant of Two Masters, The, 267
Seven Deadly Sins, The, 5
Sganarelle, 7, 21–25, *22,* 50
Shakespeare, William, 13–16, 42, 62, 100, 119, 142–144, 167–176, 176–182, 194–197, 220–225, 232, 249–258, 260
Shalhoub, Nicole, 48, 267
Shalhoub, Tony, 4, 8, 22, 32, 39
Shaw, George Bernard, 74, 179, 181, 222, 255
Shepard, Sam, 6, 114
Sher, Antony, 254–255
Sheridan, Richard, 38–40
Shlemiel the First, 11, 197–200, *199,* 228
Simon, Neil, 261
Sinclair, Upton, 207
Singer, Isaac Bashevis, 197–200
Six Characters in Search of an Author, 7, 9, 47–50, *48,* 77, 106, 265
Skarzynski, Jerzy, 173, 174
Skarzynski, Lidia, 173, 174
Skybell, Stephen, 8
Slaughter City, 207–210
Smelyansky, Anatoly, 188
Smith, Derek, *123*
Smith, Priscilla, 6, *64*
Smith, Red, 147–148
Sontag, Susan, 6, 12, 50, 56, 60–63, 113
Sophocles, 248
St. John's Night, 178
Stalin, Joseph, 188
Stanislavsky, Konstantin, 51, 97, 98, 101, 189, 190, 229

Stattel, Robert, 48
Steel, 164–167
Stendhal, Marie Henri, 103
Stern, Marcus, 11, 267
Sterne, Laurence, 57
Stevenson, Adlai, 130
Sticks and Bones, 191
Straiges, Tony, 14
Strasberg, John, 228, 231, 232
Strasberg, Lee, 228–233
Streamers, 191
Strehler, Giorgio, 59, 139
Strindberg, August, 9, 136, 144–151, 233, 239
Stuhlbarg, Michael, 11
Suvin, Darko, 155
Swan White, 146
Sweet Table at the Richelieu, 89
Swinarski, Konrad, 173–176
Szondi, Peter, 112

Taine, Hippolyte, 120
Taming of the Shrew, The, 8, 220–225, *222,* 252, 267
Tarentino, Quentin, 210
Tartuffe, 11, 132, 267
Tarvin, Emily, vii
Taymor, Julie, 7, 51, 266
Tempest, The, 42, 126
Thomas, Clarence, 185
Thomson, Bobby, 147–148
Those the River Keeps, 191–194
Three Sisters, 8, 31–33, *33*
Threepenny Opera, The, 89, 155
Timon of Athens, 251
'Tis Pity She's a Whore, 118–121
Tolstoy, Aleksei, 103
Tonight We Improvise, 9, 90, 92–93
Torres, Francine, *114*
Turandot, 51
Twain, Mark, 44–47
Twelfth Night, 8, 126, 142–144, *143*
Twilight Zone, 142
Tyrone, Mary, 245

Ubu Rock, 114
Ubu Roi, 8
Uncle Vanya, 6, *181,* 267
Unfinished Piece for Player Piano, An, 126

Vakhtangov, Yevgeni, 98
Vasilievich, Ivan, 190
Visconti, Luchino, 121